*H*IS face was close to me and I felt my throat constrict. I wished my heart would not beat so loudly. It might betray my fear or whatever it was he aroused in me.

"You are revolting. If you do not let me go at once, I can promise you that my family will bring you to the courts for this."

"Oh, that good family," he said. "Now, my fine lady, there is nothing insulting about an offer of marriage."

"There is when it comes from you."

"Don't goad me too far, I have the devil of a temper."

"And let me tell you that so have I."

"I knew we were well matched. What boys we'll have. Let's begin . . . now. The marriage vows will come after."

Philippa Carr

THE LION
TRIUMPHANT

A FAWCETT CREST BOOK

Fawcett Publications, Inc., Greenwich, Connecticut

THE LION TRIUMPHANT

THIS BOOK CONTAINS THE COMPLETE TEXT OF THE
ORIGINAL HARDCOVER EDITION.

A Fawcett Crest Book reprinted by arrangement with
G. P. Putnam's Sons

Library of Congress Catalog Card Number: 73–78602

Printed in the United States of America

First printing: April 1975

2   3   4   5   6   7   8   9   10

Contents

THE LION
TRIUMPHANT

The Spanish Galleon

From my turret window I could watch the big ships sailing into Plymouth Harbor. Sometimes I would get up in the night and the sight of a stately vessel on the moonlit waters lifted my spirits. When it was dark I would sometimes watch for lights on the sea which would tell me there was a ship out there, and I would ask myself, What sort of ship? A dainty caravel, a warlike galleass, a three-masted carrack or a stately galleon? And wondering, I would return to my bed and imagine the kind of men who would be sailing on that ship; and for a while I would cease to mourn for Carey and my lost love.

My first thought on awakening in the morning would not be for Carey (as I had such a short time ago promised myself it would be every moment of the days to come) but of the sailors who were coming into port.

I would go alone to the Hoe—although I was not supposed to do this, it being considered improper for a young lady of seventeen to go where she could be jostled by rough sailors. If I insisted on going I must take with me two of the maids. I had never been one to accept authority meekly, but I could not make them understand that it was only when I was alone that I could capture the magic of the harbor. If I took Jennet or Susan with me they would be eyeing the sailors and giggling, reminding each other of what had happened to one of their friends who had trusted a sailor. I had heard all that before. I wanted to be alone.

So I would choose the opportunity to slip down to the Hoe and there discover my ship of the night. I would see men whose skins had been burned to the color of mahogany; whose bright eyes studied the girls, assessing their charms, which I imagined depended largely on their accessibility, for a sailor's stay on land was a short one and he had little time to waste in wooing. Their faces were different from those of men who did not go to sea. It may have been due to the exotic scenes they had witnessed, to the hardships they had endured, to their mingling devotion, adoration, fear and hatred for that other mistress, the beautiful, wild, untamed and unpredictable sea.

I liked to watch the stores being loaded—sacks of meal, salted meats and beans; I would dream of where the cargoes of linen and bales of cotton were being taken. It was all bustle and excitement. It was no place for a young, genteelly nurtured girl; but it was irresistible.

It seemed inevitable that something exciting must happen sooner or later; and it did. It was on the Hoe that I first saw Jake Pennlyon.

Jake was tall and broad, solid and invincible. That was what struck me immediately. He was bronzed from the weather, for although he was about twenty-five years old when I first saw him, he had been at sea for eight years. Even at the time of our first meeting he commanded his own ship, which accounted for that air of authority. I noticed immediately how the eyes of women of all ages brightened at the sight of him. I compared him—as I did all men—with Carey and by comparison he was coarse, lacking in breeding.

I had no idea who he was at that moment, of course, but I knew he was someone of importance. Men touched their forelocks; one or two girls curtsied. Someone called out, "A merry good day to 'ee, Cap'un Lion."

The name suited him in a way. The sun on his dark blond hair gave it a tawny shade. He swaggered slightly as sailors did when they first came ashore as though they were not yet accustomed to the steadiness of land and still rolled with the ship. The King of Beasts, I thought.

And then I knew that he was aware of me, for he had paused. It was a strange moment; it seemed as though the bustle of the harbor was stilled for a moment. The men had stopped loading; the sailor and the two girls to whom he was talking appeared to be looking at us and not at each other; even the parrot which a grizzled old seaman had been trying to sell to a fustian-smocked farmer stopped squawking.

"Good morrow, Mistress," said Jake Pennlyon with a bow, the exaggerated humility of which suggested mockery.

I felt a sudden thrill of dismay; he must clearly think that because I was alone here it was in order for him to address me. Young ladies of good family did not stand about in such places unchaperoned and any who did might well be awaiting an opportunity to strike some sort of bargain with women-hungry sailors. Was it not for this very reason that I was not expected to be here alone?

I pretended not to realize that he addressed me; I stared beyond him out at the ship with the little boats bobbing around it. My color had heightened, though, and he knew that he disturbed me.

"I think we have not met before," he said. "You were not here two years ago."

There was something about him which made it impossible for me to ignore him. I said: "I have been here but a few weeks."

"Ah, not a native of Devon."

"No," I said.

"I knew it. For such a pretty young lady could not be around without my scenting her out."

I retorted: "You talk as though I am some beast to be hunted."

"It is not only beasts who must be hunted."

His blue eyes were penetrating, they seemed to see more of me than was comfortable or decorous; they were the most startling blue eyes I ever saw—or ever was to see. Years spent on the ocean had given them that deep blue color. They were sharp, shrewd, attractive in a way and yet repellent. He clearly thought that I was some serving girl who had come out because a ship was in and was looking for a sailor. I said coldly: "I think, sir, you are making a mistake."

"Now that," he answered, "is a thing I rarely do on occasions such as this, for although I can be rash at times my judgment is infallible when it comes to selecting my friends."

"I repeat that you are mistaken in addressing me," I said. "And now I must go."

"Could I not be allowed to escort you?"

"I have not far to go. To Trewynd Grange in fact."

I looked for at least a flicker of concern. He should know that he could not treat with impunity one who was guest at the Grange.

"I must call at a moment convenient to you."

"I trust," I retorted, "that you will wait to be asked."

He bowed again.

"In which case," I went on as I turned away, "you may wait a very long time."

I had a great desire to get away. There was something overbold about him. I could believe him capable of any indiscretion. He was like a pirate, but then so many seamen were just that.

I hurried back to the Grange, fearful at first that he might follow me there and perhaps faintly disappointed because he did not. I went straight up to the turret in which I had my rooms and looked out. The ship—his ship —stood out clearly on a sea that was calm and still. She must have been of some seven hundred tons, with towering fore and after castles. She carried batteries of guns. She was not a warship, but she was equipped to protect herself and perhaps attack others. She was a proud-looking ship; and there was a dignity about her. She was his ship, I knew.

I would not go down to the Hoe again until that ship sailed away. I would look every day and hope that when I awoke next morning she would be gone. Then I started to think of Carey—beautiful Carey, who was young, only two years older than myself, darling Carey with whom I used to quarrel when I was a child until that wonderful day when the realization came to us both that we loved each other. The misery flooded over me and I lived it all again; the unaccountable anger of Carey's mother—who was a cousin of my own mother—when she had declared nothing would induce her to consent to our marriage. And my own dear mother, who had at first not understood until that terrible day when she took me into her arms and wept with me and explained how the sins of the fathers were visited on the children; and my happy dream of a life shared with Carey was shattered forever.

Why should it all come back so vividly because of a meeting on the Hoe with that insolent sailor?

I must explain how I came to be in Plymouth—this southwest corner of England—when my home was in the southeast only a few miles from London itself.

I was born in St. Bruno's Abbey—a strange place in which to be born, and when I look back on my beginnings they were clearly anything but orthodox. I was light-hearted, careless, not in the least serious like Honey, whom I had always thought of as my sister. There we were in our childhood living in a monastery, which was no monastery, with that ambience of mysticism about us. That we were unaware of this in our early years was due to my mother, who was so normal, serene, comforting—all that a mother should be. I told Carey once that when we had our children I would be to them what my mother had been to me.

But as I grew older I became aware of the tension between my parents. Sometimes I think they hated each other. I sensed that my mother wanted a husband who was kind and ordinary, rather like Carey's Uncle Rupert, who had never married and I suspected loved her. As for my father, I did not understand him at all, but I did believe that at times he hated my mother. There was some reason for it which I could not understand. Perhaps it was because he was guilty. Ours was an uneasy household, but I was not as much aware of it as Honey was. It was easy for Honey; Honey's emotions were less complicated than mine. She was jealous because she believed my mother loved me more than she loved her, which was natural because I was her own child. Honey loved my mother possessively; she didn't want to share her; and she hated my father. She knew exactly where her loyalties lay. It wasn't so easy with me. I wondered whether she was as fiercely possessive of her husband, Edward, as she had been of my mother. Perhaps it was different with a husband. I was sure I would have been as eager that all Carey's love and thoughts should have been for me.

Honey had made a grand marriage—to everyone's amazement, although they were ready to admit that she was just about the most beautiful creature they had ever seen. I had always felt plain by comparison. Honey had beautiful dark blue, almost violet eyes, and her long, thick black lashes made them startling; her hair was dark, too, curling and vital. She was immediately noticed wherever she went. I always felt insignificant beside her, although when she was not there I was quite attractive with my heavy mid-brown hair and green eyes which my mother used to say fitted my name. "You are indeed a little Cat," she would be fond of pointing out, "with those green eyes, and that heart-shaped face." I knew that in her eyes I was every bit as beautiful as Honey, but this was a mother looking at her beloved child. However, Edward Ennis, son and heir of Lord Calperton, had fallen in love with Honey and married her when she was seventeen years old on her first appearance in society. Her obscure and humble birth made no difference. Honey had triumphantly achieved that which many a girl richly endowed with worldly goods had failed to do.

My mother's delight was great, for she must have feared that it might have been difficult to find a husband for Honey. She had expected Lord Calperton to raise all sorts of objections, but Carey's mother, whom I called Aunt Kate, had swept away any obstacles and she was the sort of woman who usually got her way because although she must have been about thirty-seven years old she had some indestructible charm so that men fell in love with her and Lord Calperton was no exception.

In November of the glorious year 1558, the old Queen had died and everywhere there was great rejoicing because new hope had come to England. We had suffered through Bloody Mary's reign and because the Abbey was not far from the river and a mile or two away from the Capital the pall of smoke from Smithfield would drift our way when the wind was in a certain quarter. My mother used to feel ill at the sight of it and she would shut the windows and refuse to go out.

When the smoke was no longer visible my mother would go into the garden and gather flowers or fruit or herbs, whatever was in season, and send me with them over to my grandmother's house, which bordered on the Abbey.

My mother's stepfather had been burned at the stake as a heretic in the reign of Queen Mary; that was why the fires of Smithfield were particularly poignant to us. But I don't think my grandmother continued to suffer as much as my mother believed she did. She would always be very interested in what I brought and she would call the twins in to talk to me. Peter and Paul were a year older than I—my mother's half brothers and therefore my uncles. We were a complicated family. It seemed strange to have uncles a year older than oneself, so we never considered the relationship. I was fond of them both; they were identical twins—always together and looking so alike that few could tell them apart. Peter wanted to go to sea, and as Paul followed Peter in everything he wanted to go too.

When Aunt Kate arrived at the Abbey I would go to my room, lock myself in and stay there until my mother came to persuade me to go down. Then I would do so just to please her. I would sit at my window and look out at the old Abbey church and the monks' dorter, which my mother was always talking of turning into a buttery; and I remembered how Honey used to tell me that if you listened in the dead of night you heard the chanting of the monks who had lived here long ago and the screams of those who had been tortured and hanged at the gate when King Henry's men had come to dissolve the monastery. She used to tell me these stories to frighten me because she was jealous on account of the fact that I was my mother's daughter. I retaliated, though, when I heard rumors about Honey. "You," I had said, "are a bastard and your mother was a serving girl and your father a murderer of monks." This was cruel of me because it upset Honey more than anything. It was not so much that she minded being a bastard as not being my mother's own child. At that time her first possessive love had been centered on my mother.

My nature was to let my temper flare up, to make the most wounding comments I could think of and very soon after hate myself for doing so and try hard to make up for my cruelty. I would say to Honey: "It's just a tale. It's not true. And in any case you're so beautiful that it wouldn't matter if your father was the devil, people would still love you." Honey didn't forgive easily; she went on brooding on insults; she knew that her mother had been a serving woman and that her great-grandmother had been known as a witch. She didn't mind the latter at all. To have a witch for a great-grandmother gave her some special power. She was always interested in herbs and how they could be used.

Honey came to the Abbey for the Coronation. When I asked my mother if my father would be home by then her face became a mask and it was impossible to know what she was feeling.

She said: "He'll not be back."

"You seem so sure," I replied.

"Yes," she said firmly, "I am."

We went to London to see the Queen's entrance into her Capital in order to take possession of the Tower of London. It was exciting to see her in her chariot with Lord Robert Dudley, one of the handsomest men I had ever seen, riding beside her. He was her Master of Horse and they had, I heard, become acquainted when they were prisoners in the Tower during the reign of the Queen's sister, Mary. It was thrilling to hear the tower guns boom out and listen to the loyal greetings which were delivered to the young Queen as she rode along. We had taken up our position close to the Tower and we saw her clearly as she rode in.

She was young—about twenty-five years old—with fresh-colored cheeks and reddish hair; she sparkled with vitality; yet there was a great solemnity about her which was very becoming and greatly admired by the people.

We were all very moved when we heard her speak as she was about to enter the Tower.

"Some," she said, "have fallen from being princes of this land, to be prisoners in this place; I am raised from being prisoner in this place to be prince of this land. That dejection was a work of God's justice; this advancement is a work of his mercy; as they were to yield patience for the one, so I must bear myself to God thankful, and to men merciful for the other."

This was a speech of wisdom and modesty and determination which was greatly applauded by all who heard it.

I was thoughtful as we rode back to the Abbey, thinking of Queen Elizabeth—not so very much older than myself —who now bore a great responsibility. There was something inspiring about her and I fell to thinking of her remark about the imprisonment she had suffered and how God had been merciful and brought her from her troubles to greatness. I pictured her as a prisoner entering the Tower by the Traitors' Gate and wondering, as she must have, when she would be taken out to Tower Green—as her mother had been—and commanded to lay her head on the block. How would one so young feel with death imminent? Would she, this bright young woman burning with zeal for her great task, have felt as wretched at the prospect of losing her life as I did at the loss of Carey?

But she had come through her troubles. God had been merciful; out of the great shadow of the Tower she had walked, to return as mistress of everyone and everything in this land.

Witnessing the entry of the new Queen into her Capital had lifted my spirits.

I listened to the conversation at dinner, which was led by Kate. She scintillated, and hating her as I did, I had to admit to her undeniable charm. She was the center of attraction at the table. She chattered on indiscreetly, for who could be sure what the new reign would bring forth and what servants who listened would report? At least they had during the reign of Mary. Why should we all think that Elizabeth's was going to be so different?

"So at last she has safely reached the throne," Kate was saying. "Anne Boleyn's daughter! Mind you, she has a look of her royal father. The same high temper. It's in the color of their hair. It's almost identical. I once danced with His Majesty, her royal father, and do you know I verily believe that if he had not at that time been absorbed by the charms of Catherine Howard he would have cast his eyes on me? How different everything might have been if he had!"

My mother said: "Your head and shoulders might have parted company by now, Kate. We'd rather have you in one piece."

"I was always fortunate. Poor Catherine Howard! It was her head instead of mine. What a man that was for dispossessing himself of wives."

"You speak too freely, Kate," said her brother Rupert.

Kate lowered her voice and looked conspiratorial. "We must remember," she said, "that this is Harry's daughter—Harry's and Anne Boleyn's, what a combination!"

"Our last Queen was his daughter too," put in Kate's son Nicholas, whom we called 'Colas.

"Oh, but then," said Kate, "all that mattered was that one was a good Catholic."

My mother tried to change the subject and asked my grandmother about some herbs she wanted. Grandmother was very knowledgeable about anything that grew and she and my mother were immediately deep in a horticultural discussion, but Kate's voice soon rose above theirs. She was talking about the dangers through which the new Queen had passed, how when her mother had gone to the scaffold her future had been in great danger, how she had been declared illegitimate, and how with the death of Jane Seymour she had been kindly treated by the King's three last Queens and had lived at the Dower House with Queen Catherine Parr after the death of the King.

"And I think," said Kate mischievously, "it would be unwise to discuss what happened there. Poor Thomas Seymour! I met him once. What a fascinating man! It's small wonder that our little Princess . . . but of course that is gossip. Of course she never really permitted him to enter her bedroom. That was all gossip about the Princess' being delivered of a child. Who would believe such nonsense . . . now! Why, those who perpetrated such evil tales should be hung, drawn and quartered. It would be treason to repeat them now. Imagine when they brought the news to her that he had died on the block. 'This day died a man with much wit and very little judgment,' she said. And she said it calmly as though he were just an acquaintance. As if there could have been anything deeper between them!"

Kate laughed and her eyes sparkled. "I wonder what it will be like at Court now. Gayer than under Mary. That much is certain. Our Gracious Lady will be so eager to show her gratitude to God, to her people and to Fate for preserving her for this great destiny. She will want to be gay. She will want to forget the alarms of the past. Mercy me, after the Wyatt rebellion she came as near to the block as I am to you now."

"It's all in the past now," said my mother quickly.

"One does not escape from the past, Damask," retorted Kate. "It is always there like a shadow behind us."

But, I thought, *your* miserable sins have cast a shadow over my life and you never look back to see the shadow behind you.

"Why," went on Kate, "did you see Lord Robert beside her? She dotes on him, they say."

"There'll always be gossip," said Rupert.

"He has sprung quickly into the saddle," laughed Kate. "And what would you expect of Northumberland's son?"

I watched Aunt Kate with growing resentment. How reckless she was, how frivolous! She could bring trouble to our household with her careless talk. And she would doubtless slip out of it unscathed. Whatever was said brought me back to my tragedy.

When Kate and 'Colas left for Remus Castle I felt better—not happy of course, only relieved that Kate had gone.

As it was November there was little to do in the garden. I remained listless. The Abbey seemed to me a gloomy place. The house itself—built like a castle resembling Remus, which was Carey's now—was gradually becoming more like a home since my father had gone away; it was when one looked out of the windows and saw the out-buildings, the refectories and the dorters and the fish-ponds that it seemed so alien.

My mother's interest was now focused on me. Her great desire was to end my misery and to show me a new way of life. To please her I used to pretend that I was getting over it, but she loved me too well to be deceived. She tried to interest me in the uses of herbs which she had learned from her mother, embroidering and tapestry; and when she found that I could not give my mind to these things she decided that she would tell me of her anxieties, which was the greatest help she could give me.

I was in my room when she came in, her face grave. I rose in alarm and she said: "Sit down, Cat. I've come to talk to you."

So I sat down and she said: "I am concerned, Cat."

"I see that, Mother. What worries you?"

"The future . . . I heard today that the Bishop of Winchester has been arrested."

"For what reason?"

"You can guess that the religious conflicts will continue. He supports the Pope. It is the old tug of war. Oh, God, I had hoped that we had passed through those evil times."

"They say the new Queen will be tolerant, Mother."

"Monarchs are not often so when their thrones are in danger. They are surrounded by ambitious men. There has been much tragedy in our family, Cat. My father lost his head for harboring a priest; my stepfather burned at Smithfield for following the Reformed Faith. You know Edward is a Catholic. When Honey married him she embraced his faith. That was safe in the last reign; but now we have a new Queen on the throne."

"So you are worried about Honey."

"All my life there have been these persecutions. I fear that will continue. As soon as I heard that the Bishop of Winchester had been arrested I thought of Honey."

"You think that the new Queen will begin to persecute the Catholics?"

"I think her ministers may well do so. And then we shall have all the old fears returning."

Then we talked about Honey and how happily she had married and my mother's apprehension was eased when she thought of Honey's happiness.

That helped a little.

It was Christmas time and we celebrated it in the great

hall at the Abbey. The smell of baking filled the house and it was going to be a merry Christmas, said my mother, to celebrate not only the birth of Our Lord but the accession of our new Queen. I believe she thought that by acting as though she were sure everything was going to be wonderful, it would be.

My father had been gone so long now that we no longer expected him back. Most of our servants had been monks and had known him from his childhood. They believed there was something mystic about him and they did not question his disappearance. Nobody mourned him as they did a dead person; they never had. Therefore there was no reason why we should not celebrate Christmas with all customary rejoicing.

The festival would go on for the twelve days of Christmas and what pleased my mother was that Honey and her husband would be with us.

They came a few days before Christmas. Whenever I saw Honey after an absence her beauty struck me forcibly. She was standing in the hall; it was snowing slightly and there were tiny sparkling flakes on her fur hood. There was faint color in her cheeks and the wonderful violet eyes were brilliant.

I embraced her warmly. There were at moments great affection between us and now that she had her doting Edward she was no longer jealous of my mother's special love for her own daughter. Her name was Honeysuckle. Her mother, who had entrusted her to my mother's care, had said that she smelled the honeysuckle when her baby was conceived.

My mother had heard the arrival and hurried into the hall; Honey threw herself into her arms and they looked long at each other. Yes, I thought, Honey still loves her passionately. She will still be jealous of me. As if she need be, she with her glowing beauty and her loving husband, and I with Carey lost to me forever.

Edward stood behind her, rather self-effacing, gentle; he would be a good husband.

My mother was saying that they should have Honey's old room, for she was sure that was where they would wish to be, and Honey said yes, it would be lovely; and she slipped her arm through my mother's and they went up the great staircase together.

It was a merry Christmas for all except me; and at times even I found myself dancing and singing with the rest. Kate came with 'Colas, and Rupert came too; and my grandmother and the twins were of course with us. We spent the day at Grandmother's house, which was within walking distance of the Abbey. She was rather vain of her cooking, for she excelled in the kitchen. She had roasted pigs and turkeys, great pies and tarts, and everything was flavored with her special herbs in which she took such a pride. Grandmother had lost two husbands, both murdered by the State; but there she was, red-faced, puffing and purring from the kitchen where she had been scolding her maids. One would never have guessed there had been any tragedy in her life. Should I be like that one day? Oh, no, Grandmother would know nothing of love as I knew it.

There were the usual Christmas customs; we decorated the halls with holly and ivy; we gave presents at New Year; and on Twelfth Night 'Colas found the silver penny in the cake and was King for the night; he was carried around on the men's shoulders and chalked crosses on the beams of our hall, which was supposed to be a protection against evil.

I noticed my mother's eyes as she watched him and I guessed she was thinking of Honey's Catholicism and my unhappiness over Carey; and she was secretly praying for us both.

Kate and Honey stayed with us for the coronation which was to be on January 15.

Kate, as Lady Remus, and Edward, as the heir to Lord Calperton, were entitled to ride in the royal procession and Honey invited me to accompany her; so I was there. We assembled at the Tower whither the Queen came from Westminster Palace by barge. It was a marvelous sight, and it lifted the spirits in spite of the keen winter air. The Lord Mayor was there to offer his loyal greetings and with him were the city companies. We saw the Queen land at the private stairs on Tower Wharf.

We went home after that and a few days later the Queen came into the City to receive the loyal greetings of her subjects before her Coronation. The pageants were exciting; and there was a change which was growing more and more apparent every day. No one would mention as they had freely during the last reign that Elizabeth was a bastard. It would be more than anyone's life was worth to say such a thing. In the pageants the House of Tudor was praised. For the first time effigies of the Queen's mother, Anne Boleyn, were displayed side by side with those of Henry VIII. Elizabeth of York, mother of Henry VIII, was represented adorned with white roses and she was handing the white rose of York to her husband, Henry VII, who offered her the red rose of Lancaster. All along Cornhill and the Chepe pageants were staged; and children sang songs and recited verses in praise of the Queen.

Her coronation was inspiring. I was not in the Abbey, but Kate as a peeress was and she described it to us. How clearly the Queen had spoken, how firmly she had gone through the ceremony complaining, though, that the oil with which she was anointed was grease and smelled ill; but she had looked impressive in her Coronation robes and the trumpets had been magnificent. Kate was sure that the leading nobles had been ready and willing to kiss her hand and swear allegiance—particularly her handsome Master of Horse, Robert Dudley.

"Rumor has it," said Kate, "that she will marry him. She clearly has a fancy for him. Her eyes never leave him. We shall see a royal marriage ere long, mark my words. 'Tis to be hoped her fancies are not so fleeting as those of her father."

"Tell us about her gown," said my mother quickly.

So Kate described the dress in detail and they were all as merry as they had been on Twelfth Night.

My mother, though, remained anxious and when we heard that Pope Paul had publicly declared that he was unable to comprehend the hereditary rights of one not born in wedlock, she was quite frightened. The Pope in his declaration went on to say that the Queen of Scots who was married to the Dauphin of France was the nearest legitimate descendant of Henry VII and he suggested that a court be set up under his arbitration to determine the justice of the claims of Elizabeth and Mary to the throne of England.

This Elizabeth naturally haughtily declined.

But my mother's anxiety increased.

She said to me: "There is going to be a conflict between Protestant and Catholic once more, I fear, and the Queen of Scots will represent the Catholics and Elizabeth the Protestants. Dissension in families . . . it is what I dread. I have seen too much of it."

"We shall not quarrel with Honey because she is a Catholic," I soothed. "I believe she only became one because she wanted to marry Edward."

"I pray that there will be no trouble," said my mother.

She visited Honey for a week and when she came back she seemed in better spirits. She had talked to Lord Calperton.

He was old and set in his ways, he had said, but he was going to send young Edward out to the West Country. He had an estate near Plymouth. Edward was fiercer in his beliefs than his father and if he was going to talk rashly—which he might well do—it was better for him to do it as far from the Court as possible.

My mother was distressed at the thought of not seeing Honey so frequently, but she did agree with Lord Calperton that it was safer to be far from the center of conflict.

So through that summer plans were made for Honey and her husband to leave for Trewynd Grange in Devonshire; and I was to go with them.

I said to my mother: "You'll be lonely without us both."

She took my face in her hands and said: "But you'll be happier there for a time . . . just for a time, Cat. You've got to recover yourself and start afresh." I hated to leave her, but I knew she was right.

That June about a month before we were to set out, the French King Henri Deux was killed in a tournament and his son François became King. Mary of Scotland was his wife, so she became Queen of France. My mother said: "This makes it more dangerous, for Mary has taken the title of Queen of England."

Rupert who was there at the time—as he often was these days—said that while she was in France it was safe enough. The danger would be if ever she came to Scotland, which as Queen of France she would scarcely do.

I was listless, not caring much whether I went to Devon or stayed at the Abbey. I wanted to remain because of my mother; on the other hand I thought it would be good not to have to see Aunt Kate so frequently and to get away from the scene of so many bitter memories. But I should be back in a month or two, I promised myself.

It was a long and wearisome journey and by the time I reached Trewynd Grange the summer was drawing to its end. I think that from the moment I set eyes on the Grange I felt a little farther away from my tragedy; the house was a more comfortable house than the Abbey. It was gray stone, two centuries old with pleasant gardens. It was built around a courtyard and each end was a turret tower. From these windows there was the magnificent view over the Hoe to the sea and this I found interesting. The hall was not large by Abbey and Remus Castle standards, but there was something cozy about it in spite of the two peeps high in the wall through which, without being seen, people in the little alcoves above could spy on who was below. The chapel was dank and cold and rather repellent. Perhaps I had become rather fearful of chapels because of the conflicts in our family—and indeed throughout the country. The stone-flagged floor was worn with the tread of those long since dead; the altar was in a dark corner and the lepers' squint was now used by those servants who were suffering from some pox and couldn't mingle with the rest of the household. It was a long rambling house rather than a tall one; and its grandeur really lay in its four turrets.

I was amused to see Honey chatelaine in her own house. Marriage had naturally changed her. She glowed with an inner satisfaction. Edward doted on her and Honey was the sort of person who demands love. She was unhappy without it; she wanted to be the one loved and cherished beyond others. She should have been contented, for I never saw a man so devoted to his wife—unless it was Lord Remus when he was alive with Kate.

I could talk frankly to Honey. I knew that she hated my father as she hated no one else. She had never forgiven him for not wanting her in the household and ignoring her when she was a child.

She wanted to talk of him, but I wouldn't listen because

I was unsure of my feeling for him. I knew now that not only was he my father but Carey's too and that was why we could not marry; I knew that he, while posing as a saint whose coming had been a miracle, was in fact creeping into Kate's bed at night—or she into his—in the very house where my mother slept. And all the time Kate was pretending to be her dear friend and cousin.

I think Honey had been primed by my mother to treat me with care and Honey would always attempt to please my mother. Perhaps my mother had given her other advice concerning me; I was inclined to think she had, for since I had come to Trewynd Grange Honey had given several dinner parties and invited the local squires.

It was the day after that disturbing encounter on the Hoe when she said: "Sir Penn Pennlyon and his son will be dining with us tomorrow. They are not very distant neighbors. Sir Penn is a man of power in these parts. He owns several ships and his father was a trader before him."

I said: "That ship that came in a few days. . . ."

"Yes," said Honey. "It's the *Rampant Lion*. All their ships are *Lions*. There's the *Fighting Lion*, the *Old Lion* and the *Young Lion*. Whenever you see a *Lion* ship you can guess it belongs to the Pennlyons."

"I saw a man on the Hoe and heard him called Captain Lion."

"That would be Captain Pennlyon. I haven't met him. I know he's home, though. He's been at sea for more than a year."

"So," I said, "they are coming here!"

"Edward is of the opinion that we must be neighborly. Their place is but a stone's throw from here. You can see it from the west turret."

I took the first opportunity of going up to the west turret. I could see a great house, high on the cliff, looking out to sea.

I wondered what he would say when he realized that the young woman whom he had insulted—because I insisted that was what he had done—was a guest of the Ennises. I was rather looking forward to the encounter.

It was autumn and the valerian and sea pinks were still flourishing: it had been a mild summer and I had been wondering what winter would be like in Trewynd Grange.

I could not make the journey back to London until the spring. This was a thought which depressed me; I was restless and uneasy; I wanted to go home; I wanted to be with my mother to talk endlessly of my troubles and receive her sympathy. I don't think I really wanted to forget. There was a certain luxury in being miserable and constantly reminding myself of what I had lost.

And because this man was coming to dinner I stopped thinking of Carey for a while—just as I had on the Hoe.

What should I wear? I asked myself. Honey had brought many grand dresses with her, for she was mindful of her beauty, whereas I had gathered together my garments in a somewhat listless fashion; secretly I regretted that now. I chose a velvet dress which flowed from my shoulders in a graceful manner. It was not very fashionable, for in the last year people had begun to wear whaleboned busks and hoops, which I thought not only ridiculous but rather ugly; and I could not bear to be tight-laced, which was becoming the mode. Instead of wearing one's hair in flowing curls fashionable, women were now frizzing it and wearing all kinds of ornaments in it.

But this was not Court circles and so perhaps one could afford to be out of fashion. Honey herself always dressed in what was most becoming to her beauty. She had a great sense of this and seemed to pay a secret homage to it. She too had rejected the frizzy hairstyles and the whalebones.

Just before six of the clock our guests arrived. Honey and Edward were in the hall waiting to receive them; I stood with them, and as I heard the horses' arrival in the courtyard I felt my heart begin to beat faster.

A big red-faced man was striding into the hall. He had a look of that other—who came after him—an extremely tall man with massive square shoulders and a booming voice. Everything that went with Sir Penn Pennlyon was big. I concentrated on him because I was not going to show the slightest interest in his son.

"Welcome," said Edward, looking slight and pale before these giants.

Sir Penn's twinkling blue eyes darted about him; he seemed to be amused by his host and hostess.

"Marry!" he cried, taking Honey's hand and drawing

her to him giving her a loud kiss on the lips. "If this bain't the prettiest lady in Devon I'll eat the *Rampant Lion*, that I will, barnacles and all."

Honey blushed becomingly and said: "Sir Penn, you must meet my sister."

I curtsied. The blue eyes were on me. "Another little beauty, eh?" he said. "Another little beauty. Two of the prettiest ladies in Devon."

"It's kind of you to call me such, sir," I said. "But I'll not ask you to swallow your ship if you should be proved wrong."

He laughed, great bellowing laughter. He slapped his hands on his thighs. He was more than a little crude, I guessed.

And behind him was his son, who was now greeting Honey before it was my turn to stand face to face with him.

The recognition was instant. He took my hand and kissed it. "We're old friends," he said.

I thought contemptuously: In thirty years' time he will be exactly like his father.

Honey was looking surprised.

"I saw Captain Pennlyon when I was on the Hoe," I said coldly without looking at him.

"My sister is fascinated by ships," said Honey.

"Well!" Sir Penn was regarding me with approval. "She knows a good thing when she sees it. Young lady, there's only one thing I know more beautiful than a ship and that's a pretty woman." He nudged his son. "Jake here agrees with me."

"We want to hear about your voyage," said Honey politely. "Let us go into the punch room. Supper will be served shortly."

She led the way up the three stone stairs past the dining room to the punch room and there we sat while Edward's servants brought malmsey for us to drink. Honey was very proud of fine Venetian glasses, which were very fashionable and which she had brought with her. I imagined the Pennlyons had never seen anything so fine.

We sat rather stiffly on our chairs, the tapestry back and seats of which had been worked by Edward's great-aunt. I thought the chair might break under Sir Penn, for he sat with little thought for its fragility and Honey threw a glance at me as though to say, We have to get used to country manners.

Sir Penn said what a fine thing it was to have neighbors of the quality to bring their fine Venetian glass for them to drink out of. His eyes twinkled as he spoke as though he were laughing at us and in a way despised us—except Honey of course and perhaps me. Both of them—father and son—had an insolence in their looks which suggested that they were assessing our personal attributes in a manner which was slightly disturbing.

"And how long are you staying here?" he wanted to know of Edward.

Edward replied evasively that so much depended on circumstances. His father had wished him to come and look after the estates here for a while. It would depend on what happened on the Surrey estate.

"Ah," said Sir Penn, "you noble families have your seats in every part of the kingdom. Why, young sir, there must be times when you wonder whether you're a Surrey or a Devon man or maybe there is some other county to claim you."

"My father has estates in the North," said Edward.

"Marry! Why, you've a foot in every part of the Queen's realm, young man."

"By no means," said Edward. "And might I not say that your ships sail on every known part of the ocean?"

"You can say it, sir, you can say it. And Jake will tell you that it's so. Just back he is from a long voyage, but he's too taken with the company to give voice."

Jake said: "The company delights me as you see." And he was looking straight at me, mocking because here he was and I had said it was not likely that he would be invited. "But I'll confirm it's true that I have but recently returned from a voyage."

"My sister was excited when she saw your ship come in. She sees the ships come in from her window, and never seems to tire of it."

Jake had brought his chair closer to mine. They had not the manner which we had come to expect. These people were lacking the niceties of behavior; they were more frank than we were, coarser too.

"So you liked my ship," he said.

"I like all ships."

"That's the right spirit," he said. "And you've never had the chance of seeing them before."

"We were close to the river. I often saw boats sailing by."

He laughed derisively. "Wherries and tugs," he said.

"And royal barges. I have seen the Queen on her way to her Coronation."

"And now you've seen the queen of ships."

"Yours?" I asked.

"The *Rampant Lion*, none other."

"So she is the queen, is she?"

"I'll take you out to her. I'll show you. You'll see for yourself then." He leaned toward me. I drew away and looked at him coldly, which seemed to amuse him. "When will you come?" he asked.

"I doubt I ever should."

He raised eyebrows rather darker than his hair, which made the blue eyes more startling.

"You never thought to see me here, yet here I am. And now you tell me you never will come aboard my ship. I'll warrant you'll be my guest there within a week. Come, I'll wager you."

"I do not wager."

"But you'll come all the same." He was bending toward me so that his face was close to my own. I attempted to look at him with indifference, but I was not very convincing. He at least was aware of the effect he had had on me. I drew back and his eyes mocked. "Yes," he went on, "on my ship. Less than a week today. It's a wager."

"I have already told you I do not wager."

"We'll discuss terms later."

I thought I should not care to be alone with such a man on his ship.

We were interrupted by the arrival of another guest, Mistress Crocombe, a simpering middle-aged woman, and when she had joined us in a glass of malmsey one of the servants announced that supper was ready and we went down the stairs to the dining room.

It was a beautiful room, one of the loveliest in the Grange I thought it. Through the leaded windows we could see the courtyard; the walls were hung with tap-

estries depicting the Wars of the Roses; the table was
tastefully laid with more of the Venetian glass and gleaming silver dishes. Honey had made a centerpiece of various
herbs which she grew in her herb garden and the effect
was gracious.

Edward sat at the head of the table and Honey at the
foot. On Honey's right was Sir Penn and on her left Jake;
on Edward's right I sat and Miss Crocombe on his left,
which meant that I was seated next to Jake and Miss
Crocombe next to his father.

Could it be that this Captain Pennlyon is being brought
forward as another possible suitor for me? I wondered.
The thought angered me. Did they think they were going
to make me forget Carey by producing a succession of
men who could only remind me of Carey because of the
differences between them?

Honey had certainly some very fine cooks. The food
was excellently served; there was beef and lamb as well
as sucking pig, a boar's head and an enormous pie; and
she had taken the trouble to introduce that pleasant custom of honoring the guests which we followed at home.
One of the pies was in the form of a ship and on it had
been placed by thin layers of paste the words "The Rampant Lion." The delight of the Pennlyons when they saw
this was almost childish; they laughed and ate great chunks
of it. I had never seen such appetites as those two men
had. The food was washed down often noisily with muscadel and malmsey, those wines which came from Italy
and the Levant and were growing so fashionable.

They talked too, dominating the conversation. Miss Crocombe clearly adored Sir Penn, which was strange considering she was a somewhat prim spinster in her late
thirties and certainly not the kind to attract such a man
as Sir Penn whose appetites in all things I could imagine
would be voracious. He was regarding Honey in a manner
which I thought quite lascivious and occasionally he would
throw a glance at me, amused, half-regretful, and the implication I put on that was that he was leaving me to the
attention of his son. I thought his manners unpardonable.
It seemed of no importance to him that Honey was the
wife of his host.

Honey, however, seemed not to notice, or perhaps she

was so used to blatant admiration that she accepted it as normal.

I asked Jake where his last voyage had taken him.

"Out to the Barbary Coast," he said. "What a voyage! We had our troubles. Gales and seas enough to overturn us and such damage done to the ship that at one time it seemed we would have to limp home. But we braved it and we got into harbor and we tricked ourselves out to continue as we had meant."

I said: "You must face death a thousand times during one voyage."

"A thousand times is true, Mistress. That is why we love life so much. And do you not face death on land now and then?"

I was grave. I thought of my mother's anxious face and I remembered that my grandfather had lost his head for no reason than that he had sheltered a friend and my grandmother's second husband had died at the stake because he held certain opinions.

I said: " 'Tis true. No one can be completely sure on one day that he or she will live to the next."

He leaned toward me. "Therefore we should enjoy each day as it comes along and the devil take the next."

"So that is your philosophy. Do you never plan for what is to come?"

His bold eyes looked into mine. "Oh . . . often. Then I make sure that what I wish for comes to pass."

"You are very certain of yourself."

"A sailor must always be certain of himself. And I'll tell you another thing. He's always in a hurry. You see time is something he cannot afford to waste. When will you come to see my ship?"

"You must ask my sister and her husband if they would care to make the inspection."

"But I was inviting you."

"I should like to hear of your adventures."

"On the Barbary Coast? They don't make a pretty story."

"I did not expect they would." I looked across the table at Mistress Crocombe, who was coyly begging Sir Penn to tell her of *his* adventures on the high seas. He began to tell fantastic stories which I was sure were meant to shock us all. It seemed that he had more adventures than Sinbad himself. He had struggled with sea monsters and fought with savages; he had landed his craft on the coasts and brought natives ashore to work in his galleys; he had quelled a mutiny, ridden a storm; there was nothing he had not done, it seemed; and everything he said was overlaid with innuendo. When he led a little party of his men into an African hamlet I saw those men seizing the women, submitting them to indignity, pillaging, robbing.

Miss Crocombe covered her eyes with dismay and blushed hotly. She was a very silly woman and made her designs on Sir Penn too blatant. Did she really think he was going to marry her? I found it embarrassing to watch them together.

Tenerife was mentioned. It was the largest of what were called the Dog Islands because when they were first discovered so many dogs were there. Now they were known as the Canaries.

Tenerife was in the hands of the Spaniards.

"Spanish dogs!" growled Sir Penn. "I'd beat them all out of the ocean, that I would, aye and will . . . I and a few more like me." He became fierce suddenly, all banter dropped. I saw the cruel gleam in his eyes. "God's Death!" he cried, hitting the table with his fist so that the Venetian glasses trembled. "These dogs shall be swept off the seas, for I tell you this, my friends, it is either them or us. There's no room for us both."

"The oceans are wide," I said, for there was something about these men which made me want to contradict them and prove them wrong if possible, "and much may yet be discovered."

He glared at me and his eyes had narrowed—little pinpoints of blue fire between the weather wrinkles. "Then *we'll* discover them, Madam. Not they. And wherever I see them I'll bring my guns out; I'll blow them off the sea; I'll take their treasure ships from them and bring them where they belong to be."

"Treasure which they have discovered?" I said.

"Treasure!" It was Jake beside me. "There's gold in the world . . . it only has to be brought home."

"Or filched from those who have already found it?"

Honey and Edward were looking at me in dismay.

I didn't care. I felt some tremendous surge sweeping over me. I had to fight these men, father and son, brigands and pirates both, for that was what they were; and when I talked to them I was excited, alive as I hadn't been since I knew that I had lost Carey.

"By God," said Sir Penn, "it would seem the lady is a friend of the Dons."

"I have never seen one."

"Swarthy devils. I'd cut the liver and lights out of 'em. I'd send 'em down to the deep sea bed, for 'tis where they belong to be. Don't side with the Spaniards, child, or you'll be going against what's natural."

"I was siding with no one," I retorted, "I was saying that if they had found the treasure it was theirs just as if you had found it it would be yours."

"Now don't you bring schoolroom logic into this, me dear. Findings bain't keepings when it comes to Spanish gold. Nay, there's one place where treasure belongs to be and that's in an English ship and we're going to drive the Spaniards from the sea with might and main."

"There are many of them and I believe they have made great discoveries."

"There are many of them, true, and we are going to see that there are not so many, we are going to take their discoveries from them."

"Why do you not make some yourself instead?"

"Instead! We shall make them, never fear; we shall make and take. Because I tell you this, little lady, the sea belongs to us and no poxy Don is going to take one fathom of it from us."

Sir Penn sat back in his chair red-faced, almost angry with me. Mistress Crocombe looked a little afraid. I felt the color in my cheeks; Honey was signaling with her eyes for me to be silent.

Jake said: "The old Queen died in time. Our Sovereign Lady Elizabeth is of a different temper."

"By God, yes," cried Sir Penn. "We'll defend her on sea and land. And if any poxy Don turns his snout toward these shores . . . by God, he'll wish he never had."

"We can guess what would have happened had Mary lived," went on Jake. "We'd have had the Inquisition here."

"We never would have. Thank God there are men of Cornwall and Devon who would have stood together and put a stop to that," declared Sir Penn. "And God be praised we have a new Queen and she understands well that the people of this land will have nought of Papists. Mary burned our Protestant martyrs at the stake. And by God, I'd burn alive those Papists who would attempt to bring Popery back to England."

Edward had turned pale. For a moment I thought he was going to protest. Honey was gazing at her husband, warning and imploring. Be careful! she was saying; and indeed he must be. I wondered what would happen if these fierce men knew that their host and hostess were members of that faith which they despised.

I heard myself say in a rather high-pitched voice: "My stepfather was one of those martyrs."

The tension relaxed then. We had suffered such a death in the family; the implication was that we were of one belief.

Sir Penn lifted his glass and said: "To Our Sovereign Lady who has made her intentions clear."

We could all drink to the Queen and we did so. Equanimity was restored.

We talked of the Coronation and the two men were ready to listen for a few minutes; and after that we went on to speak of local affairs, of the country and the prospects for hunting the deer; and an invitation was extended to us to visit Lyon Court.

It was late in the evening when the men left; and when I was in my room I found that I was wide awake and I sat at my turret window, knowing it was useless to try to sleep.

There was a knock on my door and Honey came in. She was dressed in a long blue bedgown and her lovely hair was loose about her shoulders.

"So you're not abed?" she said.

She sat down and looked at me.

"What did you think of them?"

"Crude," I replied.

"They are far from London and the Court. They are different of course."

"It's not only their ill manners. They are arrogant."

"They are men who command rough sailors. It would be necessary for them to show authority."

"And intolerant," I said. "How fierce the father was when he talked of the Spaniards. How foolish they are. As if there is not enough of the world for them all to have what they want."

"People always want what other people have. It's a law of nature."

"Not of nature," I said. "It's a man-made custom, indulged in by the foolish."

"The Captain was impressed by you, Catharine."

"It is of no moment to me if he was."

"He is a disturbing fellow . . . they both are."

"The father looked as though he would carry you off under Edward's nose."

"Even he would not go as far as that."

"I think he would go as far as it is possible to go—his son too. I wouldn't trust either of them."

"Well, they are our neighbors. Edward's father said we must be neighborly and particularly with the Pennlyons, who are a power in these parts."

"I hope we don't see them again in a hurry."

"It would surprise me if we did not. I have an idea that the Captain may come courting you, Catharine."

I laughed derisively. "He would do well to stay away. Honey, you have arranged this."

"Dear Catharine, do you want to mourn forever?"

"It is not what I want, Honey. It is what I must do."

"If you married and had children you would forget Carey."

"I never should."

"Then what do you propose to do? Mourn all your life?"

"What I propose to do is ask you not to parade these country boors to inspect me. Please, Honey, no more of it."

"You will change. It is just that you have not met the right one yet."

"I certainly did not tonight. How could you imagine that such a man could arouse any desire in me but to get as far from him as possible?"

"He is handsome, powerful, rich . . . at least I imagine

so. You could look far before you found a more suitable
parti."

"There speaks the smug matron. Honey, I shall go home
to the Abbey if you make any more attempts to find me
a husband."

"I promise not to."

"I suppose Mother suggested that you should."

"She grieves for you, Catharine."

"I know she does. And it is no fault of hers, bless her
dear heart. Oh, let us not speak of my miseries. Shall we
indeed be obliged to visit this Lyon Court? They would
seem to be obsessed by their connection with that animal."

"They have taken the figure of the lion as their insignia.
They say there is a lion on all their ships. They are an
amazing family. They have come to great power in the
second and third generation. I heard that Sir Penn's father
was a humble fisherman plying his trade from a little
Cornish fishing village. Then he made several boats and
sent men out to fish for him; and he had more and more
boats and became a sort of king of his village. He crossed
the Tamar and set up business here. Sir Penn grew up as
the crown prince, as it were, and he acquired more ships
and gave up the calling of fishermen and went out into
the world. He was given his knighthood by Henry VIII,
who himself loved ships and foresaw that adventurers like
the Pennlyons could bring good to England."

I yawned.

"You are tired?" said Honey.

"Tired of these Pennlyons."

"I doubt it will not be long before they are at sea, the
son at least."

"It will be a pleasure not to see him."

Honey stood up and then she gave the real reason for
her visit.

"You gathered they are fanatical in their religious beliefs."

"I did, and what astonished me was that they should
have any."

"We shall have to be careful. It would not be wise for
them to know that we celebrate the Mass in this house."

"I am so weary of these conflicts," I assured her. "You
can rely on me to say nothing of the matter."

"It would seem," said Honey, "that there is a movement from the True Religion."

"Which is the true?" I said angrily. "You say the road to Rome is the right one because Edward believes that and it was necessary for you to before you married him. We know that members of our own family take the Protestant view. Who is right?"

"Of course Edward is right . . . *we* are right."

"In matters of religion it seems all people believe they are right and all who disagree with them wrong. For this very reason I refuse to side with either."

"Then you are without religion."

"I think I can be a better Christian by not hating those who disagree with me. I do not care for doctrines, Honey. They bring too much suffering. I will go along with neither. I'm tired now, and in no mood for a theological discussion tonight."

She rose.

"All I beg of you, Catharine, is be careful."

"You may trust me."

She kissed me lightly on the cheek and went out; and I thought how fortunate she was with her adoring husband, her startling beauty and her certainty that she had found the True Faith.

But my thoughts were almost immediately back with our visitors. I looked out across the sea and there was his ship at anchor; soon I thought, I shall be at this window watching it sail away. And I pictured him on the deck, shouting orders, legs astride, defying anyone to disobey him; I saw him with a cutlass in his hand boarding a Spanish ship; I saw the blood run from the cutlass; I heard his triumphant laugh; and I saw him with the golden coins in his hands, letting them run through his fingers while his eyes gleamed as covetously as they had when they had rested on me.

I shook myself. I went to bed and was vaguely irritated because I could not get the man out of my mind.

I awoke. My room was full of moonlight. I was not sure how long I had been asleep. I lay very still listening to the sounds of the countryside—the sudden rustle of leaves; the hooting of an owl. Why had I who usually slept so soundly awakened in this way? Had something startled me?

I closed my eyes preparing to drift back into sleep when I heard the clock in the tower strike three. It was an unusual clock and all callers at the house went out into the courtyard to look at it. It was adorned with the figure of a man who resembled the late King Henry VIII, father of our Sovereign; he struck a bell to give the hour. It was quite a curio here—although at home we had one or two unusual clocks.

Three o'clock. I rose and put on my fur-edged wrap. I went to the window and looked out. My gaze went at once to the *Rampant Lion*, but it did not stay there, for farther out to sea was a magnificent sight, such a ship as I had never seen before. She towered above the water. She was majestic. I knew little of ships except what I had learned since coming here; but I did not notice that the forecastle instead of projecting over the bows rose straight up from the jutting forepeak.

I had never seen such a stately ship. Beside her the *Rampant Lion* looked small and insignificant.

I sat for some time watching this beautiful ship, and as I did so I saw a bobbing light on her and then on the water a dark speck. It disappeared and then appeared again. It was coming nearer. I watched. It was a small boat which was being rowed to the shore.

I looked at the *Rampant Lion* again. I thought: I wish he could see this fine ship. I wish he could compare his precious *Lion* with that one.

I saw quite clearly the little boat bobbing about on the water. Then it disappeared and I could see it no more; I looked in vain for it. The great ship remained and I watched and waited, but nothing more happened.

I heard the clock in the courtyard strike four and I realized that I was cold.

The ship was still there, but there was no sign of the little boat. I went back to my bed; I could not get my feet warm. I did at last and then I slept. It was late when I awoke. I remembered at once and went to the window. There was no sign of the ship or the little boat. The *Rampant Lion* was riding the waters proudly because there was no majestic stranger ship to dwarf her.

What a ship it had been! I had never seen the like before; and when I looked out across the water I asked myself: Did I truly see that glorious ship, or did I imagine it?

No. I had wakened in the night. What had awakened me? Some instinct? Some premonition? And then I had looked and seen the ship.

Or had I dreamed it? There had been such talk of ships on the previous night; those men—and particularly the young man—had forced themselves into my mind so that I could not forget them. Perhaps it had been a dream. But of course I had awakened. I had seen the ship. But because of the pictures those two men had conjured up in my mind had it seemed so grand and glorious?

I knew of course what I had seen, but I was not going to mention it. Honey and Edward would think I had been too impressed by the Pennlyons and that was the last thing I would admit.

At Trewynd I rode a frisky little mare. I had been completely at home on a horse since I was a child. We were all taught to ride at an early age, for if one were to rely on one's legs one would never get far from home.

I liked to ride out every day and alone. I hated to be accompanied by a groom, which I suppose I should have been. My little Marigold knew me well; she had traveled with me from the Abbey; we understood each other and the sound of my voice could both soothe and command her.

On that morning after the Pennlyons' visit I rode out, but as I left the stables I heard Jake Pennlyon's resonant voice. So he had called already. I congratulated myself on having escaped him. I loved the countryside; it was different from that around the Abbey. Here there were steep hills, winding paths, pinewoods and the foliage was more lush because it was warmer than in the southeast and there was so much rain. I imagined what flowers there would be in the springtime, and was looking forward to that season when I asked myself if I intended to stay away from home for so long.

While I was musing I heard the sound of horse's hoofs behind me, and turning my head, I saw Jake Pennlyon galloping up, riding a powerful white horse.

"Oh," I said flatly.

"They told me you had gone out, so I trailed you."

"Why did you do that?"

"To have speech with you, of course."

"We talked only last night."

"But we have a great deal to say to each other."

"*I* did not think that."

"Well, mayhap it is I who have a great deal to say to you."

"Perhaps some other time." I pressed my heels into Marigold's flanks and she started off, but he was beside me; I knew at once that Marigold could not outdistance his powerful steed.

"A sailor can't afford to beat about the bush. One thing he is short of . . . is time."

Realizing that I could not escape him, I slowed up.

"Well, pray say what it is and I will continue my ride."

"We can chat comfortably as we continue *our* ride."

"I did not ask you to accompany me."

"What matters that? I asked myself."

"You don't hesitate to press your company even though it may not be wanted?"

"I don't hesitate when I've made up my mind that I want something."

"And what pray do you want now?"

"You."

I gave a short laugh. "You have strange desires."

"Very normal ones, I do assure you."

"I know you scarcely at all. We have met but once."

"Twice," he corrected me. "Have you forgotten our encounter on the Hoe? That was when it all began."

"I was not aware that anything had begun."

He seized Marigold's bridle. His face was grim, cruel suddenly. "You must not deny the truth to me, Mistress," he said. "You know what has begun."

"And you it seems know more of me than I know myself —or so you would have me believe. I am not one of your friends who comes when you beckon and pants with glee when you whistle her as you would your dog."

"I should always call you by your name and you could

always have a higher place in my estimation than that I reserve for my dogs."

"When do you sail?" I asked.

"Two months from now."

"So. long?" I asked.

"So short," he replied. "There is much to be done in those two months. I have to victual my ship, overhaul her, make her seaworthy, get my crew and woo a lady . . . all at the same time."

"I wish you good fortune." I turned Marigold toward the Trewynd estate. "And now I will bid you good-bye, for I am not going your way."

"Indeed you are, for your way is my way."

"I am going back to the. stables."

"You have just ridden out."

"Nevertheless, I am going back," I said.

"Stay and talk with me."

"I must say good-bye."

"You are afraid of me."

I looked at him scornfully.

"Then if not," he retorted, "why won't you stay and talk with me?"

"Certainly I am not afraid of you, Captain Pennlyon. But pray say what it is you have to say and I'll be gone."

"I was taken with you the first time I saw you and I don't think you were unaware of me."

"There are several ways of being aware."

"And you were aware of me in many ways."

"I thought you insolent . . . arrogant. . . ."

"Pray don't spare me," he mocked.

"The sort of person I have no great wish to meet."

"And yet whom you cannot resist."

"Captain Pennlyon," I said, "you have too high an opinion of yourself and your ship."

"My ship at least is the finest that sailed the ocean."

"I saw a finer last night," I was goaded to say.

"Where?"

"In the bay."

"You saw the *Rampant Lion*."

"She was there, but there was this other which dwarfed her and was twice as magnificent."

"You may mock me but pray not my ship."

"I mock no one. I merely state a fact. I looked from my window and saw the most beautiful ship I have ever seen."

"The most beautiful ship you have ever seen is the *Rampant Lion.*"

"No, this was indeed more majestic and fine. She was so tall and lofty . . . like a castle afloat."

He was looking at me intently. "Did you see how many masts she had?"

"Four, I think."

"And her decks . . . were they high?"

"Why, yes, I suppose so. She was so tall . . . I did not know ships could be so tall."

He seemed to have forgotten his interest in me. The ship of the night had driven all other thoughts from his mind.

He questioned me avidly. I answered as best I could, but my knowledge of ships was sparse. He made no protest as I walked my horse back to Trewynd stables; he merely kept pace with me, firing questions at me, exasperated because I could not describe in detail the ship I had seen.

He burst out suddenly: "It could not be. But by God's Death, it would seem that you are describing a Spanish galleon."

I had not realized how fervently religious Edward was. At the Abbey my mother had never instilled one doctrine into me rather than another. Her ideal had been tolerance and I knew that she did not think that the manner of worship mattered so much as that one lived as Christian a life as was possible. She had once said to me: "It is in people's actions toward their fellowmen that we perceive their religion. What virtue is there in praising God if one is cruel to His creatures?"

Few people were in agreement with her. The last Queen and her ministers had burned people at the stake not because they had robbed or murdered but because they did not believe according to Rome.

And now we had turned around and the religious laws which had existed in Mary's reign were abolished and those of her predecessor's time were restored. The Protestant religion was in the ascendancy and although there might not be a recurrence of the Smithfield fires it was dangerous to go against the spiritual domination ordered by the Queen.

Whether our Queen was firm in her views or not, I could not be sure. The dangerous years when she had come close to losing her head would be remembered by her; then she had prevaricated, although perhaps she had leaned toward the Reformed Faith; and indeed had she not, she might not be on the throne this day.

Now of course she had a very good political reason for her firm Protestant views. Across the Channel was a Queen of France who was also a Queen of Scotland and who many believed was also the true Queen of England: Mary Stuart, the granddaughter of Margaret, sister of our late King Henry VIII. Thus many said she was the direct heir to the throne of England while Elizabeth—whose father had put aside his true wife, Catherine of Aragon, to marry Elizabeth's mother, Anne Boleyn—was a bastard and had no real claim to it.

Mary Stuart was Catholic, so she was the figurehead of those who would wish to see England back in the Papal fold. Elizabeth therefore must set herself up as the leader of Protestantism. I felt certain that our Queen's motives were not prompted by religion so much as by politics.

But these politics existed; and those who celebrated Mass and worshipped in the Roman manner were potential enemies of the Queen, for they would wish to lead the country back to Rome and if this were done, Mary Stuart, not Elizabeth Tudor, would be accepted as the Queen of England.

Therefore, in worshiping as Edward and Honey did, there was danger.

I knew that services were conducted in the chapel behind closed doors. I knew that beneath the altar cloth there was a hidden door, and I guessed that behind that door were images and all that was used in celebration of the Mass.

I did not join in this, but I was aware that several members of the household did. I had not thought very much about it until the night when the Pennlyons had talked so fiercely about the Dons. I thought how intolerant they would be of those who did not think as they did; and dangerous too.

I could not pass the chapel after that night without a twinge of alarm.

Jennet, the young girl whom I had brought with me from the Abbey, was putting my clothes away, smoothing her hands over the cloth of a velvet cloak with a sort of ecstasy.

Jennet was about a year younger than I was—small, lithe, with a tangle of thick dark curls. I had noticed one or two of the menservants follow her with their eyes and I thought Jennet must be warned.

Jennet's eyes sparkled as she worked and I asked if she were happy in these new surroundings.

"Oh, yes, Mistress Catharine," she replied fervently.

"So you like it better than the Abbey?"

She shivered a little. "Oh, yes, Mistress. 'Tis more open like. There was ghosts in the Abbey . . . everyone said. And you could never know what was going to come up next."

Jennet was a great gossip; I had heard her chatter to the maids; if I gave her an opportunity she would have plenty to say to me.

"So you feel it's different here?"

"Oh, yes, Mistress, why, at the Abbey . . . I'd lie trembling on my pallet at night even though the others was there. Young Mary swore she saw monks going into the church one day at dusk . . . long robes, she said, and chanting like. She said terrible things had happened there and where terrible things happen there'll be ghosts."

"But you never really *saw* a ghost, Jennet."

"No, Mistress, but I felt 'em there and 'tis the same. 'Tis more as a big house should be here. Ghosts there could be, as most houses have their ghosts, but here it 'ud be a ghost like other ghosts—a poor lady as 'ad been crossed in love or a gentleman who had lost his inheritance and thrown himself from the tower like . . . something ghosts 'as always done—but in the Abbey they were terrible ghosts. Monks and evil. . . . Oh, there was evil there all right. My Granny remembers when the men came and what they done. . . . Here, though, 'tis different. There's ships too. Oh, I like to see the ships." Jennet giggled. "And that Captain Pennlyon, Mistress. I said to Mary: 'I never did see such a fine gentleman,' and Mary she says the same, Mistress."

I felt angry suddenly. So the maids were discussing him. I pictured his swaggering past them, perhaps bestowing a kiss on the prettiest, marking her down as possible prey. The man sickened me.

And what was I doing chattering with Jennet!

I said: "Pray put those away quickly, Jennet. Don't chatter so much. Have you nothing to do with your time?"

Jennet, naturally a little bewildered by my sudden change of manner, hung her head and flushed slightly. I hoped I had conveyed firmly my indifference to Captain Pennlyon.

Jennet had stopped in her work and was looking out of the window down onto the courtyard.

"What's there, Jennet?" I asked.

" 'Tis a young man, Mistress."

I went and stood beside her. There was indeed a young man; he was dressed in a russet-colored doublet with green hose; his hair was very dark, fitting sleekly about his head, and as we gazed down at him he looked up.

He bowed elaborately.

I called down, "Who are you?"

"Good Mistress," he cried, "if you are the lady of the house I would have speech with you."

"Marry!" breathed Jennet. "But he's handsome!"

I said, "I am not the mistress of the house, but I will come down and see you."

I went down into the hall, Jennet at my heels, and I opened the iron-studded door. The young man bowed once more, very deferentially.

"The mistress of the house is not at home, I think. Perhaps you could tell me your business."

"I seek work, my lady."

"Work?" I cried. "What kind of work?"

"I am not particular as to its nature. I would be grateful for anything that came my way."

"The management of the household is not in my hands. I am a guest here."

"Shall I see if I can find the master?" asked Jennet eagerly.

He flashed her a look of gratitude and she colored prettily.

"Please," he said.

Jennet ran off and I said to the young man, "What is your name?"

"It is Richard Rackell."

"And from whence do you come?"

"I came from the North. I believed that in the South I could make my way more easily than in my native parts."

"And now you wish to work here awhile and then go off for fresh adventures?"

"It would depend. Always I look for somewhere where I can settle."

Men often came looking for work, particularly at the end of the summer at Michaelmas. There was work in the fields, threshing, winnowing, salting down cattle which could not be fed during the winter. But there was something about this young man which was different from those who usually came.

I asked him if he had any experience of harvesting; he said No but that he was good with horses and he hoped there might be a place for him in the stables.

By this time Edward had appeared. He rode into the courtyard, an elegant man who seemed to have grown more slight and delicate-looking in the last days. I suppose I was comparing him with the Pennlyons.

"Edward," I said, "this young man is looking for work."

Edward was always courteous and, I believe, eager to do a good turn. He was popular with the work people although I imagined they despised him a little. They were not used to such gentle manners.

He asked the young man into the winter parlor and sent for a tankard of ale to refresh him. Not many prospective employers treated work people thus, but Edward was something of a visionary. He did not believe his fortune placed him above others; he knew that he was more learned, more cultured, more graciously mannered than the farm laborers, but if a man had good manners and some education he would not consider him beneath himself because he was, say, the son of a doctor or lawyer and Edward was the son of a lord. Honey had often said to me: "Edward is a good man."

She was right.

I did not accompany them to the winter parlor naturally; I went back to my bedroom, where Jennet had returned to her task of putting my clothes away.

"Oh, Mistress Catharine," she said, "do you think the master'll find a place for him?"

"He does not seem to me to be fitted for hard labor in the fields and that is what will be looked for at this time of year."

"He did look a real gentleman," said Jennet, smoothing my fly cape. "They make handsome men in the North."

"You are far too interested in men, Jennet," I said severely.

"Oh, but they'm interesting folk, Mistress."

"I should warn you. You know full well what can happen to girls who don't take good care of themselves."

"Oh, Mistress, you be thinking of the sailors. Them that's here today and gone tomorrow. If this young Richard Rackell do come he's here to stay, and what he does will have to be answered for."

"Jennet, I have noticed that you are inclined to invite attention."

"Oh, Mistress." She flushed deeply and giggled.

I went on severely: "And if this young man should be fortunate enough to be given work here you would do well to wait until he shows interest in you before you betray yours in him."

" 'Tis but a boy, Mistress," said Jennet, her eyes sparkling, and I was angry with her because I knew that she was comparing the young Richard Rackell with Captain Pennlyon.

It was typical of Edward that he should find a place for Richard Rackell in the household. He came into the solarium where Honey and I sat together, she embroidering, I idly watching her, and sat down with us.

He said: "I've put him into the stables. They need an extra groom, though how he will fit in I don't know. He has not the appearance of a groom, but he certainly has a way of handling horses. In time we'll find something else for him. My opinion is that he would make an excellent scribe, though I have no need of a scribe."

Honey smiled at her husband over her needle; she was always tender and gentle with him; he, of course, adored her. She looked beautiful with her needle poised thus and a quiet, dreamy look of contentment on her face.

"Let him serve in the stables then," said Honey. "And if something other should arise he will be there to take it."

"A pleasant young man," said Edward. "Of some education, I believe."

"He speaks with a strange accent," I added.

"That is because he comes from the North. Their speech is oft so different from our own that it can be difficult to understand it."

"One can understand Richard well enough."

"Oh, yes, but he is a young man not without education . . . not the sort who normally come knocking at the doors begging for work."

"He is reticent, Jennet tells me. She has lost no time in making his acquaintance."

Edward cleared his throat and said, "Thomas Elders will be visiting us at the end of the week."

Honey paused slightly, her needle poised. I knew that remark had made her a little uneasy.

I wanted to tell them both that they had nothing to fear from me. I would not betray what I knew, which was that Thomas Elders was a priest who traveled from one Catholic household to another, that he came as a guest who was said to be an old friend of some member of the household; and that during his stay in the house he heard confession and celebrated Mass; and at the same time ran the risk of incurring the Queen's displeasure for himself and for the members of that household he visited.

He had been once before. I had thought little of his coming then although I had quickly assessed the purpose of it.

Everyone was expecting a more tolerant attitude toward religion with the new reign and indeed it could not be more severe than the last, but that extreme tolerance had not yet come; the Queen had her reasons and so did her ministers. It was, to say the least, unwise to entertain priests in the household.

When I remembered the fierce attitude of the Pennlyons I was apprehensive.

I changed the subject by talking of the newcomer Richard Rackell.

"He has gracious manners indeed," I said. "I knew someone from the North once who came to visit my father. He did not speak or act as this young man does."

"People are never cut to a pattern," said Honey comfortably.

Then she began to talk about their neighbors and, fearing that this might lead to the Pennlyons, I rose and left them together.

Every day Jake Pennlyon called. There was nothing subtle about him; he clearly came to see me.

He noticed Richard Rackell on one occasion; he said: "I've seen that fellow before. I remember. He came to Lyon Court looking for work."

"And you had none for him."

"I don't like the look of the fellow. More like a girl than a boy."

"Do you expect everyone to roar like a lion?"

"I reserve that privilege for myself."

"Or," I added, "bray like an ass."

"Which I leave to others, but I would look for neither a lion nor an ass in a servant. Some tale he had about coming from the North."

"Why should it be a tale? Edward believed him."

"Edward would believe anything. He has a mistaken idea that everyone else follows his fine mode of behavior."

"Perhaps it is more pleasant to believe the best than the worst of people before anything is proved against them."

"Nonsense. It is better to be prepared for the worst."

"As usual, I disagree with you."

"Which delights me. I dread the day when we are in complete agreement."

There was no doubt that he enjoyed our verbal battles. To my amazement, so did I.

When he was late calling one day I found myself at the

window watching for him, hoping, I kept assuring myself, that he would not come; but I couldn't help the twinge of excitement I felt when I saw his white horse in the stableyard and heard his loud voice shouting to the grooms.

We visited Lyon Court—that mansion which had been built by Sir Penn's father. On either side of the porch were lions with ferocious expressions; and a lion's face was molded over the porch. It was a younger house than Trewynd and its Gothic hall extended to the full height of the house; Lyon Court had its central block built around a courtyard and east and west wings; in these wings were the bedchambers and the living quarters. In the center block were the hall and the grand staircase leading to the gallery. It was impressive and rather ostentatious, what one would expect, I told myself, of such a family. The Pennlyons had not always been in possession of wealth and, therefore, that possession seemed something to boast of. It had been in Edward's family for years and he had been brought up to accept it as a natural right.

Still, I could not help being caught up in the enthusiasm of both Sir Penn and Jake Pennlyon for their magnificent house. In the Long Gallery there was a portrait of the founder of their fortunes, Sir Penn's father, who sat uneasily in his fine robes, and of Sir Penn, very sure of himself; his wife, a rather fragile-looking lady with a bewildered expression; and Jake Pennlyon, jaunty, arrogant, his brilliant blue eyes the most startling feature on the canvas as they were in the flesh.

The gardens were very fine. Sir Penn had numerable gardeners who were kept busy making his land the most outstanding in the neighborhood; the graveled paths were symmetrical; the flower beds immaculate, although less colorful than they would be in the heart of summer. There were still roses in the rose garden, though; and there was a herb garden which particularly interested Honey; I told Sir Penn that my grandmother was something of an authority on plants and herbs.

"There was a witch in the village," I told him. "My grandmother befriended her and before she died she gave her several recipes."

"Witches!" spat out Sir Penn. "I'd hang the Devil's spawn."

"Well, this was a good witch, I believe. She cured people."

"My dear young lady, there be no such thing as a good witch. She's damned and her purpose is to carry others to damnation. Any witch hereabouts and she'll be strung up by her skinny neck, I promise you."

"I'd not hold you to the promise," I said, wondering why I found it impossible not to spar with these Pennlyons.

"Now don't you start praising witches, me dear. There's many a woman come to grief through taking sides."

"The only safe way I see is to take the right side, which of course is yours," I said.

But irony was lost on Sir Penn.

We were shown the statues which had been erected, the sundials and the fountains, the yew trees cut into fantastic shapes. Sir Penn was very proud of his garden.

It was during this visit that Jake invited us all on board the *Rampant Lion*. I wanted to refuse to go, but that was impossible when Honey and Edward accepted the invitation.

A few days after that visit I went for my afternoon ride and when I came back Jennet was waiting for me in the stables.

"Oh, Mistress Catharine," she said. "Something terrible have happened. The mistress has taken a fall; she hurt her foot and wants you to go to her right away. I'm to bring you to her."

"Where is she?"

"She's on board the *Rampant Lion*."

"Of course she is not."

"But, Mistress, she is. She went for a visit."

"And the master?"

"He couldn't go like. He said, 'You go alone, my dear,' and the mistress went."

"Alone on the *Rampant Lion*!"

"Well, the Captain had asked them and was expecting them. It was all sudden like."

"But I was to go too."

"Well, they did say they'd go without you, Mistress.

And so . . . the master he were called away and the mistress went."

I felt angry suddenly. What was Honey thinking of, to go alone to a ship where such a man was in command?

"Then she tripped and hurt her leg and the Captain's sent a messenger and I'm to take you out there without delay."

I wondered about Honey then. I had never really understood her. I often had a notion that she harbored secrets. Could it possibly be that this swaggering buccaneer of a man had attracted her in some way and had induced her to be unfaithful to Edward?

It could not be. But if she were alone on his ship, and she had sent for me because she wished me to pretend that I had gone with her. . . .

That made sense.

I thought of Edward's sensitive face and a great desire to protect him from any unpleasant truth swept over me. I said: "I'll come at once, Jennet."

She was very relieved; and we hurried down the drive and almost ran all the way to the Hoe, where a small boat was ready to take us out to the *Rampant Lion*. We bobbed about on the sea, and looking landward, I could see the turret of Trewynd, where I had often sat to watch the craft on the water.

Jake Pennlyon was standing on the deck, clearly waiting for us. I clung to the rope ladder and was lifted up in his arms.

He was laughing. "I knew you'd come," he said.

One of his men lifted Jennet on board.

"You'd better take me to my sister," I said.

"Come this way." He held my arm as though to pilot me across the deck.

I said to him: "Why did she come here without Edward? I don't understand it."

"She wanted to see my ship."

"She should have waited until we all came. We shall have to get her ashore. It won't be easy if she's hurt her foot. How bad is it? Oh, dear, I do hope no bones are broken."

He led the way up a stairway and threw open a door.

"My cabin," he said.

It was spacious, I suppose, as ships' cabins go. There

was a tapestry on what I was to learn to call the bulkhead. There was a bookcase with books and a shelf with instruments, and on a table a revolving globe on which was depicted the earth's surface. On the wall was a brass astrolabe, a compass, hourglasses and a long cross staff which I also learned later was an arbalist.

I noticed these things vaguely while I looked around for Honey. When I saw that she was not there I felt twinges of alarm which were half excited anticipation.

"Where is my sister?" I demanded.

He laughed; he had shut the door and was leaning against it.

"In her garden perhaps. In her stillroom . . . occupying herself with those tasks which are the joy and duty of every housewife."

"In her garden! But I was led to believe. . . ."

He laughed. "Did I not tell you that you would come aboard my ship within the week?"

"But I understood my sister was here."

"You did not really believe that, did you?"

"But. . . ."

"Oh, come, you wanted to accept my invitation, did you not? And I wanted you to. So why should the means of bringing about this happy conclusion worry us?"

"I am not worried," I said.

"You should be if you are really concerned with what you pretend to be."

"I think you've gone mad."

"My sanity is something I shall never allow to desert me."

I said: "I wish to go."

"But I wish you to stay. I am the Captain of this ship. Here everyone obeys my orders."

"Those poor creatures who serve you may. They, poor souls, are at your mercy."

"And you think you are not?"

"I have had enough of this folly."

"And I could never have enough." He came toward me and put his arms about me, pinioning mine so that I was caught in a firm grip.

"Captain Pennlyon, there is no doubt that you are mad.

Do you realize that my family will never forgive this insult?"

He laughed. I noticed that his eyes were tilted slightly at the corners and that his eyebrows followed the upward tilt; this gave him an expression that was puckish and satanic at the same time. I tried to prize myself free.

"Let me go," I cried and tried to kick his shins; but he held me in such a way that it was impossible for me to do so. I thought, he has held many women thus and I pictured his raiding far-off hamlets and villages and the manner in which he and his men would treat the women they captured.

"You can't escape," he mocked, "so it's no use trying. You are at my mercy."

"Well, what do you want of me?"

"Surely you know that."

"If I am right in my assumption. . . ."

"Which I am sure you are. . . ."

"I will tell you that I consider your manners gross; I find you boorish, quite unlike—"

"The fancy gentlemen whom it has been your ill fortune to meet in the past. Well, now, my girl, you have met a man who finds you to his liking and in spite of his lack of manners you find him irresistible."

Then he took his arms from about me and caught my head; he pulled it back and his mouth was on mine . . . warm, revolting, I told myself firmly. I tried to protest, but it was useless. I could not escape from this fierce embrace.

When he at last released me I was shaking—with fury, I again reminded myself.

I said: "How dare you behave in such a way . . . I have never. . . ."

"Of course you have never been kissed like that before. But don't fret. It will not be the last time."

I was beginning to be alarmed. I was on his ship alone. I had been tricked. There were men on board, but they were his slaves.

He guessed my thoughts.

"Exciting, eh? You are at my mercy. You can't get away unless it is my wish that you should."

I could only repeat: "You would not dare to touch me."

"Now that I know that your eagerness matches my own . . . but I, being honest, make no secret of my desires while you, being deceitful, hide yours, feigning reluctance."

"I never heard such nonsense! You are a loathsome, ill-mannered pirate and I hate you."

"You protest too strongly," he said.

"You will be hanged for this. My family. . . ."

"Oh, yes," he said, "you are a girl of good family. This is a matter which we have taken into consideration."

"Who has taken it into consideration?"

"My father and I, and for what purpose you must be aware."

"I refuse to discuss this unpleasant subject."

"It is a fascinating subject. My father said to me: 'It's time you married, Jake. We want more Pennlyons. That girl will be a good breeder. Time you took her to bed. But make it legal this time. I want grandchildren.' "

"I refuse to stay here to be insulted. You must look elsewhere for your good breeder."

"Why should I when I've found her?"

"I believe it would be necessary to get her consent."

"That will not be impossible."

"Are you under the illusion that you are one of the gods come down from Olympus?"

"That may be an illusion others have about me. I know myself for a man who is clear as to what he wants and gets it."

"Not always," I reminded him. "Not if I am included in those desires."

"There are ways. Do you want me to make this plain to you?"

His face was close to me and I felt my throat constrict. I wished my heart would not beat so loudly. It might betray my fear or whatever it was he aroused in me.

"You are revolting. If you do not let me go at once I can promise you that my family will bring you to the courts for this."

"Oh, that good family," he said. "Now, my fine lady, there is nothing insulting about an offer of marriage."

"There is when it comes from you."

"Don't goad me too far, I have the devil of a temper."

"And let me tell you that so have I."

"I knew we were well matched. What boys we'll have. Let's begin . . . now. The marriage vows will come after."

"I have told you you must look elsewhere for your breeder."

"I have found her and I have sworn to God that you will bear my sons."

I said: "Stand back and open that door."

"On condition."

"What condition?"

"That you give your word to marry me . . . without delay, and that you'll be with child before I sail."

"And if I won't?"

"You give me no alternative."

I was silent and with a rough gesture he threw me onto his bunk. I stared at him in horror as he deliberately removed his coat.

I got to my feet. He was laughing at me. "You should understand, my precious virgin . . . at least I suppose you are a virgin. You are. I can spot 'em. It is something in the eyes."

"You insult me."

"In truth I honor you. I choose only those who are worthy of my manhood."

I said: "Do you really mean that if I don't promise to marry you you will force me as though I am some . . . some . . ."

He nodded. "Some wench of no consequence. Though, mind you, there have been fine ladies on occasion. It is no use looking at me with those great disbelieving eyes. You know I am a man of my word. Did I not promise you that I would have you on my ship within the week? Now what's it to be? I've told you already sailors have no time to waste."

"Let me out of here. You tricked me. I only came because. . . ."

"Because you wanted to."

"It is the last thing I wanted."

"Don't you believe it. I know you better than you know yourself."

"Jennet told me. . . ."

"Now don't blame the girl. She knew when she must do as she's told."

"Jennet!" I said. "Did she know that I was being tricked?"

"Tricked! My dear girl, I was giving you an excuse for coming here. I'm not noted for my patience."

"I must get out of here," I said.

"That is your answer." Deliberately he put on his coat.

He opened the door; he led the way down a flight of stairs. Jennet was waiting there.

I went to her and said, "You lied, Jennet. You told me Mistress Ennis was here. You knew full well she was not."

"Mistress Catharine, I . . . I . . ." She looked beyond me to Jake Pennlyon.

"You slut!" I said, and imagined the way he would look at her and lay his hands on her. No need to make her fine promises; she would be willing and eager. I knew Jennet and to my shame I had discovered that potent power in him.

Jake Pennlyon laughed, low and mocking.

"Row me ashore at once," I said.

I was trembling as we descended the ladder. I did not look back.

As we were rowed back Jennet sat with her head lowered, her hands visibly trembling. As soon as I was helped ashore I walked ahead of her back to Trewynd.

When I was in my room I was so angry that I had to vent my wrath on someone. I sent for Jennet.

She came trembling.

I had always before been rather mild with servants; Honey was far more haughty with them than I ever was; but I could not get out of my mind the thought of that man's mocking eyes and I wanted to hurt somebody; and this girl who was supposed to be my faithful maid had betrayed me.

I turned on her and cried, "Now then, girl. You had better give an account of yourself."

Jennet began to cry.

I took her by the shoulders and shook her. Then she stammered: "I meant no harm, Mistress. The gentleman he asked me . . . he talked to me like. . . ."

"Like," I mimicked. "Like what?"

"Well, he talked kind like and said I looked a good maiden. . . ."

"And he kissed you and fondled you as no man should a virgin girl."

I saw by the quick color which flooded her face that this was so; and I slapped her. It was not poor Jennet's face I was slapping: it was his. I hated him so much, because he had tricked me, because he had tried to treat me in the same way as he had Jennet.

"You lied to me. You told me Mistress Ennis was on the *Rampant Lion*. You are supposed to be *my* servant and you forget that because this libertine kissed you."

Jennet sank to the floor, covered her face with her hand and burst into loud blubbering sobs. A voice from the door said: "Catharine, what has happened to you?"

Honey was standing there, serene and beautiful.

I said nothing and she came into the room and looked down at the weeping Jennet.

"Why, Catharine, you used to be so good to the servants."

Those words spoken in that manner reminded me so much of my mother that the madness of my fury passed away suddenly and I felt very ashamed of myself, of the ease with which I had been tricked and my uncontrollable anger against poor silly little Jennet.

I said to Jennet: "You can go now."

She hastily got up and fled.

"What was all that about?" asked Honey in a bewildered voice.

"It's that man. The Pennlyon man." I told her what had happened.

Honey laughed. "You should have known I wouldn't have gone to the ship alone. How could you have been so stupid as to think I would?"

"I was surprised."

"Yet you believed it! Do you think he has such a fatal fascination for all women?"

"Jennet found him irresistible."

"Jennet is a lusting virgin. She'll be the victim of the first philanderer who crosses her path."

"You think she has already been his victim?"

"That would not surprise me. But you have a high

opinion of his irresistibility if you think I would have gone visiting him alone."

"I'm sorry. It was foolish of me. I've no one but myself to blame."

"Well, at least you escaped unscathed. It will teach you to be wary of him in future."

"I shall never see him again if I can help it. As for Jennet she sickens me. I shall have one of the others for my maid. Perhaps she could go into the kitchen."

"As you will. Take Luce. She is a girl who will cause you no anxieties and offer little provocation to any man."

"I have not told you," I said, "how I escaped."

"Well?"

"He said either I gave him my promise to marry him or he would take me there and then."

"What company you get into," mocked Honey.

"In your house," I reminded her.

"Ah, but he was already an acquaintance of yours before he came here." She must have noticed how perturbed I was because she went on soothingly: "Whatever has happened to you! He can't force you to marry him and he wouldn't dare harm you—a neighbor's daughter and a member of our family. Why, the courts would hang him. That was just bravado."

"I've heard this called Pennlyon country."

"Don't believe all you hear. Edward has some power in this land, you know. Our estates are bigger than those of the Pennlyons and we've been here longer. Who are they but upstarts from across the Tamar?"

"You are comforting, Honey."

"I'm glad. Now let me tell you my news. I am going to have a child."

"Honey!" I went to her and kissed her. "That's wonderful! And you're happy. I can see you are. You've changed. You've got that maternal serenity. Mother will be delighted. She'll want you to go back to her for the birth. Yes, you must. She and Grandmother will coo over you. They won't trust anyone to look after you. And is Edward pleased?"

"Edward is delighted and I don't intend to disappoint him this time." She was referring to the miscarriage she had had in the first year of her marriage.

"We must take the utmost care," I said; and I forgot the unpleasant incident on the ship in my excitement about the baby.

I was not allowed to forget for long.

That day Thomas Elders rode over. When he came he stayed the night, heard Mass in the chapel the following day and then probably stayed another night before going off to the next Catholic household.

He did not come as a priest but as a friend of Edward's; he supped with us and conversation at the table was never of religious matters. The next day Mass was celebrated and those trusted servants who wished to attend did so. The others were quite unaware of what was going on. The chapel was always kept locked so that the fact that it should be so during the hearing of Mass raised no comment.

I, of course, did not attend, although I was aware of what was going on, and remembering the past so well and the anxieties my mother had suffered, I was always uneasy when Thomas Elders was in the house.

I went out riding in the morning. The excitement of Honey's news had subsided and I kept thinking of those shameful moments in the Captain's cabin on the *Rampant Lion*. I returned from my ride and took Marigold to the stables. The new young man, Richard Rackell, took her from me.

I said: "I think she's losing a shoe, Richard."

He nodded. He had deeply set, expressive eyes and was quite handsome. He bowed and the gesture would have graced a Court.

I asked: "Are you getting along well?"

He replied that he thought he was giving satisfaction.

"I know it is not the kind of work to which you are accustomed."

"I become accustomed, Mistress," he replied.

He interested me. There was something rather mysterious about him. I remember that Jake Pennlyon had been suspicious that he came from the North. Then I forgot Richard Rackell for my angry thoughts were back with that man who never seemed to be out of my mind for very long.

My way to the house led around by the chapel. Mass would either be in progress or over by now.

My heart leaped in sudden terror, for the small door which led to the leper's squint opened suddenly and Jake Pennlyon emerged. I immediately thought: Through the leper's squint one can look into the chapel!

There was a fierce glint in his eyes the second or so before they alighted on me. Then they were bright with that intense blue fire.

"Well met, Mistress," he said, and came toward me. He would have embraced me, but I stepped hurriedly back and he allowed me to do so while implying that he was respecting my objections and could comfortably have ignored them.

"What are you doing here?"

"What should I be doing but calling on my betrothed?"

"And who is this . . . Jennet, the maid, who I believe has caught your fancy?"

"A serving wench, be she maid or harlot, could not be my betrothed. She whom I have chosen to honor now stands before me."

"She whom you attempted to dishonor, you mean." I turned away, but he was beside me.

He gripped my arm so that it hurt.

"Know this," he said. "My father is now at the house. I came to look for you. He is planning the celebrations for our betrothal. I had of course acquainted him with your acceptance of my proposal. He wishes to make it a grand occasion. He has invited half the neighborhood."

"Then," I cried, "he will have to cancel the invitations."

"On what grounds?"

"That there is no betrothal. How could there be without the consent of the intended bride?"

"But that has already been given." He looked at me in mock reproach. "You have so soon forgotten visiting me in my cabin. Surely you would not have come there if there had not been an understanding between us?"

"You tricked me."

"You are not going to tell me again that you did not come with the utmost willingness?" He had raised his eyebrows in mock seriousness.

I cried: "I hate you!"

"Well, that is a good start," he said.

I tried to release my arm, but he would not let me go.

"What do you propose to do?" he asked.

"Go and tell your father that he should cancel his invitations without delay."

"He'll not do that."

"Then you must find another bride."

"I have found the one I want. She is here now."

I looked around. "I do not see her."

"Why feign reluctance when you are eager? There is no need to. Let us have done with such insincerities. Let us be truthful to each other." He drew me close to him and held me so tightly that I felt my bones would break. My rage overcame all other feelings.

I kicked him; but he laughed. He held me just to show how puny were my efforts to escape.

I attempted with words what I could not do with physical strength.

"Your buccaneering methods may be effective on the high seas. They will avail you nothing in a gentleman's household."

"Wrong again, my wildcat. They will bring me what I want and at the moment I want you. I'd have had you ere this, but it must be legal this time. Our son will be born in wedlock. Not that I'll brook delay. But we'll wed first and bed after."

"Even your wife would have to make her vows of her own volition, I suppose. How will you achieve that?"

"There are ways," he said.

"You have chosen unwisely if you expect obedience from me."

"I have chosen as I must and I shall have your obedience. I shall tame my wildcat so that she will purr for my caresses."

"Your metaphors are clumsy, like everything else you do."

"Listen to me," he said. "You will come and meet my father. You will smile and tell him you are pleased to have been honored by us."

"You joke."

"I am serious. You have given me your promise and, by God, you will keep it."

"You will make me do that?"

"I will. Do not be foolish, Mistress Catharine. It could go ill with you if I were to tell what I have this day seen through the leper's squint."

I turned pale and the triumph leaped into his eyes.

"I have long suspected," he said. "I would not answer for what should happen if my father knew."

"Even though his future daughter-in-law were involved?"

"You're not a Papist. I know that well enough. If you were I'd beat the Popery out of you."

"What a nice kind husband you will be."

"So you have accepted that I shall be your husband."

"You don't let me finish. I was going to say . . . to the poor simpleton who is misguided enough to marry you."

"That will be no simpleton. It will be a wise woman. Catharine, no less, for no one else will do. I have sworn to have her and I do not swear in vain."

"And if I refuse?"

"How can you bring disaster to this house?"

"You would not be so cruel."

"I would be anything to get what I want."

"I hate you as I never thought it possible to hate anyone."

"While your eyes flash for me I'm happy enough. I will wait a week or so . . . no more. So come with me now. You will meet my father. You will smile and behave as though this match between us is a delight to you."

"How could I be so false?"

"Either be false or the betrayer of this household."

"Does that mean that you would harm them?"

"I mean every word of it."

"First attempted rape. Then blackmail."

"That is just a beginning," he said with a laugh.

I was beaten. I knew it. How foolish they were to have the priest here. Why hadn't they thought of the leper's squint? They locked the door to the chapel and forgot the one which led to the room in which those who looked through the squint assembled.

As I walked across the lawn with him beside me I was thinking: The betrothal then . . . and no more. I shall think of a way out. I will go back to my mother. Honey will have to help me. After all, she and Edward have brought me to this.

Sir Penn was sprawling in the big chair with the carved wooden back. He chuckled when I entered the hall with Jake. Honey and Edward were not there. I wondered whether they were still in the chapel.

Sir Penn hoisted himself out of the chair and came toward me; he put his arms about me and kissed me hard on the mouth. I felt bruised where his lips had touched me.

"Well," he said, "my son never was one to waste time. You're getting a bargain there, my girl. I can vouch for him."

He thrust his elbow into Jake's ribs and Jake laughed.

"No need to tell her that, Father," he said. "She's no *foolish* virgin."

They laughed together, obscenely, I thought. Jake put his arm over my shoulder; I felt his fingers pressing my flesh.

"We'll have the wedding shortly following the betrothal. There's no sense in waiting. We want you to give us a little Pennlyon without delay."

I wanted to cry out: I shall never marry this man. I'd rather burn at the stake.

But it was precisely because I feared what would happen to us all since this ruthless man knew what had taken place in the chapel this morning that I was allowing them to assume that I had accepted Jake Pennlyon's proposal.

Honey appeared then—without her usual serenity. Her face was flushed, her manner uncertain. One of the servants must have told her that the Pennlyons were here and she would be thinking of the necessity to guard Thomas Elders from such men as these.

"Good day and welcome," she said. "So Catharine is here. I have just heard that you had arrived. You will take some wine?" She went to the bell rope.

Edward came in and greeted the visitors.

"A happy occasion," shouted Sir Penn. "These young people. . . . Well, I have lost no time. There's never time to waste. We're celebrating the betrothal at Lyon Court and then we'll follow with the wedding. They're impatient, these two, and I can't say I blame them. I don't blame them at all."

Honey was looking at me fixedly. She was waiting for me to protest.

I opened my mouth to say it was all a mistake and that I had no intention of marrying when I caught Jake's eye—mocking, warning, cruelly relentless. I thought: He *would* betray them. He would have no compunction. He is without mercy.

Then I remembered my mother's telling me as she had on one occasion of how the father she adored had been a prisoner in the Tower and how one day he had been taken to the block and his head placed on London Bridge. I knew that never could she escape from the memory of that time; it had shadowed all her happiness. I had lost Carey and I believed I could never be completely happy again; and if I should be the one to betray Honey how could I face my mother or forgive myself?

A sudden exhilaration came to me. I would outwit this man who had so shortly come into my life and dominated it. I would let him believe that he had won, but he never should. At the moment I must agree to this betrothal because to fail to do so would endanger Honey and Edward. His victory should be only a brief one. If Jake Pennlyon thought I had so easily succumbed he was going to find his mistake.

He took my hand and held it tightly. His grip was a warning in itself. I could break your fingers if I wished; and I will as easily break your spirit.

"Why, Catharine," said Honey, "may I indeed congratulate the pair of you?"

"This is a time for congratulations," said Jake. "We want a speedy wedding."

Honey put her fragrant cheek against mine, her eye inquiring.

"So you have decided, Catharine?" she said. "Why, it is but a short time that you were declaring you would never marry."

"My son has that in him to break down the resistance of the most retiring damsel."

"It seems so."

The wine and cakes were brought in.

Edward poured the wine and gave the toast.

"To the betrothed pair."

Jake took his glass and drank, then offered it to me. I stared for a moment at his full sensual lips and turned my head slightly. He was thrusting the glass into my hands and I drank.

It was as though I had sealed my promise.

They began to talk about the betrothal, which was to be celebrated at Lyon Court. The wedding would take place here.

"It should be at my mother's house," I protested.

"What, on the other side of the country?" cried Jake. "Sailors have no time for such fancies. Your mother must needs come to Devon if she wishes to dance at your wedding."

"I shall make my plans," I said.

And I saw the smile turn up Jake Pennlyon's lips.

I listened vaguely to the conversation. Sir Penn was asking questions about my father's estate. Edward was answering them as best he could. There should be a good dowry, Sir Penn was saying, but even if there was not there would be no bar to the marriage. "Bar my son when he's made up his mind! That's something I could not do an' I wished it. Nor should I wish it. My son is the image of his father and I'd have that so too. He sees a filly and he's got to ride her and I know he's in no mood to wait for his bride." He leaned toward me. "He's eager. You'll find he's no laggard. That's the way to ensure sons. You're not one of these poor swooning females as will faint at the sight of a man. Not you. I saw it from the first. You're the sort who'll breed sons with spirit, for you've got spirit yourself; and you'll be as mad for him as he is for you and that's the way to get sons . . . get 'em early and get 'em in plenty. Pennlyon boys."

I hated the man as much as I hated his son. Their frank and racy conversation brought images to my mind. I was a virgin, but I knew something of the relationship of the sexes. Once I had come upon two of the servants copulating in a field. I had listened to talk. So the images came and went . . . myself and that man, with his lustful, mocking eyes. And when I was in his presence these images were always ready to intrude and disturb.

I scarcely listened to the conversation. It was about the wedding and first of all the betrothal celebration. Honey was bewildered and I was not surprised because it was such a short time ago that I had expressed my dislike of the man. Edward never betrayed his feelings; as far as he was concerned no one would have guessed that there was anything unusual about this betrothal.

It was to take place the following week; and the wedding should be four weeks later. "That will give Jake time to do his courting." The old man's chuckle was horrible. He meant of course forestall our marriage vows. "And as soon as we get them into legal bed the better. Jake will be sailing just two months after the day. But it'll not be a long voyage this time. Jake wouldn't have that when he'd a wife keeping his bed warm for him."

I felt sickened. I wanted to shout out: I will never agree. I am pretending. I have no intention of marrying this man.

But I kept silent because whenever I was about to speak I thought of Honey and Edward taken off to some miserable cell and my mother's heartbroken eyes. She had suffered too much already.

In any case, I was deceiving them. I was letting this arrogant man think he had subdued me. Nothing would induce me to share his bed as his father was fond of putting it, to bear his child, which seemed to be the main idea in the minds of both of them.

It seemed a long time before they left. I was embraced by both father and son. I hated the way they thrust their bodies close to mine.

We stood in the courtyard while they rode away.

When they had gone Honey turned to me.

"What happened to make you change your mind so suddenly?"

"We can't talk here," I said.

We went into the punch room. I said: "Not here." The punch room was approached from the dining room and there was no door to it, only a curtain over the archway.

I said: "Let us go into the chapel. Let us lock the chapel door *and* that which leads into the leper's squint."

The chapel was as normal. There was no sign that Mass had been recently celebrated.

I went to the leper's squint and peered through into the little room beyond.

"The doors are locked," I said. "What a pity you didn't lock them both before Thomas Elders officiated."

"What do you mean?" demanded Honey.

"Jake Pennlyon was in there." I pointed to the squint. "I met him coming out. He told me that unless I agreed to marry him he would make it known that Thomas Elders was here and for what purpose."

"My God!" said Edward suddenly.

Honey laid her hand on his arm. "What would happen to us, Edward?"

His fingers closed over hers protectively. How different he was from Jake Pennlyon! Must I compare every man with that one! He was gentle, protective, loving, tender.

"I don't know," said Edward. "It could be most unsafe."

"So you promised, to save us."

"I suppose so."

"Catharine!"

"Don't imagine I am going to marry him. I'll fight him." Again that wild exhilaration. I enjoyed fighting him. I wanted to defeat him, to laugh at him, to mock him. I had never dreamed it was possible to feel so strongly about one person. I had about Carey, of course, but that was the intensity of love—this was hatred. "I had to pretend then or he would have betrayed you. He is a wicked man. I loathe him and his father."

"But, Catharine, there is to be this betrothal."

"I shall make no vows. I shall fight them."

Honey was looking at me strangely. Then she turned to Edward and clung to him.

He said: "Don't fear, my love. They can prove nothing. We must be careful in the future. I must warn Thomas. If young Pennlyon knows he may well set traps for him."

I thought of my father then, who had brought so much unhappiness to our household because of what he had done to help a friend. Edward would be like that. He was such another as my father . . . born for marytrdom, which was a terrible thing to be born for in our times.

I went to my room and it was not long before Honey was there.

"Oh, Catharine, what have we all brought upon ourselves?"

She looked frail and frightened; her hand lay gently on her stomach as though she were protecting the child which was growing there.

I felt protective toward *her* and I said: "Don't fret. I'll outwit this arrogant Pennlyon."

Her mood changed suddenly.

"Why, Catharine," she said, "I have not seen you so animated since. . . ."

She did not finish; and I knew she meant since I had learned that Carey was lost to me.

She was right. I had not felt so alive since then.

The next day the Pennlyons went away for a few days in connection with stores for the coming voyages. Jake Pennlyon rode over to Trewynd before\ they left. I saw him coming and went to Honey and made her promise not to leave me alone with him.

We received him in the hall. He embraced me in that manner which made me want to throw him from me and which made him laugh as he sensed my resistance. I think he liked it; my submission, of which he was absolutely sure, would be the more rewarding if he had to force it. He was a hunter and women to him were prey.

Honey sent for wine and we went to the punch room— the three of us together.

"I have bad news for you," said Jake Pennlyon. "I have to leave you."

I smiled and he went on: "Don't despair. 'Tis but for a few days and I'll be back. Then we'll make up for our separation."

"I would not wish you to cut short your business," I said.

"I never waste time. Rest assured I'll complete with all speed what has to be done and come back to you. I should like to walk in the gardens with you. There are matters we must discuss."

"I will accompany you," said Honey demurely.

"Madam, we would not disturb you."

" 'T would be a pleasure," said Honey.

His eyes glinted. "We ask no chaperone."

"Nevertheless, propriety does."

"We don't have such ceremonies here," said Jake Pennlyon. "We're plain country folk."

"My sister must behave in the manner expected by her family," said Honey.

I smiled at her. Dear Honey, she was so grateful to me for protecting her and Edward from the malice of these Pennlyons.

I said: "We will walk in the gardens and keep in sight of the windows."

I was surprised at myself. But I did want to do battle with him—though from a safe place it was true. Nevertheless, I couldn't resist the desire to tell him how much I disliked him.

His eyes lighted up. I wondered how much he understood of me.

As we went out together he said: "So we have escaped the dragon."

"Honey is no dragon. She is merely observing the laws of propriety."

"Laws of nonsense!" he said. "You and I are as good as married. 'Tis not as though I'd tumble you in the grass, get you with child and leave you."

"In accordance I suppose with your usual practice."

" 'Tis a well-worn practice. But curb your jealousy. When I have you I'll be content."

"I doubt that."

"The contentment?"

"I was thinking of the other."

"Not trying to evade your responsibilities, I trust. It would go ill with you and yours if you did."

"You are a cruel, ruthless man. You are a blackmailer, a rapist, you are all that good and honest men . . . and women . . . despise."

"You are wrong. The men seek to emulate me; as for the women there are dozens of them who'd give ten years of their lives to be in your place."

I laughed at him. "A braggart too."

"You please me," he said.

"I'm sorry for that."

"Yes," he went on, "you please me as I please you."

"Your powers of perception are nonexistent. I hate you."

"The kind of hate you have for me is very close to love."

"You have a great deal to learn of me."

"And a lifetime to do it in."

"Do not be too sure of that."

"What, trying to evade your vows!"

"Vows . . . what vows? You threaten rape; you blackmail. Then you talk of vows."

He stopped short and pulled me around to face him. I was aware of Honey at the window and felt safe.

"Look me straight in the eyes," he said.

"I can think of pleasanter sights."

He gripped my arm in a manner which made me gasp.

"Please, will you remember that I am unaccustomed to physical violence? You will bruise my arm. You did so when you last gripped it."

"So I left my mark on you. That is well. Look at me."

I gazed up haughtily into those fierce blue eyes.

"Tell me now that you are indifferent to me."

I hesitated and he laughed triumphantly.

I said quickly: "I suppose when one despises another person as I do you that could scarcely be called indifference."

"So you despise me? You are sure of that?"

"Absolutely sure."

"Yet you enjoy despising me. Answer truthfully. Your heart beats faster when you see me; your eyes have a sparkle. You can't deceive me. I will have much to teach you, my wildcat. You will find me a very good tutor."

"As no doubt many have before."

"You should not be jealous of them. I would give up them all for you."

"Pray do not deny yourself. Go where you will. Continue to tutor others. All I ask is that you leave me to myself."

"Leave the mother of my sons?"

"They have yet to be conceived."

"A matter which causes me great impatience. Let us escape the dragon . . . now."

"I see what you mean by your tutelage. You have forgotten that I am not some tavern wench or serving girl. You would have to behave very differently if you wished to impress a lady of breeding."

"I have not of course mixed in such circles as you. You might instruct me in the manners you expect and, who knows, I might try to please you . . . if you pleased me."

"I shall return to the house now," I said. "I have walked far enough."

"What if I decided to carry you off with me?"

"My sister is watching us. Her husband would immediately come to my rescue."

"Why should I fear them?"

"If you wish to marry me you could not create a situation which would be so ignominious that they could not ignore it. They would decide that you were an unsuitable husband."

"In the circumstances. . . ."

"In any circumstances," I replied. "In a family like ours, the indiscretion at which you hint, if it came to pass, would mean that whatever the consequences we would avenge it."

"You've a sharp tongue. Marry! Methinks you could become a shrew."

"And a tiresome encumbrance as a wife."

"To some men, yes. For me, no. I'll force the venom from your tongue and make it drip with honey."

"I had no idea you could turn such phrases."

"You have yet to discover my talents."

"I have had enough of them this day and will return to the house."

He gripped my fingers.

"If you and I should marry you will have to learn to handle me more gently. You all but break my fingers."

"When we marry," he said, "I will treat you as you merit. And that is a matter for the very near future."

I had wrenched my hand away and started to walk toward the house.

The Pennlyons left that afternoon. "How peaceful it is," I said to Honey, "knowing that they are not so close."

"What shall you do, Catharine?" she asked anxiously. "You could return home. We could say that your mother was ill. While they are away is the time to go."

"Yes," I said, "that's the time."

Then I thought: If I went he would come after me. Or worse still he would betray Thomas Elders. I pictured all those who had entertained the priest being brought before a tribunal.

Edward had many rich lands; very often those who had estates to be confiscated were the ones who suffered most.

I mentioned this to Honey and she grew pale. She knew it was true.

"I'll not run away," I said. "I'll stay. I'll find some way. I swear I will. Don't worry. It's bad for the child."

I knew in my heart that I was enjoying my battles with Jake Pennlyon. It gave me a kind of inverted pleasure and although there were moments when I was afraid it was the sort of fear a child experiences, a fear of goblins and witches in the woods, terrifying but irresistible.

I would stay, I said.

Three days after the Pennlyons had gone I was at my window looking out on the Hoe when immediately below in the courtyard I saw Jennet; she was walking stealthily toward the stables and there was something concealed under her apron.

Luce looked after me now—poor ill-favored Luce whose left shoulder was higher than the right and who was more than ordinarily pockmarked. I missed Jennet in a way. Luce worked well and was devoted to me; Jennet had betrayed me and so started the whole affair with Jake Pennlyon, though I supposed he would have found some other way of starting it if that had not happened. But Jennet with her fresh young face and her soft sensual lips and thick untidy hair had interested me more. I wondered how far Jake Pennlyon had gone with Jennet. He would not be one to waste time courting a servant girl, I was sure.

And what was she doing now going down to the stables? Meeting some groom? I wanted to find out, so I slipped out of the house and went out by the small door into the courtyard.

As I approached the stables I heard voices. Jennet's

rather shrill one and others in a lowered tone.

I opened the door and there they were seated on the straw. Jennet had spread a cloth and on it were pieces of lamb and mutton with half a pie. With her were Richard Rackell and a stranger.

Jennet jumped to her feet with a cry of dismay. Richard stood up and so did the other, a dark-haired man whom I guessed to be thirty or more years of age. The men bowed; Jennet stared wide-eyed and fearful.

"What is this?" I asked.

"Mistress," began Jennet.

But Richard said: "A peddler has called with his wares, Mistress. He has traveled far and is in sore need of food. Jennet brought him something to eat from the kitchens."

"A peddler?" I said. "Why does he come to the stables?"

"He was on his way to the house and so weary that I said he should rest here awhile before taking his wares to the house."

There was something dignified about Richard, interesting too. Moreover, the advent of a peddler was always exciting, more particuarly here than at the Abbey. There we were not far from London and could take a barge to the Chepe and buy from the mercers and lacemakers and merchants.

The peddler had come forward and bowed to me.

"His name is John, Mistress," said Richard. "He craves your indulgence."

The man bowed again.

"Can he not speak for himself?"

"I can, Mistress," said John; and his voice reminded me of Richard's.

"You have traveled far?"

"From the North," he said.

"You should have gone to the kitchens. There they would have fed you. There was no need for the maid to steal food and bring it here."

" 'Tis not the fault of the maid," said Richard gently. " 'Twas I who sent her for food. Peddler John was foot-sore and sank into the straw to rest awhile."

"Well, he can eat to his fill. And, Jennet, you may go and bring some ale for him to drink. He can come to the washhouse then, and there spread out his wares for us to see. Jennet, you may take him to the washhouse when he has eaten and I will tell Mistress Ennis that we have a peddler who wishes to show his wares."

I found Honey and when I told her what had happened she was as eager as I to see what the peddler had brought. He spread out his pack. In it he had silks to make kerchiefs; he had trinkets and little boxes and combs. I saw a magnificent comb, to be placed in the hair and to stand so tall that it added three inches to the height.

I pounced on it and stuck it in my hair. Honey declared it was becoming.

I left her brooding over the peddler because I wanted to try the comb; and I thought of myself wearing it at the betrothal ceremony, which but a short while ago I was planning to escape.

I dressed myself in a russet velvet gown and I placed the comb in my hair and I liked it. I wanted to show it to Honey and was about to go to her, when it occurred to me that she might still be considering what the peddler had in his pack. I glanced out of the window and at that moment saw her with the peddler. He had rolled up his pack and they were talking earnestly. Then I saw her take him across the courtyard, through the door and into the house, not toward the kitchens but to that part where she and Edward had their apartments.

That was strange. When peddlers came they were not invited to that section of the house. They showed their wares and were refreshed and allowed to rest, while their mule or mules were fed and watered in the stables; after they had shown their goods to the mistress of the house they did the same for the servants. It was an occasion when the peddler called and an excitement to us all; but they were not entertained in the owner's apartments.

I could only imagine that she had found something in his pack which she thought might please Edward, and was filled with curiosity to know what.

I went into the punch room, which I supposed was the most likely place to find them.

They were not there. I drew aside the curtain and mounted the stone stairs to the solarium. This was a large room with a curtain placed halfway which could be pulled to divide it. The curtains were pulled and I went through to the second room. There was no one there. Then I heard their voices and guessed where they were. At the end of the solarium was a door which opened into a small chamber and inside this chamber high in the wall was a peep—a star-shaped hole which was scarcely perceptible. Through this one could look down to the hall to see who was arriving.

The door of this chamber was now shut and as I walked toward it I heard the sound of voices.

They must be there.

"Honey," I called. "Are you there?"

There was a short silence. Then Honey's voice said: "Yes, yes, Catharine. We . . . we're here."

I opened the door. Edward and Honey were seated at a table and the peddler sat with them.

Honey said: "We were just about to look at the pack. I wanted Edward to see something."

I said I would like to have another look at them. I bought some cambric to make a petticoat and Honey bought some needles and thread.

There was nothing of interest to Edward and I wondered why Honey had brought the peddler into the house.

Edward appeared to be rather tense and there was a pulse beating in his temple which I hadn't noticed before.

Three nights after the day the peddler came I saw the galleon again. The Pennlyons were still away, but I expected them to be back at any time. I awoke as I had on that other occasion. It was three o'clock in the morning. I wondered what had awakened me. There was something going on. In my sleep I had been aware of unaccustomed sounds—or had I been half awake? The great harvest moon—almost full—shone into the room; I rose and went to the window: and there was the galleon in all its glory, its four masts clearly visible—the tallest and most majestic ship I had ever seen.

The *Rampart Lion*, dwarfed beside it, made me laugh. I wished that *he* could be here at this moment. How I should like him to see that other ship! But the idea of wishing that he could be with me for any reason whatsoever was so contrary to my wishes that I must laugh at myself.

Then I saw the boat on the moonlit waters; it was clearly making for the shore. I knew then that it contained someone from the galleon.

I could hear Jake Pennlyon's voice: "By God's Death, it would seem that you are describing a Spanish galleon."

He hadn't believed I had in fact seen what I claimed to. He had pooh-poohed the idea of a Spanish galleon daring to enter the harbor.

As I watched, the rowing boat disappeared as it had on that other night. I did not return to bed. I sat watching.

Half an hour passed. The galleon was still there. Then I heard movements below. I looked down and saw a light in the courtyard. Instinct told me that the movement below was in some way connected with the galleon. Something was happening and my curiosity needed to be satisfied. I wrapped a robe about me and putting on slippers, I descended the staircase and went down to the courtyard.

As the cool night airs enveloped me I heard voices—quietly whispering. I saw the lantern and there was Edward and with him a stranger. I slipped back into the house, my heart beating fast. I ran swiftly to the solarium chamber and looked down through the peep. Edward had come into the hall and with him was the stranger. I could see them only vaguely in the dim light. They were talking earnestly; then Edward led the stranger up the stairs to the punch room and I could see them no more.

I was bewildered, but I was sure that someone had come from the Spanish galleon to see Edward.

I went to my room. The galleon had started to move. I stood there watching as she slipped below the horizon.

I was possessed by a sudden fear. Edward, who seemed so gentle, was involved in some intrigue. That much was obvious. Where would it all lead us? So far his association with the visiting priest had brought me to a situation which was distasteful and would have been alarming if it had not been so ridiculous. At the same time it was not going to be easy to extricate myself from the Pennlyon web.

I went back to bed. Sleep was impossible. I had a glimmering of what this night's visitation meant.

No, I told myself. Edward would not be such a fool. He is too gentle, too much a dreamer. But it was precisely men such as he who placed themselves in dangerous situations.

I spoke to Honey next morning.

"What happened last night?" I demanded.

She turned first red and then quite pale so I was aware that she knew something.

I went on: "I saw the Spanish galleon in the harbor."

"A Spanish galleon! You were dreaming."

"Not this time. I saw it and there was no mistaking it. And that was not all. Someone came ashore, someone who came to this house."

"You *were* dreaming."

"I was not. I saw a man come here. Honey, I am involved with your follies. Have I not placed myself in a desperate situation because of you? I won't be in the dark."

She looked at me steadily for some moments and said: "I will be back in a moment."

She came back with Edward. He looked very grave, yet his lips were firmly set as though he were determined to continue with what he had begun.

"Honey has told me that you saw something last night. What exactly was it?"

"A Spanish galleon in the bay, a boat rowing ashore and your bringing a man into the house."

"And you surmise that the man you saw was the one who came ashore?"

"I am certain of it. And I do wonder what is happening."

"We can trust you, Catharine. I know what a good friend you have been to us both."

"What are you doing, Edward? Who is the man who came here last night?"

"He is a priest."

"Ah, I thought it. Have you not had enough of priests?"

"They are good men who are persecuted in God's name, Catharine."

"And bring persecution to others," I murmured.

"We must all suffer for our faith if called upon to do so."

"It serves no purpose these days to stand in the marketplace and declare that faith, particularly if it is against that favored by the Sovereign and her ministers."

"You are right and you must know what is happening. Honey and I think that you should go back to the Abbey. We may be in some danger here."

"There is danger everywhere. Tell me who the man was who came last night."

"He is a Jesuit priest. He is English. He has been persecuted for his faith. He comes from Salamanca in Spain."

"And he was brought here on the galleon?"

Edward nodded. "He will work here for the good of his faith. He will visit houses. . . ."

"As Thomas Elders does," I said.

"First he will stay here with us."

"And so place us in jeopardy."

"If God wills it."

"Is he here now?"

"He left the house in the early hours of the morning before the servants were astir. He will arrive today in the midafternoon. I shall greet him as a friend and he will stay with us awhile until he makes his plans. He will be known as John Gregory, a friend of my youth. He will be a member of this household until he departs."

"You are placing us all in dire danger."

"It may well be, but if we are discreet we shall be safe enough. If you wish to return to the Abbey, Catharine, you should do so."

"And what will the Pennlyons do then, think you? What if I flout them? If I go home while they plan a ceremonial betrothal feast do you think they will calmly accept this?"

"They must do what they will."

"And Thomas Elders and your Jesuit and Honey and yourself?"

"We must look after ourselves. What happens here is none of your making."

Honey was looking at me earnestly. "We will not let you marry Jake Pennlyon if you are so set against it."

"*If* I am set against it! I hate the man. How could I be anything but set against it?"

"Then we must devise a plan and the best seems for you to leave here and, as Edward said, if they make trouble they must then make it."

I did not answer. I had decided against going back to

the Abbey. I was not going to let Jake Pennlyon think I had run away. I would stay and face him; I would outwit him in my own way.

Meanwhile, Edward and Honey were getting deeper into intrigue and I trembled for them.

That afternoon John Gregory arrived at the house. He was greeted as an old friend by Edward and was given the red bedroom with the big four-poster bed and a window which looked out over the country for miles.

He walked with a limp and there were scars on his left cheek and on his wrists. He was tall and stooped a little and had a certain haunted expression in his eyes which I could not forget.

He looked to me like a man who had suffered. A fanatic, I decided, who might well suffer again. Such people made me uncomfortable.

The servants appeared to accept the explanation of his visit. I watched them carefully to see if there was any suspicion, but I missed Jennet, who was such a chatterer and had often unconsciously let me into the secrets of the servants' quarters. Luce was efficient but taciturn, and I thought then of reinstating Jennet. She was contrite. I was beginning to doubt my motives, though, and I was not sure whether the sight of her angered me because she had betrayed me or because I couldn't stop thinking of Jake Pennlyon's laying his lustful hands on her and wondering, of course, whether he had seduced her already.

I did, however, take her back with me the day after John Gregory came.

I lectured her a little. "You will serve *me*, Jennet," I reminded her. "If you ever lie to me again I shall have you beaten."

"Yes, Mistress," she said demurely.

"And you should be warned not to listen to men's tales. They will get you with child and then what will happen to you, do you think?"

She blushed scarlet and I said: "Remember it." I could not bring myself to ask her for details of what had happened between her and Jake Pennlyon because I told myself it was undignified—and yet in a way I did wish to know.

A day passed. I knew that the return of the Pennlyons could not long be delayed. The period of respite was coming to an end.

The Pennlyons were back. One became aware of it at once. Even the servants seemed excited and the tension in Trewynd had increased. Since they had returned the presence of John Gregory in the house had become more dangerous.

It was not long before Jake came riding over. I was expecting him and was prepared. I had told Honey that on no account must she leave us alone together.

He sat in the hall drinking wine. Edward, Honey and myself watched him intently. He seemed bigger, more overbearing, more arrogant and sure of his ability to get what he wanted than I remembered even. I felt the surging hatred rising in me, bringing with it that wild excitement.

The betrothal ceremony was taking place in three days' time, he announced.

"It's too soon," I said.

"Not soon enough," he corrected me.

"I shall need to prepare."

"You've had all the time I've been away to prepare. You'll have no longer."

So he was commanding me already.

"The wedding takes place two weeks later," he said with authority. "And I shall sail a month after that."

"Where will your voyage take you?" asked Edward politely.

"We'll be taking a cargo of cloth out to Guinea and come back we hope with gold and ivory. It won't be a long voyage if I can help it." He gave me his lascivious grin. "I shall be missing my wife."

Edward said he wished him fair weather; and they talked about the sea for a while. Jake's eyes glowed; he talked of the sea with the same intensity that he had talked of our marriage. The sea fascinated him because it was often wild and unpredictable; he would often have to fight it with all the skill he possessed. He was a man who must fight. Always he had to subdue. Marriage with him would have to be an eternal battle, for as soon as he had won he would lose interest. But why should I contemplate marriage with him? That was for some other pitiable female. I was going to play as dangerous a game as he played on his voyages. Perhaps there was a similarity between us because I at last admitted to myself that I enjoyed the fight.

We all went out into the courtyard with him and as we did so John Gregory came out of a side door. There was nothing to do but make the introductions.

Jake Pennlyon's eyes flicked over him.

"We've met before," he said.

John Gregory looked puzzled. "I do not recall it, sir," he answered.

Jake narrowed his eyes as though he were trying to look into something which he couldn't quite make out.

"I'm sure of it," he insisted. "I don't easily forget faces."

"Were you in the North at some time?" asked Edward.

"I never was," said Jake. "I'll remember. It escapes me for the moment."

John Gregory was wrinkling his brow, smiling as though trying to recall, but I fancied that the scar on his cheek seemed to stand out more vividly.

"I was delighted to see my friend," said Edward warmly. "He has decided to stay with us for a week or so."

Jake was now looking at me, forgetting John Gregory.

He said: "We shall expect you early at Pennlyon. We can't have the bride arriving late. It would appear that she was reluctant."

He took my hand and kissed it. His lips seemed to burn my skin. I wiped it on my gown. He saw the gesture and it amused him.

Then he took his leave.

We went into the house and Edward asked John Gregory: "What did he mean about knowing you?"

"He is suspicious," said Honey in a frightened voice.

"You have never met him before?" asked Edward.

John Gregory wrinkled his brows for a moment and then said very firmly: "No."

I dressed myself for my betrothal banquet with the utmost pains. I wished to appear as beautiful as I could for, I assured myself, the sole purpose of making him more angry than ever when he realized he had lost me.

And after the betrothal? What should I do then? I could see no answer than but to go back to the Abbey and my mother. Would he follow me there? He had to leave on his voyage, so how could he come after me?

And Honey and Edward, would he betray them? Surely he would have to prove that Thomas Elders had been celebrating Mass in the chapel. But Elders would be taken and mayhap tortured and then who knew what would emerge? And this man John Gregory? He would have to go away before I left. Of course this was what I must do. I certainly could not ruin my whole life because of the trouble they had brought upon themselves.

For the moment there was the betrothal ball and banquet and I intended to amuse myself as much as I could with them.

Jennet helped me to dress. She was better at this than Luce had been. She brushed my hair until it shone and our reflections in the polished mirror were glowing. There was color in her cheeks and her mass of hair escaped from her cap; she was not exactly a handsome girl but a very desirable one, I could see that. There was something soft and yielding about her; she would be seduced sooner or later I was sure, and I thought it was time to get her married.

I said to her: "Do you like Richard Rackell, Jennet?"

She blushed—she blushed very easily—and lowered her eyes.

"You do," I said. "There's no need to be coy about it. If he had a fancy to you perhaps there could be a wedding. The master would mayhap give you one of the cottages and you could continue to work as you do now. You would like that, wouldn't you?"

"Why, yes, Mistress."

"You should be married . . . soon. I am sure of that. You are somewhat wanton, Jennet, I believe."

"Oh, no, Mistress. 'Tis just. . . ."

" 'Tis just that when they lay hands on you and tell you what a fine wench you are you'd find it difficult to say them nay."

She giggled.

"You silly girl! And you're pulling my hair."

I wanted to say to her: What did Jake Pennlyon do

when he 'had kissed you? Are you going to tell me that it ended with that? But I said no such thing.

She went on brushing my hair. Was she thinking of Jake or Richard Rackell?

I thought I would wear my hair piled high on my head and then I could crown it with the comb I had bought from the peddler.

"Frizzing be the fashion, Mistress, and I can frizz," said Jennet.

"I follow my own fashions. I do not wish to look like every other fashionable woman, nor like any serving wench."

Resigned, Jennet dressed my hair. I put on my red velvet gown cut low at the neck and the sleeves wide and flowing almost to the hem. Not the height of fashion true, but indeed becoming, and with the comb in my hair I looked regal. I should need all the dignity I could master to ward off the attentions of my intended bridegroom, I thought grimly.

Jennet stared at me wide-eyed.

"Why, Mistress, you look beautiful . . . too beautiful to be real."

"I'm real enough, Jennet," I said with a laugh.

She lowered her eyes and giggled. I spoke sharply to her. She knew that I was still resentful of the fact that she had sided with Jake Pennlyon against me. There was something knowing about her look. I wondered afterward whether Jennet, born to give pleasure to men, understood something of the nature of my feelings for this one, for try as I might to feign indifference, I was excited by him, albeit in hatred.

Honey came in and I immediately felt insignificant. But then everyone must before Honey's brilliance. She was dressed in blue—deep violet blue, the color of her eyes, which accentuated their brilliance. Since she had become pregnant her beauty had changed a little and lost nothing for it.

She wore her hair about her shoulders and there was a circle of pearls about it.

She pressed my hand and looked at me anxiously.

"I'm all right, Honey," I said.

"You look quite magnificent."

I glanced at myself in the burnished mirror. "Like one of the Valkyries going into battle?"

"Yes," she said, "a little like that."

We were to ride to Lyon Court in the carriage. Edward's carriage was a source of wonder to everyone, for few people possessed such a vehicle. Most must rely on horses or their own feet. It was uncomfortable riding in the carriage, which was drawn by two horses. People in Devon had never seen carriages before, but in view of the fact that we were dressed for the ball the carriage was very convenient. Otherwise, we should have had to take one of the mules to carry our gowns and ridden over and changed there.

I whispered to Honey as we jolted along over the rough roads: "Watch over me tonight."

"We will," replied Honey fervently. "Edward and I."

"I shall be in his house. That will give him an advantage and he'll take it, you can be sure."

"You'll outwit him."

"Indeed I shall and then, Honey, I think perhaps I shall have to go home."

"Edward and I have been talking about it. We think it is best for you. John Gregory will be leaving us and we shall be safe. He can prove nothing. Edward has influence. We shall be all right. You cannot marry to save us."

"Tonight though I shall play this game of pretense. He will think that he has won the battle. I will let him believe that, so that he may have the greater shock when he faces defeat."

"You enjoy this, Catharine. What has come over you? You were once so different."

"It is this man. He arouses such feeling in me that I hardly know myself."

"Take care, Catharine."

"I shall take the utmost care to prove to him how much I despise him and that he shall never govern me."

The carriage trundled along. Edward drove the horses and Honey and I sat behind him. Soon we were in the drive which led to Lyon Court. Under the elms we went and there was the house, lanterns on the porch lighting up the lions—gray stone and impregnable-looking in the moonlight.

Servants hurried out. There were grooms to take our horses and marvel at the carriage.

We were taken into the hall where the Pennlyons—father and son—were waiting to greet us.

The hall, lit by a hundred or so candles flickering in their sconces, looked very fine. At one end a great log fire burned although we were in September and it was not chilly. The long table was laid for the banquet and so was the smaller one on a dais at one end of the hall. In the minstrels' gallery fiddlers were playing.

I was taken in Sir Penn's arms and held firmly against his great body; he kissed me loudly and laughed over my head in Jake's direction as though he were teasing him. Jake then took me from him. I drew myself away, but it was useless. I was firmly held, pressed tightly against him and his lips on mine.

Sir Penn was laughing. "Come, Jake," he said. "You'll have time for that later." He nudged Edward in the side and Edward smiled faintly. The manners of these two must have been extremely distasteful to him.

Jake put his arm about me and swung me around. "You'll stand with me to greet the guests."

People arrived from neighboring houses. They congratulated us. It was embarrassing in the extreme and I was glad when we sat at table, which was weighed down with great pies and joints of meat. There was venison, wild fowl, tarts, marchpane fancies, sugar bread, gingerbread and every kind of food that one could think of.

Jake Pennlyon was watching me, hoping, I knew, that I should be impressed by the quantities of food with which the table was laden. It was as though he were tempting me. See how we live! Look at our fine house! You will have a part in this. You will be mistress of it—but you will always remember who is the master.

I looked beyond the table, for I would not let him know that I was impressed. His hand was on my thigh, burning, probing fingers. I lifted his hand and put it from me, but he then gripped mine and held it against him.

"Your grip is too rough," I said. "I do not wish to be covered in bruises."

"Did I not tell you that I would set my mark upon you?"

"You may have said so, but I should not wish it."

"And I must grant your wishes, I suppose.

"It is customary during wooing."

"But we have passed the wooing stage. You are won."

"Indeed I am not."

"Why, my Cat, this is our wedding feast."

"My mother calls me Cat and she alone. I would not wish anyone else to use that name for me."

"I shall call you what I like and you are to me a cat. You scratch, but you will be ere long purring in my arms."

"I would not count on that if I were you."

"But you are not me. You are your maddening self."

"I am glad I exasperate you, for that is just the effect you have on me."

"It is a fillip to our passion."

"I feel no passion."

"You delude yourself. Come try this malmsey wine. It will put you in a mellow mood and see we have Venetian glasses. We can be as fine as our neighbors."

"Gracious living cannot be found in a glass. It is good manners that count."

"And you find me lacking in them?"

"Deplorably so."

"I promise you shall find me lacking in naught else."

There had been food and to spare in the Abbey, but it had never been served in this way. To these people food was to be reverenced. The usher who brought in the boar's head was preceded by one who kissed the table before laying it down and the usher, then having set the dish on the table, bowed low before it. One scullion was cuffed about the ears for standing with his back toward it. And when the sucking pig was brought in the minstrels in the gallery played and one of the servants walked solemnly before it singing of its virtues.

We had started to eat at six and at nine of the clock we were still at table. A great deal of wine and ale had been drunk. Jake and his father had set an example to their guests and I had never seen so much food consumed.

I was amused and elated to see that the wine was having its effect on them and I guessed that they would be easier to handle in such condition than they would be completely sober.

The minstrels played most of the time and there was one with a pleasant voice who came down from the gallery and sang a love song standing before the table and addressing his words to me and to Jake Pennlyon.

While the guests were eating confections of sugared spices and marchpane Jake ordered that a dance should be played, and taking me by the hand, he led me into the center of the hall.

The others fell in behind us. Jake was not a good dancer, but he knew the steps and we circled, came back to each other and touched hands as we danced; and when the dance was over he drew me to a bench where we were a little apart from the company. He continued to grip my hand.

"This . . . is what I wanted from the moment I saw you."

"Then your wish has been granted," I said.

"The first wish. There are many to come. But they are on the way. We are as good as wed. You well know that this ceremony is binding. If you wished to marry anyone else you would have to get a dispensation from the church. You are bound to me."

"It is not so. There has been no ceremony."

"We are bound together. All you have to do now is accept your fate."

"Why do you not take someone else? There are women here tonight who would mayhap be glad to take you. You are of means obviously. You would not be a bad catch for any who fancied you."

"I have the one I fancy and who fancies me . . . why should I look beyond though she is perverse and feigns not to want me, that amused me . . . for a while? But I have had enough of it and I would have you show me your true feelings. I will take you around the house which will be your home. I will show you the rooms which will be at your disposal. Come now with me. We will slip away alone."

"We should be missed."

He laughed. "And if we were there would be smiles and understanding. We will have their indulgence. We are all but wed and the final ceremony will take place ere long. I want to take that comb from your hair. It has a

Spanish look about it which I like not. Where did you get such a bauble?"

"A peddler brought it in his pack. I like it."

"A peddler! Are they introducing plaguey Spanish fashions here now? We'll not have that."

"Know this. I shall wear what I wish."

"Don't tempt me or I shall take it from your hair here and now. That would shock your sister and her fine husband, I doubt not. But I'll be discreet. Come! I will show you our marriage bed and you shall try it and tell me if it suits you. It will, Cat. I know it. Something told me from the start that you and I were made for each other."

He attempted to pull me to my feet, but I said: "I wish to talk to you . . . seriously."

"We have years for talking. Come with me now."

I said firmly: "I don't love you. I can never love you. I am here now because of your threats. Do you think that is the way to inspire love? You know nothing of love. Oh, I doubt not that you are a past master of lust. I'll swear that many a pirate is. He ravages towns and the women in them; he forces submission, but that is not love. Don't ever expect love from me."

"Love," he said, looking intently at me. "You talk fiercely of love. What do you know of it?"

I had difficulty in controlling my features then because I had a sudden vision of what I had dreamed life would be for me: Carey and I together. Our home would have been Remus Castle; I could see the park at Remus, the walled rose garden, the pond garden with its pleached alley, and beloved Carey, with whom I used to quarrel when I was a child—as I quarreled with this man now, only differently of course—Carey, whom love had made gentle and tender as this man could never be.

He had bent closer and was looking at me earnestly.

I said: "I have loved. I shall never love again."

"So you are not the virgin I promised myself."

"You sicken me. You know naught of love; you know only of lust. I have lain with no man, but I have loved and planned to marry, but it was not to be. My father and his mother had sinned together. And he was my brother."

He studied me with narrowed eyes. Why had I attempted to talk to him of Carey? It had weakened me in some way, made me vulnerable. He had no pity for me; if he loved me, I thought, he would be gentle with me. But he had no tender feelings for me; his need for me was nothing but desire, a determination to subdue.

He said: "I know much concerning you. It was necessary for me to discover what I could of my wife. Your father was a charlatan."

"He was not that."

"He was found in the crib at Bruno's Abbey. The whole of England knew of it. It was said to be a miracle and then it was found that there was no miracle; he was the son of a wayward monk and a serving wench. Should I marry a charlatan's daughter, the granddaughter of a serving girl?"

"Indeed you should not," I retorted. "Such a refined cultured gentleman cannot be allowed to do such a thing."

"But," he went on, "this charlatan became a rich man; he was possessed of Abbey lands; your mother was of excellent family, so in the circumstances perhaps I might be lenient."

"You surely would not wish a woman of such ancestors to become the mother of your sons?"

"Well, to confess, she hath a way with her which pleases me, and since I have gone so far as to become betrothed to her I'll take her to my bed and if she pleases me I'll keep her there."

"She will never please you. Escape while there is time."

"I have gone too far in this."

"She would release you, I am certain."

"The truth is that I am never going to release her and in a short time she will be mine so utterly that she will beg me never to leave her."

"A pretty fiction," I said. "I know it to be far from the truth."

"Come with me now. Let us slip away. Let me show you what love is like."

"You are the last from whom I could learn that. I shall stay in this company until we leave. And it must almost be time that we did so."

"Tonight we will be together."

"Tonight? How could that be?"

"Easily. I will arrange it."

"Here?"

"I will ride back with you and you will open your window and I will climb through to you."

"In my sister's house!"

"Your sister is a woman. She will understand. But she need not know."

"You still do not understand that I am not as eager for you as you appear to be for me. You know full well that I despise you."

"Is that why your eyes sparkle at the sight of me?"

I stood up and went back to my seat at the table. He must perforce follow me.

Morris dancers had arrived. They had been engaged to entertain us and so they came into the hall in their Moorish costumes with bells attached to them and their capers were greatly applauded. They did a piece in which Robin Hood and Maid Marian figured and this was greatly appreciated. There was more singing and dancing, but at last the banquet and ball was over.

I rode back with Edward and Honey in their carriage, but Jake Pennlyon insisted on coming with us. He rode beside our carriage as he said he was not trusting his bride to the rough roads and any vagabond who might attempt to rob us.

I whispered to Honey: "He will try to come to my room. He has said as much."

She whispered back: "When we get back to the house I will feign sickness and ask you to look after me."

At Trewynd when we alighted from the carriage Honey put her hand to her head and groaned.

"I feel so ill," she said. "Will you take me to my bed, Catharine?"

I said indeed I would and gave Jake Pennlyon a curt good-night. He kissed me on the lips—one of those kisses which I was beginning to hate and tried hard to avoid. I turned away and went with Honey to her room.

"He'll go away now," she said. But she did not know Jake Pennlyon.

I crept cautiously to my room. I did not open the door. I put my ear to the keyhole. I could hear the window squeaking slightly as it swung open. True to his threat,

Jake Pennlyon had climbed the wall and come through it. I knew that if I went into that room I would find him there.

I pictured his leaping from behind and locking my door. I should be at his mercy and this time there would be no escape.

I turned and tiptoed back to Honey's room and told her what I suspected.

"Stay with me tonight," she said. "Edward will sleep in his own room. Catharine, tomorrow you must return to your mother. This man is dangerous."

What a night that was. I could not sleep at all. I kept thinking of Jake Pennlyon in my room, ready to spring on me. I could hear his cry of exultation when he caught me as I entered the room; I could hear the key turn in the lock, I could feel his great powerful body crushing mine. It was so vivid in my imagination that I seemed to live it.

It was not until dawn that I slept and then I was late waking.

Honey came into the room. "If he was here he has gone now," she said. "His horse is not in the stables."

I went cautiously to my room. The sun was streaming in; it showed my bed—empty but tousled. He must have slept there.

Fury possessed me. He had dared sleep in my bed. I pictured him there, waiting for the bride who did not come.

♦

When I stood gazing at my disturbed bed, I was overcome with a sense of powerlessness. I felt like a hunted animal with the baying of the dogs coming nearer, knowing that the relentless huntsman was bearing down on me.

So far I had escaped. I kept thinking how easily I could have stepped into that room last night to find myself trapped.

He was the sort of man who so far had always won. I knew that. But he should not do so this time. I knew that I must slip away and return to my home. But would that deter him? He must sail in six weeks' time, but I might well be carrying his seed at that time. I felt that if I allowed him to subdue me I should despise myself forever;

and in a way so would he. It must not happen. I must go on fighting.

I couldn't remain in the house. I guessed he would shortly be riding over. I must make sure not to be alone with him.

I went down to the stables. Honey had seen me and followed me there.

Her brow was furrowed. "You are going riding . . . alone?" she asked.

"I have to do something quickly."

"We should never have let it get to this."

"He was in my room last night. He must have waited there for me to come back. He slept in my bed."

"What . . . impudence!"

"Honey, what am I going to do?"

"Wait there," she said. "I'll ride with you. Then you won't be alone. We'll talk about it."

I went back to the house with her while she put on her riding habit and we took our horses and rode out . . . in the opposite direction of Lyon Court.

I said: "I must go home."

"I am sure you are right."

"I'll have to slip away secretly. Perhaps in a day or so."

"I shall miss you sorely. Jake Pennlyon is determined, but at least he will marry you."

I laughed. "Can you imagine marriage with such a man? He would try to reduce one to a slave."

"I don't think you are the stuff that slaves are made of."

"Sometimes I feel I'd like to make him understand that."

She looked at me oddly.

"Are you a little attracted by him, Catharine?" she asked.

"I loathe him so much that I get satisfaction in thwarting him."

"I think his wife would not be a very happy woman. He would be an unfaithful, demanding husband. I have heard stories of his father. There is not a girl in the village who is safe from him."

"I know that well. Such a man would never do for me."

We had come to the crest of a hill and were looking down on the little village of Pennyhomick, a charming sight with the little houses cluttering around the church.

I said: "How peaceful it looks. Let us ride down."

We walked our horses down the steep hill and as we came into the winding street with its gabled houses almost meeting over the cobbles I called to Honey to stop for I had seen a man crouching in a doorway; and there was that about him which was a dire warning.

"Let us go back," I said.

"Why so?" asked Honey.

"Look at that man. I'll swear it's plague."

Honey needed no more than that. Swiftly she turned her horse. At the foot of the hill we saw a woman coming toward us; she carried panniers on her shoulders and had clearly been to a brook for water.

She shouted to us: "Keep off, good folks. The sweat has come to Pennyhomick."

We rode up the hill as fast as we could, and only at the top turned to look back at the stricken village.

I shuddered. Before the night was out there would be bereaved households in that little hamlet. It was a sobering thought. And as we rode off the idea came to me. I realized then that I did not want to go home. I wanted the satisfaction of outwitting Jake Pennlyon and the stricken Pennyhomick had given me this idea.

I said: "Listen, Honey, if I go home he can take two courses of action. He can follow me and perhaps catch me. Or he may have his revenge on you. He is cruel and ruthless. You can be sure he would show no mercy. I'll not run away. I'll stay here and I'll outwit him at the same time. I am going to have the sweating sickness."

"Catharine!" Honey had turned pale.

"Not in truth, my dear sister. I shall pretend to have it. I shall stay in my chamber. You will attend me. We have been to Pennyhomick, remember. We are infected. You will nurse me and my illness will last as long as the *Rampant Lion* remains in the harbor."

Honey had pulled up her horse and stared at me. "Why . . . Catharine . . . I think we could do it."

I laughed. "Even he could not come where the sweat was. He dare not. He has to sail away with the *Rampant Lion*. He could not risk carrying the infection on board his vessel. I shall stay in my room attended only by you.

From my window I shall watch what goes on. Oh, Honey, it's a wonderful plan. He'll have to sail away without submitting me to his hateful lust. I shall die of laughing."

"It seems like tempting Providence."

"I would never have thought the great-granddaughter of witches would be so lily-livered. You shall make me some concoction—a mixture of buttercup juice and cinnamon and a paste. I shall look ill and I'll appear at the window. If he passes by he will quickly fall out of lust with me."

"No one must know except Edward and the two of us."

"Honey, I can't wait to begin. I shall go straight to my room, complaining of a headache. I shall go to bed and send Jennet for a posset. Then you will come in and from then on I have the sweat and no one must come near me except my beloved sister, who was with me at the time I was in Pennyhomick and may therefore be another victim."

We returned to the house. As one of the grooms took our horses I said: "I have such a lightheaded feeling and pains in my head. I shall go to my room."

"I'll send up a potion," said Honey. "You go and get into bed."

And that was the beginning.

The news traveled fast.

Ten people had died in Pennyhomick and the dread disease had crept into Trewynd Grange. The young mistress of the house was nursing her sister, with whom she, with great ill luck, had gone into Pennyhomick and they had brought the sweating sickness to the Grange.

Honey had ruled that no one was to penetrate the turret wing of the house to which I had moved, the better to isolate myself. Food was brought and placed in a room at the foot of the spiral stairway; Honey would descend and bring it to my room.

Edward did not come to us; for him to have done so might have betrayed us. We had to act as though I were in truth suffering from the sweating sickness and was being nursed by my sister, who might also be affected.

The first day I found exciting because it was not long, as I had guessed, before Jake Pennlyon came riding over.

Honey had ready the paste we had prepared and we coated my face with it. I looked into the mirror and did not recognize myself. I lay in my bed, the sheet pulled up to my chin. I heard his voice—resonant, suited to giving orders on the deck.

"Stand aside. I'm going up. Sweat! I don't believe it."

Honey stood by the door, trembling. I lay still waiting. He burst open the door and stood there.

"For God's sake go away," muttered Honey. "You are mad to come in here."

"Where is she? It's a trick. I'll not be tricked."

Honey tried to hold him off. "We went to Penny-homick," she said. "Have you not heard? They are dying like flies in Pennyhomick. Don't imperil your life and those of many others."

He came to the bed and looked down on me.

"Good God!" he whispered, and I wanted to burst into laughter. How grotesque I must look. He will have done with me forever! I thought.

I muttered as though in delirium, "Who's that? . . . Carey. . . . Is that you, Carey . . . my love . . . ?"

And I wondered that I could laugh inwardly while I said his name. But I did and I was exultant because I could see the incredulous fear and horror on that bold and hated face.

He had turned a different shade. It was visible even beneath the bronzed skin. He stretched out a hand and drew it back.

He turned to Honey.

"It is indeed . . . true . . ." he murmured.

"Go," said Honey. "Every moment you spend here you are in danger."

He went; I heard his heavy tread on the stairs. I sat up in my bed and laughed.

The days began to pass. They were tedious, monotonous. There was little to do. We worked tapestry, but it was not much to my taste. Often I saw Jake Pennlyon. I had to be careful, though, for he always looked up at my window and if he had caught me there and guessed at the truth I couldn't imagine what his reaction would have been. I used to laugh sometimes to think how I was deceiving him;

and that was the only thing that made these days bearable.

Once I suggested to Honey that we slip out at night and ride by moonlight. She pointed out to me that if we were discovered, even by one of the servants, all our efforts would have been in vain.

So I resisted the temptation; but how dull were the days!

My death was expected daily and it was considered something of a miracle that I was still alive. It was remembered that there had been an aura of mystery about my father. Honey was the great-granddaughter of a witch. The story went around that she had remedies which could cure even the sweat.

Jake rode over every day, but he didn't come into the house. He talked to the servants. He questioned them closely. Perhaps he was still suspicious.

The plan was working satisfactorily in more ways than one, because it was giving John Gregory time to make his plans in comfort. Everyone was chary of visiting Trewynd when the sweating sickness was there.

After three weeks of this life Honey brought news.

Jake Pennlyon had decided to leave two weeks earlier. The weather would be more favorable and he would leave before the gales set in. There could in any event not be a wedding for some time.

From my window I surreptitiously watched the activity on the Hoe. They were loading fast; the little boats were going back and forth. I was fascinated. And at last came the day when the *Rampant Lion* drew up her anchor and sailed away, taking Jake Pennlyon with her.

He had written to me and the letter was delivered while I was watching the ship fade into the distance.

"The voyage will wait no longer, so I go earlier the sooner to be back," he had written. "You will be waiting for me."

I laughed exultantly. I had won.

As soon as the *Rampant Lion* had sunk below the horizon my recovery began. In a week I was about again. It was a long week, but we had to give our subterfuge some semblance of truth. The servants were amazed. Few people contracted the sweat and lived. Moreover, Honey had nursed me and come through unscathed.

Jennet came back to me at the end of the week. It was good to listen to her gossip.

She regarded me with something like awe. "They be saying, Mistress," she told me, "that you have powers."

I was not displeased that this should be said.

"They be saying that you be the daughter of him who was a saint. Didn't he come not like others come and go in a mysterious way? And the mistress herself . . . she come from witches. That's what they be saying."

I nodded. "Well, here you see me, Jennet, almost as well as I ever was."

"It be a miracle, Mistress."

The days were long and the zest had gone out of them. The Hoe had none of the old excitement when the *Rampant Lion* no longer rode the waves and there was no danger of Jake Pennlyon's suddenly appearing.

I began to think of going home to the Abbey. My mother would be pleased to see me.

Perhaps because there was so little of interest I began to notice Jennet. She had changed in a rather subtle way. There was something a little sly about her, secretive; often when I spoke to her she would start as though she feared I would discover some guilty secret.

She often went to the stables and I had come upon her once or twice in conversation with Richard Rackell.

I was sure they were lovers. Jennet was not the sort to hold out for marriage. That hazy expression in the eyes, that slight slackening of the lips, that air of knowledge told its own story. I discussed it with Honey.

"So Eve must have looked when she ate the apple," I said.

"Perhaps we should get them married," said Honey. "Edward does not like immorality among the servants. And Jennet, if she has lost her virginity, is the sort of girl who would go quickly from one man to another."

I tackled Jennet. "I shall be going back to the Abbey very soon, Jennet."

"Oh, Mistress, and what when *he* comes back?"

"Who?" I asked sharply, knowing full well to whom she referred.

"The master . . . the Captain."

"Since when has he been master in this household?"

"Well, Mistress, he be master wherever he be I reckon."

"That's nonsense, Jennet. He is nothing here."

"But he have spoken for you."

"You don't understand these matters. What I want to say to you is this. You go down to the stables often."

The deep red stain in her cheeks told me I had come to the right conclusion. She cast down her head and her fingers plucked at her gown. I was sorry for her. Poor Jennet. She was meant to be a wife and a mother; she would never be able to hold out against the blandishments of men.

"Very well, Jennet," I said, "you are no longer a virgin. You may well be with child. Have you thought of that?"

"Yes, Mistress."

"The master—the only master of this house—will be displeased if he hears of your conduct. He expects good Christian behavior from his servants."

Her lips trembled and I put my arm about her. I had been brusque with her because with the utmost ease Jake Pennlyon had persuaded her to betray me. But now that she had become the paramour of Richard Rackell I could see her predicament more clearly. Poor Jennet was the kind of girl who was burdened—some might say blessed—with an overpowering sensuality. She was born to take and give sexual pleasure; and the reason why she would be a perpetual temptation to men was that they were a perpetual temptation to her. It was very much harder for her to stay on the path of virtue than it was for many others; therefore, one must try to understand and help her.

"Now, Jennet," I said, "what's done is done and there is no sense in mourning for virginity once it is lost, for that will not bring it back. You have been foolish and now you must make a decision. When I go back you would have come with me, but in the circumstances the man who has seduced you should marry you. I know who it is. I have seen you often together. Do not imagine that your creeping into the stables has gone unnoticed. If Richard Rackell is willing you shall marry him. It is what the master would wish. Does that not please you?"

"Oh, yes, Mistress, it does in truth."

"Very well, I will see if I can arrange it."

I was pleased really to see how relieved she was, for I was fond of the girl and I wanted to see her married and settled.

By the time Jake Pennlyon returned she would no doubt be big with child, for I imagined she was the kind of girl who would have a large brood of children. He would no longer be interested in her, so she would be saved from that ignominy; and by that time I should be at the Abbey.

I spoke to Honey about Jennet.

"It wouldn't surprise me," I said, "if she were pregnant already. Richard Rackell must marry her."

Honey agreed and she sent immediately for Richard.

When he came into the punch room and stood at the table, that air of breeding struck me afresh. I could not believe that Jennet would be a very suitable wife for him. Still, if he had seduced her he must marry her.

Honey said: "Richard, I think you might be eager to marry."

He bowed; his face was expressionless.

"You and Jennet, I believe, have been *over*friendly." She stressed the word "over" and as he did not reply she went on: "In the circumstances the master would expect you to marry her. When will you do so?"

He still hesitated. Then he said: "I will, in time."

"In time," I said. "What do you mean by that?"

"In . . . three weeks' time. I would need that."

I wondered why, but there was such an air of dignity about him that it was not seemly to press.

"Very well," said Honey. "There shall be a wedding in three weeks' time."

"We will have a celebration," I said. I was very anxious to make up to Jennet for having been harsh to her.

So it was arranged. A priest should come to the house—neither Thomas Elders nor John Gregory should perform this ceremony; it would be too public for that.

I summoned Jennet and told her the news.

"I shall give you your wedding dress and we will get Luce working on it immediately."

Jennet began to weep. "Mistress," she said, "I don't deserve such. I don't indeed."

"Well, Jennet," I said, "you have been a little too ready, but that is over. You must be a good wife to Richard and bear many children and then the fact that you did not wait for the ceremony will be forgotten."

I patted her shoulder, but that only had the effect of making her weep the more.

Because the days were inclined to be tedious we talked a great deal about Jennet's wedding. Edward had said the Morris dancers should come and we would play games and even have a cake with a silver penny in it that the one who found it might be King for the day.

Since the departure of the *Rampant Lion*, Sir Penn had been laid low with some periodic sickness the nature of which no one was sure, and we felt safe from all the troubles which might come from that quarter.

In the kitchen they had started to prepare for the feast we should have. Jennet had never had so much made of her before.

The days slipped away. I said to Honey: "As soon as Jennet is safely wed I will begin to make preparation for my journey home."

"The scene is set," said Honey. "Jake Pennlyon is on the high seas; his father is laid low; there is great excitement about the wedding. It would not be noticed for some days if you decided to leave. Heaven knows I shall hate your going. It will be so dull here without you, Catharine. But if he cut short his voyage and returned then it would be too late and we could not hope to fool him again."

"If he ever knew how he had been fooled he would never forgive us."

"His vengeance is something I would not wish to encounter."

I shivered. "Yes, as soon as the wedding is over I will leave. Do you think Richard will be a good husband to Jennet?"

"He is a quiet, good-mannered boy."

"He is strange. It is difficult to imagine his seducing Jennet."

"I'd wager most of the seducing came from her."

"Well, he is good and truly caught. I think she will be a good wife, though. She was overpersuaded by Jake Pennlyon to betray me, but I have forgiven her that, for I am sure she deeply regrets it."

"For a girl like Jennet, Jake Pennlyon would be irresistible," Honey said.

I changed the subject. I did not wish to think of Jake Pennlyon persuading Jennet. I had given too much thought to that matter already.

There came the night when for the third time I saw the Spanish galleon.

Such an ordinary day it had been—warm and sunny for the time of year, "unseasonable" they called it—a quiet, peaceful day. How was it that we could have lived through such a day unaware of the tremendous events which were awaiting us?

I was pleasantly tired when I went to bed and was asleep almost immediately.

I was awakened as I had been on other nights by unusual sounds below. I lay still listening. Shuffling footsteps, a scuffle. Some serving wench creeping out to meet a lover? I rose from my bed and went to the window.

There she was in all her glory. Closer than I had ever seen her—the mighty and magnificent Spanish galleon.

I must go down. I was not going to allow anyone to say that I had imagined my galleon this time. I would awaken Honey and Edward and insist that they look. I picked up a robe and wrapped it around me, but as I crossed to the door it was opened suddenly. John Gregory stood there.

I said: "What is wrong?"

He did not answer. He was wearing a long cloak with a hood; his face was pale, his eyes brilliant. He spoke then in a tongue I did not know and then I saw that there was a stranger with him.

"Who is this?" I demanded. "What do you here?"

They did not answer me.

The stranger had stepped into my room. John Gregory nodded toward me and spoke again.

The stranger seized me. I tried to throw him off, but he

held me firmly. I struggled. Then I screamed and immediately John Gregory's hand was over my lips. In a few seconds he had taken a kerchief and bound it around my mouth. I was powerless to make a sound. I was put onto my bed. The thought flashed into my mind: Have I saved myself from Jake Pennlyon for this?

But there was no lust about these men, only a determination to complete a task. My arms were pinioned. They had ropes for the purpose. Likewise were my ankles strapped together so that I was trussed and helpless.

Then they carried me from my room.

Down the spiral stairs we went . . . out into the courtyard.

I saw a figure lying there. There was blood everywhere. I wanted to cry out, but I could not make a sound. I was limp with horror and fear.

As they carried me past that wounded figure I saw that it was Edward.

Honey! I wanted to call out. Honey, where are you?

Edward's carriage was waiting there. Richard Rackell was holding the horses—three of Edward's best and most fleet.

Richard Rackell! Traitor! I wanted to shout, but there was nothing I could do.

I was placed in the carriage. Lying there were two other figures. My heart leaped with an emotion of relief, yet horror, for they were Honey and Jennet.

They stared at me as I did at them. We could only communicate by looks. They were as bewildered as I. I wondered if Honey knew that Edward was lying in his own blood in the courtyard.

There were voices—foreign voices. Instinctively I knew that they were speaking the Spanish tongue.

The carriage had begun to move. We were going toward the sea.

We had been abducted as women sometimes were by marauding pirates. There had been traitors in our midst and the result was that Edward was lying in his own blood in the courtyard and Honey, Jennet and I were being taken out to the Spanish galleon.

Journey to
an Unknown Destination

They carried us into the boat which was lying ready. I saw Richard Rackell's face clearly in the light of the lantern which he held. Traitor! I wanted to cry and felt a physical pain in my throat which was frustrated fury.

I was lifted into the boat and lay there helpless. They put Honey beside me, then Jennet. We could not see each other's faces clearly because it was a dark night. There was no moon, only the faint light of the stars that were visible where there was no cloud.

I tried to think of a means of escape. I guessed what was happening to us. We had been abducted as women had been throughout the years. Pirates descended on the land; they plundered; they stole; they burned down villages and townships and they took the women for their pleasure.

If only I could talk to Honey! If only I could think of some means of escape! But I was helpless, trussed and on a boat which was being rapidly rowed out to sea by strangers, and two men who had posed as a groom and a false priest were watching over us.

A wild fantasy came to me. The *Rampant Lion* would appear suddenly—returned unexpectedly from the voyage; the galleon would be discovered. Jake Pennlyon would board her; I could see his eyes flashing; see him standing there, legs apart, a bloodstained cutlass in his hands; I could hear his laugh as he uncut my bonds.

But these were but dreams.

Relentlessly the little boat pushed its way through the water to the Spanish galleon.

The men had shipped oars. We had arrived and there was no *Rampant Lion* to sight us, no Jake Pennlyon to cut our bonds.

John Gregory was bending over me. He cut the rope about my ankles and removed the gag from my mouth. He pulled me to my feet, for my arms were still bound behind me.

I stood unsteadily; the galleon loomed over us.

Honey and Jennet were beside me, pinioned as I was.

"Honey," I said, "we have been betrayed."

She nodded. I wondered again if she had seen Edward's body. Poor Edward, so gentle and kind.

I was aware of Jennet, who would have no wedding now.

A rope ladder was dangling from the side of the ship. John Gregory said: "You will climb it."

"Without use of our hands, traitor?" I asked.

"I shall untie you now, but do not attempt to do anything but climb the ladder."

"For what reason?"

"You will discover."

"You rogue!" I cried. "You came to our house. . . . You deceived us. . . ."

He said gently: "This is not the time for talk, Mistress. You must obey."

"Board that ship? For what reason? It's a Spaniard."

"Please do not force me to hurt you."

"Hurt me! Have you not brought me here by force . . . and you talk about hurting me!"

Honey said: "Don't lose your temper, Catharine. It won't help."

There was hopelessness in her voice and I believed then that she had seen Edward in the courtyard.

But I was incensed. "You are no priest," I said to John Gregory.

He did not answer. He released my hands and propelled me toward the ladder.

Richard Rackell was waiting to guide me to the rope; I made out faces above looking down.

Someone called out in Spanish and John Gregory answered in that tongue.

The boat dipped. It would not be easy to climb that ladder. I looked down at the dark water and I thought of death by drowning. Perhaps it would be preferable, I thought, but not seriously. Whatever life was I would always cling to it. The rope was put into my hands and I started to climb. Hands stretched out and I was pulled onto the deck. There were dark faces about me; I heard the excited babble of voices. Then there was silence. A figure came forward. He spoke in an authoritative voice. He must have given an order, for I was seized by two men who dragged me forward; we were followed by the man who had given the order and I was taken to a cabin in which a candle in a horn lantern gave a dim light.

A door was locked on me and I was alone. I was shivering because I was in my nightclothes and it had been cold on the boat; and even now I was not sure whether it was the temperature or fear which made me tremble so. It was incredible that yesterday Honey and I had been calmly making plans for Jennet's wedding and now all three of us were prisoners on a pirate vessel.

They had taken us—three women, for what purpose there seemed to be no doubt. But why three of us and why had they not burned down the house and robbed us? Perhaps they had. Perhaps they took us first. They had, I feared, killed Edward. It was not the first time the coasts had been raided. This was the sort of thing that Jake Pennlyon and his men did in foreign lands.

I should never have come to Devon. I should have stayed at home.

I looked into the future which all reasoning told me

was looming ahead of me. I who had stood out so fiercely against marriage with Jake Pennlyon would now be used to satisfy men—any men—who were on a long journey from home and needed diversion.

I felt ill at the prospect. I wondered whether I would not have been wiser to refuse to climb the ladder: to have chosen death rather than this.

On the floor was a rug. I lay on it because my legs were shaking. The ship rocked on the water and I lay watching the horn lantern swing with the motion of the vessel.

I thought of my mother and of what she would do when she heard that I had been abducted. How she had suffered! And now this. And not only me but Honey too and she loved us both dearly.

I thought of Honey then, beautiful, dignified Honey, who was carrying Edward's child; and to consider her submitted to a hundred indignities hurt me as deeply as did the contemplation of my own fate. I would fight. I would kick and scream. If I could find a knife I would defend myself. I would no doubt be powerless against strong men, but I would make it so that they never felt safe from me. I would make it so that when they slept they would never be sure that I might not plunge a knife into their hearts or drop some poison into their ale or whatever they drank.

I was sustained by thoughts of what I would do.

Wildcat, Jake Pennlyon had called me. They would learn that wildcats were dangerous.

The motion of the ship had changed. I knew that we had shipped anchor and were sailing out of the harbor.

The door of the cabin was opened and Honey was thrust in. She, in her night robes as I was, was clutching them about her. I saw that her robe had been ripped down the front.

Already, I thought.

The door was locked on her. I had stood up. We ran to each other and just stood holding each other tightly.

"Oh, Honey, Honey," I cried. "What have they done to you?"

She said: "They have done nothing. There was one man. . . ." She shivered. "He took me to a place like this. He tore my gown from my shoulders, then he saw the Agnus Dei. I always wear it about my neck, and he drew back as though afraid and I was brought here."

"Honey," I said, "this is a nightmare. It can't be true."

She didn't answer.

I said: "Edward. . . ."

She remained mute and suddenly put her hands over her eyes. It was a gesture of despair.

I touched her arm gently.

"He tried to stop them," I said. "Where was the rest of the household? Are they all traitors like John Gregory and Richard Rackell? What are we going to do, Honey? What can we do? They have brought us here to be as camp followers are to the army. But they go willingly. We are abducted against our will. They will use us . . . until they are tired of us. Then perhaps they will throw us overboard. Perhaps it would be better to cheat them. To take that plunge ourselves first?"

Still she didn't answer. She only stared ahead of her. I know she was seeing Edward lying in his own blood on the cobbles of the courtyard.

I went on because I had to go on talking: "Perhaps even now Jennet is being forced to submit . . . to who knows what?" I could picture Jennet, wide eyes, perhaps a little expectant. Perhaps she would take to the life. She was different from us. How easily she had agreed to betray me when Jake Pennlyon had asked her to. And where was he? Somewhere on the high seas. Perhaps he was raiding some foreign port and forcing women as we were being forced.

Oh, why had he gone so soon? Why had he always been there to plague me when I did not want him and away at the only time he could have been of use?

"Honey," I said, "speak to me, Honey."

"They killed Edward," she said. "Edward tried to save me and they killed him. I am sure of it."

"It may be that he did not die. It may be that he will come after us. They will give the alarm. They will come in search of us. We shall be rescued. If Jake Pennlyon were to come back. . . ."

"He has gone on a long voyage. It will be months before he returns."

"We may meet him at sea." I saw him boarding the Spanish galleon, his eyes gleaming. He would kill on the spot any who had dared lay hands on me.

"No one has come near you, Catharine?" she asked.

"No. I was left here."

"They are waiting until we are out of sight of England."

"And then you think . . . ?"

"What else can I think? I was saved because I am a Catholic. You must feign to be of that faith, Catharine. It will go ill with you if you do not."

"I will feign nothing."

"Be reasonable."

"I feel I have lost my reason. I have walked into a nightmare."

"This is no uncommon happening, Catharine. You should know that. Piracy on the high seas is becoming more and more commonplace. Treasure and women. That is what men go to sea to seek."

"We have to think what we can do."

"I have escaped so far. You must too. When I prayed to the Holy Mother as that man attacked me he was afraid. John Gregory came along then and must have told him that I was with child—Catholic child—and he desisted and John Gregory led me here. I believe he would be a friend to us."

"A friend . . . who betrayed us!"

"He betrayed, yes, but I believe he is uneasy to have done so."

"Uneasy. He is a deceitful liar."

"Guard your tongue, Catharine. Remember we have need of all the friends we can find. I am concerned for you. I believe you are being kept for someone . . . perhaps the Captain. You were taken away from us and brought here. If that should be so try to talk to him. He may speak our tongue. Beg him not to act rashly. Tell him that any harm done to you will be avenged."

"That might arouse in him a determination to do me harm."

"Tell him you will become a Catholic. You wish for tuition."

"In fact," I said, "betray my beliefs, go down on my knees and implore these dogs to treat us with respect. It would be of no avail, I assure you, Honey. If you had an Agnus Dei to hang about my neck I would not take it.

I will see if I can lay my hands on some weapon. If I could find a knife I would at least put up a fight."

"It would be useless." She was staring into the gloom, her face strained with grief, and I knew she was thinking of Edward.

I was not sure how long we lay there in that cabin. I think I slept a little. I was exhausted by my emotions. I started up and wondered where I was. The swaying of the ship and the creaking of its timbers quickly reminded me.

I could just make out the figure of Honey beside me. The horned lantern was swaying from side to side, its light feeble; and the horror of our position dawned on me afresh.

I knew Honey was awake, but we did not speak. There was nothing of comfort that we could offer each other.

It might be morning; how could we know? There was nothing against which to measure time. My tongue was dry, my lips parched. I supposed I was hungry, but the thought of food revolted me.

We may have lain there for another hour or more when the door opened.

We started up in terror. It was a man carrying bowls of something which looked like soup.

He said: "*Olla podrida*," and pointed to the bowls. . . .

I wanted to take them and throw them in his face, but Honey said: "Food. We'll feel better when we've eaten. We'll feel able to face whatever we have to." I knew she was thinking of her unborn child.

We took the bowls. The food smelled good. The man nodded and left us. Honey was already drinking the concoction. Her appetite had increased since she had become pregnant. She used to say it was her hungry baby demanding to be fed.

I tried it too. It was savory and warming and I found I was glad of it.

We set down the bowls and waited apprehensively. It was not long before we had another visitor. This was the man I had heard addressed as Capitan.

He came into the room and stood at the door, looking

at us. There was a dignity about him, a courtliness which aroused my optimism.

He said in halting English: "I am the Captain of this vessel. I have come to speak with you."

I said: "You had better tell us quickly what this means."

"You are on board my ship," he said. "I am taking you on a voyage."

"For what purpose?" I asked.

"That you will discover."

"You have abducted us from our homes!" I cried. "We are gentlewomen unaccustomed to rough treatment. We. . . ."

Honey laid a restraining hand on my arm. The Captain noticed and nodded approvingly.

"It is no use to protest against what is done," he said.

"Nevertheless, I protest. You have done a wicked thing."

"I have not come to speak of such things or to waste my time. I come to tell you that I am obeying orders."

"Whose orders?"

"Those of one who commands me."

"And who, pray?"

Again Honey restrained me. "Listen, Catharine," she said.

"You are wise," said the Captain. "I am sorry you were taken. That should not have been." He was looking straight at Honey. "A mistake, you understand."

"If you tell us what this means we shall be grateful," said Honey humbly.

"I can tell you that if you are wise no harm will befall you on this ship. There are sailors here who have been at sea many months . . . you understand. They could be rough. So you must take care. I would not have you submitted to indignity on my ship. That would be against my wishes and those of one who commands me."

I said: "There was another taken with us. Jennet, my maid. What has become of her?"

"I will discover," he promised me. "I will do my best to ensure your comfort . . . all of you."

I was intrigued by him. His gaze kept straying to Honey in a manner which was familiar to me. With her hair hanging about her shoulders she could not fail to look beautiful; she looked vulnerable too; all men were seized with the desire to protect her. I suppose that applied even to Spanish Captains of pirate ships.

"You are uncomfortable here," he said. "I would talk with you in more suitable surroundings. Come with me and we will eat. You have had a little food, I believe."

Honey and I exchanged glances. The manner in which the Captain had spoken to us had brought us a little comfort. He was no rough sailor, that much was clear; and he was treating us as though we were guests on his ship, which was reassuring.

The smell of grease and cooking was strong in the alleyway. The ship lurched so that we had to cling to a rail which ran from one end of the alley to the other. We stumbled after the Captain as best we could and he opened a door and stood aside for us to enter.

This was his cabin. It was spacious and the bulkheads were paneled. It was like a small room. There were books and instruments everywhere. Dominating the cabin was the long wooden table which was bolted to the floor; I noticed also a piece of ordnance which was mounted on a carriage and pointed out through a gunport. A tapestry hung on the paneling. I was later to discover that it represented the surrender of Granada to Queen Isabella and King Ferdinand.

At that first view I was astonished that there could be so much comfort on a ship.

"Pray be seated," said the Captain. "I will order food."

We sat down and a barefooted sailor came in and prepared the table. It was not long before steaming plates of something like beans and salted meat was brought in.

The Captain held the chairs for us as we sat down.

"You do not perhaps feel hungry," he said, "but it is well to eat a little."

"Can you tell me why you struck down my husband?" asked Honey.

"I cannot tell you. I did not leave the ship."

"You knew others had come to take us away?"

"It was the purpose of our mission."

"To raid our coasts to take women . . ." I began.

"No," he said. "To take you. You will understand in due course."

Honey spoke gently then: "And *you* will understand

that we are bewildered. We want to know what this means. We fear you have brought us here to. . . ."

He smiled at her courteously. "No harm shall come to you on my ship if you obey orders. I have issued a command that no one is to touch you." He was looking at me. Then he turned to Honey. "I will command the same immunity for you."

"She has already been attacked," I said.

"I trust. . . ."

Honey touched the Agnus Dei. "This saved me," she said. "This and John Gregory."

"Any man who dares touch either of you will pay for it with his life," said the Captain.

"Then I demand to know for what purpose we have been brought here," I said.

"This is something you will know in time."

"You have snatched us from our homes," I began, but again Honey restrained me.

"For Heaven's sake, Catharine, let us discover all we can. The Captain is anxious to help us." Pregnancy had brought a serenity to Honey which in the circumstances seemed unnatural. She was thinking of her baby and playing for time.

He gave her a grave smile.

"It is my duty to see that you shall not be harmed. I shall do my duty. But I ask your help. You will not go where I do not wish you to. You will never go unescorted. The man Gregory will be with you. Do not go on deck without him. The men will have been warned, but it is not always possible to control them, and although they know they risk their lives there may be some wild enough to thrust their attentions on you."

"Where are we going?"

"I cannot tell you. It is not a long voyage. You will understand when you reach our destination. There you will learn the purpose of your coming. If you are wise you will forget what has happened and look forward. As far as this ship is concerned I offer my protection and any comforts I can give you. The ship resembles a castle, some say—a floating castle—but it is not a castle, you must understand. We are at sea and life at sea is not like that on land. There are luxuries we cannot have. Nevertheless, I would wish you to be as comfortable as I can make you. Clothes, for instance. You have come ill prepared for a journey. I must find some cloth for you. Perhaps you can make it into gowns. You will eat in this cabin—sometimes with me, sometimes alone. My advice is that you accept what has befallen you—accept with serenity and understanding that on this ship if you follow my instructions no harm can come to you."

He applied himself to the meat and beans on his plate. I could not eat much, nor could Honey.

I could not believe that this was really happening to me. I would wake up soon, I promised myself, the Spanish galleon would become the *Rampant Lion,* the Captain change to Jake Pennlyon and it would be just another dream of which I had had several, about that domineering character.

But this dream—this nightmare—went on and on and it was reality that had faded.

Very soon after Honey became violently ill. It was small wonder. We were unused to the roll of a ship; we were exhausted mentally and physically; we were bewildered and uncertain of what was happening to us. And Honey was pregnant.

I looked after her and that was a good thing to do because it made me forget everything but that I feared she would die.

John Gregory was never far away. How I hated that man who had slyly come to our house, posing as a priest, and who had led our captors to the house and to us. A spy! A traitor! What could be worse? But he was now our protector. I could not bring myself to look at him without expressing my contempt. But he was useful.

I said to him: "I fear you are killing my sister. You know the state of her health; this shock has been too much for her, as indeed was to be expected. I should have believed those who had been befriended by us would never have betrayed us, but I was mistaken. We had liars and traitors in our midst." When I berated him he would stand before me, his eyes downcast, contrition in every gesture. Honey always tried to stop me, but I couldn't stop myself and there was some relief in giving vent to my feelings.

On the second day when Honey was so sick and I feared for her life I said to John Gregory, "I need our maid here. She must help me nurse my sister."

He said he would speak to the Captain and very soon Jennet joined us.

She looked much the same. Is it possible, I asked myself, that she could adjust herself so soon?

She was in an old gown which she had snatched up before she was taken; and already she was regaining that complete placidity which was a feature of hers.

The sight of her face irritated me once I had felt the relief that she was alive and well. She looked as though she were satisfied with her lot. How could she be? And what had happened to her?

I said: "The mistress is very sick. You must help with her, Jennet."

"Oh, poor lady," she said. "And in her condition."

Honey's pregnancy was visible now. I thought anxiously of the child and I fervently wished that we had both gone home to my mother the day aftter Jake Pennlyon had sailed.

Honey seemed comforted because the three of us were together, and Jennet was undoubtedly a good nurse. There were rough stools on which we could sit and we were beginning to grow accustomed to the roll of the ship and the smell of cooking. Honey slept a great deal during those first days, which was a good thing for her; and Jennet and I talked together as we watched over her.

I learned that Jennet had been seen by one of the men who had raided the house. He was strong and lithe and had come upon Jennet on her way to my room. He had seized her and spoken to her, but she could not understand what he had said. He had picked her up and carried her under his arm as though she were a bundle of hay.

Jennet giggled and I knew what had followed on the ship.

"Just him," said Jennet. "There were others that wanted me, but he brought out a knife. And although I couldn't understand what he said, I knew he meant I was his and he'd use that knife on anyone that touched me."

She cast down her eyes and blushed and I wondered

that she so wanton—for it was clear that she was not displeased with her state—could appear so coy, for she was not assuming modesty; she was too simple for that.

"I do think he be a good man, Mistress," she murmured.

"He was not your first either," I said.

Her blush deepened. "Well, Mistress, in a manner of speaking, no."

"In a manner of acting either," I said. "And what of Richard Rackell, whom you were going to marry?"

"He were but half a man," she said scornfully.

Jennet was undoubtedly satisfied with her new protector.

She talked a good deal about him as we sat watching Honey. It took my mind off what was happening to us all as I listened.

She had not in truth been eager to marry Richard Rackell, only it was good for a wench to be married; and having given in like, well, there might be results.

"And what if there are results now?" I asked.

She said piously that that was in the hands of God.

"Rather in yours and your pirate lover," I reminded her.

I was glad to have her with me. I said we should keep together, the three of us; she should help to look after Honey because Honey was going to need care.

So she was with us during those uneasy days though she crept away at night to be with her lover.

It is strange how quickly one can grow accustomed to a new life. We could only have been at sea for three days when I was no longer filled with incredulous dread on awakening, when I had grown accustomed to the creaking of timbers, the pitching and tossing of the ship, the sound of foreign voices, the nauseating smell which always seemed to come from the galleys.

Honey began to improve. She was suffering from the sea rather than any dreadful disease, and the color began to return to her face and she looked more like herself.

When she was able to stand we went to the Captain's cabin and ate there. We did not see him again for some days, and that cabin, strangely elegant among its surroundings with its paneled walls and tapestry, became familiar to us. Jennet ate with us and we were waited on by the Captain's own servant, dark and dour, who never said a word in our hearing.

After meals, which consisted mainly of biscuits, salted meats and a kind of crude wine, we would go back to our sleeping quarters and there would speculate on what this strange adventure meant.

John Gregory brought us some cloth—two or three bales of it—so that we could make ourselves some gowns, and this was a good occupation, for we grew quite animated discussing what styles we would make.

Jennet and Honey were good with their needles and we all set to work.

Honey used to talk a great deal about the baby, which would be born in five months' time. It was quite different now. She had dreamed of the child's being brought into the world either in Trewynd or the Calpertons' place in Surrey or perhaps she would do as my mother wished and go to the Abbey for the birth. That was all changed. Where would her child be born now? On the high seas or in whichever mysterious place for which we were destined?

"Edward and I planned for this child," said Honey. "We used to say we shouldn't mind whether it was a girl or a boy. He was so good and kind, he would have been such a loving father and now. . . . I dream of him, Catharine, lying there. I can't get him out of my mind."

I soothed her, but how could I stop her grieving for Edward?

As for myself I could not really believe in this life. It was too fantastic. If we had been ill used by crude sailors at least we could have understood what our abduction meant. But it was not so; we were protected and treated with courtesy by our abductors.

"It simply does not make sense," I said to Honey.

We made gowns for ourselves with speed; they were by no means elegant, but they sufficed. At times we were allowed to walk on the deck. I shall never forget emerging for the first time and standing on deck, high above the water. I was astonished by the rich decorations and the towering forecastle. To hold the rail and look out to the horizon and let one's eyes run around that great blue-gray curve filled me with an excitement which I could not suppress in spite of my apprehension and my anger against the circumstances which had brought us here.

And as I stood there straining my eyes always I looked for a ship on the horizon. In my heart I said: It will come. He will come in search of me. And I was exultant because I was sure this would come to pass.

I only had to close my eyes to see him there. He would shout to our Captain. "Spanish dog!" he would call him and he would board the ship, though the decks were high and strong nets were stretched between the sides and central gangway that joined forecastle to quarter deck. I looked at the great cannon, which one could not fail to notice. Such cannons, I knew, could blow a ship out of the ocean. But not the *Rampant Lion*.

He will come, I told myself. Before we reach our mysterious destination, he will come.

A few days after our capture I saw a ship on the horizon. My heart leaped with delight I had rarely known.

Honey was standing beside me. "Look," I cried. "A ship. It's the *Rampant Lion*."

There was pandemonium on deck. The sound of chattering voices filled the air. The ship had been sighted.

It was the *Lion*, I was certain of it.

"*Inglés*." I caught the word.

"He has come," I whispered to Honey. "I knew he would come."

We stood there clinging to the rail. The ship had grown a little larger, but it was many miles distant.

"He must have returned," I said. "He came back more quickly than he believed possible. He would hear what had happened immediately and he would set sail to find us."

"How can you be sure?" asked Honey.

"Is it not just what he would do? Do you think he would let me go?"

The Captain was standing beside us.

"You have seen the ship," he said quietly. "She is an English ship."

I turned to him triumphantly. "She is coming this way."

"I think not," he said. "Merely a caravel. She's limping a little. No doubt she is going into harbor."

"She is the *Rampant Lion*," I cried.

"That ship! I know her. Nay, it is no *Rampant Lion*. It is but a little caravel."

Disappointment was a pain; my throat constricted and I felt a great anger toward this Captain and those traitors who had led the pirates to us.

"She would not dare approach us, that one," went on the Captain. "We'd blow her out of the water. She'll get away as quick as she's able and when she's having the barnacles scraped off her in some English harbor her crew will tell the tale of how they escaped from a mighty galleon."

"It may not always be so," I said.

"No," replied the Captain, perhaps willfully misunderstanding, "they do not always escape us. But we have a cargo of a certain nature on board and I do not wish it to be endangered."

He was looking at Honey and then asked her how she fared.

She said that she felt much better and he expressed his gratification for that. They behaved as though he were a friendly neighbor paying a call rather than the Captain of a pirate vessel who was carrying us off against our will.

He bowed and left us. And when he had gone Honey said to me: "Did you really think it was the *Rampant Lion*?"

"I did! Oh, that it were."

"It is such a short time ago that you said you would give anything to escape from Jake Pennlyon."

"I would give anything to escape from these villains who now hold us captive."

She said: "You should stop thinking of Jake Pennlyon. He is dead to you."

Then I covered my face with my hands because I could not bear to look at Honey.

It was she who comforted me then.

The Captain was indeed a courteous gentleman. When we dined with him he talked to us, asking questions about England. He had successfully conveyed to us the implication that he had nothing to do with the raid on Trewynd. He had merely been carrying out orders. He was to take

his ship to the coast of Devon; a woman would be brought
to his ship and he would take her to a stated destination.
He was merely doing his duty. He had taken no part in
the actual abduction. One could not imagine his doing so
in any circumstances.

Accepting this, we grew quite friendly.

For Honey he had a very special kind of devotion.
I think he was falling in love with her.

Ever since he had learned she was pregnant he had
been anxious for her to have every care.

One day she asked him if he knew whether her husband could have lived even though she feared he could
not possibly have done so; he said he did not know, but
he would question those who had been at the house at
the time of the abduction.

A few days later he told her.

"Your husband could not possibly have survived," he
said.

Honey nodded in a calm, hopeless kind of way. I felt
quite differently. I wanted to rage. That good, kind man
to be done to death by robbers and pirates!

Honey took my hand. She was reminding me of what
we owed the Captain. His protection stood between us
and we could guess what terrible fate.

I remembered and was quiet; but there was a sick
despair in my heart and I mourned Edward deeply.

Then the storm overtook us. I am sure we were never
so near death as we were in that wild sea. Our galleon
was mighty; she was seaworthy; she rode the water in
her proud, gallant, dignified way, but even she must falter
before the fury of such an onslaught.

All day the wind had been whipping up the white
horses. We heard the excited voices of the sailors as they
lowered the sails and closed the gunports and hatches.

The Captain ordered us to his cabin and said we were
to stay there. We staggered down. We could not stand
and the stools on which we sat were flung from one side
of the ship to the other.

Jennet clung to me. Her lover was busy at his tasks.
He had no time to spare for her now.

She was terrified. "Be we going to die, Mistress?" she asked.

"I doubt not the Captain will save the ship and us," said Honey.

"To die . . . without confessing our sins," said Jennet. " 'Twould be a terrible thing."

"I doubt your sins were very great, Jennet," I soothed her.

"They be, Mistress," she said. "They be terrible."

"Nonsense," I retorted. "I wish there was something we could do."

"The Captain said we were to stay here," said Honey.

"We could be drowned like rats in a trap."

"What else should we do?" demanded Honey.

"There must be something. I'm going up to see."

"Stay here," said Honey.

I looked at her, now so obviously pregnant; I looked at Jennet, filled with a fear of dying with her sins on her; and I said authoritatively, "You will stay here, Honey, and Jennet will stay with you. Make sure that the mistress is as comfortable as it is possible for her to be," I added to Jennet.

They stared at me in amazement, but I could not remain inactive, just waiting for death.

I was flung against the sides of the ship as I came onto the deck. The galleon was groaning her protest. Fortunately I was on the lee side or I should have been blown overboard. It was a stupid thing to have done to come on deck against the Captain's orders, but it was more than I could endure to stay in that rattling cabin. The rain lashed the decks mercilessly; the wind shook the ship as a dog might shake a rat. I was saturated, for as the ship dipped the waves broke over her; the deck was slimy and dangerous. I knew that it would be folly for me to attempt to cross it and although I preferred the fresh air to the depth of the ship I knew that it was doubly dangerous to stay up there.

I fell against a man who was struggling with a bag of tools in one hand and a horn lantern in the other.

He did not recognize me in the gloom and must have thought I was a cabin boy, for he shouted something which I realized meant I was to take the lantern, so I did so and stumbled after him.

I followed him down into the bowels of the ship. It was eerie down there. I had escaped the roar of the wind and the torrential rain, but the air was close and fetid; the rancid smell of food was everywhere, and the groans and creaking of the ship seemed to proclaim her distress at the treatment she was being given and her inability to go on if the torture did not abate.

Men were working at the pumps. So we had sprung a leak; their faces gleamed in the light from the lantern.

I stood and held the lantern high. The man who had led me here was, I discovered, a carpenter's mate and was there to find where the ship was leaking and to patch her up if possible.

The men cursed the ship and the sea and prayed for salvation all in the same breath.

I watched the men pumping with all their might, the sweat running down their faces.

They screamed at each other in Spanish, which I was beginning to understand a little.

They were all calling on the Mother of God to intercede for them and as they prayed they worked the pumps.

I saw Richard Rackell among them.

He noticed me too and gave me that rueful smile which I suppose was meant to imply contrition.

I retaliated with the contemptuous look I reserved for him and then I thought: This could well be our last hour on earth. I must at least try to discover what had made him deceive us so. I half smiled at him and the relief on his face was apparent. Someone shouted at me, for I had lowered the lantern. I was able to recognize what was required and held it high again.

That nightmare seemed to go on for a long time. My arms ached with holding the lantern, but at least that was better than inactivity. The galleon had taken on a new character; she was like a living person. She was taking a furious beating and standing up to it. I realized then a little of what Jake Pennlyon felt toward his *Rampant Lion*. He loved that ship perhaps as much as he could love anybody, and witnessing the fight for survival the galleon was making, I could understand that.

Two cabin boys came down to the pumps and one of

them recognized me, for I heard him say something about the Señorita.

One of the men came over and looked at me closely. My hair hanging in wet strands down my back betrayed me.

The lantern was taken from me. I was pushed toward the companionway.

All about me were the rhythmic sounds of the pump; the carpenters were patching parts of the ship with thin strips of lead and ramming oakum into the spots where the sea was coming in.

I found my way back to the cabin.

Honey was distraught and when she saw me her face shone with relief.

"Catharine, where have you been?"

"I've been holding a lantern." I was flung against the side of the cabin as I spoke. I got up and clung to the leg of the fixed table. I told the others to do the same. At least we could not be dashed about if we could keep our grip on that.

I thought the ship was going to turn over; she rose and leaned so that her starboard side must have been been beneath the sea. She shivered as though she were being shaken and then seemed to remain in the position for minutes before she crashed down.

There was the sound of heavy objects being flung about. There were shouts and curses. If I had been on deck at that moment I should certainly have been swept overboard.

Honey murmured: "Oh, God, this is the end then."

I felt my entire being crying out in protest. I would not die. There was so much I had to discover. I must know for what purpose we had been abducted. I must see Jake Pennlyon again.

After that, although the storm raged, it began to abate a little. It was terrifying yet, but the ship was still standing up to the storm and the worst appeared to be over.

For hours the wind continued to shake us; the ship went on creaking and groaning; we could not stand up, but at least we were all together.

I looked at Honey; she lay exhausted, her long lashes beautiful against her pale skin. I was overcome with a kind of protective love for her; and I wondered when her child would be born and what effect these terrible happenings might have on it.

On an impulse I bent over and kissed her cheek. It was a strange thing for me to do, for I was not demonstrative. She opened her eyes and smiled at me.

"Catharine, we're still here then?"

"We're alive still," I said.

"And together," she added.

For two days and nights the storm had raged, but it was over now. The waters had lost their fury; they were smooth blue-green and only the occasional white horse ruffled them.

There was cold food only—biscuits and salt meat—and we were hungry enough to enjoy it.

The Captain came to the cabin while the storm was still raging and inquired for us. I noticed how he looked at Honey, tender, reassuring.

"We are riding the storm," he told us. "The ship has come through. But we shall have to put into port to repair the damage."

My heart leaped. In port. It would not be an English port, of course. No Spanish galleon would dare risk that. But the word "port" excited me. We might escape and find our way back to England.

"While we are in port I shall have to keep you confined to this cabin," he said. "You will understand the necessity of this."

"If you could tell us where we are being taken we could perhaps understand it," I said.

"You will know, Señorita, in time."

"I want to know now."

"It is necessary sometimes to wait," said the Captain. He turned to Honey. "I trust you were not afraid."

"I knew you would bring the ship through to safety," she answered.

Something seemed to pass between them: an understanding; a rapport. I had never really understood Honey. It came of her connection with a witch and the strange way she had come into our household.

Edward was dead, it seemed, and she had mourned

him, but for not as long as might have been expected. He had been a good husband to her and she had grieved, but she was not prostrate with her grief as I had thought she might be. Her main preoccupation was with the baby and the Captain's solicitude had brought her great relief.

"As soon as the galley fires can be set burning there will be hot food," he said.

Honey murmured: "Thank you." And he left us.

"A maddening man," I said when he had left us. "He knows where he is taking us and why, and he will not tell. I could shake him."

"He has been good to us," said Honey, "and it is another's secret he keeps."

"He has certainly found favor with you," I said.

She did not answer.

The storm had died down; the ship, though battered and not quite her former dignified self, had come through. She was still afloat and capable of voyaging. It was a matter for rejoicing.

The Captain told us that there was to be a thanksgiving service on the deck and as every soul on board had been saved all were commanded to attend.

We should take our stand on deck with the others. John Gregory and Richard Rackell should stand on either side of us. We should come up on deck after the ship's company were assembled and leave as soon as the service was over.

There was a keen wind following the ship and it was an impressive moment when we mounted the companionway, John Gregory before us and Richard Rackell taking up the rear. The men were lined up on deck: men of all ages and sizes. A wooden box served as a pulpit and on it stood the Captain. He looked a fine man with his rather pleasant face, yet stern. He was a mild man, but one had the impression that if the occasion demanded he could be fierce and forbidding.

It was a moment I would remember for many years— the chill wind billowing the sails, blowing our hair about our faces, ruffling our garments and seeming good after the stuffiness of the cabin; the sky a light blue with the clouds visibly drifting across; everywhere the smell of damp wood and sweating bodies and musty garments, to make one rejoice even more in that clean fresh air.

Life was good; one knew that when one had come near to losing it—yes, even to captives on a pirate ship who were being carried to some unknown destination it was good to be alive.

I knew in that moment that my zest for living would never fail me. Whatever was in store for me I should endure and remember that I intended to go on living to the full every minute of my life until I died.

The Captain read from the Bible; I did not now know what but it was beautiful; and the silence broken only by the wind in the sails and the sound of his voice.

I suppose everyone there on deck was giving his heart-felt thanks for life.

Then I was aware of the glances which were coming our way and that in the main these were directed at me, strange, almost furtive looks, looks which implied a certain hatred . . . yes, and fear! What did this mean? I glanced at Honey, but she was oblivious of whatever it was and a tremor of apprehension ran through me. I was deeply aware of how vulnerable we were.

The Captain was no longer speaking; John Gregory touched my arm lightly.

It was time for us to go below.

We had shipped anchor a mile or so from land and the Captain had come to talk to us.

"I regret," he said, "that I cannot allow you to go ashore. It is important that while we are in port I make sure that you are well guarded. I trust you will understand."

Honey assured him that she did.

I demanded: "Could we not at least go on deck for fresh air?"

He said that he would see what could be arranged, but we should have to give our word not to attempt any folly. "Folly being to attempt to return to our own home?" I asked, for I could never resist implying how these people had wronged us.

"That would not only be folly but an impossibility," he replied gently. "You are in a land alien to you. How would you without means find your way back to England? You would be beset by dangers on all sides, so it is for your own good that I guard you."

"And for him whose orders you obey?"

He nodded.

We were allowed to go on deck with John Gregory and Richard Rackell to guard us. We were about two miles from the coast. I saw trees and grass and a cluster of houses. It was good to look on them after seeing nothing but the ocean.

To her great delight Jennet was allowed to go ashore. We watched her climb down the ladder into the bobbing boat; her sailor caught her in his arms and she was laughing. I saw him pinch her buttocks affectionately and she laughed up at him. She seemed to have no regrets for her abduction. She was the most adaptable creature I had ever known.

I said to Honey: "Give her a man and she will be content."

"She seems fond of her Spaniard," said Honey tolerantly.

How I should have liked to step ashore. I wondered whether Jake Pennlyon had ever come here. It was possible, for I guessed it was part of Spain and that we were en route for the Barbary coast. He had talked of these waters. I looked to the far horizon where the sea and the land appeared to meet and I said to myself: One day a ship will appear. The *Rampant Lion*. He will come, I know it.

We leaned over the rail and watched the coast. We were not near enough to see people, but we could see the boats bobbing to and fro.

Jennet came back with tales of what she had seen.

"People jabbering away in Spanish!" she said. "I couldn't catch what they did say. But my Alfonso he could."

"I should hope so since he is a Spaniard," I retorted.

She had been taken into a wine shop and had drunk wine accompanied by little savory cakes which had been "rare tasty." She was full of the sights her Alfonso had shown her.

The next day we were taken into harbor and there we stayed while the repairs were attended to. The rigging had to be overhauled; seams had to be freshly calked; the shipwrights were busy.

All day long there was activity on board. Not only were the repairs carried out but fresh stores loaded. Some members of the crew deserted; the storm had no doubt cured them of their desire to go again to sea; there had to be replacements.

It was a busy time for them, an irksome one for us, and out of sheer boredom I began to consider plans for escape. They were absurd, I knew, because we were foreign women in a foreign land, without money and unable to speak the language—though we had by now picked up a few words —and one of us pregnant! But I found some comfort in planning. My mother had always said that I was impulsive. "Count ten before speaking, Cat darling," she used to say. "And think well before acting."

But it was a comfort to plan. I said: "We could dress ourselves as sailors. We could slip ashore and in no time we would be out of that little town."

"Without clothes, without money, without knowing where we are?" asked practical Honey.

"We would soon find out."

"It would be a worse fate than that which awaits us now. We have been lucky. The Captain is a good man."

"He will protect you, Honey, because you have charmed him and he implies that he is protecting me for some purpose."

"I do wonder what is awaiting us."

"Could you not lure it from him?"

"He will never give a hint."

I was frustrated. Constantly I looked for that ship on the horizon, but it never came.

Once I talked to Richard Rackell, for I was on deck alone with him.

"Why did you lie to us?" I asked. "Why did you pretend to be what you were not?"

"I did what I must," he answered.

"You were ordered to come?"

He nodded.

"For what purpose?"

"I cannot tell you."

"You deceived us, you lied to us, you accepted our

bounty and because of you a good man now lies cold in his grave."

Richard Rackell crossed himself and murmured: "May God rest his soul."

"And you are his murderer."

"I would never have laid hands on him."

"But because you came and worked with our enemies he is now a dead man."

Richard Rackell's lips moved; he was murmuring a prayer.

"You murder and ravish, you pirates and rascals and rogues!" I cried. "Yet you are all very religious men, I observe." He did not speak and I went on: "And your affianced bride—what of her? You seduced her; you promised to marry her knowing full well that you never would. Am I right?"

He bowed his head.

"You have need of your prayers," I said with sarcasm. "I hope you are repaid a thousandfold for what you have done to us."

"Mistress," he said, "I ask forgiveness."

"There is no harm in asking."

He sighed and looked out to sea.

I said after a while: "Tell me who sent you to us with your lies of coming from the North."

"That I am forbidden to do."

"But you were sent, as that rogue Gregory was sent."

"We were sent."

"And the purpose was to take us away."

He was silent.

"Of course it was. But why . . . *us!* If you wanted women could you not have raided any coastal town and taken them? Why did you have to come, you and Gregory, and this great galleon to take us away?"

Still he did not answer.

"You came in the galleon, did you not? I awoke in the night and saw it. It was when the *Rampant Lion* lay in the harbor. I saw a boat rowing ashore. You were in that boat. And first you went to Lyon Court and they would have none of you. So you came to us. That's so, is it not?"

" 'Tis so, Mistress."

"And the galleon came again and this time it brought John Gregory. He came with his lies and was given shelter. Then the galleon came for the third time and this time we sailed away with it. You are not going to lie to me, to tell me this is not so?"

"No, Mistress," he said humbly.

"But why, why?" I demanded.

He would give no answer; and I had come no nearer to finding the solution than I had ever been.

The Captain's chaplain came to stand beside me as I leaned over the rail. He spoke a little English so that we were able to converse. He told me that the Captain would like me to take instruction in the Catholic Faith.

"I shall not do so," I said vehemently. "Why should I? I have been forced from my home, but at least I shall insist on freedom of thought."

"It would be for your own good and protection," he told me.

"So you think! I am weary of Intolerance. My mother believed in tolerance. She taught me to believe the same. I do not wish you to change your religion. Why should you wish me to change mine?"

"It would be well for you to come to the True Faith."

I think I spoke more loudly and fiercely than I would normally have done. I was suddenly so angry that these people should attempt to force their faith on me. I did not notice immediately that one or two sailors had come nearer and were listening intently.

"I shall not be coerced," I cried. "I shall think as I wish. I am not going to be told I must worship God in this or that way."

The priest took the cross which hung about his neck on a chain and gazed at it.

"One is no less Christian," I cried, "because one does not believe in exactly the way you have decided all men should."

He stepped toward me and with an impatient gesture I thrust him aside. As I did so, the cross fell from his hand.

One of the watching sailors cried out something which I did not understand. I was not particularly interested because I did not realize then how significant this could be.

We had sailed into smooth warmer seas.

Now it was a pleasure to be on deck. The Captain was anxious, for there was not enough wind to sail this mighty ship.

For two days the weather remained fair and warm with a slight breeze; then even that dropped. There was no breath of air; the sea was so calm it looked as if it had been painted—no ripple, no stirring of wind; the sea cooed quietly about us; we could walk about the vessel as though we were on dry land.

The following day when we awoke the ship was still; there was no vestige of wind; her sails were useless; she was a floating castle on still and silent sea. Before that day was out we knew that we were becalmed.

The sun was warm; we had traveled many miles south. How pleasant it seemed at first to walk decks and companionways which were as steady as they would have been in dock.

We were on the deck every day—in the company of Gregory and Rackell; Jennet worked often with the sailors; I had seen her barefooted, swabbing the decks, singing as she did so; I had seen her in the galleys, ladling soup into the dishes.

I had seen too men's eyes following her; and Jennet was aware of it too; she blushed constantly, as much as ever, but her big Spaniard was never far off with his knife ready. He was a king among the sailors; he had got a woman, which was what none of the others had. I knew they thought he should have shared her, but I was glad for Jennet's sake that he would have none of that. Still, I thought how unsafe it was for her to go among them. They eyed us sometimes—beautiful Honey, now quite large with child; and myself, the flashing-eyed virgin, who they would know would fight with tooth and claw if attacked. It was not Honey's pregnancy or my fiery spirit which saved us; it was the Captain's orders. Lashes for those who attempted to molest us and for any who succeeded in doing so, death. So John Gregory had told us.

We ate in the Captain's cabin and he talked of his anxieties.

The storm had been violent and threatened to shatter our vessel and throw us all into the merciless sea; but in such an emergency it was necessary to work all the time. There was no giving up, no time to spare. Every man was fighting for the life of the ship and that meant his own.

But to be becalmed was different. There was nothing to be done but look out on that sea which was like one painted on a canvas, so still was it. There was little to be done but watch a clear bright sky for the sign of a cloud and a little wind. The sails hung uselessly. The sun was growing warm; if the calm continued there would not be enough food to carry us to our next port of call, where we could replenish stores. And worst of all, idle men were dangerous men.

The Captain prayed for a wind.

"A wind," I said to Honey, "will carry us to that mysterious destination. Should we pray for a wind? Or are we better off on this ship?"

Honey said: "We must pray for a wind, for the men grow restive and restive men are dangerous."

And she too prayed for a wind.

We were on deck for the fresh air. Another day and night had passed and still no sign of a wind. The tension was growing; it was becoming increasingly obvious. Groups of idle men stood about on the decks, murmuring together.

Food would have to be rationed; water was to be used with greater care than ever. And there was little that could be done but wait for a breeze. The great galleon was powerless; she was nothing but a hulk full of anxious, discontented men.

I had noticed one of the men eyeing me speculatively. I knew the meaning of that look. I had seen it in Jake Pennlyon's eyes. Perhaps John Gregory noticed it too, for he hurried us down below.

Later that day I saw the man again; he was close to the rail where I was accustomed to stand. I heard his muttering and believe his words were directed toward me.

I was afraid. But I assured myself that the Captain's

orders must be obeyed and that I was safe from all men
on this ship. What awaited me at the end of the journey
I could not know, but I was protected here because I was
being preserved for some mysterious mission.

I had reckoned without the boredom of a becalmed
ship—and the anxieties which mingled with the boredom.
Little to do all day but watch for a wind and the possibility of death from the elements which, fierce or quiet,
could be lethal.

When men are in such a situation they take risks.

I was aware of him; there were rings in his ears, and
his black eyes flashed in his dark brown face. He sidled
closer. John Gregory moved toward me, but the man
came too. I turned to John and said: "Should we go
below?" As I moved forward the dark man put out his
foot; I tripped; he caught me and for a moment I was
held close against him. I saw the dark, lustful eyes close
. . . the flash of yellow teeth.

I screamed, but he did not release his hold; he started
to drag me away.

But John Gregory was there. They were both holding
me, pulling me this way and that.

The Captain appeared I did not know from where, unless
he was always watching when we were on deck. He shouted
an order to a group of men standing by. For a few terrifying moments everything seemed to be as still as the
ocean. No one moved. The thought flashed into my mind:
This is mutiny. The Captain spoke again. His voice rang
out clear and firm with an authority to which those men
were accustomed to respond.

Two men came forward; they seized the dark man and
held him firmly. He was marched away.

"You should go below," said the Captain to me.

He was flogged and the ship's company were assembled
to see it done.

We of course did not witness this. We remained below
in the Captain's cabin, but we knew what was happening.
I could picture it as though I were there—that man tied
to the whipping post; his back bare, the terrible whip
descending, leaving his flesh torn, raw and bleeding. I

could imagine his agony and I wanted to run up and stop it.

The Captain came down to the cabin later.

"He has had his punishment," he said. "It will be a lesson."

I shivered, and he went on: "He will survive. Thirty lashes. Fifty would have killed him."

"Was so much necessary to teach a lesson?" I asked.

"Lashes are the only lessons which they understand."

"And all because he touched me!"

"I have my duty," he said.

"And that is to protect me."

He nodded.

"He will never forget me, that man," I said, "and he will never forgive me."

"He will, let us hope, never forget the need to obey orders."

"It is disturbing that such a thing has happened because of me."

"Let us renew our prayers for a breeze," said the Captain.

Another day passed, a day of breathless calm.

I was afraid to go on deck after what had happened; I knew I should not meet this man because he would be too sick of his wound to stand about and stare at me.

"The men said he nearly died," reported Jennet. "The whip is a terrible thing. 'Twill mark his back forever."

"Poor man, I'm sorry for him."

"He'd been boasting he'd take you. He said he didn't care what you were. He said he didn't care if you'd come from the Devil, he was going to have you."

She was wearing a little image of the Virgin around her neck. Her lover had given it to her as a talisman to keep her from harm.

"What's that?" I had asked.

" 'Tis the Virgin," she had told her. "She protects women."

Now she was uneasy and wanted to give it to me.

"Mistress," she pleaded, "take my Virgin. Wear it around your neck."

"You need it, Jennet. You go among the sailors."

She shook her head fearfully.

"What's the matter, Jennet?" I asked.

" 'Tis what they're saying, Mistress. 'Tis what they're saying about you."

"What are they saying about me?"

"When they were lashing him he called out. He said it was the Devil in you that had urged him on. He said you were a witch and a heretic. You'd cast down the priest's holy cross, he said, and you'd brought evil onto the ship. He said witches brew up storms and didn't we have such a storm as they'd rarely seen before! Then they all said a man had nearly died through you and now there's the calm. They frighten me, Mistress. So . . . take the Virgin. She'll protect you."

A cold fear took possession of me then. I recalled that moment of hesitation when the Captain had commanded them to seize my attacker. I knew that mutiny was in the air and for me there was a personal terror for many of these men believed me to be a witch.

What did they do to witches? I asked myself.

And the calm continued.

I was out on deck gazing toward that far horizon; the sky was a delicate blue, the sea like a sheet of silk, not a ripple; silence everywhere.

On the deck a group of men watched us furtively. John Gregory was nervous. Richard Rackell was pale.

"It is very hot up here," said Gregory. "I think we should go down."

"Not hastily," I said. "But presently."

Somehow I knew that a hurried retreat would have pressed those men into action.

I had been afraid many times since I had stepped onto this ship, but I think I was then living through some of the most terrifying moments.

I gazed across that great arc of the sky; I stared out to the horizon; I asked John Gregory if there was any hope of a change in the weather—and all the time I was conscious of those men watching me.

At length I said: "I've had enough. Let us go below."

Slowly I walked to the companionway. Every second I expected a rustle from behind, a scurry of feet, strong arms about me. I knew that they were ready and waiting for some sort of signal. Perhaps I would hear the words: "Heretic! Witch!" What did they do in Spain to heretics? They tied them to a stake; they placed wood at their feet; then they lighted the fagots. The bodies of heretics were consumed by the flames, a foretaste on earth of that fate which many believed would pursue them through eternity.

I was in revolt, as I always had been since my mother had taught me, against such bigotry. I could never believe that leading the good life depended on a single mode of belief. But I was now afraid.

The Captain came to his cabin, to which we had been taken.

He said: "I think it would be wise if you remained here until we sail. It is not good for the men in the mood they are in to see you."

I nodded. I was in agreement with him now.

The door was locked. John Gregory remained on guard with Richard Rackell and we stayed in the cabin.

Night came. Every sound set my heart beating wildly. I could picture them all storming the cabin, battering down the door and seizing me. I could almost hear their shouts of "Witch" and "Heretic."

They wanted to destroy me because I was on board and kept apart from them. Women on board—three of them, and only one serving the purpose for which these men would consider they were meant. Jennet—the property of Big Alfonso. Honey and myself kept under strict guard by the Captain's orders. And everywhere that calm which was more devastating than the storm.

I slept but fitfully.

I whispered to Honey: "The Captain cannot guard us forever."

"He will guard us for as long as he must," she answered. She had a blind faith in him.

I wondered afresh about Honey, who it seemed was a widow. But her plight and the baby she carried seemed to have kept the loss of Edward from her mind. I pondered too on this deep feeling of which I was conscious between herself and this Captain. It was there, some understanding. I wondered whether it was love.

Then I thought of Jake Pennlyon and my heart leaped,

for I thought constantly: He will come for me. He will look for me and find me.

No ship could sail on this calm sea; was that the reason why this fear was with me? He could not come to me because the *Rampant Lion* would lie as still and helpless as the galleon.

Fear was back. We were trapped in a miniature floating castle; there was acute danger all about us and our protectors would be helpless against a band of desperate men.

I must face the fact that it was only a matter of waiting.

Morning came—the still and beautiful morning. The sun rose touching the sea with scarlet and began its climb into the sea.

Another day—of breathless calm and growing tension.

We stayed in the cabin. Every time there were footsteps outside the door we started.

The Captain had set the men tasks to perform. They could not swab the decks because there was a shortage of water, but they could carry trays of burning pitch through the mess decks to fumigate them. The odor which came from them was fetid and nauseating. He set them trying to catch fish—a useful occupation, for they could cook what they caught and share it with their comrades.

But even so the tension grew. While they fished they talked of the heretic witch who had set a spell on their ship and was bringing disaster to them all.

Jennet brought news to us.

"The men be getting together this afternoon," she said. " 'Tis a plan of action. They be working out what they'm going to do."

Her eyes were wide and frightened. She was fond of me.

"Wear the Virgin, Mistress," she said. "It'll save 'ee."

And I put it on, as I said, to please her, but in truth I was ready to clutch anything that could help me and it might do me some good.

They were meeting that afternoon. I was in the cabin and Honey was with me. I did not tell her what Jennet had told me. It would be bad for the baby if she were too frightened.

I imagined what would happen: the sound of feet on the companionway, the hammer of fists on the door.

I made an excuse to leave the cabin. Jennet was at the door, her eyes round with horror.

"What's happening, Jennet?" I asked.

"They're up there on the deck," she said. "None will stop them, Mistress, not even the Captain. They say it's black magic. . . ."

"They're coming for me . . . !"

"Oh, Mistress, it be terrible."

I started up the conpanionway. She was pulling at my arm. "Don't go. If they do see you they'd go mad. You've got the Virgin, Mistress. Pray to the Virgin. She protects women."

I could hear the shouts of the men.

Jennet whispered: "They'm saying you're a witch. They blame you for all that's gone wrong. Oh, Mistress, they be building up the fagots on the deck . . . there. They've got the stake to tie you to. It's what they do to witches."

"Oh, God, Jennet," I said. "This is the end . . . the terrible end."

"Nay, Mistress, it must not be. I know somewhere we could hide. Alfonso showed me. He puts me in it sometimes . . . when he won't be there to look after me. Come quick."

I followed her, not noticing where we went. In my imagination I could hear the crackle of flames, I could feel my scorched and burning flesh.

I was near to death—horrible death—and the realization was terrifying.

Jennet opened a hatch and we were in a dark hole. The smell was nauseating, but the dark brought comfort.

But for how long could we remain hidden?

Jennet was praying to the Virgin, the protectress of women; and never was a woman more in need of protection.

I prayed with her . . . prayed for a miracle.

I don't know how long we stayed in the dark hole. I only know that the miracle happened. After we had been there for what seemed a very long time, the realization came to us that something was happening. The ship was moving.

Jennet cried: "It's over. The calm's over."

She lifted the hatch and stepped out, but she would not let me follow her.

"You stay there where you'm safe. I'll come back."

In a short time she returned.

Her face was shining with joy.

"It's over," she cried. "There's a fine breeze. They're all excited. Nobody's thinking of you now. You're safe."

Yes, the miracle had happened.

What a glorious sight was a ship with its sails billowing out in the wind, seeming to dip with joy into the ocean as she forged ahead. The wonderful wind was carrying us onward. The sea had become alive again. The calm was over.

Tension eased. There was too much to be done to give the men opportunities to plan mutiny. Orders were shouted and cheerfully obeyed; there was extra food and drink for all to celebrate; there was a thanksgiving service which we did not attend.

A week after the calm we sighted land. We first saw a snow-topped mountain far off, a landmark in the ocean.

The Captain said: "You should prepare to go ashore now. This is the end of your journey."

We took our few belongings—they were not much, only the clothes we had made for ourselves—and we climbed down into the boat and were rowed ashore. We looked back at the galleon—majestic in the waters—and we knew that we had said good-bye to the old way of life and were embarking on the unknown.

At the Hacienda

On the shore a party of men with mules were awaiting us. We were clearly expected. I supposed our ship would have been sighted a day before it arrived. We had seen the conical snow-topped mountain jutting out from the ocean; very soon after they must have seen the galleon from the land.

The Captain, Richard Rackell and John Gregory were among the small party which accompanied us; and as I looked back at the galleon and thought of those days when we had lain becalmed and the terrible fear which had come to me then I could not suppress a feeling of relief and an immense curiosity and excitement. I believed that soon we would discover what our abduction was all about.

As usual I scanned the horizon for the sight of a sail, but there was nothing but an expanse of blue ocean.

The sun was warm, though it was only February. I looked at the others; Honey was within two months of her confinement; she had, in spite of everything, retained a certain serenity. Jennet had that bewildered look on her face; I supposed she was wondering whether her sailor would come ashore. He was not with the party but had remained on board ship. It was no doubt due to this that she felt this anxiety.

The Captain asked us to mount the mules. "We have some short distance to go," he said.

We obeyed and we set out from the shore.

The animals' progress was slow and it took us some two hours to cover what could not have been more than six or seven miles. The Captain called a halt at the top of an incline and from there we were able to look down on the town. On the edge of this he pointed out a large white building which appeared to be surrounded by parkland.

He said: "This is the residence of the Governor of this island, Don Felipe Gonzáles. The house is known as the Hacienda and it is there we are going."

"For what purpose?" I asked.

"You will discover," he answered.

Our mules carried on down the slope toward the town and the white house and at length we came to iron gates. These were opened by a man who bowed to us and we went through them into a drive on either side of which grew tall flowering shrubs, pink, white and red. Their heavy perfume hung in the air.

We came at length to the portico; three white steps led to a door, which was opened by a servant in yellow and black livery. We went into a hall which was dark after the brilliance of the sun outside.

We were taken to a small room and there we were left—the three of us—almost in the dark, for the tinted windows and heavy drapes shut out the sun.

We did not speak; our tension was too great. I had gathered this much: that I had been the object of the abducting. Jennet had become the mistress of one of the sailors and because he was a strong man and carried a knife she had had but one master; Honey would have been ravished but for the Agnus Dei at her neck and perhaps that aura of divinity or maybe her own witchcraft; but I had been guarded; the man who had dared touch me had suffered violent lashing because of it. So it was clear that the purpose of this mission concerned me.

The Captain returned. He spoke to Honey: "Have no fear. You will be looked after until such time as the child is born." His voice was tender; there was a sadness about him. They smiled at each other. I knew there was a bond of love between them, a love that would never be fulfilled but which had touched their lives briefly and had meant something to them.

"Jennet shall be your maid while you need her," he said. "Remain here." Then to me: "Come."

I followed him up a staircase. There was a strange brooding silence about this house. It was dark everywhere; it was full of shadows. I knew something strange and dramatic was about to happen to me.

I followed the Captain along a corridor. The tinted windows threw a faint yellowish color into the gloom and I had the impression that the owner of this house wanted to shut out the light because he could not bear it to show what went on within these walls.

I had a desire then to turn and run. Where could I run to? How could I leave Honey and Jennet behind? But it was because of me that we had been brought here.

The Captain had paused before a door. He rapped lightly on it, someone spoke from within and we entered.

At first I could see little in that darkened room and then I was aware of the man. This was my first glimpse of Don Felipe Gonzáles. I felt the cold shiver run through my body. Perhaps it was a premonition, perhaps it was that there was something so forbidding, almost awe-inspiring about the man. He was not tall, compared with Jake Pennlyon, for instance, nor was he small for a Spaniard. He was dressed in a black doublet which was trimmed with fine white lace, his breeches were of padded satin, at his side was a short sword in a velvet scabbard, and never had I been aware of dignity such as he possessed, never had I seen eyes so cold. He would terrify by a look, this Don Felipe Gonzáles. His skin was of olive color; his nose large aquiline, lips thin, a straight line, cruel, ruthless lips.

He said: "So this is the woman, Captain."

I knew enough Spanish to understand that.

The Captain answered in the affirmative.

He came forward and bowed to me, coldly, yet politely. I acknowledged his greeting.

"Welcome to Tenerife," he said in English.

Because I was afraid I must answer boldly. "Not well come," I said, "since I am brought here against my will."

"I rejoice in your safe arrival," he replied.

He clapped his hands and a woman came in. She was young--about my own age—considerably smaller, with dark skin and big dark eyes.

He nodded to her and she came toward me.

"María will attend you," he said. "Go with her. We shall meet later."

It was bewildering. The girl took me along the silent corridor. We came to a big room, dark as the others in spite of the big window. The heavy embroidered hangings shut out the light although they were not fully drawn. In the room was a large four-poster bed, about which hung embroidered curtains; the posts and canopy were finely carved; the coverlet of silk. The chairs were finely carved too, and there was a massive oak chest on one side of the room. On the wooden floor were two large mats of unusual designs. I had never seen such beautiful rugs.

I quickly discovered that María knew no English and that I could learn little from her. She drew me through a door which led from the bedroom and there was a toilet room such as I had never seen before. A sunken bath was in the floor and there were Venetian mirrors on the wall.

María pointed to the bath and to me; she pulled at my clothes and I could see that she was suggesting I should take a bath.

I was nothing loath. I felt I needed it; and I had a great desire to be cleansed of the all-pervading odors of the ship.

She disappeared and I unbound my hair and let it fall about me. She came back shortly with cans of water, with which she filled the bath. She pointed to me and I indicated that I wished her to leave me. She did. I locked the door, threw off my clothes and got into the sunken bath. It was a delicious sensation. I lay full length and let my hair fall into the water. Then I washed it and my body too and as I stepped up onto the tiled floor María was there holding out towels for me. I could not understand how she had come in, for I had locked the door; she saw my surprise and pointed to the curtains behind her. I realized there was another door behind them which led into the toilet room.

I dried my body and she brought scented oils, with which she massaged me. The scent was pungent, overpoweringly sweet like the flowers I had noticed in the drive.

She wrapped a toweled robe about me and spread my hair around me. She giggled and drew back and, throwing back the curtains, opened the door through which she had come.

The bedroom window opened into a balcony and she beckoned me. I went out; it was small and there was just room for two or three people. I looked over the wrought-iron balustrade onto a patio in which grew highly colored flowers. There was a seat on the balcony. María turned it so that my back was to the sun; I could see the purpose was to dry my hair.

She hunched her shoulders as though amused and disappeared. I sat still shaking out my damp hair, in spite of everything enjoying the luxury of being clean again. It gave me courage. I had ceased to speculate as to my fate, for I was aware that I would know very soon why I had been brought here. I wondered what was happening to Honey and Jennet and whether the Captain had returned to his ship.

The warm sun was pleasant; I felt my spirits rising a little because I could not associate violence with the dignified man whom I had seen so briefly and who I knew was the master of everything here.

María came out; she felt my hair; she brought a comb and combed it, holding the strands of hair up to the sun's warmth. I tried to ask what she knew, but it was impossible.

I was on the balcony for what must have been more than an hour. The sun was lower in the sky. It would be almost sunset. I calculated that it would be about six of the clock.

María beckoned me into the bedroom. There was a polished metal mirror and a chair before it. I sat down and she dressed my hair. She piled it high on my head and placed in it a comb very similar to the one I had bought from the peddler; and I felt it was symbolic in a way. That had been at the very beginning. Now we were at the climax.

She took a velvet robe from a cupboard. It was a deep mulberry shade and edged with miniver. There was something regal about it. She put it about me.

I said, "Whose is this, María?"

She giggled. She pointed to me.

"But whose before?" I asked. There was a faint perfume about it. The same as that of the oil with which I had been anointed.

She kept on pointing to me and I gave up the interrogation as hopeless.

There was a knock on the door. María scuttled to it; there was a hurried exchange of words. Then she came back and beckoned to me.

I followed her out of the bedroom along the dim corridor into a room. It was dark now; the sun had disappeared below the horizon and there was not the twilight we had at home.

María pushed me into the room and shut the door. I saw the table laid for a meal. There were flowers on it. Candles flickered in their sconces on the walls.

I advanced and I knew as I did so that I was being watched.

Don Felipe Gonzáles rose from a chair in the shadows and bowed to me.

I said: "Where is my sister?"

He replied: "We dine alone." He took my hand and with a graceful gesture led me to the table.

I sat in the chair at one end of the table; he took one at the other end.

"We shall converse in your barbaric tongue," he said, "for I am acquainted with it."

"That will be an advantage," I replied, "for I know only a few words of your savage one."

"You will not indulge in useless vituperation. It will serve you ill."

"I am a prisoner here. I know that. You can hold me here I have no doubt, but you cannot force me to silence or to speech."

"You will learn grace and courtliness here. You will

learn that pointless badinage will help you not at all."

I was irritated by his habit of saying, "You will do this and that." He made it sound like a command. I had the impression that he was stressing the fact that I was in his power and would be forced to obey him. It frightened me. There was something cold and implacable about him.

"We will eat now, and afterward we will talk. I will then explain what is expected of you."

He clapped his hands and servants appeared.

They carried hot dishes, which they placed on the table. We were served with some sort of fish.

It smelled good after salt meat and beans and biscuits in which there were very often weevils.

"We call this *calamares en su tinta*," he told me. "You will enjoy it."

I did, marveling that I could eat with such enjoyment in such a situation and strange company.

He talked of the food of the countryside. "You will enjoy it when you have grown accustomed to it. Taste is a matter of cultivation. Custom plays a large part in what we enjoy."

A kind of pork followed, served with tiny green vegetables which I had not seen before. *"Garbanzos con patas de cerdo,"* he told me. "You will repeat it."

I obeyed.

"Your accent shocks me," he said. "It is unharmonious."

"You could not expect one of my barbaric tongue to speak yours well," I retorted.

"You speak with wisdom," he said.

"Then I have at last won your approval."

"You will learn that words can be wasteful. You will eat and after that we will talk and you will learn the reason for your coming."

I said nothing and ate the food. There were fruits afterward—dates and little yellow fruit which I learned were called bananas. They were delicious.

"You will want to know where you are. There is no reason why you should not. You are on one of the chief of a group of islands once known as the Fortunate Isles."

"And were they?" I asked.

"You will not speak unless asked to do so," he said.

"These islands were in the far-off days called Canaria because when the Romans came here there were many dogs. They called them the Islands of Dogs. Now you will hear them spoken of as the Canaries and you will understand why. The dogs have disappeared. The islands were inhabited by a race known as the Guanches—a warlike people. There are some left. They are savages and stain their bodies with the dark red resin of the dragon trees. We have subdued them. The flag of Spain now flies over these islands. The French settled here first, but they were unable to keep order. We understood how important they were to our navigation. We did not fight for them; we bought them from the French and since then we have settled here and are subduing the Guanches."

"At least I know where I am."

"We are on the outskirts of the town of La Laguna, which we built when we settled here. You may be allowed to go into the town. It will depend on your behavior."

While he had been talking the food had been cleared away; but the silver jug containing a kind of mead which we had been drinking was left on the table.

The door shut; we were alone.

"You will hear now why you are here and why your path has crossed mine. You are necessary to a plan."

"How could that be?"

"You will not be impetuous. You must be silent. You would not wish to play your part without knowing why. Nor would I wish you to. I would not have you think that I resemble the barbarians of your island home. You will be quiet therefore and learn the reason for your abduction. You will be reasonable, pliable, do what is expected of you and therefore save yourself much trouble and degradation. I am no rough pirate. I am a man of breeding. I come from a noble family; I am distantly connected with the royal house of Spain. I am a man of taste and sensibility. What I must do is distasteful to me. I trust you will make it as tolerant as possible. I will continue."

I bowed my head submissively.

"I am the Governor of these islands, which I hold in the name of Spain. I have told you how they came into our possession. They belong to Spain, as the whole world should and shall one day. But there are marauding pirates on the seas; and there is one nation which is particularly offensive to us. They have bold seamen, adventurers without grace, crude men who raid and pillage our coastal towns and ravish our women."

"It is not only one nation who is guilty of these practices," I said. "I speak from personal experience."

"You will learn to curb your tongue while you are here. It is not seemly for women to use that organ so constantly. They should be gentle and gracious in the presence of their masters."

"I have yet to learn that you are my master."

"You have yet much to learn and the first lesson will be just that. You are here to obey me and that you will do. But silence, or you will rob me of my patience and you shall not know why but only that you must do as bidden."

That did silence me.

"Let us to the point," he said. "Five years ago I came here. I was betrothed to a lady of a noble family. Isabella was carefully nurtured and when I left Madrid she was a child of thirteen, too young for marriage, but we were betrothed. She would come out to me when she was fifteen. There were therefore two years to wait. Those two years passed and she was fifteen. She and I were married in Madrid by proxy. The King himself attended the ceremony. Then she set out on the journey from Spain. We prepared to receive her. Our true wedding would take place in the Cathedral of La Laguna within two days of her arrival. We were ready to receive her. The journey was long, for the ship had been becalmed for a week. You will know what that can mean. I waited eagerly and while I was waiting a message was brought to me that the Guanches were rising in another of our islands. It was imperative for me to leave La Laguna to sail across to the troubled island. I was there for three weeks; and in the meantime Isabella arrived. I was not there to greet her, but my household was in readiness. My young bride was received with honors; she was a bewildered child of fifteen, delicately nurtured, ignorant of life. I knew that it would be my task to teach her gradually and with care. But that did not happen. It was two nights after Isabella and her duenna arrived with their retinue that the pirates came. I was not there to defend her—my poor ravished

Isabella—humiliated, degraded, terrified."

I shivered. "Poor child," I murmured.

"Poor child indeed, and you have not realized all. The effect on her has been terrible."

There was silence—a great moth fluttered up suddenly from the curtains and flew to the candlelight; it flew madly around, singeing its wings until it fell. We both watched it.

"She had to be nursed back to health," he said. "But that was something beyond our powers."

"She died?" I asked.

He looked beyond me. "Perhaps it would have been better so."

We were silent for a second or so. I was thinking of the leering faces of men during the calm; and I saw the poor little girl of fifteen in their power.

"I am not a man to accept insult and injury," he said. "I seek revenge . . . nothing will satisfy me but revenge. I want an eye for an eye, a tooth for a tooth. No more. But that I want and that I will have. Tell me that you understand."

"I do."

"You would feel as I if so wronged?"

"I believe I should."

"There is anger in you. I sense that. It is good. It will make you pliant."

"Explain to me more."

"It is simple. I know the name of the ship which raided our coast on that night. I know the name of Isabella's ravisher. The ship was the *Rampant Lion*. The man who ruined her life Captain Jake Pennlyon."

I had caught my breath; I felt the color rushing into my face. I stared at him. I know my lips formed the name Jake Pennlyon although I did not speak.

"Now you begin to understand. My affianced bride was cruelly treated by this brigand. *His* affianced bride is in *my* hands. You are not a fool. You understand."

"I begin to."

"I shall tell you of Isabella, beautiful Isabella, an untutored child. Our brides are young . . . younger than yours perhaps. Fifteen years old. She knew nothing of life, what marriage would be. I should have led her gently to understanding . . . tenderly. You are made of stronger stuff. You are no child. You have knowledge of the world. It may be that you are not a virgin. But I shall take my revenge. He took my woman, so shall I take his. You are not, I trust, carrying his child already?"

"You are insulting."

"Nay. I respect your pride; but I know his kind. I would not wish to insult you. We are not brigands here. We live graciously and in a becoming manner I shall secure my revenge if you permit this. I know that you were not his mistress. My spies kept me informed."

"The false Rackell, the falser Gregory."

"Faithful to me," he said, "as they should be. I have vowed to take my revenge and shall do so whatever the cost. I shall rejoice if you are a virgin, for that will make my revenge complete."

"That is your purpose then?"

"Our wedding took place as we arranged. She was demented. She would awaken screaming from her sleep; her dreams terrified her. None but her duenna could comfort her. When I approached her she shrank from me. She associated me with him, you see. We discovered that she was with child . . . that brigand's child. You can not realize this tragedy until you have seen it. I vowed revenge. I have sworn before all the saints that I shall not rest until that revenge is complete."

"A strange vow to take in holy places," I said.

"I have sworn," he said, "in the name of God the Father and the Holy Virgin; I have sworn on my family's honor, and I know that I have divine help in this, for now you are delivered into my hands."

"And so the drama is to be reenacted. I take the part of Isabella and you Pennlyon." I recoiled from him—this strange cold man. "Do you think you could ever be like him? You could not be more unlike . . ."

"And you like her. It matters not. You are here by God's grace. We have brought you out of your island. You have come safely through the perils of the sea. And I swear by my ancestors and all the saints that you shall not leave this island until you carry my child in your womb. You shall take my child to him as he has left his to me."

"So you think that I will submit with docility?"

"I think that you have no choice but to submit."

"And allow myself to be treated as of no consequence as merely a means of giving you your revenge!"

"As Isabella was a means of satisfying that man's lust."

"You call yourself courteous, sensitive! I call you a rogue, a pirate, for although you are too fastidious to sail the seas and capture women for yourself you have your servants bring them to you. You are as bad as he is."

"I have vowed a vow. I intend it to be carried out. I am indeed different from the man who was to have been your husband. I offer you a choice. Gracious submission or force."

"I've no doubt he offered her that."

I stood up and moved to the door. He was beside me.

"This is distasteful to me," he said. "Do not imagine I lust for your body."

"Can I hope that I am as repulsive to you as you are to me?"

"You can believe that I have as little pleasure in what must be done as you have. But it shall be done and whether our encounter is to be conducted with seemly discretion or in a manner which will be humiliating and degrading to you is for you to decide."

I looked at him; he was slender and he did not give the impression of great strength, as Jake Pennlyon had. A woman would know at once that she had no chance against him. I could fight this man. And if I escaped him where should I go?

He followed my thoughts. "I have many servants here. I have but to summon them. Strong men who would truss you up as a chicken for the pot. But I do not wish for that. I want the matter to be conducted expeditiously and with as little discomfort to you and myself as possible. I do not blame you for what happened. But you are a necessary instrument of my revenge."

I thought I could like him better if he were goaded by that lust—anything would be better than this coldly scheming approach.

He said: "I will send for María; she shall conduct you to the bedchamber; she will prepare you. I will visit you there. I beg of you consider. You know you are here and powerless to resist. This *shall* come to pass. *How* depends on you."

He went to the door. María must have been waiting. She came in and knew what to do. I followed her back to the bedroom.

I suppose always before I had acted on impulse. I had forcefully expressed my agreement or refusal to do anything. I had rarely been undecided. "Count ten before speaking," my mother had said. I could go on counting day and night now and I should not know what to do. I was going to be this man's mistress. It was as inevitable as the rise and setting of the sun. I could see nothing that would prevent it. I was a prisoner on this island and there was nothing that would save me. If I attempted to resist him he would resort to force as he had said; and he was not the man to apply force himself, any more than he was to take part in the actual abduction. Others did that for him.

María slipped off my clothes; over my head was put a night shift of silk. It had that pungent odor about it.

María turned down the sheet. She indicated that I was to get into bed. I did so shivering. I was fighting with myself. I saw men tying my ankles together. I saw myself forcibly taken as Jake Pennlyon had taken Isabella. I could not endure that—just to reach the same end.

María was blowing out the candles. The room was in darkness. She went out and shut the door.

I leaped out of bed. I tried the door. It was locked. I went to the window. I drew back the curtains so that a little starlight penetrated. I opened the window and stepped out onto the balcony. I wondered if I could climb down into the patio. I could find Honey, run to her for shelter.

I pictured rough hands on me. He was right. I had to make a choice. Would I make a pretense of submission or would I wait to be degradingly forced?

It was too late. I could hear the key in the lock. I ran back to the bed and lay there, my heart beating quietly.

He came into the room. I saw him in the starlight standing by the bed. He was wrapped in a robe, which he took off. I closed my eyes tightly.

Then I was aware of his body, his hands on me, his face close to mine.

I tried to calm myself and I thought: Oh, God, I saved myself from Jake Pennlyon, from the lustful men on the galleon . . . for this.

A week had passed. I could not believe that this was happening to me. I saw little of him during the day, but each night he came to me. He never stayed. "The matter," as he called it, was as distasteful to him as to me. I had never thought it possible to have such a cold-blooded lover—but he was not a lover; this had nothing to do with love; it was revenge.

There was a certain passion—the passion of revenge—and for me the passion of hatred. I hated him for this humiliating use of me. He had robbed me of my dignity as a human being. I was not a woman to be loved or to be hated; I was a means to give him the revenge he needed. My hatred grew when I considered that. He was trying to create a life; he would bring a child into the world to satisfy his revenge and make me the instrument of reproduction. Could anything be more humiliating than that?

Only a man of extreme arrogance could dream of using others for such a purpose. He was every bit as bad as Jake Pennlyon. I hated them both. How dared they treat women in such a way!

When this man came to me I thought of Jake Pennlyon and I could not shut out of my mind the thought of his coming to this house and finding Isabella and in my imagination I was Isabella and the man who was humiliating me was Jake Pennlyon.

I was treated with respect during the day. There were servants to wait on me. During that first week I was not allowed beyond the house. But I did see Honey. The very first day I was taken to her. I was very shocked on that day by what had happened on the previous night; and as the days passed I was shocked in another way to discover how quickly I had grown accustomed to his visits.

The first encounter had horrified me—after all, I had been a virgin and, although not ignorant of sexual relationships, had never experienced such. It was at this stage that I talked to Honey.

She had been well received and had been given a pleasant room with Jennet to act as a kind of maid to her. She was bewildered as to why we had been brought there until I told her what had happened to me.

She listened incredulously. "It is too fantastic. It can't be true."

"This Felipe is a vindictive man. He is cold and cruel. He would go to any lengths to gain his revenge. When I carry his child we shall be taken back to England . . . and not till then."

"So it was all planned."

"What sort of mind would make such a plan? You can guess the sort of man he is. An eye for an eye. He has to pay back in exactly the same manner. It is Jake Pennlyon who has ruined my life, Honey. I knew it from the moment I saw him."

"His young wife taken like that! It's horrible, Catharine."

"What became of her I don't know. All I know is that he must have been heartbroken when he came back and found her . . . a child of fifteen, think of that, Honey; and Jake Pennlyon."

Then I began to laugh hysterically. "I have been raped. As surely as anyone I have been violated, and in this most courteous manner." I covered my face with my hands.

Honey shook me. "Don't, Catharine," she said. "Don't laugh like that. It's happened. Let us think on from there. This man. . . ."

"He will visit me each night. He has said so. Oh Honey, when I think of it. . . ."

"Don't think of it. It is happening and nothing can change it. We are prisoners here and we know now for what purpose. At least he has not ill-treated you."

"He has only misused my body," I said fiercely.

"Catharine, we have come through violent adventures. This has happened. Edward is dead. My baby will soon be born. We are far from home. This man has taken you against your will, but not roughly as he might well have done."

"As Jake Pennlyon must have taken Isabella. But perhaps she had a chance of passivity or the consequences. I chose passivity. I wish I'd fought him now."

Honey said: "Be calm. Let us wait and see what happens. We don't know from one moment to another. This man has had his will of you. It has happened to girls before. Let us try to bear what is in store for us."

All that day I was with Honey and I could not get out of my mind what had happened to me. I thought of it all day—myself and this cold strange man—Isabella and Jake Pennlyon. And the evening came and María came for me and I bathed and was anointed with the perfumed oil—he was such a fastidious gentleman—and again that night he came to me.

Everyone in the household knew I was the Governor's mistress. He did not wish to see me during the days, but at night he visited me. He did not stay. His visits were brief—only long enough to achieve the purpose.

I was treated with respect. So was Honey. The hushed household was far more comfortable than the galleon and Honey was getting to the stage when she needed comfort. Jennet slipped into the new life with ease; she mourned Alfonso for a day or so, but I knew it would not be long before she took up with someone. There were menservants and I had seen the looks that came her way. Such looks would always come Jennet's way.

I was too deeply concerned with myself to think much of them during that first week. Often I could not believe that it was truly happening. I must wake up and find it all a dream—from the night the galleon had been in the bay and the men had called.

Then what astonished me was that I was beginning to accept everything. The quiet daily life; the house; the beautiful gardens with flowers such as we did not grow in England; the warmth of the sun; the fruits growing in the enclosed gardens. We were free to walk about, but there were guards at the gate who prevented us leaving the house and the gardens. There was a sewing room in which were frames and canvases to be embroidered. Honey was allowed to make clothes, but I was not. I was to draw what I wanted from the cupboards in the bedroom. Clothes were put there for me to choose from. I was allowed freedom in that. They were beautiful clothes, feminine clothes, and most of them were scented with the perfume of the oil which María rubbed into me at the end of each day.

Where did these clothes come from? I demanded to know. But María only shook her head.

I saw him now and then. He would ride out on a fine white horse. He looked magnificent mounted. He would often be away the whole day, but he always came back at night. He always came into my bedroom at the appointed time and rarely did he speak to me.

My moods varied—sometimes I would try to convey to him my contempt for a man who could behave so, sometimes I wanted him to know how I hated him. I wanted to shout: "Get me with child quickly that I may be rid of you." At others: "I will be barren to spite you. What then, my revengeful lord?"

But I never spoke either and so that first strange week passed.

I had ceased to look for the ship on the horizon. I had accepted my fate. I had fought for myself and lost. I had been taken, ill-used; and I began to wonder how I could take revenge on men such as Don Felipe and Jake Pennlyon, who believed that women were there for their pleasure whether it be to satisfy lust or revenge, it mattered not.

I hated Don Felipe Gonzáles as I had hated Jake Pennlyon.

We had made a kind of pattern of our days, Honey and I. It was March of the year 1560, and her baby was due in a few weeks' time. I suppose impending childbirth makes everything else seem insignificant. Honey's thoughts were all for the child. She was constantly making clothes from the materials she found in the sewing room. I was not much use with my needle, but I improved a little during those first days merely because I had to do something. I used to wonder that in a house such as this one there should be a sewing room; Honey took it for granted and was grateful for it. I supposed that these rooms had been prepared for the bride Isabella. Had she ever used them?

I would sit making idle speculations, but Honey scarcely listened; she was absorbed by her child.

It was a week after we had arrived at the Hacienda

that we ventured into the Casa Azul. This was a small house standing in the grounds surrounded by a high wall. We had seen it from a distance and wondered what it was and on this particular morning I made up my mind to find out.

I insisted on Honey's accompanying me and when she saw that I was leading her to the Casa Azul she wanted to turn back.

"Why?" I demanded.

"There is something repellent about it."

"You are fanciful."

"I don't want to do anything that would harm the child."

"Why, Honey, what's come over you? What more can happen? Any child who could survive the last months will manage the next few weeks."

She came with me to the wrought-iron gates; we looked through them to a courtyard which had been made with stones of varying shades of blue which had no doubt given the house its name. There were flowering shrubs of all kinds—brilliant colors among the green foliage.

"It's beautiful," I said.

"It's gloomy," insisted Honey.

I pushed open the wrought-iron gate and beckoned Honey. Rather reluctantly she followed me.

There was an air of silent mystery in the courtyard. Windows looked down at us, all with their balconies shut in by wrought iron. They were picturesque and one imagined girls wearing red petticoats and black lace mantillas seated there. Against the wall was a wooden seat with a trellis back. I tiptoed into the courtyard and sat down.

Honey followed me reluctantly. "Has it occurred to you that we might be trespassing?"

I said: "This is part of *his* estate. I will see all I can of it."

Honey looked distressed as she did when I talked of him, and I did not wish to talk of him either. By day I wanted to forget those furtive visits.

As we sat there I was aware of a movement at one of the windows and a child stepped onto the balcony. She was like a doll, I thought; she wore black velvet with a white lace frill at her neck and wrists; her long dark hair hung about her shoulders. I guessed her to be about eleven or twelve years old.

She called out something in Spanish which I gathered to be "Who are you?"

I answered in English. "We are at the Hacienda."

She put her fingers to her lips as though warning me to silence; she said something else and disappeared.

"What a beautiful little girl!" said Honey. "I wonder who she is."

The girl had come into the courtyard. She was holding a doll in a red satin petticoat and a black mantilla. It was rather like herself.

She held the doll out to us and made a bow; I curtsied and she laughed aloud. There was something arresting about her besides her beauty, for there was a strangeness about her enormous dark eyes.

She held out her hand and took mine. We all sat down together on the seat. Then she noticed that Honey was pregnant, or so it seemed; her face puckered suddenly and she began to cry out: "No. No." She hid her face in her hands on which several rings sparkled; I noticed gold bracelets on her wrists. Then she turned her back on Honey as though she were determined to forget she was there and when she looked at me she was smiling happily.

She muttered something in which I caught the words *bella* and *muñeca* and as I thought she was talking about her doll I replied in stumbling Spanish that the doll was a very beautiful one. She started to rock it as one would a child and I thought then that she looked too old for this kind of play.

Then at the door from which she had emerged a figure appeared.

"Isabella!" said a voice shrill and commanding.

Although I had begun to guess, the shock was none the less great. This was his wife then. This was the girl who had suffered at the hands of Jake Pennlyon.

Isabella rose obediently and went to the woman. She put her arms about her, the doll held by one arm dangling down as she did so. A flood of words came from the woman, scolding and tender, I judged from the tones. Over the girl's head the woman studied us. Her eyes were sharp, piercing under straggling black brows in which the occasional white hair was visible.

She took the girl's hand and drew her toward the door, but Isabella suddenly became petulant, crying, "No. No," and turned to stare at us. She extricated herself from the woman's arms and came over to stand before us. I was aware then of a scent which was familiar to me; it was the same as that which was in the toilet room and of which the clothes I wore smelled faintly. It was in the bedroom where I suffered my nightly humiliations. I wondered what it was.

The girl spoke to us, but as it was in Spanish I could not understand; then the woman came and took her by the hand and led her firmly away.

She turned to us at the door and spat out a word which I assumed meant "Go away."

The door shut and we were alone in the courtyard.

"What a strange scene," I said.

"We deserved all we got. We had no right to be here. I wonder who the girl was."

"She must be *his* Isabella," I said.

"You mean . . . his wife? But she was a child."

The door into the courtyard had opened and Richard Rackell stood there.

"Come away," he said quickly. "You should not have gone there."

"Is it forbidden?" I asked coldly. I could never forget the part he had played in betraying us.

"There have been no express orders," he said holding open the door. He went on: "Please."

As we walked away he went on: "It was a terrible tragedy."

"Whatever happened," I said fiercely, "does not excuse what has been done to us, nor those who helped to do it."

"You have seen the Lady Isabella," he said. "She is as a child. She became so after the *Rampant Lion* came here. It affected her mind. She lives like a child with her duenna."

I said: "She is beautiful."

"You see a beautiful shell which holds nothing. Her mind is incapable of retaining anything; she has reverted to her childhood. Her interest is in dolls. It is a great tragedy. You understand."

I wanted to be alone. I could not get out of my mind the memory of that beautiful face which was devoid of the light of understanding.

The perfume too. I began to understand more. He tried to imagine that I was Isabella. I had to wear her clothes; use her perfume; he wanted to delude himself that the woman to whom he came each night was Isabella.

My attitude toward him had changed. I was sorry for him. I pictured his returning from his expedition expecting to find his beautiful bride waiting for him; the marriage ceremony would have been fixed; he and his lovely highborn Isabella were to be husband and wife. Isabella may have been a child of fifteen, but they married young in Spain; and Felipe Gonzáles was a gentleman; with great courteousness he would have wooed his wife and initiated her into the bedchamber rituals in such a manner as would have been acceptable to her. Instead of which Jake Pennlyon had come with his crude buccaneering ways and he had taken this delicately nurtured creature and crushed her, for crushed she was, poor little bud who had been cruelly deflowered before the blossoms came. And her mind had become unhinged.

I hate you, Jake Pennlyon, I thought; and my feelings against that man were intense while I could only feel pity for Felipe Gonzáles.

Jake Pennlyon! How I wished I had never seen him. He had brought me nothing but disaster. Here I was a prisoner, each night submitted to an intolerable humiliation—because of Jake Pennlyon. My pride was ignored; my body was used to satisfy revenge. I was a substitute for a beautiful young girl whose mind had been destroyed by Jake Pennlyon and my seducer had to imagine that I was this girl in order to make love—if one could use such a word in this connection—to me.

In addition to my humbled pride I was getting anxious about Honey. Her time was near. In the first year of her marriage she had had a miscarriage and I remembered my mother's saying that the next time she must take the greatest care. In a few weeks now her child would be born; and what would happen if it came before its time? Who would care for her?

I decided to see Felipe Gonzáles. I had seen very little of him really. I wondered whether he avoided me by day. Ours must have been one of the strangest relationships which ever existed.

I knew that at certain times of the day he was often in the room which was called his *escritorio* and I decided that I would see him there. When I considered my feelings I realized that they had changed since I had seen Isabella. I was piqued because of what was implied in the fact that I had to wear Isabella's clothes and use her scent; at the same time I felt a certain sympathy for him. I could imagine so much of what must have taken place: his arranged marriage which would have been ideal; his return to find his beautiful wife reduced to a shell. I imagined the ceremony of marriage which had followed and Isabella's screaming terror when he approached her; and then the knowledge that she was to bear a child— Jake Pennlyon's child. It was a tragedy and I understood how he must have called forth the wrath of heaven on the man who was responsible. I even understood his vow of vengeance.

I was also angry that I, so desired by Jake Pennlyon and others, should have to be tricked out as someone else before this man could be sufficiently aroused to carry out his purpose. It was a vain and stupid emotion, I suppose, but I felt it.

I had to see him and it was a fact that I was anxious about Honey.

He was seated at a table with papers before him. He rose as I entered.

"I gave orders that no one was to disturb me," he said.

"I have to see you," I replied. "There is something of importance that I must say to you."

He bowed again—always courteous. I was glad of the darkened room. I felt embarrassed; I could have sworn he did too. Here we were two strangers by day but who by night shared the ultimate intimacy.

I said: "I have come to see you on behalf of my sister."

He looked relieved. I sat down and he resumed his seat.

"As you know she is shortly to have a child. At any

moment her time may come. I should like to know what can be done for her."

"We have many servants," he said.

"She will need a midwife."

"There is a midwife in La Laguna."

"Then she must be brought here. It was no fault of my sister's that she was taken away."

He conceded this. "Nor of any of us," I went on angrily, hating his cold manner and thinking of his deluding himself that I was Isabella. "We have been dragged from our home to suit your evil purpose."

He held up his hand. "Enough," he said. "The midwife shall be sent for."

"I suppose you would like me to thank you, but I find it difficult to thank you for anything."

"It is not necessary. Suffice it that the midwife shall come."

He half rose in his chair—a gesture of dismissal. But I did not wish to be dismissed. I was angry to be used in this manner and seeing him there in his elegant clothes, his cold face expressionless, his manner so precise, and thinking again of those nightly encounters and the way in which I had been used, robbed of my dignity, my will, everything to serve his revengeful purpose, my anger was so intense that I wanted to hurt him.

I said: "I can only pray that ere long I shall be free of you."

"It is too soon yet," he said. "But I pray with you that we shall both soon be relieved of this irksome duty."

My anger was so great that I could have struck him.

I cried: "You appear to have no great difficulty in performing this irksome duty."

"It is good of you to concern yourself on my behalf. May I assure you that we have substances which if taken judiciously arouse desire in the most reluctant."

"And how long am I expected to submit to this distasteful duty of yours?"

"Rest assured that as soon as I am certain that my efforts have borne fruit I shall with the utmost pleasure and relief abandon my visits to you."

"I think I may well by this time be with child."

"We must be sure," he said.

"It is such an effort for you. I thought but to spare you."

"I have no wish to be spared from my revenge. The sooner I can effect it, the better."

"And when you are certain that your loathsome seed is growing within me I shall be taken back to my home?"

"You will be returned to your affianced husband in the same condition that Isabella was left to me."

"You are indeed a vengeful man," I said. "Others must be trampled underfoot for the sake of your revenge."

"It is often so."

"I despise you for your cruelty, your indifference to others, for your cold and calculating revengeful nature. But I suppose that is of no importance to you."

"None whatever," he replied; and this time he stood up and bowed.

So I left him. But I kept thinking about him all day and wondering how I could be revenged on him.

Later that day the midwife rode into the courtyard on a mule and was brought to Honey. To our delight the woman could speak a little English. She was middle-aged and had been with a family in Cádiz which had had two English servants. Her English was of course limited, but it was a great relief to find she could understand a little.

She told us that Honey's condition was good and that the child was due in the next week or so. She would ask that she might stay at the Hacienda so that they would not have to send for her in the night.

Jennet was present and suddenly the woman asked her when she was expecting.

Jennet blushed scarlet. I looked at her in astonishment. Now that I knew it seemed clear, but she had certainly successfully hidden it from us.

Jennet said she thought she was five months gone. The woman prodded her and said she would examine her. They went off together into the room leading from Honey's where Jennet slept.

"I'm not surprised," said Honey. "It had to happen sooner or later. It will be Alfonso's."

"I thought at first it might have been Rackell's. What a strange affair that was. I'll swear she has scarce been near him since we left."

"She couldn't bear him after Alfonso."

"I think Jennet would be able to bear any man rather than none."

"You are often a little hard on her, Catharine. It can hardly be called her fault if that Spanish sailor has got her with child."

"I don't think she was very reluctant."

"It would have been no good if she had been. She submitted, that was all."

"With a very good grace."

I began to laugh suddenly. "The three of us, Honey . . . think of it! All to have children. For I shall soon be in like case, I doubt not. And I am the only one who has had a child forced on me. How does one feel, I wonder, toward one's bastard when rape has been the cause of his arrival? Of course it was a very courteous rape. I never thought it would be like that." I started to laugh and suddenly the tears were on my cheeks. "I'm crying," I said, "for the first time. I'm sorry for myself. There is so much hate in me, Honey . . . for him and for Jake Pennlyon. Between them they have done this. But for them I should be at home in the Abbey with my mother."

I covered my face with my hands and Honey was soothing me.

"It was to have been so different. The way Carey and I planned our life together. It was going to be so wonderful."

"The things we plan rarely happen as we plan them, Catharine."

Her face was sad and wistful and I thought of Edward, her kind husband, lying in his own blood on the cobbles.

"What is going to become of us all?" I asked.

"Only the future can tell," she replied.

Jennet came back to us, her face flushed, a certain demureness in her expression.

Yes, she was with child.

"And knew it and kept it secret," I accused.

"I couldn't bring myself to tell you," said Jennet bashfully.

"So you concealed it. You've been letting out your petticoats."

"Well, the need were there, Mistress."

"And you are five months with child."

" 'Twas six in truth, Mistress," said Jennet.

I narrowed my eyes and looked at her.

"Why," I said, "it was before you left England."

"These midwives they can be mistaken, Mistress."

I said: "Jennet, will you go to my bedroom? I have just thought of something I wanted to say to you."

She went out and left us.

Honey was saying what a relief it was to know that the midwife was near. I let her go on talking. I was thinking of what I would say to Jennet.

Jennet looked at me shamefaced.

"The truth, Jennet," I said.

"Oh, Mistress, you know."

I was not sure, but I said: "Don't think you can deceive me, Jennet."

"I knew it'ud come out," she said distressed. "But he were such a man. Why, not even Alfonso. . . ."

I took her by the shoulders and looked into her face. "Go on, Jennet," I commanded.

" 'Tis his all right," she murmured. "No mistake 'tis his. I wonder if my son 'ull be another like the Captain."

"Captain Jake Pennlyon, of course." I spoke of him as I would speak of a loathsome snake.

"Mistress, there were no saying no to him. He wouldn't take it. He were the master and who could say him nay?"

"Not you, Jennet," I said angrily.

"No, Mistress. You see he'd had his eye on me, and I knew 'twould come sooner or later. And I was helpless like. 'Twouldn't have been no good, so I said what's to be will be."

"As you did with Alfonso. You'd never be the victim of rape, Jennet. You'd be only too eager to submit. That was it, wasn't it?"

She did not answer. She kept her eyes downcast and once again I was amazed by her innocent looks.

"When?" I demanded. For some reason I wanted to know in detail. I told myself I hated what had happened but I had to know.

" 'Twas on the night of the betrothal, Mistress. Oh, I

was not to blame. I was took like . . . in place of you, it were."

"What nonsense you are talking, Jennet."

"Well, Mistress, 'twas the betrothal and I came to your room though I'd heard you say you were spending the night with the mistress, for he'd ridden over with you. I went in. The window was open wide and as I closed the door he stepped out from behind it and caught me. I was holding a candle and it dropped to the ground and went out. Then I heard him laugh."

She giggled a little and I shook her and said: "Go on."

"He took my chin in his hand and jerked my face up; he was roughlike. He were always roughlike in his ways. He said: 'So it's you. Where's your mistress?' And I said, 'She bain't here, Master.' He said, 'I can see that. Where is she?' And I said, 'She won't be here tonight. She be with the other mistress.' And he got it out of me what I'd heard that because he was here and you didn't trust him to stay away you were staying with the mistress. He was angry and I was frightened. He cursed and swore and it was against you. He was wanting you, Mistress, bad he was. He was wild he were because when he'd heard my footsteps he'd thought they were yours."

I laughed aloud. "So he was cheated, was he?"

"He reckoned so. And he was angry. And I said I'd go and tell you he were here and he said: 'You little fool, do you think that will bring her?' And I believe he was in two minds to come and get you. But even he couldn't do that in his neighbor's house, could he? So he made me stay and he said, 'We'll make believe, Jennet. You'll be your mistress tonight.' And then it happened, Mistress. I was powerless. There never was such a time."

"In my bed!"

"I'd meant to straighten up, Mistress. But there weren't time. He went at dawn; and I fell into such a sleep. Well, Mistress, it had been such a night . . . and when I woke it was late and I went to my room to get myself looking shipshape like . . . and by the time I came back you'd seen the room and the bed and. . . ."

"The scene of your triumph, Jennet."

"What's that, Mistress?"

"And because of that he got you with child."

She was again bashful. "There were other times. When you had the sweat he used to come over . . . and he'd command me to go to Lyon Court, he would."

"And you did of course."

"I dursn't disobey him."

"Jennet," I said, "you are a false servant. This is the second time you have betrayed me."

"I wouldn't have, Mistress. It was just that it were beyond my power."

"From him to Alfonso and I'll warrant you sneak into someone's bed in this place!"

" 'Tis into the stables, Mistress. One of the grooms."

"Spare me your disgusting details." I kept thinking of Jake Pennlyon waiting in that room for me and taking Jennet. And I thought of the similarity of my own affair with Felipe Gonzáles, who pretended that the woman he visited each night was Isabella instead of me.

"And it did not occur to you that because of your lust you might bring some unfortunate infant into the world?"

"Oh, it did, Mistress, but then Sir Penn have had many such, but he always looked after 'em. They always had a good place somewhere and I said to myself 'twill be the same with Captain Jake."

"You were mistaken."

"It changed, though, Mistress. Who could have known that we'd be on the high seas and in this place? Who could have foretold that?"

She stood before me forlorn, yet her eyes were alight with the memories of her liaison with that man.

I wondered why I had failed to notice that she was pregnant. It seemed so obvious now.

Jake Pennlyon, I thought. Everything comes back to Jake Pennlyon. I wished that I could shut out from my mind memories of him and Jennet together.

I said: "Get out of my sight. You disgust me."

She crept away.

I hated Jake Pennlyon. I hated Felipe Gonzáles. I hated my father and Kate for spoiling my life. So much hatred was like a sickness of the body. There was a tight feeling in my throat which was like a pain; I wanted to relieve it which I could only do by taking some action. I wanted revenge chiefly on Jake Pennlyon; but he was out of my reach. By comparison I almost felt a sympathy for Felipe Gonzáles. At least he was revenging himself on Jake Pennlyon. A feeble revenge perhaps. He did not understand that Jake was a different kind of man from himself. Jake could content himself with Jennet when he could not get me. Jake would never understand the devotion Felipe felt for his Isabella.

But I hated Felipe for humiliating me and I hated him for not desiring me, for forcing himself to do what he did and tricking me out so that he could delude himself into thinking I was Isabella.

Everything came back to Jake Pennlyon; but he was out of my reach and I could not revenge myself on him.

I wanted to hurt someone. To beat Jennet was of no avail. Besides, she was pregnant and I had no wish to harm an innocent child even though it was the fruit of Jake Pennlyon's lust. I thought of Felipe and wondering about this strange, silent man took my thoughts from my bedroom in Trewynd and Jake Pennlyon's waiting there behind the door to seize Jennet.

I began to consider those dark nights when Felipe Gonzáles came to me. I would not admit it, but they no longer shocked me. I had become accustomed to his visits. I received him passively and since I had seen Isabella my sympathy for him had grown.

But a desire began to grow in me—perhaps I wished for my revenge on him, perhaps my feminine vanity was affronted. I was not sure, but I began to think of him more than I had and my attitude toward him was changing.

Once when he came in I pretended to be asleep. I lay quite still. The room was always dark, but there was faint light from a crescent moon and the brilliant stars. I kept my eyes closed, but I was aware of his standing by the bed looking at me.

He always left his candle outside the door. I fancied that he was ashamed and did not wish to be embarrassed by the light. Still keeping my eyes closed, I felt him get into the bed. I lay still. I knew that he was watching me. On impulse I put out a hand and touched his face. I let my fingers linger on his lips and I could swear he kissed them.

I made no sign. I just lay there as though sleeping. He watched me for some minutes. Then silently he went away.

I lay listening to his receding footsteps. My heart was beating wildly. I felt a certain exultation. Our relationship was beginning to change. Faint stirrings of a desire were in me—not for love but for revenge.

Honey's time was near and the midwife came to settle in.

I went to Felipe's *escritorio* ostensibly to thank him for what he had done for Honey, but in fact to speak to him and see if I could sense any change in his attitude toward me.

He had returned on other nights, but not every night. I would never know when he was coming and would lie awake listening for his steps. I was angry when he came and angry when he did not. I could not understand myself.

He rose from his desk as I entered and stood courteously.

Then he indicated a chair.

I sat down. "I have come to thank you. The midwife is here. My sister will have need of her shortly."

He bowed his head.

"It is good of you to treat us as human beings." I injected a little sarcasm into my voice, but he did not seem to notice it.

"It is no fault of hers that she is here. Certainly she must have attention. She will bring a good Catholic into the world."

"I have a strong suspicion that I am with child."

"Suspicion is not enough. I must have certainty."

"How soon shall I leave when it is known?"

"That is a matter which will have my consideration. Your sister will not wish to travel for a while. Your maid, I hear, is also soon to give birth."

I was not going to tell him who the father of Jennet's child was.

I said: "She was raped by one of your sailors."

"That is deplorable," he said.

He half rose in his chair, the gesture of dismissal.

I went on: "We are kept as prisoners here. Are you afraid that we will find our way to the coast and swim home?"

"There is no reason why you should be kept prisoners. Once you are with child you will have more freedom. You are kept in seclusion because the child must be of my giving."

I flushed hotly. "And you think I am a woman to take lovers here and there from your Spaniards of La Laguna? You are offensive, sir."

"I ask your pardon. I meant no such thing. Your serving woman was taken against her will. There is a strangeness about you . . . a foreign look . . . which might put you in danger. I might not be at hand to protect you."

"I trust soon that I shall be beyond your protection."

"You cannot wish for that more than I do."

I thought of his coming to me and how he had watched me and how he responded when I laid my fingers on his lips.

I had imagined the whole thing. There was no moving this strange silent man.

Honey had a long labor and it was day and night before her child was born—a puny girl, small but living.

It was not to be wondered at after all she had endured.

She lay back in her bed, looking unbelievably beautiful with her dark hair flowing loose and the maternal look in her lovely violet eyes.

She said: "I shall call her Edwina. It's the nearest to Edward. What do you think of that, Catharine?"

I liked the name, but I was so relieved that Honey had come through the ordeal safely that anything would have sounded good. There had been times when I had begun to fear for her and then I realized how much she meant to me. I had gone over our childhood together in the Abbey and wondered what my mother was doing and whether she was thinking of us—her two daughters lost to the Spaniards.

The baby occupied our time and our thoughts. Its arrival was a turning point, I think. I had to rejoice when I looked at those miniature fingers and toes, and the child became the center of our lives. We ceased to think of revenge and home while we asked ourselves how much the baby had grown since yesterday.

A week or so after the birth of Edwina I was sure that I was pregnant.

Triumphantly, I faced him in the *escritorio*.

"There is no doubt," I said. "I have seen the midwife. Your unpleasant duty is finished."

He lowered his head.

"Now is the time for us to return home."

"You shall do so at a convenient time."

"You said this is all you wanted of me. You have defiled me, humiliated me, impregnated me with your seed. Is that not enough? Am I not free now?"

"You are free," he said.

"Then I wish to go home."

"You will need a ship."

"You have ships. You sent for me, now take me home."

"There is no ship in the harbor at this time."

"Yet you sent the galleon."

"It was convenient to do so."

"Then pray find it convenient to keep your bargain."

"I made no bargain with you. I made a vow to the saints."

"You have promised that I shall go home."

"In due course you will sail for your barbaric land and you can tell your pirate lover what you have seen here. You can tell him of what happened to a noble lady and what has happened to you. You can tell him that he ruined her life and that I have had my revenge on him. You will take your bastard to him as he left his here with me."

I stood up. "So when a ship comes, I shall go?"

"It shall be arranged," he said. "But I want to be sure that there is a child."

"He never saw his. Why should you see yours? Is that in the vow?"

"His child was born," he said. "I must be sure that mine is."

"You have not gained your revenge completely," I said. "I am not as Isabella. You have insulted and humiliated me, but you have not robbed me of my reason. Your revenge is incomplete."

"You will have this child," he said. "You will not leave

this island until that child is born. I will make sure that there is a child and then you shall be taken back."

I walked out of the *escritorio*. I thought: He said that I might leave when I was with child. But he does not wish me to go. I laughed exultantly and I thought: He is vulnerable. When I can discover how vulnerable I can have my revenge.

Revenge is sweet, there is no doubt. It gives one a reason for living when life becomes too tragic.

I was beginning to understand Felipe.

Our lives had undergone a change; it was due mainly to the fact that he no longer came to me; I felt as though I was in complete possession of myself again. And the fact that there was a baby in the household was not without its effect.

A certain normality had come upon us. Strangely enough we had settled down, which was something I now and then marveled at. But such is human nature that it can become accustomed to anything however extraordinary. One adjusts oneself—or at least we seemed to.

I now had the bedroom to myself—and a pleasant room it was. Since it was no longer the scene of my nightly humiliation my feelings changed toward it. I could enjoy the tasteful, yet somber decorations: the tapestry which hung on one of the walls; the heavy arras which shut out the light; the arch with the curtains across it which led to the toilet room with its sunken bath. There was an Eastern touch about it and I learned later that Felipe's family had lived in that part of Spain which was dominated by the Moorish influence.

Perhaps it was because I was pregnant that a certain serenity had come to me. I had noticed this in both Honey and Jennet though with Jennet it was a constant attitude. I was surprised that I was excited by the thought of bearing this child which had been forced on me. But already I was forgetting the means of its begetting and was conscious only that a new life was stirring inside me and that I should be a mother.

I would dream of my child and be eager for its arrival . . . not only because it meant that when I had it

I should go home, but because I longed to hold it in my arms.

We were allowed to go into the town. Honey left the baby in Jennet's care and she and I set out riding on mules, accompanied by Richard Rackell and John Gregory, who, because they spoke English perhaps, had been made our guards.

They rode one in front and one behind and I felt my spirits lift as we saw the town lying in the valley. The sun was brilliant and it shone on the white houses and the Cathedral, which John Gregory told us had been built at the beginning of the century. We could not see the great mountain peak from this spot, but we had seen it at sea when we had approached the island—the great Pico de Teide which the ancients had believed supported the sky and that the world ended just beyond it. Perhaps one day, he suggested, we should be permitted to go farther inland and there we should see this miraculous mountain.

We left our mules at a stable and we went on foot into the cobbled streets, closely guarded by the two men. The women mostly wore black, but on the balconies of some of the houses there were ladies who leaned on the wrought-iron balustrades to take a close look at us, and some of those wore colored skirts and mantillas.

"They are interested in us," said Honey.

"They know you are foreigners and come from the Hacienda," said John Gregory.

"Do they know," I asked, "how we were brought here?"

John Gregory replied: "They know you have come from a foreign land."

He took us into the Cathedral. The three of them crossed themselves before the magnificent altar while I looked at the sculptures and the fine ornaments that decorated it. I had never seen such a great cathedral. The smell of incense hung heavy on the air. The figure of the Madonna was the most startling object, though; she was in an enclosure of wrought iron and wore a dress of some silken material on which sparkling gems had been sewn. On her head was a crown of jewels and on her fingers diamonds and brilliantly colored stones of all kinds.

John Gregory was beside me. He said: "People give their wealth to the Madonna. Even the poorest will give what they have. She refuses nothing."

As I turned away he whispered: "It would be better if you acted as a good Catholic. It would not be wise for it to be seen that you are what would be called a heretic."

I said: "I have had enough of the Cathedral. I will wait outside."

He accompanied me and I left Honey on her knees with Richard Rackell beside her. I wondered what she was thanking the Virgin for—the death of her good husband; her abduction; the safe arrival of her child?

Outside the sun was brilliant.

I said to John Gregory: "So you are a devout Catholic. I wonder have you confessed what harm you have done to two women who did nothing to hurt you?"

He flinched slightly. He was always uncomfortable when I upbraided him, which I did often. He folded his hands together and as he did so I noticed again the scars on his wrists and wondered how he had acquired them.

"I did what I was obliged to do," he said. "I had no wish to harm you."

"So you thought we could be dragged away from our homes, ravished and humiliated and no harm done?"

He did not answer and we were joined by the other two.

There was such a sense of freedom in walking those streets; there was an air of excitement in the town too. The shops enchanted us. It was long since we had seen shops. They were open onto the streets, like enchanted caverns. There was spicy food and hot bread, different from the variety we had at home; but what fascinated us most were the bales of various sorts of cloth which we saw in one shop.

We could not resist handling them. Honey ran her hands over them ecstatically, and a dark-eyed woman in black came to us and showed us materials—one was velvet, deep midnight blue.

Honey said: "Why, Catharine, that would become you. What a gown that would make you!"

She held it up against me and the woman in black nodded her head sagely.

Honey draped the material around me. I said: "What

are you doing, Honey? We have no money." I was conscious then of wearing Isabella's gown and I determined that I would do so no longer. Honey had made gowns for herself. So should I, but how I should have enjoyed wearing the velvet!

"Come away, Honey," I said, "this is absurd."

And I insisted on walking away.

At the inn we were given a beverage which had a strange flavor of mint. We were thirsty and drank it eagerly and after that we mounted our mules and returned to the Hacienda.

It was later that day when going to my room I found a package on my bed. I opened it and there was a roll of velvet. It was the material I had seen in the shop.

I stared at it in amazement. I held it against me. It was beautiful. But what did it mean? Did the woman in the shop think we had bought it? It would have to be returned at once.

I went to find Honey. She was as surprised as I was and we decided that the woman had misunderstood and thought we had purchased the material.

We must find John Gregory at once and explain to him. When we did so he said: "It is no mistake. The material is for you."

"How can we pay for it?"

"It will be arranged."

"Who will arrange it?"

"The shop woman knows you come from the Hacienda. There will be no difficulty."

"Does it mean that Don Felipe will pay for this?"

"It would amount to that."

"I shall certainly not accept it."

"You must."

"I have been forced to come here. I have been forced to submit, but I will not take gifts from him."

"It would be impossible to return it. The woman believes you to be under the protection of Don Felipe. He is the first gentleman of the island. It would be a slight to him if you returned the velvet. That would not be allowed."

"It can be taken to him then, for I shall not use it."

John Gregory bowed and took the material which I thrust into his arms.

Honey said: "It's a pity. It would have made a most becoming gown."

"Would you have me accept gifts from my seducer? It would be tantamount to giving him my approval of what has taken place. I shall never forgive him for what he has done to me."

"Never, Catharine? That is a word one should use with care. It could have been so much worse. He has at least treated you with some respect."

"Respect! Were you present? Did you witness my humiliation?"

"At least it was not what Isabella suffered at the hands of Jake Pennlyon.'

"It was the same . . . the method may have been slightly different. She bore Jake Pennlyon's child and I am to bear his. It nauseates me, Honey, to think of it."

"Still," said Honey, "it's a pity about the velvet."

A summons came for me to dine with Don Felipe. It was the first time since that other occasion when he had told me for what purpose I had been brought here.

I wondered what it meant.

I dressed myself with care. Honey and I had made a gown for me from the material we had found in the sewing room. As I put it on I thought how illogical it was to accept that material and haughtily decline the velvet which had come from the shop. Everything in this house belonged to him, so naturally did anything in the sewing room. We lived on his bounty.

But the velvet was a kind of gift direct from him and that I would refuse.

He was waiting for me in the cool dark salon in which we had dined before, and as on that other occasion I sat at one end of the table, he at the other. In his black doublet trimmed with that dazzlingly white lace he looked every bit the fastidious gentleman. When we had last dined thus, none of those embarrassing encounters had taken place; now they stood between us—memories which I imagined he no more than I could efface.

He was aloof in his manner but courteous, and we were

served as before by silent-footed servants with the food with which I had now become familiar. I was aware of a certain excitement which I had not known before. I was very much conscious of him. I wondered about him and I kept thinking of that night when I had touched his face gently and tenderly and pretended to sleep.

He talked of the island while the servants were there. He spoke without enthusiasm for it nor any great show of interest, but beneath that cold manner I sensed that he had a great feeling for it. He commanded it. He was holding it for his master, Philip the Second, a strange silent man such as himself. They were different these Spaniards; they did not laugh aloud as we did; they thought us barbarians.

He told me then how the Guanches who were the natives of the island stained their skins the dark-red resin of the dragon trees and how they mummified their dead.

It was interesting and I wanted to know more and more of the island. He said that Pico de Teide was regarded by the Guanches as a kind of god who must be placated, and a fine sight it was towering above the plains with its snowcapped top which never changed even where there was burning heat below.

It was when the meal had been finished and we were alone that I realized the reason he had invited me to sup with him.

He said: "You went into La Laguna and saw the Cathedral."

"Yes," I said.

"You must not act as a heretic in La Laguna."

"I shall act as I please and as I am doubtless what you will call a heretic I shall perforce act as one."

"When you visit the Cathedral you must show *Catholic* respect for the Virgin and the altar; you must kneel and pray as others do."

"Would you have me a hypocrite?"

"I am determined that you shall bear the child. I would not wish aught to happen to you that would prevent it."

I put my hands on my body. I used to delude myself into fancying that I could feel the child. It was absurd, it was much too soon; but I was already so much aware of it.

"What should prevent it?" I demanded.

"You could be taken before the Inquisition. You could be questioned."

"I! What have I to do with the Inquisition?"

"This is Spain. Oh, I know we are an island far from Spain; but Spain is wherever we settle and that will be in every part of the globe."

"Never in England," I said proudly.

"There too. I assure you it will be so in due course of time."

"Then I assure you it will never be so." I had a vision of Jake Pennlyon, his eyes flashing scorn, brandishing his cutlass and crying out to the Spanish Dons to come and see what they would find.

"Listen to me," he said, " 'ere long the whole world will be ours. We shall bring the Holy Inquisition to your land . . . as it is here and in every place on earth where Spain has laid its hand. No one can escape from it. If you were taken, even I could not save you. The Inquisition stands above all . . . even above our Most High King, Philip."

"I am no Spaniard. They would not dare touch me."

"They have touched many of your countrymen. Be wise. Listen to me. You will start instruction in the True Faith tomorrow."

"I will do no such thing."

"You are more foolish than I thought. You must be shown what happens to those who defy the truth."

"Whose truth? Yours? You who trample over the innocent to gain your revenge. You have taken three women from their homes; you have submitted them to degradation and pain; you have killed a good man because he tried to protect his wife. And you talk to me about your faith, the True Faith, the only faith."

"Be silent." For the first time I saw him moved. "Know you not that servants may hear?"

"They do not speak my barbarian language, remember, except the two villains whom you employed to bring us here."

"I will be tolerant. I will beg of you to be calm. I ask you to listen in a civilized manner."

"*You* talk to me of civilized behavior. It is as funny as

speaking of your religious virtues."

"I speak for your good. I speak for you and the child."

"Your bastard which was forced on me." Yet even as I said those words I murmured a reassurance to the child. "Nay, nay, little one, I want you. I'm glad you are there. Wait until I hold you in my arms."

My voice must have faltered, for he said gently, "That is past and done. Nor can it be undone. It was your misfortune that you were the betrothed of this brigand. You have the child. Bear it and accept your fate. I swear to you that from now on I mean no harm to you. Will you accept that?"

I did; but I said: "Having harmed me in such a manner that must leave its mark on me forever, perhaps you do mean that."

"I assure you it is so. I never meant harm to you. You were necessary to the fulfillment of my vow. Now I would give you the comfort you will need until the child is born."

"You promised I should go home when the child was conceived."

"I have said I must see the child is born. For that reason you will stay here; but while you are here I wish to live securely and in peace. And for that reason you will listen to me."

I cried: "Do not think I can be placated with gifts of velvet."

"It was no gift of mine. The shop woman sent it for you."

"Why should she?"

"Because we buy much cloth from her and she wishes to please me by offering you this gift."

"Why should it please you?"

"Surely you understand. She believes, as many will, that you are my mistress. That you have been brought here to live with me and in such case what pleased you will please me and put the donor in favor."

"Your mistress! How dare she."

"It is what you are in a sense. Let us face the facts. And in these circumstances you will have some protection. But as I told you even I cannot protect you from the mighty Inquisition. That is why I wish you to be

instructed in the True Faith. John Gregory, who is indeed
a priest, will instruct you. You must listen. I do not want
you to be taken away . . . before the child. is born."

"I refuse," I said.

He sighed. "You are unwise," he answered. "I will
tell you what has happened in your country while you have
been away. Your Queen is a foolish woman. She might
have married Philip when her sister died. It would have
been an opportunity to have united our countries. It
would have saved much trouble."

"She could not take her sister's husband. Moreover,
he did not give a very good account of himself as a husband, I fancy."

"The fault lay in that poor barren woman. And now
her foolish half sister, the bastard Elizabeth, has the
throne."

"In which her country rejoices," I said. "Long may she
live."

"It is long since you left home. Her throne is shaking
now. She will not long occupy it. The true Queen Mary
of France and Scotland shall take it and when that has
been done the True Faith will be restored to England."

"With the accompaniment of your Holy Inquisition?"

"It will be necessary. There will be a great purge of
heretics in your island."

"God forbid," I said. "We have had enough. We remember the Smithfield fires. We'll have no more of them."

"The faith will be restored," he said. "It is imminent."

"The people are firmly behind the Queen." I was remembering her accession, how nobly she had spoken as
she entered the Tower. "I must bear myself to God thankful and to men merciful. . . ." And my heart swelled with
loyalty toward her and hatred toward all her enemies.

"They will no longer be so," he told me. "Certain
events have changed the people's feelings for the Queen."

"I do not believe it."

He studied me coolly in the light of the candles.

"The Queen made Robert Dudley her Master of Horse.
Rumor has it that she wished to marry him. He had a
wife. He had married earlier, impulsively, some said, for
as events turned out he could have been destined for a
high place. King no less—though mayhap in name only—

for the Queen doted on him. She is a coquette, a frivolous woman; she is coy toward all men, but we hear that the feeling she has for Robert Dudley goes deeper. Now his wife, Amy Robsart, has died somewhat mysteriously. Her body was found at the bottom of a staircase. Who shall know how she died? Some say she threw herself from the top of the staircase because she could no longer bear the neglect of her husband; those who would placate your Queen and Lord Robert will tell you that she suffered an accident. But there are many who will say she was murdered."

"And the Queen will marry this man?"

"She will marry him and there is an end of her. On the day she marries Lord Robert she stands a self-confessed accomplice to murder. She will lose her kingdom, and who will take her crown? The Queen of France and Scotland, who is the true Queen of England. We shall support her claim. She will become our vassal. I command that you take instruction from John Gregory. I insist on this for your own welfare."

"You cannot make a Catholic of me if I will not have it."

"You foolish one," he said quietly. "I tell you this to save you."

Over the candles I looked into his face. He was moved in some way; and I knew that he feared for me.

After that began my daily sessions with John Gregory. At first I refused to listen to him. He said I must learn the Credo in Latin. He used to chant it again and again.

He said: "If you could not do that, you would be condemned as a heretic without further ado."

I turned away from him, but I could not keep up my silence; I was not silent by nature.

"You are an Englishman, are you not?" I demanded.

He nodded.

"And you have sold yourself to these Spanish dogs." I jeered inwardly at myself for talking like Jake Pennlyon.

"There is much I could tell you," he said. "Perhaps then you would not despise me so much."

"I shall always despise you. You took me from my home, you submitted me to this, you came to us, accepted our hospitality and lied, that is something I shall never forget."

"The Virgin will plead for me," he said.

"Her prayers would have no effect on me," I retorted grimly.

Later I said to him, "You will never convert me. I was never eager to take one side against another, but the more you force me, the more I shall turn away. Do you think I can ever forget the reign of her whom they called Bloody Mary? Let me tell you this, John Gregory: My grandfather lost his life because he sheltered a friend—a priest like you, of your faith, for that was my grandfather's faith. My mother's stepfather was burned at Smithfield because books concerning the Reformed Faith were found in his house. Someone informed on him, as my grandfather was informed against. And all this in the name of religion. Does it surprise you that I want none of it?"

He spoke vehemently: "No, it does not surprise me. But you should listen. You should prepare yourself lest danger should come."

"Then I am preparing to save my body, not my soul."

"There is no reason why you should not save both."

We talked a great deal and I wondered about him; and during the weeks that followed my attitude toward this man began to change. Everything was changing. It was almost as though a mist were clearing before my eyes.

Days passed and became weeks. I surprised myself. I was becoming happy in this alien land. I understood the serenity of Honey, her preoccupation with Edwina. Jennet was growing near her time. She would sit with us sometimes in the Spanish garden which Don Felipe had had made by a gardener come from Spain. During the hot days there was a sense of peace in the gardens. We would sew together, for fine linens and lace had appeared in the sewing room; and although I hated to take these things for myself I would accept anything for my child.

Sometimes the incongruity of it all came over me; and I thought of my mother in her gardens or visiting my grandmother. They would talk of us. My poor mother would be sad, for she had lost both her girls. Did they think of us as dead now? Then I was mournful, for she had suffered much and loved us both dearly—particularly me, her own daughter.

But that was far away, like another life; and here we were in the Spanish garden, my baby stirring within me, reminding me that each day it grew and that the happy moment when I should hold it in my arms was coming nearer.

Jennet was complacent—very large, completely undisturbed, accepting life as I supposed I never would. Now that she had rid herself of the burden of her secret, she seemed to have cast off her cares. She had a habit of humming to herself, which I found mildly irritating because they were the tunes which I remembered from home.

As we sat in the shade out of the sun, which was warmer than ours at home, Honey was playing with her baby, Jennet was humming over her sewing and I sat there stitching. Suddenly I began to laugh. It was so incongruous—three women—one a mother and two soon to be—who had gone through violent adventures and were now serene.

Honey looked at me and smiled. This laughter did not frighten her. It was not hysteria. There was an element of happiness in it. We had come to terms with life.

I loved Honey's child; she was small and delicately made; I doubted she would be as beautiful as her mother; at this time her eyes were china blue, her skin delicate. I liked to have her on my own and I would take her to the Spanish garden and rock her gently. She would watch me with great wondering eyes. I believed she knew me. She was very good with me. I used to sing to her songs that my mother used to sing to me. "The King's Hunt's Up" and "Greensleeves," which were said to have been composed by our great King Henry himself.

One day I was seated in the trellised arbor in the Spanish garden rocking the baby when I was aware of being watched.

I looked up and Don Felipe was standing a few yards from me.

I flushed hotly; he continued to regard me in the detached manner to which I was accustomed. I looked down at the baby, pretending to ignore him; but he continued to stand there. The baby began to whimper as though she were aware of some alien presence.

I murmured: "Hushaby, 'Wina. You are safe. Catharine is here, darling."

When I looked up he had gone. I had not known that he was at the Hacienda because I had heard that he had gone to another part of the island.

I was always disturbed when he was in the house. It was not that he forced his presence on me, but I was aware of him. The household changed when he was there. The servants went about their duties with renewed vigor; there was a sense of tension everywhere.

I had a fright in that night, for as I lay in my bed I heard steps in the corridor, slow, stealthy steps. I started up in bed and listened. Slowly they came nearer and nearer. They paused outside my door.

I thought: He is coming to me, and I remembered how he had stood in the garden watching me.

My heart was beating so wildly that I thought it would choke me. Instinct made me lie back and feign sleep.

Through half-closed eyes I saw the candlelight; I saw the shadow on the wall.

It was his shadow.

I lay very still, my eyes shut. He was at the bedside, the candle wavering slightly in his hand. Keeping my lids lowered and pretending to be in a deep sleep, I waited for what would happen next.

I knew that he was at the bedside watching me.

It seemed a long time that he stood there; then the candlelight disappeared; I heard my door close gently. I dared not open my eyes for some time because I was afraid that he was in the room; but when I heard his footsteps slowly receding, I looked and saw that I was alone.

Jennet's time had come. The midwife came to the Hacienda and Jennet's labor, unlike Honey's, was brief; a few hours after her pains started we heard the lusty bawling of the child.

It was a boy and I'll swear that from the first it had a look of Jake Pennlyon.

I said to Honey: "Shall we ever escape from the man? Now there will be Jennet's bastard to remind us."

I thought I should dislike the child, but how could I do that? In the first weeks he was bigger than Edwina. He showed his temperament too. I had never believed a child could bawl so lustily for what he wanted.

Jennet was overcome with pride. He was not only her baby; he was Captain Pennlyon's too. She was sure there never had been such a child.

"That's what all mothers think," I said.

" 'Tis so, Mistress, but this be true. Only a man like that could make a baby like this 'un."

Each day he grew more like his father.

Jake Pennlyon would indeed be with us forever.

"As soon as my child is born," I said to Honey, "there will be no excuse for keeping us here. We shall go home. I shall go back to the Abbey. I long to be with my mother. There is so much I want to say to her. Before, I was so ignorant of everything. I often think of her life with my father. Children never know their parents, I suppose; but because of what has happened to me and those violent adventures that she has endured we shall be closer than ever when we meet."

I could see in Honey's eyes that she too longed for home.

We talked as we sat in the gardens of the old days at the Abbey and how my grandmother used to come over with her basket laden with ointments and goodies and flowers; and how she used to talk of her twin sons, who came with her sometimes.

And when we spoke of the old days Honey began to confide in me.

"I was always jealous of you, Catharine," she said. "What I wanted always came to you."

"You jealous of me! But you were the beauty."

"I was the daughter of a serving girl and the man who despoiled the Abbey. My great-grandmother was a witch."

"But you did very well, Honey. After all, you married a rich man who doted on you. You were happy then."

"I was always happy in my fashion. It was a makeshift sort of way. I was the adopted daughter, not received by the master of the house. . . ."

"But your beauty freed you from that. Edward Ennis would have been Lord Calperton and you a lady of high rank."

"I took Edward because he was a good match."

"I should think he was. Mother was delighted."

"Yes, everyone was delighted. The orphan had climbed out of her poverty; she had made a good match, she had the kindest and most tolerant of husbands. Is that being happy, Catharine?"

"If you loved him."

"I came to love him. He was so kind and good. I had affection for him. He was the best I could hope for."

"What are you telling me, Honey?"

"That I loved . . . even as you loved, but he was not for me. I made my plans. But he did not love me. He loved someone else. That was apparent for a long time before he or she realized it. I saw it and I hated you, Catharine, as I had never in my childish jealousy hated you before."

"You hated *me?*"

"Yes, I did. Our mother loved you as she could never love me. You were her own child. And Carey loved you. He always looked for you. He teased you, he bullied you, you used to fight together . . . but he always looked for you; he was only gay and happy when you were there. I knew. I used to cry at night."

"*You* loved Carey?"

"Of course I loved Carey. Who could help loving Carey?"

"Oh, Honey," I said. "You too."

We were silent thinking of him—Carey, beloved Carey, who was to have been my very own. But I lost him and Honey lost him.

"Our love was doomed," I said. "There is no reason why yours should have been."

She laughed. "Because the loved one is denied that does not mean that anyone else will do."

"But he was fond of you."

"As a sister. And I knew that he loved you. So I

accepted Edward. It was only after we married that I knew the truth."

I turned away from her. I looked at the dazzling sky, at the palm trees on the horizon; and I thought of the tragic twists and turns in our lives which had led us to this moment.

We had come closer through this confession. Once we had both loved and lost Carey.

Jennet's baby, like Honey's Edwina, was baptized in the Catholic ritual. Honey had been a Catholic before she had left England and Jennet was quite ready to adopt any religion that she was asked to. Alfonso had started her on the road; John Gregory had prodded her along. I wondered what Jake Pennlyon would say if he knew his son—bastard albeit—was being baptized in the Catholic Faith; and the thought gave me a certain pleasure.

Jennet called him Jack, which was as near to his father as she dared go, and he quickly became known as Jacko.

Our lives were now dominated by the two children; and then another came into them.

It was I who discovered Carlos. Poor little Carlos, he was enough to wring any woman's heart, the more so because there was something jaunty about him, something gay and adventurous.

I had been thinking more of Don Felipe than I cared to admit. He was away a great deal even if he only went to La Laguna. When he was in the house I would take great pains to avoid him; but I liked to watch him when he was unaware of me. Sometimes I would see him from my window and stand in the shadows looking out. Often he would glance up so that I felt he was aware of me there.

I wondered a great deal about his relationship with Isabella. She was his wife. Did he visit her often? Of what did they speak when he did? Was she aware of my presence at the Hacienda? And if so, what did she think of that? Did she know I was to bear her husband's child?

I often walked past the Casa Azul; I would look through the wrought-iron gate onto the patio where the oleanders threw shadows on the cobbles and I would think of the beautiful face of the girl who played with dolls, and wonder what her life was like with her sour-faced duenna.

The house had become a kind of obsession with me. I found my footsteps leading me there every time I was alone. I would peer through the wrought-iron gate and wonder about Isabella and what happened when Don Felipe visited her.

One day the gate was open and I stepped inside. It was afternoon siesta hour. The house looked as though it were sleeping, as I supposed most of its inhabitants were. I enjoyed walking out at this time; I liked the stillness of everything, the silence, and in spite of the heat I came back refreshed in my mind. On my lonely walks I would think about my home and my mother and I would hope that she was not grieving too much for me. I was beginning to feel that the old life was over and I had to make a new one here, for I wondered whether Don Felipe would ever let us go.

It was because that strange man was dominating my thoughts that I had to come to this house. I wanted to know more about him. What had his life been in Spain before he came here? Had he in truth loved Isabella passionately? This must have been so since he had gone to such lengths to be revenged. Yet that could be due to his pride.

The stillness in the patio enveloped me. I looked up at the balcony on which I had seen Isabella. The doors were shut; there was no sign of life. I went quietly around to the side of the house; there was a pergola shady and made cool because the plants were trained over the trelliswork. I was facing a gate—wrought iron like that other—and beyond this lay a patch of land and a small hutlike dwelling.

As I stood looking through this gate a child emerged from the house; I judged him to be about two years old; he was dirty and barefooted, and he was dressed in a shapeless garment which came to his knees. He was rubbing his eye with his fist and he was obviously in distress because every few seconds a sob shook his body.

I had become passionately interested in children and his misery touched me deeply and made me want to alleviate it if possible.

He saw me suddenly and stopped; he stared at me and

I thought for a moment he was going to run. I called out to him: "Good day, little boy." He looked bewildered and I repeated my greeting in Spanish. My voice must have reassured him, for he came toward the gate and stood there. A pair of brown eyes were raised to me; his hair which was thick and straight was of a medium brown, his skin olive. He was an attractive little boy in spite of the grime; and the jauntiness was there in spite of his misery.

I smiled at him and knelt down so that our faces were on a level. I asked in rather stumbling Spanish what was wrong. His lips quivered and he showed me his arm. I was shocked by the bruises. He sensed my sympathy and held out the arm to me. I touched it gently with my lips and he smiled. His smile was dazzling, like but one other, and I knew at once who he was. He was Jake Pennlyon's son, the result of the rape of Isabella.

With all my heart I hated Jake Pennlyon then, who spread his bastards around and never thought of what became of them. In this remote place there were two of them. And because I hated Jake Pennlyon my sympathy for this unfortunate child was intensified. But I should have been angry at the sight of any neglected child.

Through the bars I laid my lips on the bruises.

I heard a voice call: "Carlos! Carlos." And a string of words I could not understand. Some patois, I supposed. The child turned and ran away. There was a bush in this patch of land; he scuttled behind it and hid. I backed from the gate as a woman came out. Her hair hung around her face; her mouth was cruel; her black eyes fierce; her flaccid breasts nearly fell out of her loose low-necked dress.

I heard her repeat the name "Carlos." And I watched, wondering what I should do if she found the child, for I knew she was responsible for those bruises.

I wanted to open the gate and go through. I wanted to remonstrate with her, but I knew that would only make things worse for the child.

She seemed to content herself with shouting and after a while went back into the cottage. I waited for the child to come out, but he did not do so and I wondered whether he had fallen asleep in the bushes.

I went back thoughtfully to the Hacienda.

I talked to Honey. "I think I have seen Jake Pennlyon's child," I said, and told her about the boy Carlos.

"You shouldn't have gone there. You were shown clearly that you weren't wanted."

"What a strange ménage this is, Honey," I said. "What do you think happens in that house? Does Don Felipe go there often?"

"What is it to you?"

"Nothing, of course. Oh, Honey, when my child is born we shall go home."

I could not get Carlos out of my mind. Those great brown eyes and the look in them when I had kissed his bruises, and the show of fear at the sound of that voice. I pictured his cowering before her blows. The next day I took with me a little rag doll which Honey had made for Edwina. The child had ignored it. She was no doubt too young to know what it was.

Strangely he was waiting at the gate and I knew that he had hoped that I would come again. When he saw me he grasped the bars and started jumping up and down. I knelt down and he held out his arm for me to kiss. The gesture brought tears into my eyes.

I gave him the rag doll. He seized it and laughed. He held it against him and then held it out to me. I realized it was for me to kiss.

"Carlos," I said. He nodded.

"Catalina," I said, the Spanish version of my name.

Then he ran away looking around all the time, which I knew meant that he wanted me to stay. He came back with a flower—an oleander—which he gave to me. I took it and tucked it into my bodice. He laughed. We were friends.

I wanted to ask him questions, but the language barrier was difficult, and suddenly I heard the sound of voices and once again the little boy scuttled away and hid behind the bush. I drew back into the shelter of the oleanders and watched. Two children came out of the house, one of about eight I should say, the other about six. They ran to the bush and dragged Carlos out. I heard him scream. They took the rag doll and the elder of the boys started to pull it apart. Carlos screamed his rage; but he was powerless and the mutilated rag doll lay in pieces on the grass.

Carlos lay on the ground and lamented miserably. The elder of the boys came up and kicked him. Carlos sprang to his feet. The two boys rolled on the grass; then the woman appeared. The elder of the boys ran away. Carlos was struggling to his feet when the woman kicked him.

This was too much for me. I pushed the gate with all my might and to my amazement it opened. I ran through. Her attention turned from the child; the woman stared at me and let forth a stream of abuse.

Carlos had stopped screaming and moved behind me; I could feel his hands clutching my skirt.

The woman attempted to seize him, but I held her off, protecting the child. She was ugly, that woman—low, atavistic; there was no intelligence in her face; only cunning; and there was cruelty there too—horrible unreasoning cruelty, and this was the woman who had charge of Jake Pennlyon's son.

Her eyes flashed with sadistic delight. I knew she was planning what she would do to the child. A trickle of saliva dribbled from her mouth. I drew back. She was repulsive and horrible and I would not leave any child to her mercy.

Without thinking what I would do, I picked up Carlos in my arms and walked through the gate. I felt his hands clutching me tightly, his hot dirty face close to mine.

The woman ran after us. I tried to shut the gate in her face, but I was too late, so I hurried with the child into the patio.

I saw then that there was someone there. It was the duenna whom I had heard called Pilar.

Pilar stared at me with those sharp eyes under the straggling brows. I said: "This child is in need of care."

Pilar came to me and tried to take Carlos from me. He screamed and clutched to me more tightly.

"It's clear," I said, "that he is terrified of you all, which is an indication to me of the ill treatment he has received from you. I shall take him to the Hacienda with me."

Pilar could evidently understand one or two words. "To the Hacienda," she cried. "No, no." She screamed something about Don Felipe.

I said: "I care not for Don Felipe!" which was a foolish thing to say when he was the master of us all.

Isabella came into the patio. She took one look at the child and she ran to us. She tried to take him from me.

Carlos began to scream in real terror.

Pilar cried: "Isabella, Isabella *favorita*."

I knew that I must protect the child. I knew that I must not let his mother lay hands on him. She was mad. I had never seen a madwoman before. Some would say that she was possessed by devils and if ever I saw possession it was then. She started to scream; Pilar was beside her or she would have dropped to the ground; I saw her lying there and Pilar was forcing something between her lips; she was writhing as though tormented.

I ran out through the gate across the grass back to the Hacienda.

I said: "It's all right, Carlos. You are with me now."

Don Felipe was away, which was perhaps well. I knew that everyone in the household was astounded by the enormity of what I had done. I could not have done anything which would have been more outrageous. The terrible tragedy of this house had begun on the day the *Rampant Lion* came to Tenerife; the shadow of those events had hung across the house for three years; they had changed the way of life of everyone there. And in true Spanish fashion this matter which had changed everything was to be ignored; they were to behave as though it had not happened; even though Don Felipe's bride lived in a house apart because she was mad, and he had taken an alien woman to complete his revenge. And I—that alien woman—had now brought into his house the result of this disaster. I did not care. I was to have a child of my own and I loved all children. I would not stand by and see them ill-treated to save any Spanish Don's pride.

It was pathetic to see the manner in which Carlos regarded me. I was clearly a kind of goddess who could do anything. I was the one who had kissed his bruises, who had carried him out of squalor to a beautiful house. I bathed him in my sunken bath and treated his bruises and there were many on his little body and the sight of them aroused my fury to such an extent that I was ready to inflict the same punishment on that evil-faced woman. I soothed him with lotions and wrapped him in a cotton shift; and he slept in my bed. When I awoke next morning he was lying close to me and his hand gripped my nightgown firmly. I believed he had held it while he slept, so terrified was he that he was going to lose me. I knew then I could never fail him.

Oh, Jake Pennlyon, I thought. I am going to fight for your son.

Jennet couldn't make enough of him. The likeness between her child and this boy was apparent. Though one was fair and the other dark . . . they were half brothers.

No one in the Hacienda protested, although there was a tension all about us.

"They are waiting," said Honey, "for Don Felipe to return."

He came back three days after I had brought Carlos to the Hacienda. By that time the child had ceased to be afraid; he followed me but no longer appeared to feel it necessary to cling to my skirts. Under my treatment the bruises were beginning to disappear from his body and also from his mind. In a short time I hoped those miserable days of his early life would become like a bad dream that disappears with the light of day. That was what I intended should be.

Everyone was waiting for what would happen now. I sensed they believed that my brief show of authority was over.

Nothing happened all day. I was tense, starting every time a servant approached me, waiting for the summons. The one who was least perturbed was the one most concerned: Carlos. He had complete faith in me. Moreover, he had no idea of who he was.

It was early evening when Don Felipe sent for me. I was to go to the *escritorio*.

He rose as I entered; he looked impassive as ever; there was no sign of anger on his face; but then I had never seen any emotion there.

He said: "Pray be seated." So I sat down.

I looked about the *escritorio* at the paneled walls and the emblem of Spain above his chair.

"You show great temerity in bringing the child into the Hacienda. You know full well who he is."

"It is obvious."

"Then you will know too that he is an embarrassment to me."

I laughed angrily. "And do you know that you are diabolically cruel to him? For the last three days that child has been happy for the first time in his life."

"Is that reason to flout my orders?"

"It is the best of reasons," I said unflinchingly.

"Because he is your lover's child?"

"Because he is a child. He is not my lover's child. Jake Pennlyon was never my lover. I hate that man as much as you hate him. But I will not stand aside and see a child ill-treated." I stood up, my eyes blazing. I was determined to keep Carlos as I had rarely been determined before. Someone had said of my mother—I think it was Kate—that when my mother had a child she became a mother to all children. Well, I was about to have a child. I had always been fond of children, but now I was ready to lead a fervent crusade on their behalf. Carlos had turned his appealing gaze on me—and even though I was aware of his resemblance to Jake Pennlyon every time I saw him I was going to save him from misery. I was going to make him a happy child no matter what the cost.

Don Felipe said: "You were betrothed to Captain Pennlyon. You would marry him."

"I would never have done it. You see your plans for revenge have failed. I was betrothed to him because he forced me to it. He would have betrayed my sister and her husband if I had not agreed to it."

"You are a defender of others," he said, and I was not sure whether he spoke with a touch of irony.

"He has no compassion, that man. He would have forced me as he forced your Isabella. I eluded him although the betrothal was necessary. Later I feigned to be suffering from the sweating sickness until his ship had sailed. That is what I felt for Jake Pennlyon."

He was looking at me strangely.

"How vehement you are! How fierce!"

"I have found it necessary to be so. But know this:

You have no call to judge Jake Pennlyon. He has ruined lives through his lust; you will do so through your pride, and I believe one sin to be as deadly as the other."

"Be silent."

"I will not be silent. Don Felipe, your pride is so great that you have taken a woman from her home. You are guilty of rape. You have given her a child. Moreover, you have inflicted torture on the innocent result of another man's lust. And all this to appease your pride. The devil take your pride . . . and you too."

"Take care. You forget. . . ."

"I forget nothing. Nor ever shall I forget what you and Jake Pennlyon have done to women and children. You great men! So powerful, so strong. Yes! When suppressing the weak and those who are not in a position to fight you."

"I see little weakness in you," he said.

"Do you not when I was forced to submit to your evil motives?"

"Tell me, were you not quickly reconciled?"

I felt a slow flush creeping over my face. "I do not understand you, Don Felipe Gonzáles.'

"Then we will dismiss the subject and return to the reason for my summoning you here. The child must go back. I cannot allow him to be here."

"You cannot send him back . . . not now. It would be worse for him than before."

"There! You see what you have done."

I went to him and I felt the tears in my eyes because I was thinking of Carlos back in that compound with the evil woman waiting for him. I would humiliate myself a thousand times to save him from that.

I laid a hand on his arm. He looked down at me.

"You have wronged me . . . deeply. I ask you now. Give me this child."

"You will have a child of your own."

"I want this one."

"You should never have brought him here."

"Please," I said. "You have ill used me. I ask you this. It is the only thing I have ever asked of you. Give me the child."

He took my hand which I had placed on his arm; he

held it for a moment and then dropped it.

He turned back to his desk. I went out of the room. I knew that I had won.

It was indeed victory. Everyone was expecting the child to be sent back. That night I was still fearful as I lay with him in my bed; but in the morning he was still with me. For two days I was anxious, but my fears were without grounds. Don Felipe had decided to let the child stay.

I warmed toward him. Once I saw him in the gardens and I spoke to him. I had the child with me, for he still hated to let me out of his sight.

I said: "Thank you, Don Felipe."

"I hope you will keep the child away from me," he said.

"I will," I promised. "But thank you for him."

I felt Carlos' hand on my skirt and I took it firmly in mine and we walked away.

I sensed that Don Felipe watched us as we did so.

A few weeks passed. I was noticeably pregnant now. Edwina was taking on a personality of her own—she was a contented baby. I used to look at her in her cradle sometimes and think: Dear little Edwina, chuckling there, who has no notion that her father was murdered by marauding pirates and that her mother carried her precariously through terrifying adventures.

Carlos was already settling into the nursery as though he had lived there all his life. I had had a little pallet brought for him and it was placed in my room beside my bed. He was happy there although he would still come into my bed in the morning and I believed that at first it was to reassure himself that I was still there.

Don Felipe went away again and we resumed our normal life, but before he left he sent for me. I was afraid that he was going to rescind his decision to let the child stay, but I was mistaken. It was another matter of which he wanted to speak.

"I learn from John Gregory that you are not progressing well with your instruction."

"My heart is not in it," I told him.

"You are foolish. I tell you it is necessary that you become a good Catholic."

"Does one ever become good at anything against one's will?"

He looked at the door. He said: "Keep your voice low. People listen. There are some here who understand English. It would go ill with you if it were known that you were a heretic."

I made an impatient gesture.

"I do not think you realize what benefit you enjoy under my protection."

"I have no desire for your protection."

"Nevertheless, you have it. I have told you before that there are certain forces over which I have no power. I would ask you for your sake and for the child you will have and that other whom you have taken under *your* protection to be careful of yourself."

"What do you mean?"

"That you could be in acute danger if you do not profit from John Gregory's instructions. You have enemies. You have made more in the last few weeks. You will be watched, spied on; and as I tell you, it might not be in my power to save you. Think about this. You are impetuous. Have a care. That is what I would say to you."

I smiled at him and he avoided my smile. It was as though he feared it as something evil.

"I suppose I should thank you," I said. "You speak for my good."

"I am anxious that you should bear this child."

"And when I have borne it you have promised that you will return me to my home."

He did not answer. Then he said: "There are some months before the birth. In the meantime it will be necessary to take care."

I was dismissed.

It was two days later when John Gregory said that I was to go into La Laguna. It was on the instructions of Don Felipe.

"Why should he wish me to go?" I asked.

"There is to be a spectacle which he wishes you to see."

"And my sister?"

"You only, I believe. You are to go with me and with Richard Rackell."

I was puzzled.

It was a warm day and the sun beat down on us as we rode our mules into the town. There were crowds coming in from the countryside, all making their way into the city.

I said: "I have never seen so many people here. It must be a great festival."

"You will see," said John Gregory quietly.

I studied him; I had come to know since our sessions together that he was a man with secrets. For one thing he was English. Why then should he have Spanish masters? I had already noted the marks on his cheeks and wrists. I had seen another on his neck. Sometimes in his instruction he seemed overfervent, at other almost languid. I had tried to ask him questions about himself, but he was always evasive.

Now I realized that he was deeply moved.

I said: "Has something happened to disturb you, John Gregory?"

He shook his head.

There were crowds of people in the square. Several stands had been erected; I was led to one of these most ornately decorated with an emblem blazoned on it.

I mounted to the platform. There was a bench on which I sat. John Gregory was on one side and other members from the household on the other.

"What is going to happen?" I asked Gregory.

He whispered: "Do not speak in English. Speak Spanish and quietly. 'Tis better that it were not known you are alien."

A sense of horror then began to take hold of me. I guessed now that what I was about to witness was something so horrifying that I had only visualized such happenings in my nightmares. I recalled those days when the smell of smoke had come drifting down the river from Springfield. I had now seen the piles of fagots and I knew what they meant. Recalling my last conversation with Don Felipe, I realized now why he had wished me to come here.

I said to Gregory: "I feel ill. I want to go back."

"It is too late," he said.

"This will be bad for my child."

He only repeated: "It is too late now."

Never shall I forget that afternoon. The heat, the square, the chanting of voices, the tolling of Cathedral bells; the figures in their robes, their hoods covering their faces and their eyes looking out through the slits, menacing and terrifying. None could have been unaware that something horrifying was about to be enacted.

I wanted to shut out the scene. I longed to get up and go. As I half rose in my seat John Gregory's arm was firm around me, holding me in my place.

"I can't bear this," I whispered.

He whispered back: "You must. You dare not go. You would be seen."

I half closed my eyes, but something within me forced me to open them.

Even now it is vivid in my memory; it is like a kaleidoscope changing first here, first there, until the complete horror was before me.

People had crowded into the square; only the center was left clear for the hideous tragedy to be played out. I looked into that sea of faces and I wondered if any among them had come to look on the dying agonies of a loved one. Were they all "good Catholics"? Did their faith in their religion which was said to be based on the love of their fellowmen blind them to the misery they were about to behold? Could they reconcile themselves to this cruel intolerance because they believed that men and women who thought differently from them should die? I wanted to get up and shout to these people, to rise up against cruelty and intolerance.

And then they came—the wretched victims in the tragic sanbenito—that shapeless gown with flames and devils painted on it—their faces gray from long incarceration in dank foul cells; some had been so cruelly tortured that they could not walk. I was about to cover my face with my hands when John Gregory whispered: "No. Remember you will be watched."

So I sat there, my eyes lowered that I might not look on this fearful scene.

Suddenly all had risen; they were chanting words which I realized was the Oath of Allegiance to the Inquisition. John Gregory had moved in front of me so that I was hidden from view. I felt sick and ready to faint. My child stirred then as though to remind me that for its sake I must feign to be one of these people and pretend to accept their beliefs. This was why I had come here. It was Don Felipe's way of telling me in what danger I stood. *I* could so easily be one of those people below in the yellow sanbenito; I could be led to my pile of fagots to be bound there while they crackled into flame below me.

I owed it to the child to live. Nor did I wish to die. Once again I knew that I would cling to life no matter what it held for me.

I was there when the fires were lighted. I saw that the authorities were merciful to some because they strangled them before committing their bodies to the flames. The unrepentant, those who declared they would cling to their beliefs, were not given that benefit; the flames were lighted under them while they still lived.

I sat there and I remembered the fires of Smithfield and the day when my mother's stepfather was taken away. I remembered that my grandfather had died by the ax for sheltering a priest and my mother's stepfather had burned at the stake for following the Reformed Religion; and a fierce hatred was born in me for all abuse of religion, Catholic or Protestant.

We must never have the Inquisition set up in England. I would tell them of this day when I reached home. We must fight against it with all our might.

And as I sat there I felt a great desire to crush all intolerance, to fight all cruelty.

I heard the cries of agony as the flames licked already mutilated mangled bodies.

"Oh, God," I prayed, "take me away from this. Take me home."

I lay on the bed in my darkened room. I had felt faint on the way home and found it difficult to sit my mule. As soon as I was in the house I went to my bedroom and lay on the bed.

I could not get the sight of what I had seen out of my mind.

Don Felipe came in and sat by the bed. He was in riding habit, so he had evidently just returned to the

Hacienda. It was significant that he had come first to me.

"You attended the *auto-da-fé*," he said.

"I hope never to witness such a spectacle again," I cried. "And most of all I marvel that this is done in the name of Christ."

"I wished you to see for yourself, to realize the danger," he said gently. "It was to warn you."

"Would you not be glad to see me among those poor creatures? It would be a new turn to your revenge."

"It does not come into my plan," he said.

I lay very still looking up at that ceiling carved with angels ascending to heaven and I said: "Don Felipe, I hate what I have seen today. I hate your country. I hate your cold and calculating cruelty. You believe yourself to be a religious man. You say your prayers with regularity. You thank God daily that you are not as other men. You have influence and riches and, chief of all, you have pride. Is this goodness, think you? Those men who were murdered today, do you think they are so much more sinful than you are?"

"They are heretics," he said.

"They dared to think differently from you. They worship the same God but with a difference; therefore, they are condemned to the flames. Did not Jesus Christ tell you to love your neighbor and is this not your neighbor?"

"You have seen today what happens to heretics. I ask you to take care."

"Because I am a heretic. Must I change my faith because I fear the cruelty of wicked men?"

"Be silent. You are foolish. I have told you there may be those to overhear. What you have seen today is a warning. I want you to understand the danger in which you could be placed. You waste your sympathy on these heretics. They are doomed to burn for eternity in hell. What can twenty minutes on earth matter?"

"They will not go to hell—those martyrs. It is the cruel men who have gloated on their misery who will go to eternal damnation."

"I have tried to save you."

"Why?"

"Because I wish to see the child born."

"And when he is born he and I shall leave your hateful

land. I shall go home. I long for that day."

"You are overwrought," he said. "Rest awhile. I will send them up with a soothing draft for you."

When he had gone I lay there thinking of him; it was relief to stop brooding on that terrible scene; and I marveled at his tolerance toward me. I had said enough to condemn me to the questioning and the torture by the Inquisition; yet he was gentle with me. He had given me little Carlos . . . and when I thought of that child and the one not yet born I despised myself for giving vent to my feelings. I must be careful. I must preserve myself . . . for them. I must do nothing to imperil my position. I should be grateful to Don Felipe for showing me the danger into which I could so quickly fall.

I listened to John Gregory. I could say the Credo. I could answer the questions he put to me. I was making progress.

We talked a little now and then. He was a sad and haunted man and I was certain he regretted having taken part in that operation which had brought me here.

One day after the instruction I said: "You would have a story to tell if you would but tell it."

"Aye," he agreed.

"You are sad sometimes, are you not?"

He did not answer and I went on: "You, an Englishman, to sell yourself to Spanish masters?"

"It came about in such a way that I could have done no other than I did."

And gradually he told me his story.

"I was an English seaman," he said. "I sailed under Captain Pennlyon."

"So you did know him?"

"I was fearful when we came face to face that he would recognize me; and he did know me. I was terrified that he would realize who I was when he saw me in Devon."

"He said that he believed he had seen you before."

"Aye, he had, but in different garb. He knew me as an English seaman, a member of his crew. This I was and this doubtless I should have been to this day, but I was captured. We had come through a storm, great seas lashed about us. Nor should we have expected to live through it but for our Captain, Jake Pennlyon. To see him roaring up and down the deck, giving orders, promising those who disobeyed him that damnation in hell would be preferable to the punishment he would give them, was a grand sight to weary frightened sailors. There is a legend among sailors that the Pennlyons are invincible."

They were not wrecked, which seemed somehow due to the skill of Jake Pennlyon. They needed to limp into port though to refit and while they were there John Gregory with others of the crew set off in a pinnace to explore the seas to discover what manner of place they were laid up in.

"We were boarded by a Spaniard," said John Gregory, "and we were taken back to Spain."

"And there?"

"Handed over to the Inquisition."

"There are scars on your cheek and wrists . . . on your neck . . . and there are doubtless others."

"There are. I have been tortured as I never thought to be. I have been condemned to the flames."

"You have come near to terrible death, John Gregory. What brought you back from it?"

"They realized that they could make good use of me. I was an Englishman who had embraced their religion under duress. I asked that I might become a priest. They had tortured me, remember. I knew what it meant to die a horrible death. I recanted. And I was given my freedom. I could not understand why. They were rarely so lenient; and then I realized that I was to be used as a spy. I made several trips to England during the last Queen's reign. And then I was put into service with Don Felipe and he sent me on this mission."

"Why did you not stay in England when you had the opportunity?"

"I had become a Catholic and I feared what would happen to me if I ever fell into their hands again."

"What if you had been caught spying in England?"

He raised his shoulders and lifted his eyes.

I went on: "And Richard Rackell?"

"He is an English Catholic working for Spain."

"And Don Felipe sent you over to help him complete his revenge. And you were willing to come!"

"Not willing, but knowing no alternative. For the sake of your child you will forget your pride and your principles. So it is with the others. My life is precious to me. Remember that I suffered torture at the hands of the Inquisition. Because of that I changed my faith. I worked against my own countrymen to save my body from further torture and that I might go on living."

"The temptation was great," I said.

"I trust you will think a little less hardly of me."

"Suffice it that I understand your dilemma. It was your body to be saved from torture, your life from extinction."

He breathed freely.

"I have wanted to tell you for so long and as we sat there on that afternoon in the plaza I determined that I would."

I nodded and he rested his chin on his hands and looked back . . . far into the past, I imagined, before he had entered the prison of the Spanish Inquisition, before he had come to England and abducted three innocent women; long before, when he was an innocent sailor under Captain Jake Pennlyon.

I went to the Cathedral; I confessed my sins to the priest who was in residence at the Hacienda; I lit my candles to the saints and sprinkled myself with Holy Water.

I would feign to do what was expected of me until my child was born.

I longed for the day. I talked of little else. I yearned now for the long months of waiting to be over.

Don Felipe now and then invited me to sup with him. I looked forward to these encounters. I knew that he was not as indifferent to me as he would have me believe, or why invite me to sup with him?

I was now heavy with child. The summer months had passed and I expected my confinement to be in January. The midwife visited me regularly. It was on the orders of Don Felipe that she did so. She used to laugh and shake her head. "This child is to have everything of the best," she said. "Don Felipe's orders . . . none less." She was proud of her English and liked to air it. "It was a different matter when that other poor infant came into the world."

She meant Carlos and I wondered what had happened when the poor mad Isabella was expecting her son. And it seemed ironical that the child of his wife should have been so ill received while mine was to be ushered into the world with everything to ease his coming.

His pride again, I thought, for after all, this child is his.

A new relationship had sprung up between us.

He told me now and then what was happening at home, always with a biased flavor which I learned to ignore. Our suppers were an escape from the company of Honey and Jennet. Not that I sought to avoid that. Honey's serenity, Jennet's delight in her situation were a continual solace to me. Carlos had taken to them too. Jennet adored him. He was only second to her own Jacko; and indeed the two boys were growing more alike every day. It made me laugh for the very incongruity of it. Two sons of Jake Pennlyon were here with us and he did not know of their existence.

Don Felipe clearly had an immense interest in England, and so it seemed had others in Spain, for it was through Spain and the visitors who called at the Hacienda from that land that he received his information.

He was chagrined to admit that events had not turned out as he had prophesied. He had believed that the end of Elizabeth's reign was in sight when the wife of Robert Dudley, the man on whom she had set her heart, was found dead at the bottom of a staircase. But Elizabeth had come through that affair with an unquestionable ease. There might have been rumors, but nothing was proved against her, and there was no marriage with Dudley.

"She is cleverer than so many of us thought," ruminated Don Felipe as we sat at the table together. "To have taken Dudley as her husband could only have been done at the cost of her crown and she knew it. She has made her decision clear. Dudley is not worth a crown."

"So you admire her cleverness?"

"She has shown a certain wisdom in this matter," he said.

On another occasion he talked of the death of the

young King of France, François Deux, which took place in December of the last year although it was only now that we heard of it.

Don Felipe was excited by this news because of the effect it had on the Queen of Scotland.

François had died of an imposthume of the ear; and his young Queen, Mary of Scotland, had found there was no place for her in France. So she must return to her kingdom of Scotland.

"She will be less powerful now," I said.

He answered: "She will be more of a threat to the woman who calls herself Queen of England."

"I doubt our Queen cares overmuch for the people beyond the border."

"She will have supporters everywhere, not only in Scotland but in France; and I am of the opinion that there are many Catholic gentlemen in England who would rally to her standard if she were to travel south."

"So you wish for a civil war in my country?"

He did not answer; there was no need.

Life passed by smoothly; the days of my pregnancy were drawing to a close and I longed for my child to be born. I was shut into a little cocoon of contentment.

The preparations for the birth were almost ceremonious. The midwife was already installed in the house when my labor began; I went to the bedroom—that room of many memories—and it was there that my child was born.

I shall never forget the moment when he was laid in my arms. He was small . . . much smaller than Jacko had been, he had dark eyes and there was a down of dark hairs on his head.

I thought as soon as I saw him: My little Spaniard!

I delighted in him. I held him against me and I felt love overwhelm me, love such as I had never known for any other living being—except perhaps once for Carey. But there was no barrier between me and this child. He was my very own.

And as I held him in my arms Don Felipe came into the room. He stood by the bed and momentarily I remembered his standing there with the candle in his hand when I had feigned to be asleep.

I held the baby out for him to see and he looked at him in wonder and I saw the faintest color in his olive cheeks. Then his eyes met mine; they glowed with a luminosity I had never seen in them before.

I thought: It is the fulfillment of revenge.

Then he was looking at me; his gaze embraced us both and I was not sure what was in his thoughts.

Don Felipe ordained that the child should be called Roberto. I said that for me he should be Robert; but somehow I was soon calling him Roberto. It suited him better.

He was baptized in the chapel of the Hacienda with all the pomp that would have been to the son of the house.

During the first weeks after his birth I thought of nothing beyond his welfare. Remembering how Honey used to feel because she had come before me and was not my mother's own, I wanted no such heartaches for little Carlos. I tried to make him interested in the child, and he was; he took a protective attitude toward him because he was mine and was gentle with him. We were a happy little nursery. Jennet was in her element with babies; the fact that hers and mine were illegitimate worried her not in the least.

"Law bless us," she said on one occasion, "they'm babies . . . little 'uns. That be good enough for the likes of I."

Don Felipe often came to the nursery to see the child. I had seen him, bending over the cradle, staring at him. I knew that it satisfied his pride to have such a son.

One day I went into the *escritorio* and said to Don Felipe: "Your plan is complete. I have your child. Is it not time for you to keep to your promise? You have said we should go back to our homes."

"The child is too young to travel," he said. "You must wait until he is a little older."

"How much older?" I asked.

"Would you take a child of a few months on the high seas?"

I hesitated. I thought of the storms and calms; I thought

of the faces of sailors driven a little crazy by long days at sea.

I said: "We should have gone before the child was born."

"Wait awhile," he said. "Wait until he is older."

I went back to my room and brooded on what he had said.

I laughed inwardly. He loves his son and does not want to lose him. Love! What does such a man know of love? He is proud of his son. Who could not be of Roberto? And he doesn't want to lose him.

We lacked nothing. Anything we wanted we had. The only condition that was asked of us was that we show ourselves to be good Catholics. That was easy for Honey and Jennet because they were. As for myself: I had my children, Roberto and Carlos, to think of, and children were more important to me than my faith. I was not of the stuff that martyrs were made.

Don Felipe's attitude changed toward me. He wished me to dine with him frequently. He would come into the garden where I sat with the children; and he even spoke now and then to Carlos, who began to lose his fear of him. But it was Roberto who enchanted him. There could be little doubt that the child was his. Already Roberto had a look of him. Strangely enough it did not repel me, only amuse me; and I loved Roberto nonetheless for that. In the same way I could see Jake Pennlyon clearly in Carlos and that somehow endeared the child to me.

And the months began to slip away without incident. Roberto was six months old and the winter was almost upon us.

I said to Don Felipe: "He is older now. We shall be going soon."

"Wait for the winter to pass," said Don Felipe.

And then the spring came and Roberto was one year old.

The Wives of Don Felipe

I had dined with Don Felipe and we sat in the light of the candles and talked of Roberto: how he had a tooth, how he was crawling; how I was sure he had said: "Madre."

Then I lifted my eyes and looking at him intently, I said: "I often think of my home. What news is there of England?"

"Nothing of interest. All I can think of is that the spire of St. Paul's Cathedral was burned down and that although it was supposed it was struck by lightning a workman had now confessed—on his deathbed—that a pan of coals was carelessly left in a steeple."

It must have been a mighty conflagration. They would have seen it in the sky along the river. My grandmother would have come into her garden to watch; and perhaps my mother would be with her. They would remember perhaps the way the smoke used to drift along from

Smithfield. And my mother would remember her two girls who were lost to her.

"Darling Cat and Honey," she would say. There would be tears in her eyes. How lonely she must be without us.

He said: "Of what are you thinking?"

"Of my mother. She will be sad thinking of me and my sister. Both of us to have been snatched away. What a tragedy for her and there have been so many tragedies in her life."

I was silent and then he said: "You are smiling now."

"I am thinking of our going back. She will love Roberto, her grandson. Dearly she loves children. I think I inherited that from her. And Carlos shall not be forgotten. I shall say, 'Mother, this is my adopted son as Honey was your adopted daughter. He belongs with us now.' We shall be happy again."

His face was impassive and I went on: "Roberto is one year old. He is old enough to travel. Now you must keep your promise. It is time for us to go back."

He shook his head. "You cannot take the child," he said.

"Not take my son!"

"He is my son too."

"Your son. What is he to you?"

"He is my son."

"But this child is part of me. He is my own. I would never give him up."

"He is part of me. Nor shall *I* give him up." He smiled at me gently. "How your eyes blaze! There is an alternative. I would not rob a mother of her child, and as I will not give up my son, if you will keep him you must stay here."

I was silent. Then I said: "Always you have led me to understand that you wished me no ill."

"Nor do I."

"You have told me that it is only because of a vow you made that I am here. You led me to believe that when you had fulfilled that vow I should be at liberty to go."

"You are at liberty . . . but not to take the child with you."

I stood up. I wanted to get away to think. He was at the door before me, barring it.

"You will never leave your child," he said. "Why not accept what cannot be avoided? You can be happy here. What is it you want? Ask me and it shall be yours."

"I want to go home, to England."

"Ask anything but that."

"It is what I want."

"Then go."

"And leave my child behind?"

"He shall lack nothing. He is my son."

"I believe you are glad that he is born."

"I was never more pleased with anything."

"You could have been had he been born of Isabella."

"He would not have been Roberto. He has something of you in him."

"And that pleases you?"

"It pleases me, for if you ever went away there would be something to remind me."

"And you *wish* to be reminded?"

"I do not need the reminder. I shall never forget."

Then he drew me to him and held me against him.

"I would," he said, "that we could have more sons like this one."

"How could that be?"

"It is not beyond your power to understand."

"You have a wife. Have you forgotten?"

"How could I forget?"

I said: "You never see her."

"She screams at the sight of me."

"She could be cured."

"She can never be cured."

"You loved her once."

"I have loved one woman," he said. "I still love her. I shall do so to the end of my life." He looked steadily at me.

"You cannot tell me that you feel love for me, your victim? You hated coming to me as much as I hated it. You had to pretend I was Isabella. You had to remind yourself constantly of your vow."

He took my hands and held first one to his lips and then the other.

"If you loved me," I said, "you would wish to please me. You would let me go."

"Ask anything but that," he said.

I felt exultant. It was a victory. Fate had turned the tables. He was at my mercy now, not I at his.

"Tell me," he went on, "that you do not harbor resentment against me. Tell me that you do not hate me."

"No," I said, "I don't hate you. In a way I'm fond of you. You have been kind to me . . . apart from your violation of me, and that I will admit was conducted in a courteous manner . . . if one can imagine rape so being. You have tried to save me from the evil laws of your country. But you do not love me well enough to make me happy, which you would do by letting us go."

"You ask too much," he said. "It will be different now. You do not hate me. Could you grow fond of me?"

I said: "You cannot offer me marriage, Don Felipe, which could be the only gateway to the path you suggest."

"Tell me this," he said, "if I could. . . ."

"But, Don Felipe, you cannot. You have a wife. I know she is mad and no wife to you and that is a grievous state of affairs. I know that Jake Pennlyon was in part responsible. But was he entirely so? How mad was Isabella before she came here? Let me go now. I want to think of what you have said."

He stood back, but he still held my hands; then he kissed them with a passion unfamiliar to him. I withdrew them and with a wildly beating heart went to my room and shut myself in to think of this revelation.

Don Felipe left next morning. I had spent a disturbed night. That I could consider the possibility of marriage with him seemed absurd. Yet it was not so. He was the father of my beloved child and the child was a bond between us. Roberto was already beginning to show an awareness of him and Don Felipe was always gentle and tender toward him.

It's ridiculous, I said; but I had to confess that I was intrigued by the situation.

I was a little disappointed to learn that he had left the Hacienda. I was restless and wanted to know more about his feelings for Isabella.

That afternoon, when most people were indulging in the siesta, I left Jennet in charge of the children and wandered off in the direction of Isabella's house.

The sun was warm; everything seemed sleeping behind the wrought-iron gate; and as I stood there the subject of my thoughts appeared in the doorway. She was carrying the doll I had seen before and as she walked across the patio she saw me. She hesitated. I smiled and she came toward me, murmuring a greeting. I knew enough Spanish now to be able to converse a little, so I replied. She stood looking at me, which gave me an opportunity to study her features. If beauty is perfection of feature, then she was indeed beautiful. Her face was without blemish and without expression; this was indeed a beautiful shell; there was no intellect to give character to the face.

She held out the doll to me. I smiled and she smiled too. Then she opened the gate and I went into the patio.

I had not been there since that day when I had taken Carlos away. She took my hand confidingly and led me to the seat. We sat down and she chattered about her doll. I gathered that she took the doll everywhere with her. She kept saying the word *muñeca*. Pilar made clothes for it which came on and off.

Then suddenly her face puckered; she showed me that the doll was wearing only one shoe.

"She has dropped it," I said. "We'll look."

She nodded conspiratorially and I began to search the patio while she followed me around. I was delighted to find the shoe near the gate. She clasped her hands and we went back to the seat and put it on the doll.

Suddenly she stood up and, taking my hand, drew me toward the door and led me into the house. I noticed the faint perfume with which I had become familiar; it was dark inside, for the house, like the Hacienda, had been built to shut out the sun.

There was an imposing staircase leading from the hall with its blue mosaic floor. The banisters were exquisitely carved and the ceiling of this hall was painted with angels floating on clouds. It was more splendid than I had thought it would be.

Isabella, still holding my hand, took us into a room which led from this hall; it was dark as I had come to expect and there was in it a brooding sense of mystery —or perhaps that was my mood.

Isabella indicated that I should sit down. Pilar appeared suddenly and hovered at the door. Isabella began to talk excitedly about the doll's shoe which I had found and then she announced that she wanted to show me more of her dolls. I should come up and see.

"Bring them down, Isabella," said Pilar.

Isabella pouted.

"Oh, yes, that is best," said Pilar. "Come, we will go and get them."

She took Isabella by the hand and I was left alone in the room. I looked about me at the rich draperies and the elegant Spanish furniture. This was his house, I thought, and she is his wife for all that she had the mind of a child.

It was a strange situation into which I had been thrust. I kept thinking of the passion in his eyes when he had said he would marry me. How could he while this childlike creature stood in his way?

The door opened suddenly and a young girl came in. She had dark hair and big dark eyes in an olive-colored heart-shaped face.

She said: "Señorita, forgive me."

"Who are you?" I asked.

"I am Manuela and I work here. I wish to speak to you if I may, Señorita."

"What is it you wish to say?"

"It is the boy . . . the little fellow." Her face was illuminated by a pleasant smile. "Carlos."

"Oh, yes."

"I wanted to know. He is happy now?"

"He is happier than he has ever been."

She smiled. "He is a good boy," she said. "What a boy. María was so cruel to him."

"María? Is that the woman who lives here?" I waved my hand in the direction of the courtyard where I had first seen Carlos playing.

She nodded. "She was the boy's foster mother. It was wrong. She is a stupid woman. . . . She has no love for children though she has five of her own. The boy should not have been put with her. I used to speak to him."

I warmed to her. She had been kind to Carlos; I could see by her face.

"You need no longer worry," I told her. "I shall see that Carlos is well looked after."

"I used to take him sweetmeats. Poor child, he had no love, and children need love as they need sweetmeats. Thank you for taking him away, Señorita."

"You must come and see Carlos for yourself."

"May I? You are good."

I said: "What work do you do here?"

A faint frown appeared between her eyes. "I help in the boudoir. I am Doña Isabella's maid."

"You are not happy?"

"I love children, Señorita. Doña Isabella is a child in so many ways."

"I see," I said. She curtsied suddenly and hurried out. I wondered whether she had heard footsteps, for very shortly afterward the woman Pilar came in. Isabella was not with her.

"She is sleeping," said Pilar. "You understand. When she reached her room she had forgotten you. It is thus sometimes."

"Poor soul," I said.

"Poor soul indeed."

"Did I do wrong to speak to her?"

"She was happy to speak with you and you found the doll's shoe, which pleased her. But she forgets from time to time."

I said: "This did not happen overnight."

She was silent for a while. Then she said: "She was always a little simple. She could not learn her lessons; it was not important with a lady of such high degree. She was destined to make a good marriage; her dowry was great; her family had connections with the royal house."

"So her simplicity did not matter."

"It was thought she would be a good wife . . . she would produce children and she was betrothed to Don Felipe. He is a nobleman of some wealth and he was high in favor at Court. It was a good match."

"Even though she still played with her dolls."

"She was a child. Fifteen. We used to say: Wait until she has a child of her own; then she will grow up." Pilar's eyes narrowed. "If I could lay my hands on her ravisher I would inflict on him such tortures that the world has never known. He has ruined this young life."

"Was it not ruined before he came? From birth she was not as other children are."

"She would have grown out of it; she would have had children."

I was not convinced. I did not wish to defend Jake Pennlyon; he had wantonly satisfied his lust and this girl was the victim. But the blame for her plight did not lie solely with him, yet he had shocked her into some sort of awakening which was like a nightmare; he had crudely broken into her half-formed mind.

I said: "Would you prefer me not to come here?"

"No," she said. "Come when you wish. You understand her. You do her good. You have taken the child. That is good. He is no longer a burden to us. I cannot understand how you persuaded Don Felipe to keep him at the Hacienda."

She looked at me searchingly and I wondered how much she knew. Would she be aware that I had been brought here to satisfy Don Felipe's lust for revenge?

As I went out I saw a man working in the gardens. He was very tall and broad for a Spaniard. He stood up and touched his cap when he saw me. Pilar led me to the gate.

"That was Edmundo," she said. "He is strong and can help me if need be. He knows what to do if Isabella is ill. He can pick her up and carry her with the greatest ease."

I said good-bye and told her I would come and see Isabella very soon.

I told Honey what had happened, but she did not yet know, of course, that Don Felipe had talked to me of marriage.

We thought it sad that Isabella had been simpleminded and that it was incongruous that she should have been given in marriage to such a fastidious and intellectual man as Don Felipe.

I told her about the girl Manuela who had asked after Carlos.

"She was rather wistful," I said. "She must have been fond of him."

"We could do with help in the nursery. Do you think she could come here?"

"I'm sure of it," I said, certain that Don Felipe would not refuse me such a request.

We discussed Isabella's preoccupation with her dolls and Honey suggested we make doll's clothes and take them to her. We did this—making a gown from some pieces of velvet and a lovely ruff in stiff lace.

Isabella was delighted when we took them to the Casa Azul. That was a peaceful afternoon. We sat in the patio and she had two dolls which she proudly showed us. She cried out with delight when she tried on the velvet gown which fitted the doll perfectly.

Pilar brought out a mint drink and with it some little spiced cakes. Isabella laughed gaily and prattled as a child will about the doings of her dolls.

The fact that Isabella was made happy by our coming meant that Pilar welcomed us.

After that afternoon we frequently called. Isabella would be waiting for us in the patio. Now and then we saw the big Edmundo at work in the gardens keeping his eyes on Isabella. Manuela was there sometimes, which gave Honey an opportunity to assess her. She thought she would make an excellent addition to our nursery.

And so the days passed until Don Felipe came back to the Hacienda.

The day he returned he asked me to come to the *escritorio*. Our meetings always took place there. Other rooms would not have afforded us the secrecy we needed; and the apartment which had become mine held too many memories of our first encounters which I knew would have been distasteful to him.

As soon as I entered he came to me and took my hands in his and kissed them with fervor.

"There is much I have to say to you," he said. "I have been turning over these things in my mind while I have been away. I must find some way of bringing about our union. If I do not my life is as wasteful as the desert. I know that you do not hate me, Catalina." He said my name lingeringly, giving it a quality it had not had before. "You could bring yourself to marry me."

"But there is no question of marriage. How could there be?"

He sighed. "I have debated the matter with myself. A dispensation from the Pope would be impossible, I fear. Yet I have no hope of legitimate sons if I do not remarry; I could give sons to the church, to my country. Isabella's family is influential, more so than my own. A dispensation would never be granted."

"Then it is useless to continue these suppositions."

"There must be a way. There is always a way. I must tell you this—in a short time Don Luis Herrera will be arriving. He is going to take over the governorship from me, but not immediately. He will need a year, perhaps more, to learn what I have to teach him. These islands are of the utmost value to Spain; they are the gateway to the new world. We must hold them and we are continually assailed. Therefore, the new Governor must understand what is expected of him. In a year . . . two at most , , , I shall return to Madrid. Catalina, I am going to take you with me . . . as my wife."

"Do Spanish Dons have two wives then?"

"She is not healthy, poor Isabella," he said slowly. "These fits are becoming more frequent."

"You are willing to let her die."

He was silent for a moment and then he said: "What can her life be? What has she?"

"She seems happy enough with her dolls."

"Dolls—and she a grown woman!"

"She is not a woman. She is a child. You loved her once."

He looked at me steadily. "I have loved but once, and I shall go on loving one woman to the end of my days."

"Don Felipe!"

"Do not say Don Felipe. To you I am Felipe. Say it as though you are close to me. It would give me great pleasure to hear you."

"When I say it I will say it naturally."

"It will happen," he said. "I know it."

"So you never loved Isabella," I insisted. "Tell me the truth."

"It was a worthy match. Hers is one of the greatest families in Spain."

"So it was for this reason only that you wished to marry her?"

"It is for such reason that marriages are arranged."

"And when you came back and found her after Jake Pennlyon had been, you were mad with rage, not for love of this simpleminded child but because of the affront to your pride. This had happened to her when she was under your protection. That was why you vowed to be revenged."

"Yet," he said, "all this has brought me to you."

"It is better to say no more of that. Let me go back to England. My son is old enough to travel now."

"And lose you both!"

"It is better for you. You are a man of great standing. You will go back to Madrid and take up a post of great importance. Perhaps in due course you will be in a position to marry. Who can say? But you should let me go."

"I cannot lose both you and the child. You are more to me than anything on Earth."

The fact that he spoke these words in a quiet, restrained manner gave them force. I was suddenly afraid of the passion which I had aroused in this cold man.

He began to talk eagerly. "If we were married I could legitimize Roberto. I have rich lands and estates in Spain. He should be my heir and there would be a goodly portion for other children we might have. We should live graciously. Perhaps I should retire from the Court. Our children would have every comfort that you would wish for them."

I let myself dwell on the prospect, which was strange because although I loved Roberto beyond everything and in a way wanted those rich estates for him, I longed for home. I wanted to see my mother, to witness the happiness in her face when she knew that her girls were safe and alive; I wanted to see the fruit trees in blossom in the spring. In short, I wanted to go home.

I said to him: "You speak of dreams. You have a wife. I am sorry for you. I am sorry for us all. But Isabella stands between you and what you hope for."

And I left him because I wanted to brood on my feelings which were by no means clear to me. There were times when I felt a great relief because Isabella stood between us and there could be no change in our relationship because of this; but at others I was not so sure.

Weeks grew into months. There was an uneasy tension in the house. I was constantly aware of Felipe's brooding eyes on me. He often visited the nurseries and Roberto, who knew him well, used to clap his hands when he saw him.

Manuela had joined Jennet there and although the two of them were not as friendly as I would have wished them to be there was no outward friction.

My son was nearly two years old. So it was three years since we had left England. Much of it seemed far away, but there were moments which I could remember with such clarity that they might have happened but a day before; and most of these concerned my mother. If I could have seen her and if she could live close to me and if there had been no Isabella I think I would have agreed to marry Felipe.

I was not in love with him; but it was impossible to live in the Hacienda and not respect him. His dignity was unquestionable. His justice was apparent in his treatment of those who offended—not that many dared. He was admirable. He was a man of power and a man in command appealed to me. I knew what marriage would entail with him; he would be no stranger in my bed. I knew that I could expect courtesy, gentleness and now a tenderness in our relationship. He loved me with a quiet intensity which I found comforting. I could see a pleasant life opening out before me. I did not expect to love, as I had loved Carey, but I could accept Felipe, and I thought of all the advantages he could bring to me and my son. Roberto would be heir to vast estates. He would receive the best of educations. He would be brought up in the Catholic church, of course, and he would go to Spain and the fact that he had an English mother would be no hindrance with the power of Don Felipe behind him.

During one of my talks with Felipe I said as much. It would be different if Isabella were not there. On the other hand, I was thankful to her. She prevented my having to make a decision which would have been immensely difficult for me.

So during that time I was living in a period of indecision. I knew now that Don Felipe would never allow me to return to England—either with or without my child. Not that I would consider going without Roberto. And I knew too that Isabella stood between our making any decision.

That this was just an intermediary period was brought home to us by the arrival of Luis Herrera, the man who would in time take Felipe's place.

Don Luis was a handsome man, slightly younger than Felipe—charming, good-looking, courteous. It was apparent from the first moment that he saw Honey that he was deeply affected by her.

Whenever I looked at her I wondered why Don Felipe should have set such store by me when Honey was there. She was superbly beautiful with her violet eyes and dark hair. I knew that she lacked my vitality; she was no fighter, as I was; it had always been her way to let life flow over her, or if she did feel strongly to brood over it and withdraw into herself.

However, she did none of this with Don Luis and it was clear that they liked each other's company from the start.

Don Luis brought news from the outside world. The four of us dined together—Honey and Luis, myself and Felipe. Felipe's excuse for this was that it made a pleasant party.

Luis talked a great deal about England. Since we had left, the rivalry between Spain and England had intensified. We heard that the Queen, so unsafe did she feel on the throne, had imprisoned the Lady Catherine Grey—who had some claim—in the Tower for marrying without royal permission.

"She is afraid that there will be offspring to challenge her rights," said Don Luis. "Yet she remains unmarried. And how can an unmarried woman beget heirs?"

I winced, but only Felipe noticed.

"She has been mightily sick of the smallpox and it was feared in England, though hoped in Spain, that she would die. Even then she refused to appoint an heir."

"You forget, Don Luis," I said, "that you speak of our Queen."

"A thousand pardons. I thought but to give you the truth."

"Of course we want the truth," I replied. "But if our Queen refuses to appoint an heir it is because she knows that many years are left to her and she will beget her own."

Don Luis was too polite to debate the point.

Honey laid a hand on his arm. "Don't let Catalina"— they had all begun to call me Catalina—"stop your telling us the news. We long to hear it."

"I'll tell you something else," said Luis. "One of your Captains, John Hawkins, has started dealing in slaves."

"Dealing in slaves!" I cried.

"Indeed he has. He has fitted three ships and taken them to the Guinea Coast. There he captures Negroes and takes them to that part of the world where he thinks to get the highest price for them."

"You mean he just picks people as though they were . . . plants and takes them away from their families. It's monstrous."

Felipe was regarding me steadily.

I saw myself . . . a slave. I saw my little Roberto snatched from me . . . perhaps taken from me to be a slave himself or left behind while I was carried away in chains. I have always, I think, more than most people, put myself in the places of others; it was one of the reasons I waxed vehement when I thought justice had failed to be done.

Felipe said: "Your English Captain Hawkins has done this. You should not hanker for that island of yours. Is it not true, Luis, that some of the ships used by Hawkins belonged to the Queen of England? And this, Catalina, sets her seal of approval on this horrible trade."

Luis said: "You should be thankful that you are here. . . ." And he smiled at us both. "Perhaps we all have reasons to be thankful." He threw a soulful look in Honey's direction. "For life goes on uncertainly in your island. Each day the English become a greater menace to us on the high seas. We are a great and powerful nation. We intend to colonize the whole world. And one day we shall take over your island too. You will become a vassal of Spain."

"You do not know us," I said fiercely. And I thought of Jake Pennlyon then. I would stake all I had on him when set against these courtly gentlemen. Even hating him as I did, I knew that his courage was supreme and his love of his country as natural to him as drawing breath.

"We begin to," said Luis, smiling gently. "A formidable enemy. Our most formidable! There should be peace between us. We should unite without fighting."

"That could never be," I said.

"I think so too," put in Felipe gently, "but it is a pity."

"Your country is losing her possessions on the continent of Europe," went on Luis. "Warwick has surrendered Le Havre to the French. The English will never regain a foothold in France and the only spoils of war which Warwick has brought back to England from France are the plagues. Twenty thousand persons have been carried off by one in and around the city of London."

I turned pale thinking of my mother and the old days when the sweating sickness had visited the Capital.

It was good to hear news of England though, even if it was not good news. I believed that it was colored to be advantageous to Spain and I could understand that; but how strange it was that the men who loved us (for Luis clearly was in love with Honey) should have been so gratified by the misfortunes which befell those who were dear to us.

Honey explained to me: "I have been without a husband so long, Catalina. I am young."

"You are older than I."

"But young. Admit it, Catalina. And I am fond of Luis."

"You are not in love with him."

"I can settle for him."

"And Edward?"

"Edward is dead. You know, don't you, that we are never going to leave this place. We shall spend the rest of our time here. Even if Don Felipe were willing to let us go, how could we? Could we sail to England in a Spanish galleon and be rowed ashore! 'Here are your women now returned to you!' Imagine that. They would have forgotten us at home. What should become of us?"

"You think Mother would ever forget us? Grandmother too. I long to be home with them."

"I want that too, but it is not to be. We know it is not to be. That is clear. Don Felipe loves you and he loves Roberto. He will never let you go. Be reasonable. He is a good man."

"A man who is so determined on revenge that he forces a woman to share his bed—not out of lust for her but for revenge."

"That is over."

"Over! For you perhaps. You were not violated."

"And that violation gave you Roberto, whom you love dearly. Try to look at life reasonably, sister. Sometimes good comes from evil. You were brought here against your will and the result is the son whom you love so deeply. The man who sought revenge has found love. Be reasonable. Life does not give you exactly what you most want, but it serves a very palatable dish. Be wise, Catalina, don't turn away from it."

"And become his mistress?"

"You would have all the honors of a wife."

I said coldly: "Talk of yourself, Honey, but leave me out of it."

"Well," she said, "I am going to marry Luis."

"A foreigner, and enemy of our country."

"What are countries to women who love? I am a woman. I have been long without a husband. I need a husband and Luis is good. He will be a father to Edwina."

I was silent, and she went on gently: "Perhaps you will go away from here after a while but, I shall stay, for Luis will be Governor in due course."

"Then we shall say good-bye."

"Only *au revoir*. Because, Catalina, when our spell is done, and it will not be more than eight years, we shall come to Madrid and there we shall see you in your beautiful home with Roberto and Carlos playing there with their brothers and sisters. Just think of it."

"A pretty picture," I said. "Marry your Luis if you so need to marry. Have your children. What matters it, one man is as good as another to some."

"Why do you speak thus? Ah, I know. It is because my way is plain. Yours is not. You are not indifferent to Felipe. You change when he is in the house. I am sorry, Catalina, that Isabella stands in your way."

"Isabella stands in your way." The phrase haunted me. I dreamed of Felipe often. And he was there at the side of my bed and Isabella was beside him—a pale, shadowy child with a doll in her arms.

Honey and Luis were married in the Cathedral. She was the most beautiful bride I had ever seen and there was about her that serene happiness which had been there before Edwina's birth.

Honey had always wanted to be loved, had blossomed with love; and there was no doubt that Luis adored her.

The wedding was celebrated at the Hacienda and there was feasting and the people of the surrounding villages were invited to come and dance which they did in the gardens. It was a wonderful sight with the girls and young men in the traditional costumes dancing the Andalusian dances which had been brought from the mainland. They danced and sang to the tunes played on the timple and I heard for the first time the *Isa* and the *Folias*.

Songs were sung praising the newly married couple and marriage in general, and afterward the bride and groom returned to the bedchamber and there was none of that ribaldry which would have accompanied such a ceremony at home.

That night I lay sleepless for a long time and I thought: We are farther from home than ever. Honey has accepted her fate and if we could go home now she would not leave her husband. Honey has become one of them. And how could I go and leave Honey here?

I thought: If my mother knew where I was; if I might see her now and then, I could do worse than marry Felipe. He would be a good and devoted husband; Roberto loved his father—how could I separate them?

I was becoming more and more convinced that my life lay here.

In my dreams I took Don Felipe's hand and I was to be married in the Cathedral, for I would adopt his faith; and then I heard the childish tinkling laughter of Isabella.

And I awoke with the words "Not while Isabella lives" ringing in my ears.

Felipe wished us to take a trip inland. . . .

It would be good for the children, he said. I had only seen the great mountain Pico de Teide from the sea. I should see how truly magnificent it was. He himself had to go to another part of the island, and while he was away our nursery should be transported to a house in the valley which he used sometimes. His servants would look after us. We would come back refreshed after our little holiday.

I knew that there was some motive behind this suggestion. Don Felipe was a man of mysteries. One would often wonder how much his inner feelings belied those which he expressed, but this, in a manner, was a source of fascination to me.

When I learned that there was to be an *auto-da-fé* in La Laguna I thought I understood. Members of his household would be expected to attend and I was known to be an important member of that household—the Governor's mistress. If I were absent, this would be noted. He did not wish to expose me to that which he knew was abhorrent to me; moreover, he would doubtless fear that I might betray my repulsion. Hence our trip into the mountains.

I was touched by his concern for me. I was beginning more and more to enjoy basking in his care for me.

We set out on mules with packhorses to carry all that we wished to take with us. We had a litter in which the children traveled and Honey, Jennet, Manuela and I took it in turns to ride with them. Sometimes we would carry one before us on our mule. It was a great game to them.

Carlos, with Jacko in his wake, was adventurous. What one would expect, I thought, of Jake Pennlyon's sons. I believe he had completely put behind him those nightmare days in the shack behind the Caza Azul. He was a child who would come through life unscathed, like his father. There was nothing of poor Isabella in him; he was all Jake Pennlyon. Jacko would be the same, for he followed Carlos in all things.

It was not a long journey, some thirty miles in all, and I was struck by the exotic beauty of the land. We passed a magnificent old dragon tree which was said to be over two thousand years old. I remembered that it was from the resin of this tree that the native Guanches stained their skins when they went in to do battle with their Spanish conquerors. John Gregory—with whom I had formed a kind of understanding—told me of this. Richard Rackell also accompanied us and we took about six servants and a party of half a dozen strong men in case we should need protection.

I was amused by the amount of trouble Don Felipe had taken to get us away from La Laguna.

We arrived in due course at the house in the mountains where we were to stay. We were treated with great respect since we had come from the Governor's Hacienda. And there in the shadow of the white-topped Pico de Teide we spent some pleasant days.

We rode out into the mountains; we gathered golden oranges; we played games with the children. It was a happy time. Honey missed Don Luis, who had remained behind to take charge in Felipe's absence. As for myself I was content to be there in those impressive surroundings dominated by the great conical mountain. Felipe had given me books in Spanish so that I might learn something of Spain and improve my knowledge of the language. In these I had read of the Canaries too and of Tenerife in particular, which had been given the name of the Garden of Atlas in which golden apples grew. These were the oranges and the dragon trees were set there to guard this delightful spot.

It was with some regret that I turned my mule homeward toward La Laguna.

There a shock awaited us.

Isabella was dead.

A terrible fear came to me and hung over me like a dark shadow, for Isabella had fallen from the top of the staircase on the Casa Azul and broken her neck. It had happened five days after we had left—on the day of the *auto-da-fé.*

I was aghast. It had happened so neatly. I was away; Don Felipe was away. How many times had he said: "If it were not for Isabella"?

I wished that he had never mentioned marriage to me. I wished that Isabella was still in the patio at the Casa Azul playing with her dolls.

Don Felipe had come home. He greeted me courteously but coolly; but I was aware of the intensity of the passion which he suppressed.

Jennet was agog with excitement. It was she who told us how it had happened. She had a detailed account from her lover in the stables.

I made her tell me all she knew.

" 'Twere like this, Mistress," she said, " 'twere the day of the *auto* and the whole household had gone into Laguna."

"Pilar would not leave her."

"She did. She did this once. You see it was the day of the *auto* . . . a sacred duty to go."

I closed my eyes. Oh, God, I thought. Everyone was sent away . . . because it was the day of the *auto-da-fé*. It was a sacred duty to attend. Everyone was afraid of not attending . . . and even Pilar went. Had he planned it just so?

"And what of her . . . the poor young creature?"

"Well, she didn't go, Mistress. None 'ud expect her to. She was to stay behind with her dolls."

"Someone was with her?"

"Edmundo, the big man. . . ." Jennet could not help the lilt in her voice, even when recounting such an event as this, at the mention of Edmundo, the big man. "He were there. Working in the garden. He could see to her if she was took bad. They say he could lift her when she was kicking and screaming as easy as though she were a rag doll."

"Someone else was in the house, surely?"

"Two of the maids . . . silly little things."

"Where were they?"

"They said they'd left her sleeping. It was hot . . . and she was taking her siesta. The next thing she was found at the bottom of the staircase."

"Who found her?"

"The two maids. They went to her room and she weren't there. Then they came down the stairs and there she was lying there. They said there was something strange about the way she lay there. And then they went and looked and they ran screaming to Edmundo. He saw what was wrong and left her just as she'd fallen. 'She's gone,' he said. 'Poor mad soul. She's gone.'"

I had closed the shutters and was lying on my bed. I wanted to lie in the darkness, but even the brilliant sun penetrated between the shutters and there was some light in the room.

The door opened slowly and Felipe was standing by the bed, looking down at me.

I said: "You should not be here."

"I had to see you."

"There are other places."

"To see you alone," he said. "Now she is dead. . . ."

"So recently dead, so strangely dead," I interrupted.

"She fell and killed herself. It is a wonder she did not fall before."

"She fell when she was more or less alone in the house. Everyone but the two maids and Edmundo had gone to the *auto-da-fé*. Pilar had gone."

"It was their duty to go. It was rarely that she was left almost alone in the house."

"It needed only once."

"She is dead. You know what that means. I am free."

"It is not wise to say such things. The servants listen."

He smiled faintly. "Once I so cautioned you."

"It is of more importance now than then."

"You are right. We will wait, but the waiting will be easy because in the end I shall have my heart's desire."

"You remember my Queen and her lover. He had a wife, Amy Robsart. She died. She fell down a staircase. Why, how like this! It could almost seem that one who had been impressed by that incident had decided to repeat it."

"Lord Robert Dudley murdered his wife with your Queen's connivance."

"Did he? I think you are right. Some say it was suicide. Some an accident."

"But many knew the truth."

"The Queen dared not marry him."

"It was because she would not stomach a rival on the throne."

"That . . . and because to have married him would have been to connive at murder . . . and maybe run the risk of being suspect."

"That may be."

"Don Felipe," I said, "you are in like case. Amy Robsart's servants went to a Fair; yours went to an *auto-da-fé*. Then when the house is almost empty your wife dies."

"Many times she has been saved from inflicting harm on herself."

"And this time there was no one to save her. There will be people to talk. If you married now, Don Felipe, there might be some to say you had rid yourself of a wife to do so."

"I am the master here . . . Governor of these islands."

"My Queen was the mistress of England. She was wise."

He looked momentarily forlorn; then he lifted his head and I saw the stern pride of him, the determination to succeed. It was this which had made him undertake the intricate operation of bringing me to Tenerife. He was now equally determined to marry me, to proclaim Roberto his legitimate heir. He would stop at nothing.

And I asked myself: Felipe, what part did you play in this? You were not here when Isabella died. But you did not come to England to bring me here. You are a man who sets himself a goal and employs others to carry it out. Have a care, Don Felipe.

He held out a hand to me, but I did not take it.

"Go now," I said. "Take care. Let no one see in what direction your ambitions lie."

He left me then and I lay on in my darkened room.

Isabella was buried with accompanying pomp.

It was said that she had been possessed by devils as she had attempted to descend the stairs and as she had been seen to do so many times fell and so met her death.

Death set a shadow over the household. Only in the nursery did it fail to penetrate and Honey and I spent a great deal of our time there. The weeks began to pass; we fell back into our routine.

Often I would think about Isabella and wonder what

had really happened. Had she suddenly missed Pilar? Had she gone to look for her? I thought of her often, standing at the top of that staircase and then suddenly falling to the bottom. I pictured her lying there. Poor little Isabella.

How often had he said: "If it were not for Isabella"? But he had been away.

Lord Robert Dudley had been away from Cumnor Place at the time of his wife's death; but that did not exonerate him from murder.

Men such as Sir Robert and Don Felipe did not do evil deeds themselves. They employed others to do them for them.

Edmundo was at the Casa Azul; he was the strong man; he had picked up Isabella and carried her as though she were a rag doll. He was Felipe's servant. Would he do anything his master asked . . . anything?

So ran my tormented thoughts.

Six months had passed and Felipe said to me: "It is time we married."

"It is too soon," I said.

"I cannot wait forever."

"Six months ago you had a wife."

"I have no wife now . . . nor did I ever have a wife."

"I know it to be unwise."

"I will protect you. Shortly we shall go to Spain. I must take you with me."

"We should wait awhile."

"I will wait no longer."

"I am undecided. I think often of my house. My mother will never forget me. She mourns me now."

"Tell me you will marry me and I will have a message sent to your mother. It is folly. It is dangerous. But this I will do to show you how much I care for you."

I looked at him and I felt a great tenderness surge over me. He held out his arms and I went toward him. I was held firmly against him. I could no longer resist love such as he was offering.

Had I not learned most bitterly that one does not hold out for the perfection of one's dreams? Honey knew it. She had taken Edward and enjoyed some happiness and now with Luis. And this man had proved to me that he regarded me with a tender devotion which amazed even himself. I could not reject that.

He said: "My love, you shall write a letter to your mother. You will tell her that you are well and happy. John Gregory shall take it. We will arrange it. The next ship that leaves shall carry him. There is one stipulation: You must mention no names; you must not mention where you are. I must run no risks. But, my Catalina, this shall be done. You will see how I love you!"

And so I promised to marry Don Felipe.

We were married quietly in the little private chapel of the Hacienda. I was not unhappy; sometimes I laughed within myself, for I could not help remembering the occasion of my humiliation when I had no alternative but to submit to him; I remembered how he had ordered that I should wear gowns made for Isabella, use scent which was hers, so that as he lay with me he should imagine I was the beautiful girl bride. There was no one but myself he wished to think of now. But Isabella was a shadow between us. More so for him than for me.

How changed everything was. How he loved me, this strange quiet man! How strange that he, whose emotions were so rarely aroused, should feel this searing passion for one of an enemy race, a race he despised as barbarians; and here was one who was typical of that race—and yet he loved her.

I never forget that he had allowed me to send a letter to my mother. I used to dream of her in the old Abbey garden and I held imaginary conversations with her. I believed I was never far from her thoughts.

Perhaps by now, I would promise myself, she is receiving that letter. She is weeping over it; she would tuck it into her bodice and say: "My darling Cat's hands have touched this!" And it would never leave her.

So I must be grateful to Felipe.

He loved me and he loved our son. To us alone did he show that part of his nature which was capable of loving. It had once occurred to me that when he loved it would be with a single-minded devotion. How right I had been! He now gave to love that intensity of passion which he had once given to revenge.

He abandoned himself to moments of great happiness

and at the very heart of that happiness was myself and our son.

He loved to lie on our bed with me in his arms and talk of our future. I loved to hear him say our boy's name. He said it differently when we were alone together. I felt an emotion welling up within me because such a cold stern man could love so much.

"Catalina, Catalina, my love," he would whisper to me.

He was indeed happy and it is gratifying to realize one has brought such joy to another human being.

His first task was to legitimize Roberto. Ships came now and then from Spain to Tenerife bringing men from Escorial, where Felipe's master lived in spartan state. Papers came from Madrid and he gleefully showed them to me.

"Roberto is my firstborn," he said. "It is now as though we had been married when he was born. There will be no barriers to his inheritance."

"And Carlos?" I asked.

His brow darkened. He had never liked Carlos although he had accepted his presence in our nurseries to please me.

"He shall have nothing of mine, but his mother's family will make him a rich man."

That contented me.

Felipe talked often of the time when we would go to Spain. He was anxious to return now. Don Luis was ready to take over his responsibilities. There was no reason why we should not go.

We were blind to imagine that we could have married and none question it. The Queen of England had not dared to marry her lover after her lover's wife had died mysteriously. Should the Governor of a small island be less immune?

There were whispers.

It was Manuela who first brought them to my knowledge.

"Mistress," she said, her brow puckered, "they are saying you are a witch."

"I . . . a witch. What nonsense is this?"

"They are saying that you have bewitched the Governor. He were never as he is with you, before."

"Why should he be? I am his wife."

"He had a wife before, Señora."

"This is nonsense. You know what the Governor's first wife was like."

"She were possessed by devils."

"She was simpleminded, half-mad."

"Possessed, they say. And that you commanded the devils to possess her."

I burst out laughing. "Then I hope you tell them what fools they were. She was possessed before I ever knew of her existence. You are aware of that."

"But they says she was possessed and you sent the devils to possess her."

"They are mad themselves."

"Yes," she said uneasily. But that was the beginning.

They watched me furtively. When I went into La Laguna I was aware of averted eyes and if I turned sharply I would find people were looking back at me. Once I heard the whispered word "Witch."

At the Casa Azul the shutters were closed. I heard that Pilar walked through the house lamenting. She stood at the top of the stairs and called to Isabella to come back to her, to tell her what happened on that fateful afternoon.

Felipe pretended to be indifferent to the tension which was building up, but he did not deceive me. He came to our bedroom one evening and his face was set and anxious. He had spent most of the day in La Laguna.

He said: "I would we were in Madrid. Then this nonsense would end."

"What nonsense is this?" I asked.

"There has been much talk. Someone has been to La Laguna and talked recklessly. There is no alternative. A certain course will be taken."

"What course?"

"I am speaking of Isabella's death. There is to be an inquiry."

Manuela sat mending Carlos' tunic. Her hands trembled as she did so.

I said: "What ails you, Manuela?"

She lifted her great sorrowful eyes to my face.

"They have taken Edmundo away to be questioned. He was the one to find her. She was lying at the foot of the staircase with her neck broken. He was the one. They will question him."

"He will satisfy them with his answers," I said, "and then he will come home."

"People who are taken for questioning often do not come back."

"Why should not Edmundo?"

"When they question," she said, "they will have the answer they want."

"Edmundo will be all right. He was always so good with Isabella. She was fond of him."

"She is dead," said Manuela, "and he is taken for questioning."

I had learned since Manuela came to us that she and Edmundo had both been in the retinue Isabella had brought with her from Spain. Manuela had been one of her maids and Edmundo had known how to look after her when she was "possessed." When the raiders had come Manuela had hidden and so saved herself; and she had been with Isabella during the months of pregnancy and the birth of Carlos. She had loved the child and tried to protect him from the alternate devotion and dislike of his mother; and when the boy had been put in charge of that dreadful harridan she had done what she could to help him.

It was understandable that she should be sad because Edmundo had been taken in.

I was astonished at the outcome of the questioning. Edmundo confessed that he had murdered his mistress. He had stolen a cross studded with rubies from her jewel box to give to a girl whom he wished to please. Isabella had caught him in the act of taking the cross and because he feared the consequences he had suffocated her by placing a damp cloth over her mouth. Then he had thrown her down the stairs.

He was hanged in the plaza of La Laguna.

"That is the end of the affair," said Felipe.

I could not get out of my mind the memory of big Edmundo lifting poor Isabella so gently in his arms as

I had seen him do when she was suffering.

"He was so gentle," I said. "I cannot believe him capable of murder."

"There are many sides to men and women," Felipe answered.

"It is hard to believe this of Edmundo," I said.

"He has confessed and the matter is at an end, my love."

I was disturbed but glad that I could consider the mystery solved.

Christmas came and went. I thought of home and the mummers, the wassailing and the Christmas bush. I wondered whether John Gregory had reached England yet and whether my mother had my letter.

What a Christmas gift that would be for her!

To Felipe's disappointment I had not conceived. I was not sure whether I was disappointed or not. I longed for children, and yet I could not forget Isabella; even though Edmundo had confessed to murdering her, she still seemed to stand between me and my husband. Sometimes I felt that my husband was a stranger to me. I never thought for one moment that he had ever loved Isabella. I believed him when he said that there had been one love in his life and that I was that love. That was something he could not hide. His love for me was expressed a hundred times during a single day. It was in the very inflection of his voice. Moreover, I had given him Roberto—a sturdy little fellow now three years of age. . . . But there was something Felipe held back even from me, and perhaps for this reason I willed myself not to conceive. The fact remains that I did not, although I was not unhappy.

It was never cold in Tenerife, for there was very little difference between the winter and summer; the only unpleasant days were those when the south winds blew from Africa and this was not frequent. I liked the damp warm atmosphere and I did not want to leave it for the extremes of temperature which I believed we should experience in Spain. I often thought of the cold winter days at home in the Abbey. Once the Thames had frozen and we had been able to walk across it. I remembered sitting around the great log fire in the hall and how the mummers had slapped their frozen hands into life before beginning their performance. I remembered so much of home; and sometimes I felt a dull pain in my throat, so great was my longing for it.

Yet here I had a husband who loved me and a sweet son.

In January the Cavalcade of the Three Wise Men took place and we took the children into La Laguna to watch it. What excitement there was and I listened with delight to the chattering children.

Yes, there was so much that I enjoyed.

Time slipped away and it was Holy Week and this was a time of great celebration. There were more processions in the town and when I saw the white robed figures coming from the Cathedral I was reminded so poignantly of the day I had sat in the plaza and looked on the misery of men, I felt suddenly nauseated; and a poignant longing for home swept over me.

I had talked of my sudden desire for home to Honey and she admitted that she felt this too. She was adored by Don Luis; she had her little daughter even as I had my son; but our home was something we should never forget; and I believe that at the very heart of it was my mother—for Honey as well as for me.

We had ridden into La Laguna on our mules to see the Holy Week procession and left the children at home because we feared they might be hurt in the crowds. Honey and I stood side by side. There were two grooms with us; we were never allowed to go far without protection. And as we stood on the edge of the crowd I felt someone press against me.

I turned sharply and looked into a pair of fanatical eyes which looked straight into mine.

"Pilar," I said.

"Witch," she hissed. "Heretic witch."

I started to tremble. Crowds in this plaza brought with them such hideous memories.

I said to Felipe: "I saw the woman Pilar in the town. She hates me. I could see by the way she looked at me."

"She was devoted to her charge. She had been with her since her birth."

"I think she believes that I am responsible for her death."

"She is distraught. She will grow away from her grief."

"I have rarely seen such hatred in any eyes as was in hers when she looked at me. She called me a witch . . . a heretic witch."

I was unprepared for the change in Felipe's expression. Fear was clearly to be seen as his lips formed the word "heretic." Then suddenly that control which was so much a part of his character seemed to desert him. He took me into his arms and held me tightly against him.

"Catalina," he said, "we are going to Madrid. We must not stay here."

A terrible fear had begun to overshadow me. When darkness fell I would often fancy I was being watched. I could not specifically say how. It was just that I would hear footsteps which seemed to follow me; or the quiet shutting of a door when I was in a room, so that it seemed that someone had opened it to watch me and then quietly shut it and gone away. On one or two occasions I fancied someone had been in my room. Some familiar object had been moved from its place and I was sure I had not done this.

I admonished myself. I was allowing my imagination to take possession of my good sense. Since Isabella's death and my marriage—the one a natural sequence of the other—the tension had been gradually rising. I could not forget Pilar's face when she looked at me and whispered those words: "Witch. Heretic witch" and in my mind had conjured up such horror as I dared not brood on.

It came into my mind that there was hatred around me. Some evil force was trying to destroy me. I knew this was so when I found the image in my drawer.

I had opened it unsuspectingly and there looking up at me was the figure. It was made of wax and represented a beautiful girl with black hair piled high and in that hair was a miniature comb. Her gown was of velvet and the resemblance struck me immediately. Isabella! It could not be meant to resemble anyone else.

I picked it up. What horror possessed me then, for

protruding from her gown, at that spot beneath which her heart would have been, was a pin.

Someone had put the thing in my drawer. Who? Someone had made that thing in the image of Isabella. Someone had stuck a pin through the heart and put it in my drawer!

I stood there with it in my hand.

The door had opened. I looked up startled and saw a dark reflection in the mirror.

To my relief I realized that it was only Manuela.

I held the figure crushed in my hand and turned to her. I wondered whether she noticed how shaken I was.

"The children are ready to say good night," she said.

"I'll come, Manuela."

She disappeared and I stood staring at the thing in my hand; then I thrust it to the back of the drawer and went to the nursery.

I could not listen to what the children were saying. I could only think of that horrible thing and its significance.

Who had put it there? Someone who wished me ill. Someone who was accusing me of bringing about Isabella's death. I must destroy it with all speed. While it was there I was unsafe.

As soon as I had tucked the children in and kissed them good night I went back to my room.

I opened my drawer. The figure had disappeared.

I told Felipe what I had found and I was immediately aware of the terrible fear this aroused in him.

"And it was gone?" he cried. "You should never have put it back in the drawer. You should have destroyed it immediately."

"It means that someone believes I killed Isabella."

"It means," he said, "that someone is trying to prove that you are a witch."

I did not have to ask him what that meant.

"I was accused of that on the ship," I said. I shivered. "I came near to a horrible death."

"Some of the sailors must have talked. We must get away from here quickly."

He speeded up preparations for our departure.

Fear had certainly entered the Hacienda. The great

shadow of the Inquisition hung over us. Sometimes I would awaken shouting, having dreamed I was in that square. I was looking on from the box . . . looking on at myself in the hideous sanbenito. I could hear the crackle of flames at my feet. I would awake crying out from my dream and Felipe would take me in his arms and comfort me.

"Soon," he said, "we shall be safe in Madrid."

"Felipe," I asked, "what if they should come and take me . . . how would they come?"

He answered: "They come often at night. There would be the knock on the door. We should hear the words: 'Open in the name of the Holy Office.' Those are the words none dare disobey."

"And they would take me away then, Felipe. They would question me. I should answer their questions. What have I to fear?"

"All have something to fear when they fall into the hands of the Inquisition."

"The innocent, . . ."

"Even the innocent."

"If they believe you to be a witch they would take you," he said. "If they should come by night I shall hide you. We must pretend that you have disappeared, that you are indeed a witch and you have invoked the Devil to aid you. There is a secret door in the bedchamber." He showed it to me. "You will hide in here until such time as I can save you."

"Felipe, would Pilar inform against me?"

"It may well be," he answered. "And if she does they will come for you."

"Do you believe she has?"

"I cannot say. People are wary of going to the Holy Office even to lay information against others, for it has happened that in so doing they have become involved themselves. We will pray that Pilar has not said to others what she said to you."

I trembled in his arms and he said soothingly: "It is not like you to be afraid, my love. We will outwit any who come against us."

"If you hid me, Felipe," I said, "would that not be an act against the Inquisition?"

He was silent.

I went on: "You would act against the Inquisition for my sake? You would preserve a heretic in your house because you love her?"

"Hush. Do not say that word, Catalina, even when we are alone. We must be watchful. I will speed on our departure. Once we have left this place we shall be safe."

The days passed. We were waiting for a ship. When it came we would say good-bye to the Hacienda and Honey, Don Luis and little Edwina. I had prevailed upon Felipe to allow Carlos to come with us. Manuela would accompany us too, with Jennet and young Jacko.

I was desolate at the thought of leaving Honey; but I knew that from now on I was in jeopardy and the tension created by the realization that at any moment there might be that knock on the door was such that one must long to escape from it at all costs.

I heard that Pilar was sick and had taken to her bed. I sent Manuela over to see her. Manuela had been a good and faithful servant and grateful to me for rescuing Carlos whom she adored. I thought that she might discover how far Pilar had gone with her accusations.

When she came back I summoned her to my bedroom where we could talk without being overheard and asked her what she had found.

"Pilar is indeed sick," she said. "She is sick of heart and sick of body."

"Did she talk of Isabella?"

"All the time. The maids told me that she wanders about the Casa Azul at night calling for Isabella, that she will not allow them to touch the dolls. She has them there in her room."

I nodded.

"Manuela, I wish to know all," I said, "no matter what. I know that she hates me because I married Isabella's husband. But Isabella was no wife to him. You know that."

"Always she talks," said Manuela. "She goes from one thing to another. She curses Edmundo. 'All for a cross,' she said, 'a ruby-studded cross. You remember it, Manuela. She wore it so seldom.' "

"You did remember it, Manuela?"

"Yes, I did. It was a beautiful thing. I noticed it particularly, for I have a special liking for rubies. And it was not found either."

"Edmundo gave it to someone, I believe that was the assumption. A woman he loved."

"Who was this woman? They never found her."

"You would not expect her to come forward. She would be afraid to. Or it may be that he hid the cross somewhere. Perhaps he buried it in the garden. He would have to hide it I suppose. But what does the cross matter?"

"Edmundo was such a gentle man. It seems strange that he should kill for a ruby cross."

"One never knows what people will do. Perhaps he loved someone and wished her to have the cross. Who can say? And he did it on an impulse and then he was caught and his future threatened. They would hang him for stealing a valuable cross. So he killed to save himself."

Manuel shook her head. "It was awful when she cursed him. I wanted to run out. But then she talked of you, Mistress."

"What did she say of me, Manuela?"

"She said that she wished to see you. She said that she would have come to you but because she is ill you must go to her."

"I will go," I answered.

Manuela nodded.

I did not tell Felipe I was going. I thought he might prevent me. But I knew I had to speak to Pilar. I must try to explain. I wished I had done so during our encounter in the street, but I had been too taken aback to do so then. I wanted to ask her what she meant by calling me a witch. I wanted to assure her that I was no such thing.

It occurred to me that she knew something about the image. Had she put it there? How could she have done so? She did not come to the Hacienda. Perhaps she had people working for her there, people who hated me as much as she did, who wanted to prove that I was guilty in bringing about Isabella's death.

I packed a basket with some delicacies from the kitchen and went to see her.

As I opened the gate a terrible revulsion came over me. It was as though my whole being were crying out a warning to me. There was the patio. There was the window and the balcony at which I had seen Isabella with her doll. Here Edmundo had picked her up so gently when she fell. In my mind's eye I saw Edmundo's lifeless body hanging from a rope in the plaza of La Laguna.

How quiet it was! I pushed open the door. I could scarcely bear to look. There was the staircase. I pictured her poor broken body lying at the bottom of it.

I stood hesitating.

Go away, said a voice within me. Run . . . while there is time. Leave this place. You are in imminent danger.

Someone was standing behind me. One of the servants must have seen me enter the house and followed me.

She looked at me, her eyes wide. I could see that she was afraid of me.

I said: "I came to see Pilar."

She nodded and turned her eyes as though she feared she might be contaminated by some evil.

She started to run up the stairs. I followed her.

On a landing she opened a door. I went in.

The room was dark, for it had been built to keep out the sun. On the bed lay Pilar; her hair streaming about her shoulders gave her a wild look.

I took a step toward the bed and tried to speak normally.

"I'm sorry you are ill, Pilar. I have brought you these. I heard that you wanted to see me."

"Do you think I'd eat anything that came from the Hacienda . . . that house of sin? Do you think I'd eat anything *you* brought me? You . . . witch! You have done this. You have cast your spells. You lusted for him and you bewitched him. And her death is at your door."

"Listen to me, Pilar. I am no witch. I know nothing of witchcraft. I was not here when Doña Isabella died."

Her laughter was horrible, cruel and sneering.

"You knew nothing! You know everything. You, and those like you, are wise in the ways of the Devil. You marked her down, my innocent child. Had she not suffered enough? Nay. You wanted him. You cast a spell. And she died . . . my poor innocent lamb . . . my poor sweet child."

"I cast no spells. . . ."

"Don't tell me your lies. Save them for others . . . when the time comes. They'll not believe you any more than I do." She thrust her hand under the pillow and when she brought it out she was holding something. To my horror I saw that it was the figure of Isabella.

"Where did you get that? Who gave it to you?" I demanded.

"I have it. The evidence. This will prove to them. And you will die . . . die . . . even as she died . . . and more cruelly."

"Where did you get that?" I repeated. "I saw it but once when I found it in my drawer. You put it there, Pilar."

"I? I have not left this bed."

"Then someone working for you. . . ."

"Tell them that when you stand before the tribunal. Tell them that when you feel the flames licking your limbs."

I could not bear to stay longer. I knew there was nothing I could say to her. I turned and ran out of the room, down the staircase and out into the fresh air. I did not stop running until I reached the Hacienda.

Felipe was horrified when he heard what had happened.

"If she has informed against you they will strike at any time. We must be ready as soon as the ship comes."

And so the uneasy days passed. One cannot live at such high tension day after day. One grows accustomed even to that.

Felipe said: "I can't understand it. If she had informed against you they would have come by now. It is because she is sick that she has taken no action. While she is confined to her room she cannot move against us. While she is ill we are safe. And the ship will be here any day."

I visualized the life which awaited us in Spain.

We should live in Don Felipe's country estate. He would be in attendance on the King at times and have to pay his visits to the gloomy Escorial and perhaps be sent off on missions to other lands, in which case we should accompany him.

It would be a life not dissimilar to that which I had led at the Hacienda. I should never grow accustomed to Spanish solemnity, for I could never become a part of it; nor did I believe that Felipe wished me to, for he had loved me as I was and perhaps because I was so different from the women of his land.

I must try to forget England. I was married to a Spaniard; my son was half Spanish.

If I could but hear that my mother was safe and well and that she knew that I was, I suppose I could in time become reconciled and I wondered often what had become of John Gregory.

Soon the ship must come and we would leave this house in which I had experienced so many emotions. I would try to start afresh when I left it—as I must.

I talked a great deal to Honey of the future. She had adjusted herself more easily than I. She was less tempestuous—or perhaps she was more successful in disguising her feelings. Just as she had appeared to be completely happy with Edward now she seemed so with Luis.

Her attitude was that we must accept life and do our best to be happy in it.

Our parting would be a bitter blow to us both, but we must accept it. We must think of our reunion which both Felipe and Luis had promised us should come in time.

My fears were almost lulled to rest when on that never-to-be-forgotten night there came the knocking on the door.

The candles had been lighted. We sat in that gracious room—myself and Felipe, Honey and Luis. Honey was playing the lute; and how beautiful she looked with her graceful head bent a little and her eyes downcast so that her thick lashes made a dark shadow against her skin— Honey of the indestructible beauty which no hardship could impair.

She was singing a Spanish song. We did not sing the

English ones, only when we were out together in the open where none could hear.

Then we heard the sound from without.

We started up. Felipe came swiftly to my side. He put his arm around me. He wanted me to go up to our bedroom so that he could hide me there.

But already we could hear the voices and knocking on the door in the portico. Someone screamed and then there were the sounds of footsteps.

The door of the salon was flung open. I saw John Gregory and a great joy swept over me.

"He comes from England," I cried.

And then I saw the man I had pictured so many times, his eyes flashing blue fire and there was mockery and murder in them. Jake Pennlyon had come to the Hacienda.

He was looking at me and he laughed triumphantly when he saw me. "I've come for you," he cried. "Which is the fellow who took my woman?"

He was terrifying, magnificent and invincible. How many times, when I had first been brought to Tenerife, had I imagined his coming just like this.

He had turned to Felipe. Some instinct seemed to tell him that he was the one. Then I saw Felipe throw up his arms and fall to the floor.

"Oh, God," I cried, for Jake's sword was dripping with blood.

I felt sick with horror.

"Did you doubt I'd come?" he cried. "God's Death, it's been a long time."

How difficult it is to remember the details of that bewildering and horrifying night. My thoughts were dominated by one terrible truth. Felipe was dead and Jake had killed him.

When I shut my eyes I can see the salon—the blood-stained tapestry, the bodies of men, bloody and inert lying on the mosaic tiles. Honey's husband was among them; he lay close to Felipe. I was aware of Jake's men stripping the walls and I realized they were taking away all objects of value.

As I stood there staring down at the body of Felipe whom I knew now I had deeply loved, I thought of the children and ran out to the stairs which led to the nursery. Jake Pennlyon was beside me. It was so long since I had seen him, I had forgotten the power of the man.

He said: "Where go we then? To our bed? Why, girl, you'll have to wait for that. We've work to do this night. We've got what we came for, but there's no need to go back emptyhanded."

"There are children," I said.

"What?"

"My son."

"Your son?"

"Yours too," I answered.

I tried to escape from him, but he gripped me firmly. We went up to the stairs. The children were awake. Roberto ran to me and I caught him in my arms.

"Your son . . . this black brat," cried Jake Pennlyon.

"It is all right, Roberto," I soothed. "No harm shall come to you, my son."

Jake Pennlyon's blue eyes blazed with fury. "So you were got with child by a poxy Don. I'll have no Spanish vermin on my ship."

I held the child firmly in my arms.

Carlos and Jacko had come up. Carlos stared at Jake Pennlyon with frank curiosity.

"And these?"

"Yours," I said. "Your sons, Jake Pennlyon—one got on a Spanish lady and the other on a serving wench."

He stared down at the boys. Then he put out a hand and let it rest on the shoulder of Carlos. "God's Death!" he said. Then he took Carlos' chin and jerked his face up. Then he did the same to Jacko. They met his gaze fearlessly. Jake Pennlyon burst into great laughter. Carlos, uncertain, laughed too. Jake took a handful of Carlos's hair and pulled it. There was a certain emotion in his face.

He released Carlos and slapped him on the back. The boy staggered but was looking eager and expectant still. Jacko had stepped a little forward, not wishing to be left out.

"Why," said Jake, "I'd have known you two anywhere."

Then he looked at me, his eyes narrowed. "These boys should have been yours and you got with child by a poxy Don!" He looked down at the boys. "Get warm clothes on," he roared. "Bring what you can—everything you can lay your hands on. You're going on the finest ship that ever sailed the seas."

Honey, weeping quietly, had come in for Edwina. She picked her up and held her in her arms.

"Make ready," growled Jake Pennlyon, "and follow me."

We went down the stairs; packhorses were waiting for us. They had been taken from Felipe's stables. Already articles of value were being loaded onto them. It must have been midnight when we started to ride to the coast.

There was a faint moon to show us the way and the going was slow.

Jake Pennlyon rode beside me and I held Roberto on my mule. Jennet was there, her eyes wide with excitement; Manuela kept close to the children, quietly determined to follow them; Honey, widowed twice and in a like manner, her beautiful face now impassive, held Edwina on her mule. Jacko rode with Jennet and Carlos had a mule to himself.

I felt as though I were living in a nightmare. I could not forget Felipe lying in his blood, he who, a short while before, had been alive and so concerned for my safety, and all that had happened in the last hour seemed quite unreal. I was certain I would wake up soon.

There was Jake Pennlyon—I had forgotten how vital a man could be—the murderer of Felipe, whom I had grown to love.

I should never forget Felipe's gentle courtesy, his deep and abiding kindness to me. And Jake Pennlyon had killed him. How I hated Jake Pennlyon.

And so we came to the coast and there, a mile or so from the land, lay the *Rampant Lion*.

We rowed out to her; we scrambled aboard.

The spoils which Jake Pennlyon's men had taken from the Hacienda were stowed away.

It was beginning to be light when the *Rampant Lion* shipped anchor and we sailed for England.

Homecoming

The familiar creaking of timbers, the rolling and pitching of a ship at sea—it came back to me so vividly. Jake Pennlyon's cabin was not unlike that of the galleon's Captain. It was less spacious and the deck head was lower. The same kind of instruments were there. I saw the astrolabe and the cross staff, the compasses and hourglasses.

We were taken to his cabin, Honey, Jennet and I with the children. Edwina clung to her mother as Roberto did to me but Jake Pennlyon's boys were examining the cabin; they were into everything, trying to understand how the astrolabe worked and chattering in a kind of half English and half Spanish language of their own.

Jennet was smiling to herself. "Well, fancy, 'twere the Captain himself," she kept murmuring.

Honey sat limply staring in front of her as though she were in a trance. I knew how she felt. She had lost a husband whom she loved—even as I had. Hundreds of memories must be crowding into her mind as they were into mine.

Felipe, I thought, I loved you. I never let you know how much because I didn't realize it myself until I saw you lying there.

Then it was back in my mind—that hideous memory. I could see the blood staining his jacket, making a pool about his body. I could see the blood on the walls and Jake Pennlyon's dripping sword.

I must try to shut that terrible picture out of my mind.

"The children should be sleeping," I said.

"Oh, Mistress, do you think they could after such a night?" asked Jennet.

"They must," I replied. I was thankful that at least they had not seen the murders. I wondered what was happening now. How many of the servants had survived, what they would say in the morning. Pilar at the Casa Azul would cry out that it was the witch's work—the English witch who had fascinated the Governor and brought him to his death.

The door of the cabin opened and John Gregory came in.

"Well," I said, "here is the double traitor."

"Did you not want to go home?" he demanded. "Was it not what you hoped and prayed for?"

I was silent. I was thinking of Don Felipe. I could not stop thinking of him.

"You are to be taken to a cabin where you will sleep. I will show you."

We followed him along an alleyway and into a cabin which was considerably smaller than the one we had left. There were blankets on the deck.

"You may all rest here. Captain Pennlyon will see you later. He will be busy for some hours yet."

I followed John Gregory into the alleyway.

"I want to know what happened in England," I said.

"I left in good faith," he said.

"Did you ever know good faith? Which master do you serve?"

"I serve Captain Pennlyon who is my true master and was ere I was taken by the Spaniards."

"You betrayed him once."

"I was taken and submitted to torture. I was made to obey but when I saw once more the green fields of home I knew where my loyalty lay. I never want to leave my country again."

"You found my mother? You gave her my letter?"

"I gave her your letter."

"And what said she?"

"I never saw such joy in any face as when I placed your letter in her hands and told her you were well."

"And then?"

"She said you must be brought home and she bid me take a message to Captain Pennlyon, your betrothed husband, to tell him where you were. She said I must take him to you and that he would bring you safely home."

"And this you did. You were a traitor to him and to your new master. And now you have returned to the old. How long will you be faithful to him, John Gregory?"

"You are sailing for home, Mistress. Are you not content to do so?"

I said: "There was bloody murder in Trewynd Grange on that night when we were taken away. There was bloody murder at the Hacienda. These murders are at your door, John Gregory."

"I understand you not. I have expiated my sin."

"Your conscience must trouble you," I said. I asked myself: How near had I come to loving Don Felipe? I did love him. Surely this emptiness I now feel, this numbed despair was due to love.

I went back to the cabin. Roberto was looking anxiously for me, so I took him in my arms and soothed him. Edwina was fast asleep. Carlos and Jacko were whispering together.

I said: "We should all lie down. Though I do not expect we shall sleep."

In a short time Jennet was breathing noisily. I looked at her contemptuously and asked myself of what she dreamed. Of further tumbling with the Captain? How wantonly her eyes had shone at the sight of him.

Honey lay still.

I whispered: "Honey, what are you thinking?"

She answered: "I keep seeing him lying there. A man who has slept at your side . . . in whose arms you have lain. . . . There was so much blood, Catharine. I can't forget it. I see it wherever I look."

"You loved Luis?"

"He was gentle and kind. He was good to me. And you Felipe, Catharine?"

"He took me against my will, but he was never brutal. I think he soon began to love me. Sometimes I think I shall never be loved as I was by Don Felipe."

"Jake Pennlyon . . ." she began.

"Do not speak of him."

"We are in his ship. What will happen do you think?"

I shivered. "We must wait and see," I said.

We must have dozed a little, for it was morning. The ship rocked gently, so the weather was calm. There was food for us—beans and salt meat with ale. It was brought by John Gregory. As on that previous occasion he had been given the task of guarding us.

"All's well," he said. "There is a fair wind and we are on course for England. The crew have had a double ration of rum for last night's work. The Captain has promised them a share of his booty when we're safe in the Hoe. He wishes to speak with Mistress Catharine when she has eaten."

I was silent and in no mood for food. Roberto said he did not like the food, but I noticed Carlos and Jacko ate heartily. Edwina ate some beans and Jennet did justice to her share, but Honey could not eat. We drank a little of the ale, which tasted bitter, but at least it was cooling.

John Gregory conducted me to the Captain's cabin.

Jake Pennlyon roared, "Come in," when he knocked. I stepped inside.

"Come and sit down," said Jake Pennlyon.

I sat on the stool which was fixed to the deck. He said: "This is your second sea voyage. A little different from the first, eh?"

"The galleon was a finer ship," I said.

He pursed his lips contemptuously. "I'd like to meet her. Then I could show you who is master."

"She had an armament of eighty cannon. I doubt you could match that."

"So we have become a sailor, since we sailed with the

Dons! You'll never see that one again."

I shuddered. Once more I saw him clearly there on the floor, his blood mingling with the mosaic tiles.

"John Gregory told me you had been questioning him."

"Do you expect silence from your captives?"

"Captives! Who speaks of captives? I have rescued you from God knows what. I am taking you home."

I said: "Don Felipe Gonzáles was my husband."

The color flooded his face.

"I know he got a Spanish brat on you."

"We had a son," I said.

"Married you!" he spat out. "That was no marriage."

"Solemnized according to the rites of the church," I went on.

"The Catholic Church. How could you sink so low!"

I laughed at him. "You are a very religious man, I know. You lead a life of piety. All your actions are those which one would expect of a holy man."

"I am a man of tolerance. I am even ready to take my wife back even though she has played the whore with a filthy Don."

"He was a man of fine and cultured manners such as you could never understand."

He took me by the forearm and shook me; I thought at once of the gentle hands of Felipe.

"You were betrothed to me. That betrothal was binding. It was as good as marriage."

"I did not regard it as such. If I had I would never have entered into it."

"You lie. You wanted me. You would have been my wife, you would have been at Pennlyon Court had you not been sick of the sweat."

"I never was sick of the sweat."

He stared at me. Oh, I had deceived him completely then.

"It was a ruse. It was a way of keeping you off. Now, Jake Pennlyon, was I eager for you? When I kept to my bed for weeks to escape you?"

"You were suffering from the sweat. I saw your face."

"A concoction . . . a paste, spread lightly over the face. Even you lost your lust when you saw that!"

"You . . . devil!" he said.

"In Tenerife they called me a witch and you call me a devil. In truth, all I am is a woman seeking to escape from a man she does not want."

He was shaken. So he had not really believed in my reluctance, so great was his conceit.

He said at length: "I shall marry you when we reach Devon. In spite of everything I will honor my bond."

"I will release you," I promised him. "I will leave Devon and take my son with me to my mother. She will be happy to have us."

"I have not risked much to bring you home for that. You will honor your promise and when you have a son of whom you can be proud you will forget that you so demeaned yourself as to go through a ceremony of marriage with a Spanish dog."

"You are to blame for everything that happened," I cried. "You with your lust and your cruelty and your wickedness. It was no ordinary raid which was made that night. It was for revenge because of what you had done to Don Felipe. You had ravished the innocent child he was to marry; you left your seed there. Carlos! Oh, yes, your eyes light at the sight of him. There is no doubt that he is your son. It is due to this and a proud Spaniard's desire for revenge that I was taken as you took that girl. Because I was betrothed to you. Betrothed to you through blackmail. There never was a more unwilling partner in such a bond! So because of your wanton lust I was taken and submitted to similar treatment."

He clenched his hands. I knew he was imagining me fighting with all my strength and finally being overcome.

"He was not like you," I said. "He did not want violence. It was not lust for a woman but for revenge. You are responsible for everything. You . . . . *you* . . . from the moment you came into my life you have destroyed my peace. Because of you this has happened to me."

"You liked him. You agreed to marry him. Or was that for the child?"

"You would not understand this man. There could not be one less like you. He explained to me what was to happen. He did not come himself to get me and it was not until I reached the Hacienda that I was forced to submit. He offered me a choice. He did not wish to use violence. I was trapped. So I was passive. Then . . . he loved me and he married me . . . and life was not unpleasant."

"So my wildcat was tamed . . . tamed by a dirty poxy Don."

I turned away. As always I was, to my fury, excited by the presence of Jake Pennlyon. I felt alive now as I had not since I left England. I was actually enjoying the battle with him and I was disgusted with myself—particularly that this could happen so soon after Felipe's death.

He sensed this, I know. For suddenly he had me pinioned; he held me against him.

He kissed me then and I felt an excitement which Felipe had never aroused in me.

He said: "I'll not let the fact that you were a Spaniard's whore stop our marriage."

"Dare say that again."

"Spaniard's whore," he said.

I lifted a hand to strike him, but he caught the hand by the wrist.

He bent me backward and again his mouth was on mine. He said: "Ah, Cat, 'tis good to have you back again. I was too kind to your Spaniard. I should have brought him back to the ship and had sport with him before I dispatched him to the torment of hell."

I said, "I hate you when you speak of him. He was a good man."

"We'll forget him, for I have you back and to hold you thus and know that 'ere long you and I will be as one gives me such delight I have not known since you went away."

When he said those words I felt a lifting of my spirits. I knew that I had missed him, that I had thought of him often, that although I hated him my hatred was in itself a fierce enjoyment. It was like coming out into keen fresh air after a long stay in prison. I was exultant, and I must be true to myself and admit that Jake Pennlyon had done that to me.

I knew that he would not allow me to escape him during the long voyage home. I knew he would force me to become his mistress within the next few days.

It was as inevitable as night following the day. Yet even as I mourned for Felipe I could not suppress a wild exultation.

For three days I held him off. I believe that was how he wanted it to be. He wanted to tease himself; to let me think I had a chance of winning in this battle, for battle it was. But it was inevitable that this would not go on. There he was in that floating world of which he was the indisputable master; he could have taken me at any time he wished. But he held off . . . just for three days.

He wanted to keep me in suspense. He enjoyed his verbal battles with me. Physically I was no match for him, but I was more than a match with my wits. I was trapped, of course. There was no way in which I could hide from him on his ship.

For those three days the weather was ideal. There was enough wind to keep us on course. It was a wonderful sight to stand on deck and see those sails billowing out. Despite myself, I began to be proud of the *Rampant Lion* and admit that she had a quality which the stately galleon had lacked. The *Lion* was a faster vessel; she had less to carry; she was jaunty, confident; and I knew too that Jake Pennlyon was her master as the Captain had never been of his galleon. I guessed there would never be near mutiny on Jake Pennlyon's *Lion*.

It was dusk. We had eaten and I came upon him in the alleyway near his cabin.

He barred my way and said: "Well met."

"I am going to the children," I told him.

"Nay," he replied, "you are coming with me."

He took my arm then and pulled me into his cabin.

The lantern swinging from the deck head gave a dim light.

"I have waited long enough for you," he said. "Look, the wind is rising. It could mean stormy weather."

"What has that to do with me?"

"Everything. You're on the ship and the weather is of great concern to you. I could be occupied with my ship. I want time for dalliance with my woman."

"I had thought you had begun to understand that I wished to be left alone."

"You thought nothing of the sort."

He pulled the comb from my hair so that it fell about my shoulders.

"That is how I fancy you," he said.

I said: "If you are looking for someone on whom to satisfy your lust may I recommend you to the maid Jennet."

"Who wants the substitute when the real thing is there for the taking?"

"If you imagine that I shall submit willingly . . . and eagerly . . . and that I am of a like mind to Jennet. . . ."

"You lack the girl's honesty. You suppress your desires, but you don't deceive me into thinking they are not there."

"It must be comforting I dare swear to have such a high conceit of yourself."

"Enough of this," he cried and at one stroke stripped my bodice from my shoulders.

I knew of course that the moment which I had resisted for so long had come. I was not the innocent girl I had been when I had first come to Devon. Already I had been taken in humiliation—for revenge not for lust—and later I had become accustomed to my life with Don Felipe. I had borne a child. Indeed I was no innocent.

But I fought as any nun might have fought for her virginity. I could not deny to myself that I experience a wild exhilaration in the fight. My great concern was to keep my feelings from him. I was determined to resist for as long as I could as I knew the climax was foregone. He laughed. It was a battle which of course he won. I could not understand the wild pleasure that he gave me; it was something I had not experienced or imagined before. I was murmuring words of hatred and he of triumph; and why that should have given me greater satisfaction than I had ever experienced before I cannot say.

I broke free from him. He was lying on his pallet laughing at me.

"God's Death!" he said. "You don't disappoint me. I knew it was meant from the moment I clapped eyes on you."

"I knew no such thing," I said.

"But you do now."

"I hate you," I said.

"Hate away. It seems it makes a better union than love."

"I wish I had never come to Devon."

"You must learn to love your home."

"I shall go back to the Abbey. As soon as I reach England."

"What?" he said. "Carrying my son? You'll not do that. I'm going to be gracious. I'm going to marry you, in spite of the fact that you've been a Spaniard's whore and mine too."

"You are despicable."

"Is that why you can't resist me?"

He was on his feet.

"No," I cried.

"But yes, yes," he said.

I fought him; but I knew that I could not resist. I wanted to stay; but I would not let him know it.

And so I stayed with him and it was late when I crept back to the cabin I shared with Honey.

She looked at me as I came in. "Oh, Catharine," she whispered.

"He was determined," I said. "I knew it would come sooner or later."

"Are you all right?"

"Scratched, bruised. As one would expect after a fight with Jake Pennlyon."

"My poor, poor Catharine! It's the second time."

"This was different," I said.

"Catharine. . . ."

"Don't talk to me. I can't talk. Go to sleep. It had to happen. He was determined. It is not as though I were a young inexperienced girl like Isabella. . . ."

She was silent and I lay there thinking of Jake Pennlyon.

The journey was long and not uneventful. Was any voyage on the unpredictable seas? The storm Jake had prophesied came and we battled through it. It was not as violent as that which had hit the galleon; or was the *Lion* more able to withstand the elements? Was it due to her Captain, the undefeatable Jake Pennlyon? The mighty and imposing galleon was unwieldy compared with the jaunty *Lion*. The *Lion* defied the seas as she was tossed hither and thither; her timbers creaked as though sorely tried, but she stood up defiantly against the driving rain. The wind shrieked in the rigging and she was shaken by the seething waters as gust after gust caught her top-hamper.

Jake Pennlyon was in charge. He it was whose seamanship made the *Lion* turn toward the wind so that the upperworks gave shelter to the leeward side, where he was shouting orders above the roar of the wind. Did everyone on board feel as I did? We are safe. Nothing can stand against Jake Pennlyon and win—not even the sea, not even the wind.

So we rolled in the Bay and the storm persisted through two nights and a day and then we were calm again.

When the wind had subdued there was a thanksgiving service on deck. How different it was from that other. There was Jake Pennlyon actually giving thanks to God for the safety of his ship in a manner which suggested that it was the ship's Captain rather than the Deity who had brought us through the storm. He talked arrogantly to God, I thought, and I laughed inwardly at him. How like him! How conceited he was, how profane! And how grand!

That night of course I was in his cabin.

He had come to the cabin which I had turned into a nursery and there demanded of Carlos what he had thought of the storm.

"It was a great storm," cried Carlos.

"And you whimpered, eh, and you thought you were going to be drowned?"

Carlos looked astonished. "No, Captain. I knew you wouldn't let the ship sink."

"Why not?"

"Because it's your ship."

Jake pulled the boy's hair. It was a habit he had adopted with Carlos and Jacko. Sometimes I thought he hurt them, for I saw them steel themselves to hide a wince. But both the boys were proud when he spoke to them. They clearly revered him. They were his sons and he reveled in the thought. Men like Jake Pennlyon passionately wanted sons. They thought themselves such perfect specimens of manhood that the more often they were reproduced, the better; and they always looked for signs of themselves in their children.

I could see it already in Carlos and Jacko. They had changed since they came aboard. They aped him in many ways.

"And you think I could stop it, eh?"

"Yes, sir," said Carlos.

"You're right, boy. You're right, by Heaven."

He pulled Carlos' hair and Carlos was happy to bear the pain because he knew it meant approval.

Jake Pennlyon then gripped my arm.

"Come now," he said.

I shook my head.

"What, would you have me force you here before the boys?"

"You would not dare."

"Don't provoke me."

Roberto, whom Jake always ignored, was looking at me fearfully, and because I knew that Jake was capable of anything if he were, as he would put it, provoked, I said: "Give me a few moments."

"See how I indulge you."

So I kissed the children and said good night to them and I went to Jake Pennlyon.

When we were in his cabin he said, "You come readily now."

"I come because I do not wish the children to see your brutality."

"I am indeed a brute, am I not?"

"Indeed you are."

"And you love me for it."

"I hate you for it."

"How I enjoy this hate of yours. You please me, Cat. You please me even more than I dreamed of being pleased."

"Must I endure this. . . ."

"You must."

"As soon as we are home. . . ."

"I will make an honest woman of you. I'll swear I've got you with child by now. I want a son . . . my son and your son. That boy Carlos, he's a fine boy. So is Jacko. They're mine, you see . . . but mine and yours, Cat, by Heaven, he'll be the one. I doubt not he has begun his life now. Does that not lift your heart to think on it?"

"If I should have a child by you," I said. "I would hope I do not see its father in it."

"You lie, Cat. You lie all the time. Speak truthfully. Was your wretched Spanish lover like me?"

"He was a gentleman."

Then he laughed and fell upon me and gave vent to his savage passion which I told myself I must needs endure.

And I was exhilarated and exulted and I told myself no one ever hated a man as I hated Jake Pennlyon.

Through the treacherous Bay of Biscay into the almost equally treacherous Channel we sailed and what emotion we felt—Honey and I—when we saw the green land of Cornwall!

And then we were entering Plymouth Harbor.

So much had happened to us—I had become a wife, a mother and a widow. I was surely a different woman from the girl who had sailed away on that strange night five years before. Yet nothing seemed to have changed here. There were the familiar waters, the coastline. Soon I should be able to make out the shape of Trewynd Grange.

We dropped anchor. We went ashore with the children; Jake Pennlyon came with us. He had never looked more arrogantly proud. He was a sailor returning home with his booty, and he had taken his revenge on the Spaniard who had dared thwart him.

I was unprepared for what I found on the shore, for there was my mother.

She held out her arms and Honey and I ran to her; she hugged first me and then Honey and she kept saying, "My darling girls!" over and over again, while she laughed and cried and kissed us and touched our faces and held us at arm's length to look at us before she held us again.

The children stood looking up at her wonderingly. We introduced her to them—Edwina, Roberto, Carlos and Jacko. Her eyes lingered on Roberto. She picked him up and said: "So this is my little grandson." Then she did not forget to show equal interest in Edwina—her little granddaughter as she called her.

She was staying at Trewynd Grange, which Lord Calperton had put at her disposal. No member of his family had used it since the tragedy of Edward's death. When Jake Pennlyon had set out to bring us back, my mother had prepared for the journey to Devon, so determined was she to be there to greet us as soon as we stepped onto English soil.

How strange to walk into the Grange again, to look up at that turret window from where I had first seen the galleon. My mother and I walked arm in arm, hands clasped. She could not speak of her emotion just then, though later doubtless she would.

As soon as the *Rampant Lion* had been sighted she had set the servants preparing a banquet, and the smells of savory meats and pies greeted us. It was so long since we had smelled such food and in spite of our emotion we were eager for it.

I went up to my old room; I stood at the turret window and looked out on the Hoe and the *Rampant Lion* dancing there on the waves.

My mother was behind me, and we were at last alone.

"Oh, my dearest Cat!" she said. "If you but knew."

"I do know," I said. "You were in my thoughts all the time."

"What terrible experiences for you—and you little more than a child."

"I am a mother too now."

She looked at me anxiously. I started to tell her why we had been abducted, but she already knew. John Gregory had told her.

"And this man . . . you say he was good to you."

"Yes, Mother."

"And you married him!"

"In the end it seemed the best thing to do. I had my son. Roberto was made heir to his estates. And I was fond of him, for he was good to me."

She bowed her head. "I too married, Cat."

"Rupert?" I asked.

She nodded.

"And my father?"

"He will never come back. He is dead, Cat. I have long known he was dead."

"He was said to have disappeared mysteriously."

"There was nothing mysterious about your father, Cat —at least no more than there is about all men and women. He was placed in the Abbey by the monk who was his father and so the legend was built up. He acquired his riches by selling the treasures of the Abbey and he died by an accident in the Abbey tunnels. That is all in the past and I have married Rupert."

"You should have married him long ago, Mother."

She said: "I am happy now. He wanted me to come here because he knows of my love for you, but he is eagerly awaiting my return."

"And Kate?"

"She is as ever."

"She did not marry again?"

"Kate does not wish to marry, though there are many who try to persuade her. She wishes to keep her freedom. She is rich, independent, she wants no man to govern her."

"No man would ever govern her. She would govern him."

"You still speak of her bitterly, Cat."

"I still remember. And Carey?"

"He has a place at Court."

"So you see him now and then?"

"Yes."

"Does he speak of me?"

"We all spoke of you when we lost you."

"Carey too?"

"Yes, Carey."

"And is he well, Mother?"

"He is indeed. Now, Cat darling, what will you do? Will you marry Jake Pennlyon? I want you to be happy, dearest Cat. More than anything I want that. Jake Pennlyon brought you back. He plans to marry you. He was betrothed to you before and he has waited for you."

I laughed aloud. "I think I may be going to bear his child."

"Then you love him."

"Sometimes I think I hate him."

"Yet. . . ."

"He insisted," I said. "He was the Captain. He offered me marriage, but he was impatient."

She took me by the shoulders and looked into my face. "My dearest Cat," she said, "you are changed."

"I am no longer your virgin daughter. Twice I have been forced to submit. It's odd, Mother. They both offered marriage."

"Now you must build up a new life for yourself, Cat. Come home with me to the Abbey."

"I thought of it. There I should see Carey perhaps. I do not want to open that old wound. Perhaps he will marry. Has he married?" I asked swiftly.

She shook her head. "You married the Spaniard," she reminded me.

"I married him because I thought I would stay there forever. I wanted to assure my son's position."

"And this child you are carrying?"

I hesitated. Was I beginning to ask myself if I could overcome my grief for Felipe, which stirred sadly in my heart, by my hatred of Jake Pennlyon?

I said: "I will marry Jake Pennlyon. He is the father of the child I am carrying. I shall stay here, Mother, for much as I long to be with you I could not return to the Abbey."

She understood as she had always understood.

Jake Pennlyon was triumphant. The preparations for the wedding began at once.

"We want our son's birth to take place at a respectable time after the wedding day."

During the previous year Jake's father had had an apoplectic fit and died instantly. He had lived so lustily that he had shortened his span, was the general opinion. So Jake was master of Lyon Court and I was to be its mistress.

I made conditions.

The children were to remain with me. He wanted Roberto to go to the Abbey when my mother went. "For to tell the truth," he said, "the sight of that brat makes my gorge rise."

"He is my son," I said. "He shall never be parted from me as long as I live."

"You should be ashamed of consorting with our enemies. A brat that was forced on you!"

"That could be said of the child I am to bear."

"Not so. You were willing. Do you think you deceived me?"

"It is you who deceive yourself. My son stays or there will be no marriage."

"There will be a marriage," he said. "Don't think you'll cheat me twice. No plaguey sweat this time, my girl."

I laughed at him. "Roberto stays," I said.

"And the other two," he said. "By God, I've got no objection to a nursery. We'll fill it. Those two boys are game little fellows. I like them."

"You would. They resemble you. Manuela and Jennet will take care of the nursery, but let me tell you this: There will be no more merry games with my servants."

He took my chin in his hand and jerked up my face in one of his ungentle gestures. "You must see to it that there is no one but you. I warn you I am a lusty man."

"I do not need the warning."

"You need to *heed* it. You can keep me solely yours, Cat, and you will."

"Do you think I can manage to retain such a prize?" I asked with sarcasm.

"If you are wise, Cat, you can."

"Who is to say? Who knows I might welcome your lust for others? All I say is it shall not be in my house and with my servants."

"I have never had difficulty in finding willing companions."

"A pretty subject for a man about to marry."

"But we are not as others, are we, Cat? We know that, do we not? It is what makes the prospect of our union so enthralling. Tell me how does my son today?"

"I am not at all sure that he exists. If he does not . . . there may not be the need for this wedding."

"If he is not there rest assured he soon will be."

I said: "I would like to see the house. There may be changes I wish to make."

He laughed at me, exulting. I knew he was longing for our wedding with deep intensity.

The day dawned when I was married to Jake Pennlyon. The ceremony took place in the chapel where once Jake had spied through the leper's squint. There was feasting in Trewynd Grange and afterward I went back with Jake to Lyon Court.

It is no use pretending that I was not excited by this man, and to enter that house of which I should be mistress, to go with him to our bridal chamber, and stand there with him. In those first moments I believe he was moved almost to tenderness. I knew that he had achieved that which he had long desired and when he put his arms about me he was momentarily gentle. This was different from those adventures which were familiar to him.

The moment did not last. His passion was fierce; and because I knew that there was a need in him to subdue, to fight, I resisted him.

But I shared his passion. He knew it. Yet I did not want him to realize how overwhelming were these encounters, how they drove everything from my mind but this intense physical satisfaction.

My relationship with Jake was entirely physical. I could not uphold my refusal to admit my pleasure in them, but it was always the pleasure of the senses and I did not attempt to hide this. If he had no tenderness for me, I had none for him. I was not going to pretend to love him. I was not even going to pretend I had need of him. I found him coarse, crude, arrogant and I was not going to pretend otherwise. I had married him because I was to bear a child he had forced on me. I was a woman with strong natural impulses and his tremendous virility matched a similar quality in me. It was possible to share a sexual encounter and yet not to love one's partner.

I made this clear to him, but he laughed at me. He had always known, he told me, that I wanted him as he wanted me. He had always been aware that he only had to beckon and I would be in his bed.

"There was much beckoning," I reminded him, "but I never was in your bed till forced to be there on your ship when there was no escape for me."

"I could see you longed for me."

"As silly Jennet did. I'm no Jennet, remember."

"I know it well. But you are a woman even as she is and a woman like you needs a man like me."

"Nonsense!" I retorted.

"Let's prove it."

And there was no holding him back.

Yes, I was exhilarated by our encounters. I could not hide it. "We were made one for the other," he said. "I knew it. From the moment I clapped eyes on you on the Hoe, I said to myself, 'That's your woman, Jake Pennlyon. She'll be the best you ever knew.' "

But afterward we would argue and I usually won and he was pleased to let me.

He had only to seize me and although I would often resist he would always have his way . . . at any time, anywhere.

I said he was shameless and he answered that I was equally so.

And so passed the first month of my marriage to Jake Pennlyon.

Then my mother said she must go home. She had left Rupert too long.

Honey would go with her. Trewynd had too many unhappy memories for her. She would live with my mother at the Abbey and they both said that this was a consolation for saying good-bye to me.

So with Edwina, she set off for the Abbey; Roberto, Carlos and Jacko stayed behind and in the nursery Jennet and Manuela were their nurses.

I was certain by this time that I was pregnant.

Soon, I promised myself, there would be another in my nursery.

Roberto was pining. His dark eyes grew larger in his little olive-skinned face.

"Madre," he said, "I want to go home."

"Roberto, my precious," I answered him, "we are home."

He shook his head. "This is not home. Home is not here, Madre."

"It is now," I told him. "Home is where I am and that is where you belong."

He conceded this.

"I want my father. Where is my father?"

"He is gone away, Roberto. He is dead. You have a new father now."

"I want my own father, Madre. Who is my new father now?"

"You know."

He shrank in terror. "Not the man. . . ."

"He will be your father now, Roberto."

He shut his eyes tightly and shook his head. I had said the wrong thing. I had frightened him.

I took him onto my lap and rocked him. "I am here, Roberto." That did comfort him. He clung to me. But he was terrified of Jake, and Jake, who had no under-standing of children, did nothing to alleviate the situ-ation. Carlos and Jacko had been taken over the *Rampant Lion*; they played wild games which involved ships and captains. Carlos was always Captain Pennlyon and this pleased Jake. He was proud of those two . . . his boys. He didn't seem to care that one of them was the son of a Spanish lady of high degree and the other of a serving girl. They were Pennlyons and that was good enough for him.

How different it was for my little Roberto!

I was so concerned about the child that I spoke to Jake about him. I even went so far as to plead with him to show a little interest and kindness to the boy.

"Interest in that man's son?"

"He is mine also."

"That does not endear him to me."

"It should. I have taken your sons and cared for them."

"You're a woman," he said.

"If you have any decent feelings in you. . . ."

"But you know I have not . . . only indecent ones."

"I beg of you. Be kind to my son."

"I must act as I feel."

"Oh, so you have become honest, have you?"

"In this matter, yes." He turned to me suddenly, "I tell you, I hate the boy. When I see him I think of you with that Don. I want to break every bone in his body; I want to destroy anything that reminds me of that."

"You're inhuman. To blame a child."

"You should have let him go with your mother."

"My own son!"

"Will you stop talking of *your* son? Soon you'll have mine and then that dark-skinned brat can be sent away.

I might take him with me when I sail and drop him off at his old home. How would that be?"

"You dare touch that boy."

"And?" he mocked.

"I'd kill you, Jake Pennlyon."

"So we would become a murderess."

"Yes, if any harmed my son."

"Oh, come, what's a bastard now and then? You're going to have that nursery so full of real boys you'll not miss this one."

I hit him across the face. This sort of encounter always excited him. He had me pinioned and forced me down.

There was the inevitable ending, but it solved nothing.

He hated my son because of his father and I was worried.

When Roberto became ill I was with him all the time. I think it was the cold east wind which blew up suddenly and which was too much for him.

Jennet and Manuela were worried about him and I spent a day with them in the nursery.

He was a little better as the dusk fell.

"He do seem comforted to have you with him, Mistress," said Jennet.

It was true, when I sat beside his bed he slept a little, holding my hand; and if I attempted to release it momentarily his hot little hands clung.

I decided I would stay with him.

When night fell Jake came to the nursery. Jennet and Manuela hastily disappeared.

"What means this?" said Jake. "I am waiting for you."

"The child is sick," I answered.

"Those two women can care for him."

"He is uneasy when I'm not here."

"*I* am more than uneasy when you are not with me."

"I am staying here for the night."

"Nay," he said, "you are coming to bed with me."

"I shall stay with my son tonight."

"You will come," he said.

He caught my arm and I stood up and threw him off. "You will wake the child."

"Why should I care?"

"I care," I said.

I stepped out of the room with him, for I greatly feared the effect a scene would have on Roberto.

"Go away," I said. "I have made up my mind."

"And if I have made up mine?"

"You must needs unmake it."

"You are coming with me."

"I am staying with my son."

We looked unflinchingly into each other's eyes.

"I could carry you there," he said.

"If you touch me, Jake Pennlyon," I said, "I will leave this house. I will take my son to my mother and never see you again."

He hesitated and I knew that I had won.

"Go away," I said. "Don't shout. If you wake the child, if you frighten him now I shall never forgive you."

"Are you not afraid that if you deny me I might turn to others?"

"If you are so desperately in need you must do so."

"You would not wish that."

"I tell you I care for nothing tonight but that my son sleeps peacefully and I shall stay with him to make sure that he does so."

"Cat," he said. "I want you . . . now . . . this minute."

"Go away."

"So you don't care what I do?"

"Do what you please."

He caught my arm and shook me. "You know full well that I have a fancy for no one but you."

I laughed at him. Exultantly, yes. I had won of course. I went back to Roberto.

In the morning the child was better, but I knew that he was terrified of Jake Pennlyon.

The summer came. Tenerife seemed a long way behind. I had settled in to life at Lyon Court. Soon Jake would go away on a voyage. He had postponed this because of our marriage and I knew he wished to be with me; but of course he could not stay ashore forever. I think sometimes he planned to take me with him, but I was pregnant and the sea was no place for a woman in my condition. He was a sailor who loved the sea and his ship was near to his heart as any living being I was sure, and yet he lingered on shore. I laughed at him. He could not leave me.

He could never shut out of his mind the memory of the raid which had taken place while he was away. He was afraid that it might happen again. He was torn between his desire for adventure on the high seas and his life with me.

Often I would see him down at the Hoe; he would be rowed out to his ship and spend some time on her. He finally decided that he could stay behind no longer.

A Captain Girling came to visit us from St. Austell— a man some twenty years older than Jake. He was a keen man, Jake told me, one of the few whom he cared to trust on one of his ships.

Captain Girling stayed with us for a month and he and Jake went out to the *Lion* every day; and there was a great deal of bustle on the Hoe while her stores were taken aboard. She was taking out a cargo of linen.

At dinner the conversation was generally of the sea and ships and I became increasingly knowledgeable in these matters, particularly as I had firsthand experience of two voyages. They used to question me at length about the galleon and I could never resist praising her and pointing out her superiority over the *Rampant Lion* and English ships I had seen, which exasperated and intrigued them.

Captain Girling was as fierce in his denunciation of the Dons and Catholicism as Jake was and they were at one on this as on most matters.

They hated the Inquisition, which had seized a number of English sailors, submitted them to torture and even burned them at the stake. John Gregory was an example of a man who had been captured and only freed on condition that he spy for them. Oddly enough Jake seemed to have forgiven him although he had helped in carrying me off in the first place. He had, however, made it possible for Jake to bring me back.

"There's good news from the Netherlands," said Captain Girling. "There's a rising there and by all accounts it's a success. The Spaniards had set up the Inquisition there, and because of this the country is in revolt. By God, the sooner we blow them all off the seas, the better."

Jake regarded me with some amusement. "I'd slit the

throat of any Spaniard on sight . . . no matter who."

"Throat slitting's too good for them," growled Captain Girling.

And I trembled for Roberto, who looked more like his father every day.

"If ever they attempt to come to England . . ." began Captain Girling.

Jake's face was purple at the thought, yet his eyes shone with excitement.

"That would be the day!" he cried. "We'd see them finished off forever then. Why, Girling, do you think there's a possibility the rascals would be so foolhardy as to try it?"

"Who can say? You know they've taken possession of lands all over the globe. They're taking the rack and the thumbscrews among the savages and trying to make Papists of them."

"Let them come here!" cried Jake. "Oh, God, let them come here. Let them bring their thumbscrews here. We'll show them how to use them."

"They fear us . . . they respect us. They prefer to play with savages," Girling said.

"I swear they shall continue to fear us. When they meet one of my ships on the high seas they'll show some respect too."

"You talk much of what you will do if certain things happen," I said. "We know exactly how they would act and how you would. But why should they come here? What hope would they have?"

"They would build a fleet of ships. They would come to our coasts. They would attempt to land," said Jake. "Let them try it. Oh, God, let them try it."

"There are traitors here," said Captain Girling. "We must be aware of the traitors within."

"Plaguey Papists," said Jake. "And now with this Queen above the Border! The Queen of Scots, recently Queen of France, could lead an army into England if she could find the support from traitors here on land and the King of Spain from the sea."

"War!" I said. "Oh, I pray not war."

"There are continual forages on the Border," said Girling. "Our Sovereign Lady Elizabeth is shrewd. She seeks to cause friction among the Scottish nobles and, by God, they are a quarrelsome crowd. 'Tis said that she herself did all possible to further the marriage of the Scottish Queen with Lord Darnley, while pretending to oppose it. That fellow is no good to Mary. He's a swaggering braggart, a lecher, a coward, and he greatly desires the Crown Matrimonial of Scotland. If the Queen of Scots is wise she'll keep him in his place, which is not on the throne with her."

"While I have been away," I said, "the situation has become grave between England and Scotland."

"It was so since Mary's husband, the young King of France, died and she lost her position overnight," said Captain Girling. "The Medici woman made it clear that she must get out and where could she go but to her own country of Scotland?"

"Let us not forget," added Jake, "that she dared call herself the Queen of England. Our Lady Elizabeth will not forget that, I am sure."

"For that alone she deserves to have her head cut off."

"Mary's point is that our Queen is the daughter of Anne Boleyn, whom the Catholics call a whore because they say she was never in truth King Henry's wife, whereas Mary herself is descended legitimately through Henry's sister," I reminded him.

Jake threw me a warning glance. "You talk like a Papist." He narrowed his eyes. "And let me tell you, I'll have no Papist in this house. If I find any it will be the worse for them."

I knew he was referring to Roberto, for he had been watchful of the boy. I trembled for my son, but I replied boldly: "I speak without religious bias. I merely state that this is the case."

"Our Lady Elizabeth is Queen by right of inheritance, a true daughter of King Henry," retorted Jake, "and we'll fight for her. There is no Englishman worthy of the name who would not give his life for her—and keep the Papists from the land."

We drank the Queen's health—I as fervently as the others.

But I was uneasy. There would always be disquiet in the land I supposed. There would always be this conflict;

and when I thought of the quiet determination and religious fervor of Felipe and those whom he commanded, and the might of the Spanish galleons, I feared the breaking out of a mighty conflagration.

In the night I awoke and Jake stirred beside me.

He said: "You know why I've sent for Girling?"

"He is going to command one of your ships, I doubt not."

"Which ship think you?"

"That I cannot know."

"The *Rampant Lion.*"

"*Your* ship?"

"Well, she is lying idle there in the Hoe."

"I did not know that you allowed others to command her."

"Nor have I till now."

"But why so?"

"Need you ask? I have found a more desirable mistress than adventure. She is as unreliable as the sea, but by God, she can be whipped to sudden fury; she can be soft sometimes—though she tries to hide it. There are times when I am at the helm and she is as soft and gentle as any could wish—but I can never be sure of her."

"Your fancies are beyond your imaginative powers to express. I should not attempt them if I were you."

He laughed. "Know this. I am letting Girling take the *Lion.* It's a short voyage. And when he comes back I shall go away. I would take you with me, Cat. You and the boy. But he'd be too small, wouldn't he? Who knows what we might meet on the seas? Here's a problem. If I leave you I shall dream every night, and in the day too, of Spaniards raiding the coast. If I take you with me. . . . How could I take you with me?"

I said: "You will have to go as other men go."

"What a reunion it'll be when I come back. You'll be on the shore waiting for me. No games, my love, while I'm away."

"Do you imagine everyone is like you? I wonder how many games *you* will play on your voyage?"

"You must not be jealous, Cat. I am a man who must needs game. But there will only be one for whom I truly care and for her I would cast aside all others."

"Do not deprive yourself," I said. "Game all you wish."

"Nay, you would be jealous, but we have to part in time. I am a sailor. For the first time I almost wish I were not. See how I love you. I love you so much that I give Girling command of my ship that I may stay with you."

I was silent being moved by such a declaration. For the first time I felt a certain tenderness toward him.

Girling had sailed away. Poor Jake, he stood watching until she was out of sight—his love, his ship, his *Rampant Lion*.

He said: "It is like seeing another man with your woman."

He was moody for a day or so, wondering why he had allowed Girling to go in his place. He busied himself with the comings and goings of others of his ships, but there was only one *Lion*.

He would follow the voyage in his mind, studying charts and working out where the ship would be. He would say: "If the winds have been favorable, if she has not been becalmed, if she has not met up with any with whom it has been necessary to do battle she will be here."

At times he wished he were with her. At others he was clearly delighted to be at home. In the midst of some of our battles he would say: "To think I gave up a lion for a shrew."

But there were the moments of deep satisfaction. I began to be satisfied with my life. Was this again the serenity of pregnancy? Perhaps it was. My mother sent a messenger to me fairly frequently with letters.

"If only you were not so far away," she mourned. "How I long to be with you at this time."

My grandmother sent recipes and even concoctions she had prepared. After having been so far away we seemed moderately close now in spite of the miles which separated us.

The months began to pass. My child was due in February.

Jake was beside himself with glee. He visualized the sturdy son we should have. He continued to despise Roberto, but Carlos and Jacko never ceased to delight him. They were growing wilder and more untamable every day. They rode, went hunting with Jake and studied archery and fencing. They played truant from the tutor whom I had engaged to teach them, which amused Jake.

He had done it all before. Anything they did which reminded him of his own exploits was applauded and they knew this. My Roberto was clever in the classroom, a fact which made me rejoice, for it gave him this advantage at least. I kept him away from Jake as much as possible and often arranged that they did not come into contact for weeks at a time, a fact which pleased them both so it was not very difficult to maneuver.

"The boy should be here when the *Lion* returns," said Jake. "We'll call him Lion."

"There is no such name," I said.

"We'll make one."

"Would you saddle the boy with such a name? He will be laughed at throughout his life."

"Much he'll care."

"As a compromise we'll call him Penn after your father."

Christmas came and with it the messenger from the Abbey bringing gifts but most welcome of all letters. Honey was happy at the Abbey. Edwina was well. "How peaceful it all is, Catharine," she wrote. "Tenerife seems far away."

And Luis? I wondered. Did Honey ever think of the two husbands who had been murdered—one before her eyes? I myself could not forget the sight of Felipe lying in his blood, slain by the man who was my second husband. I missed his courtesy; sometimes I found myself comparing Jake with him.

We lived in violent times and life was cheap. Men such as Jake Pennlyon thought little of running a man through the heart. I trembled to think of the slaughter there would be when the *Rampant Lion* met a Spanish galleon on the sea.

This hatred of men for men, when would it end? I

hoped that by the time my little Roberto was a man it would be over.

It was the end of January when the *Rampant Lion* came home. It had been a bleak month with cold winds blowing in from the east. Then it had turned warm and with the warmth came the inevitable rain. There was a heavy mist and out of this suddenly there loomed the ship. She was dangerously near the shore and the mist clung eerily to her masts; Jake at the window saw her first.

"God's Death!" he cried and stared at her.

I looked at him and saw that his deep color had faded. "What's wrong?" I cried.

"God's Death!" he cried. "What have they done to the *Lion*?"

Then he was out of the house. He was running down to the Hoe. I followed him. I stood on the shore watching the small boat row out to the shattered ship.

What a day that was! I shall never forget the dampness of the mist and that still, almost lakelike sea. And there she was, his beloved ship, with one of her masts shot off and a hole in her side.

It was a mercy she had managed to limp back to the Hoe.

I saw the faces of men, blackened by sun, gaunt from near starvation and many of them wounded.

There was little I could do.

I felt tender toward Jake as I saw the bleak horror in his face. He loved this ship and she had been ill-treated.

I knew then how he must have looked when he came back from his voyage to find that the Spaniards had taken me.

It was an old story. The ship had encountered a mightier one. There was no need to say that that ship had been a Spaniard.

She had sought to take her, but by mercy that had not happened. The *Rampant Lion* had suffered almost mortal wounds, but she had given a good account of herself. She had inflicted such deadly havoc on her enemy that the Spaniard had had to limp away, thus enabling the *Lion* to do likewise.

Captain Girling had been fatally wounded, but he had lived for four days after the attack. He had nobly directed his crew from the pallet which he had had brought on deck. He had known he was dying, but his great concern had been to bring the poor wounded *Lion* back to her master. Only when he knew that could be done did he die.

One of the sailors kept saying: "It were as though he keep his strength till then, Captain 'Lyon. It were as though he clung to life till he knew she could make port."

Jake was quieter than I had expected. I had imagined he would fly into recrimination; but he was seaman enough to understand exactly what had happened.

The *Lion* had not disgraced him or herself; she had stood up nobly against a more powerful adversary. She had given as good as she had taken. Perhaps better, he promised himself. He took satisfaction in picturing the sinking of the Spaniard. He was certain she had gone to the bottom of the sea.

He called curses on her and her crew. But his great concern was with the *Lion*. He stayed on her throughout the rest of the day and far into the night while he tried to satisfy himself that she could be made seaworthy again.

Then he came back.

"It shows what she can do, Cat," Jake said to me. "I'd always known it. There's not another of her class who wouldn't have gone down, but here she is and in a matter of months she will be herself again. I'll see to that."

This was indeed a time of disaster. The day after the *Lion* had arrived home, my pains started. It was too early and my child was born dead.

What made the tragedy more hard to bear was that the child had been a little boy.

I was desperately ill. The fact that I had lost my longed-for child did nothing to help my recovery, and for two weeks it was believed I could not survive.

Jake came and sat by my bed. Poor Jake! I loved him then. His *Rampant Lion* all but a wreck, the son he had so desired was lost to him. And I, whom he loved in his fashion, was about to die.

I heard afterward that he was almost demented and threatened the doctors that if I died he would kill them, that he spent his time between my sickroom and his ship; it was not until the end of the second week when it became apparent that I had a good chance of recovery and that the *Rampant Lion* would sail again that he became his old self.

I was delirious often; I was not entirely sure where I was. Often during that period I believed I was in the Hacienda and that soon Don Felipe would come into the room. Once I thought I saw him standing by the bed, holding the candle high while he looked at me. At another I was holding my son in my arms and he was watching us.

One night I came out of my delirium and saw that it was Jake who stood by my bed. I saw his clenched fists and heard his muttered words.

"You are calling to *him!* Stop it. You gave him a son. Yet you cannot give me one."

I was afraid suddenly, afraid for Roberto because I understood in that moment how violent Jake's feelings could be. I knew the fact that I had borne Felipe a son would be like a canker in his mind, and that his fierce hatred of Felipe, of Spain and all things Spanish would be concentrated on my son.

I wanted to appeal to him. "Jake," I said, "I am going to die. . . ."

He knelt by the bed and took my hand; he kissed it fiercely, possessively. "You are going to live," he said, and it was like a command. "You are going to live for me and the sons we shall have."

I understood something of his feelings for me. He needed me in his life; he could not contemplate being without me. His lips were on my hand. "Be well," he said. "Be strong. Love me, hate me, but stay with me."

I felt secure then, but when I began to get better my anxieties about Roberto returned. What would have happened to him if I had died? I asked myself.

It was in this mood that I sent for Manuela.

Manuela had been unobtrusive since her arrival in England; if she was homesick for Spain she had never shown it; and she and Roberto had something in common because they were both of Spanish blood.

So while I lay weakly in my bed, I summoned her

and bade her sit beside me and assure me that there was
no one in earshot.

"Manuela," I said, "tell me, are you happy in England?"
She answered: "It has become my home."

"You have been good to Roberto. He trusts you more
than he does the others."

"We speak Spanish together. It is pleasant to speak as
though one is at home."

"I have thought a great deal about him while I have
been lying here. He is young yet, Manuela, and not able
to take care of himself."

"The Captain hates him, Señora. It is because he is the
son of Don Felipe and you are his mother."

"I have come close to death, Manuela. I clung to life
because I feared for Roberto."

"Your passing would be in the hands of Almighty God,
Señora," she said reproachfully.

"I am still here, but weak. I want you to make me a
promise. If I should die I wish you to leave here at once
with Roberto. I wish you to take him to my mother. You
will tell her that I asked that she should care for him.
She must love him because he is my son."

"And the Captain, Señora?"

"The Captain does not love Roberto, as you know."

"He hates him because he is a Spaniard."

"He is a little impatient with him," I prevaricated.
"Roberto is not like Carlos and Jacko. I know you once
loved Carlos dearly. I remember when you came to the
nursery at the Hacienda. . . ."

My voice faltered and she said vehemently: "Carlos
has become the Captain's boy. He shouts. He boasts he
will slit the throats of Spaniards. He is no longer of his
mother's faith."

"He is his father's boy now, Manuela."

I saw angry tears in her eyes. I knew that she was
fiercely true to her faith and that she practiced it regularly
but in secrecy.

"And Roberto," she said softly, "he is different. Roberto
would stay true. He will never forget that his father was
a gentleman of Spain."

"You love the boy, don't you, Manuela? Carlos can
take care of himself now, but if anything should ever

happen to me look to my little Roberto."

"I will do anything to save him," she said vehemently, and as she spoke I knew that she was sincere.

I awoke to find my mother sitting by my bed.

"Is it really you?" I asked.

"My dearest Cat. Jake sent for me. I came at once and I shall stay until you are well again. Your grandmother has sent you many remedies and you know her cures always work."

I took her hand and would not release it. I wanted to be absolutely sure that I had not dreamed she was there.

From the moment she arrived my recovery was rapid. I felt that I must get well with her to nurse me. I had always felt this when she nursed me through my childish ailments. She used to say: "All's well now. Mother is here." And I believed it now as I had then.

She and my grandmother had made garments for my child. "We shall leave them with you for the next," she told me.

I felt wonderfully optimistic then. The next! I thought. Of course! What had happened to me was a disaster which befell many women during the course of their childbearing years. I had had one son. I could have another.

She brought into the house a sense of peace. I liked to hear her talking to the servants.

I told her of my interview with Manuela.

"My darling Cat," she soothed me, "you need have had no fear. If this terrible tragedy had befallen us I should have come here and taken Roberto away with me. But, God willing, his mother will live long into his manhood."

She asked me earnestly whether I was happy in my marriage and I did not know how to answer her truthfully.

"I doubt there was ever a marriage like ours," I told her.

"He sent another man out with his ship, I hear, because he could not leave you."

I laughed. "Dearest Mother, do not attempt to understand what my marriage is. It could never happen to one as gentle as you are. There is a wildness in me which matches that in him. Yet there is a good deal of hate in us."

"But you love each other?"

"I would not call it love. He was determined that I should bear his sons. He selected me for that purpose. I have failed him now . . . and at the time when he all but lost his ship! I can find it in my heart to be sorry for him, which surprises me. Mother dear, do not look so put about. You could not understand us. You are too good, too kind."

"My dear daughter, I have lived and loved and life has seemed strange to me often."

"But now you have Rupert and everything is as you always longed for it to be."

"Yet I could have taken Rupert years ago and did not. You see nothing is simple for any of us."

"I used to think it would have been wonderful for me," I said, "if I could have married Carey."

She was a little impatient with me. "You delude yourself," she answered. "All that is past. You have one child and you will have others. You are still living with an obsession of Carey, when you *have* Jake. You love him. You know you do. Stop thinking of the past. You loved your Spaniard, too, but now you have Jake. Face reality, Cat."

Was she right, this wise mother of mine?

Jake came in and sat with me.

"You will soon be well," he said, "now you have the best possible nurse."

"Thank you for sending for her."

"Now she is here I am going away for a short time. I have been thinking a great deal about Girling's family."

"What family has he?"

"His wife died recently—the sweat, I think. He has children who may be in need. He served me well. I must not fail him."

"You must make sure that they are not in want," I said.

"So thought I. I shall go to St. Austell and see for myself what is happening there. I know I shall leave you in good hands."

He left the next day.

The house seemed peaceful without him. I was able to get up. I sat at the window and looked out over the Hoe. I could see the *Rampant Lion* there. Men were working on her. Her canvases and rigging were being overhauled. The shipwrights were going back and forth in the little boats; they would be busy repairing her faulty timbers.

I wondered how long before she would sail again and when she did I knew Jake would go with her.

I drank the broth my mother prepared for me; I swallowed my grandmother's special remedies and I was soon taking my first steps into the fresh air. It was the end of April and the daffodils were in bloom. My mother, who delighted in flowers and who was herself named after the damask rose, gathered them and arranged them in pots to fill my bedroom. We walked under the pleached alley together with the sun glinting through because there were only buds and tiny leaves on the entwined branches at this time; we sat in the pond garden and talked.

It was while we sat there that she gave me the news which must have lain heavily upon her. I knew that she had been awaiting the time when I should be well enough to receive it.

We had taken our seats near the pond when she said to me: "Cat, there is something I have to tell you. You must be brave. You must understand. You will have to know."

"What is wrong, Mother?"

"It's Honey," she said.

"Honey? She is ill?"

"Nay. You love her well, do you not, Cat?"

"You know I do. She is as my sister."

"It is how I always wished you to be."

I knew that she was even now delaying the moment of telling.

"Please, tell me quickly," I begged. "What has happened to Honey?"

"She has married again."

"But why should she not? She is so beautiful. Many men would wish to marry her. It is good news, is it not? Why should she not marry?"

My mother was again silent. I turned to her in astonishment. She seemed to steel herself. Then she said: "Honey has married Carey."

I stared at the green grass, at the sun glinting on the pond. I pictured them together. Beautiful Honey and Carey, my Carey. . . . Why should I feel this sudden anger? I could not have him and it was inevitable that he should marry one day. Had I not done so . . . twice? And if he was to have a wife, why should it not be Honey, who had long loved him?

My mother had reached for my hand and pressed it warmly. She said: "I asked Manuela to bring Roberto to us. I think I hear her coming now."

I knew she was telling me: You have your son. Forget the impossible dream. That is the past. Here is the present. It is for you to make the future.

And Manuela came leading my son and when he saw me he ran to me.

"Madre, Madre," he cried; and I knew that while I lay ill and cut off from him he had suffered deeply.

I said: "I am well again, Roberto. Here I am. Why, we have missed each other."

And I was comforted.

My mother would talk of everything except Honey and her marriage, but I could not forget it. I pictured them in Remus Castle, laughing happily together, talking of the old days, making love. Did they ever mention me? I wondered. And how would Carey feel if they did?

Honey was both beautiful and lovable. There was a serenity in her beauty which I think made it doubly appealing to men. There was nothing of the wildcat about Honey; she was adaptable. She had been a good wife to Edward although she had loved Carey; she had appeared to forget Edward and had devoted herself to Luis; and now she would have forgotten them both for Carey. And I had to confess that she had always loved Carey.

My mother talked of what was happening at home. How her half brother twins were eager to go to sea and how my grandmother was trying to dissuade them, of the flowers my grandmother was growing and the many bottles that lined the shelves of her still room. "She is becoming quite an apothecary and people come to her for cures."

My mother was a little easier in her mind because there was less fear of a Catholic rebellion. The marriage of the Queen of Scots to Lord Darnley had been a good thing for England. The young consort was such an over-bearing, arrogant, dissolute and generally unsatisfactory man that he was causing a great deal of dissension above the Border.

"It is better for them to quarrel among themselves than to seek conflict with us," said my mother. "That is what everyone is saying."

The turmoil up there had increased when the shocking murder of the Scottish Queen's secretary had taken place at her supper table.

My mother shuddered. "People have been speaking of nothing else. Mary is with child and was supping privately at Holyrood when certain of her nobles burst in and dragged the young man from the table. Poor fellow, they say, he clung to the Queen's skirts and begged her to save him. What an ordeal for a woman six months with child! It was said that Secretary Rizzio was her lover. This seems unlikely. Poor woman! Why, Cat, she is but your age."

"Perhaps we should be thankful we are not born royal."

My mother said soberly: "There are dangers enough for all folk, royal or not. But it seems that matters are less tense because of this conflict in Scotland. Our good Queen Elizabeth is highly thought of and surrounds herself with able statesmen, and what we need is a good stable monarch. There is of course the religious conflict. They say the Queen is Protestant because she could be no other and it is for expediency's sake she is so. But I must whisper that, Cat. One must guard one's tongue. We are fortunate in our Queen. But as long as the Queen of Scots lives there will be danger. It is wrong to hope for trouble for others, but it does appear that the more disasters which befall the Court of Scotland the more peacefully will English men and women sleep in their beds."

It was a lovely May day when the fruit trees were in blossom and the hedges full of wild parsley and stitchwort and the birds everywhere were in full song. A glorious time of the year when nature renews herself and there is a song of thanksgiving from the blackbird and chaffinch, the swifts and the swallows.

And at this time Jake brought Romilly Girling into the house.

She was twelve years old—a sad little waif when he brought her, very thin with great green eyes too big for her small white face.

They arrived late at night after the journey from St. Austell and the girl was almost asleep when they came into the hall.

"This is Romilly," said Jake. "Captain Girling's daughter. She'll live with us. This is her home now."

I understood at once. The girl had lost both parents. She would be without a home and I was glad that Jake had brought her. I ordered that a room should be made ready for her and she was given hot food and sent to bed without delay.

Jake explained. "There was very little left. The two of them . . . she and her brother . . . were in the house alone. The servant had gone. They were almost starved to death. A distant cousin of the Captain's took the boy. All I could do was bring the girl here. Her father served me well."

"We will care for her," I said warmly.

It was wonderful to see the girl react to good food and comfortable living. She filled out a little; but she was still rather waiflike—a dainty elflike creature with quiet manners. Her great beauty was her eyes, they were big and such a strange green color that they immediately attracted attention. Her hair was dark and thick and straight. She had short, stubby lashes even darker than her hair.

June came and my mother said she must return home. Rupert was the most patient of husbands, but naturally he missed her. We said farewell and I watched her for as long as I could ride off with her party for the first stage of the long journey home.

By August of that year the *Rampant Lion* was ready to put to sea. Jake had been ashore too long. News had at length reached us that in June the Queen of Scots had given birth to a son. He was called James and this boy would be said to have a right to the throne of England.

Jake said: "The plaguey Spaniards would put his mother on the throne. You know what that means. We'd have the Papists here in no time. It would be the Smithfield fires before we knew where we were. They've got to be driven off the seas and it's up to English sailors to show them who are the masters."

I knew what this meant.

He was longing to put to sea again; and this time the *Rampant Lion* would be trusted to none but himself.

I was once more pregnant.

And in September of that year Jake sailed out of Plymouth.

The Birth of a Boy

A few weeks after Jake had left I made a disturbing discovery. I could not find Roberto. I had asked the boys where he was and they could not tell me. I was not unduly worried until a few days later he was missing again.

Knowing how close he was to Manuela, I decided to ask her if she knew where he was and I went up to the room she shared with the servants. She was not there, but one of the others told me they had seen her going up to the turret.

I mounted the steep spiral staircase to the rooms in the turret which were rarely used and as I approached I heard the sound of murmuring voices.

I opened a door and as soon as I did so I knew exactly what was happening. An altar had been set up; a candle burned at either end and kneeling at it were Manuela and Roberto.

They started up and Manuela's arm went protectively about Roberto.

"Manuela," I cried, "what are you doing?"

Her olive skin darkened and her eyes flashed defiantly.

"It is for me," she said, "to look after Roberto."

I was afraid. I knew that she was instructing Roberto in the Catholic Faith, her faith and that of his father. Had we stayed in Tenerife Roberto would naturally have followed that faith, but we were not in Tenerife and I knew what would happen if Jake ever discovered that any under his roof were as he would say "Papists."

I said: "Manuela, I have never interfered with your beliefs. As far as you yourself are concerned you are at liberty to act as you please in this matter, though you must be careful not to attract attention to yourself. You know I have always believed in tolerance. I would more people did. I know your deep faith. But if you practice it in this house, Manuela, you must do so alone and in privacy. Leave my son out of it. He must follow the faith of this house in which, with the rest of the children, his tutor instructs him."

"You ask me to look after him, to care for him, to save him. It is his soul that is important."

Roberto looked startled and I said: "Yes, Roberto, when I thought I was dying I asked Manuela to take you to my mother who would care for you. But I am well again and there is no question of my dying. I am here to look after you now."

I went to the altar and blew out the candles. Manuela stood aloof, her eyes downcast.

"I wish to follow my father's faith," said Roberto.

How much had Manuela told him of his father—that courteous gentleman who was even now so often in my thoughts? I saw the firm set of Roberto's jaw when he mentioned his father. He would never accept Jake in that role. He hated Jake. There was a fierce animosity between them. And if Jake ever discovered that he was harboring a Catholic under his roof what would he do?

Oh, God, I thought, is there no escape from this intolerance?

One thing I knew; there must be no more of these secret sessions with Manuela. When Jake returned Roberto would have to go to church with the rest of us—a good Protestant subject of our Protestant Queen.

"Take these things away, Manuela," I said. "And there must be an end of this. You are no longer in Spain. Captain Pennlyon would turn you out of the house if he discovered what you are doing."

She did not answer, and taking Roberto by the hand, I said: "Come with me." I turned to Manuela. "Leave no trace of this and never attempt to do the like again."

I took Roberto to my bedroom and reasoned with him. I explained how dangerous it was to do what he had done.

"I am a Spaniard," he answered proudly and how like his father he looked. "I am not of this country."

I put my arms about him and held him close. I wanted to tell him that we must be tolerant with each other. We must follow the true Christianity, which was to love our fellowmen. I repeated what my mother had said to me.

"It is enough to be good and kind, to love your neighbor. That is what being a Christian means."

He listened thoughtfully and I hoped I had made some impression on him.

Soon after that I miscarried. Jake had been five months at sea. I had been uneasy in my mind ever since I had discovered Manuela and Roberto together, but I don't think this had anything to do with my miscarriage.

What was wrong with me? I asked myself. Why had I borne Felipe a son when I appeared to be unable to bear Jake one?

I tried to forget my disappointment and my anxieties over Roberto by devoting myself to the children. They seemed different with Jake away. Carlos and Jacko lost something of their swagger as Roberto lost his fear. The tutor I engaged for them, a Mr. Merrimet, appeared eager to do his duty, yet with a certain gaiety which matched his name, and I was delighted that he should be so impressed with Roberto.

Edward's cousin Aubrey Ennis had come down to Trewynd to manage the estate and it was pleasant to have him and his wife, Alice, as neighbors. From them I learned that Honey had given birth to a son.

We visited Trewynd and the Ennises visited us.

There was a great deal of talk of course about political events and Scotland was the scene of the most sensational.

The Queen's husband, Darnley, had died violently in a house at Kirk o'Field, murdered undoubtedly, some said, by the Queen's lover, the Earl of Bothwell. It was hinted that the Queen of Scots herself had had a hand in the crime. News was constantly coming from Scotland. The Queen had married Bothwell, her husband's murderer, and by doing so, was the general opinion, had made her guilt plain. So much was happening in the outside world, so little in our domain, that I felt shut in with my little family of children, for I looked upon Carlos and Jacko as mine too.

Roberto was growing taller, though he lacked the stature of the other two. He was becoming more and more like Felipe and he could chatter as fluently in Spanish as in English. This perturbed me, particularly as I knew he was spending a good deal of time in the company of Manuela. Had they heeded my warning?

I think I was guilty of shutting my eyes. I did not want Roberto to turn against me. I believed he thought often of his father and the life he might have had and I wondered whether Manuela had told him that Jake had killed his father.

Yes, I was guilty. I wanted to forget what was past. I did not want to look into the future. I tried to make Roberto more interested in outdoor sports. Carlos excelled at archery and I knew he rejoiced in this because he was looking forward to showing off his skill to Jake when he returned. With a six-foot bow and an arrow of a yard in length he could shoot almost two hundred yards, which was a great feat for a boy of his age. At Pennlyon we had a tennis court and both the boys played good games. They could toss the bar and throw the hammer and were fond of wrestling. We often had visitors from the other side of the Tamar to wrestle with them, for the Cornishmen were the best wrestlers in England.

"When the Captain comes home I shall show him this or that." Those were words I often heard on both boys' lips. "When the Captain comes home." I would notice too the shadow which passed over Roberto's face at the thought of Jake's return.

Aubrey and Alice Ennis had no children. They told me that in due course Edwina would come to Trewynd. The

Grange would be hers when she was eighteen years, as she was Edward's only daughter.

I said: "I doubt if she would wish to come down to Devon after the exciting life she must lead with her mother and stepfather near the Court."

"We'll have to wait and see," was the answer to that; and meanwhile the months slipped by.

There was more news from Scotland. Mary and Bothwell had attempted to stand against the nobles of Scotland at Carberry Hill and the result was that Bothwell had fled and Mary was taken prisoner. She was incarcerated in Lochleven, where, we heard, she was forced to abdicate; her son, James, was declared King James VI of Scotland and James Stuart, Earl of Moray, Regent of that unhappy land.

"This is good for England," said Aubrey Ennis at our dinner table. "There's little to fear from the fair devil of Scotland now."

One afternoon I was in the schoolroom with the boys, Mr. Merrimet and Romilly Girling when Carlos, who happened to pass the window, gave a sudden shout of excitement.

"It's the *Lion*," he cried.

We were all at the window. And there far out to sea was a ship.

"We could be mistaken," I said.

"No," cried Carlos. "That's the *Lion*." He and Jacko jumped about madly, embracing each other. I had seen the look of fear in Roberto's eyes and it worried me. I took his hand to reassure him.

There was no doubt that it was the *Rampant Lion*. She was not limping this time. She lay proudly on the calm waters waiting for the wind.

I went into the house and gave orders in the kitchen. There should be beef and lamb, capons and partridges. They must bestir themselves with the pastry. They must prepare a banquet such as they had not produced for two whole years. The master was home.

All afternoon the ship lay there in sight of land and it was dusk when she sailed into the harbor.

We were on the shore waiting.

I watched Jake being rowed ashore. Bigger than I remembered, his face darkened by sun, his eyes more vividly blue than ever.

He leaped out of the boat and seized me. I was laughing. Yes, truly glad that he was safely back. Carlos and Jacko were jumping madly around us.

"The Captain's home," sang out Carlos.

He turned to them and shook them by the shoulders.

"Lord, how they've grown!"

He was looking around. There should have been one other to greet him. The child who had been on the way when he left.

I said nothing. I did not wish to spoil these first minutes.

"So you're glad to see me, eh? So you've missed me?"

"We had begun to feel you had been away a long time. You've had a good voyage, doubtless."

"A profitable one. You shall hear. But all in good time. Let me look at you, Cat. I've thought of you . . . day and night I've thought of you."

I was gratified, yet I felt the old need to do battle. It was like coming alive again. There was no doubt that I had missed him.

Carlos was leaping up. "Captain, a good voyage was it? How many Spaniards did you kill?"

Oh, Carlos, I thought, have you forgotten that you are half Spaniard!

"Too many to count, boy."

"Enough of killing," I said. "The Captain has come home. He wants to talk of home."

He gripped my arm. "Indeed I do," he said. "I want to be with my wife. I want to think of home."

He looked at the house and I could see that he was moved. So must it be after an absence of two years.

"I believe," I said, "that one of the most exciting things about going to sea is coming home."

"Home," he said. "Yes—home." And I knew he meant me.

Being Jake, the first thing he needed was the physical satisfaction of our union. He came straight up to our bedroom holding me firmly as though he feared I would try to escape him.

"Cat," he said. "Still the same. I've wanted you so much I've almost turned the *Lion* around and come back to you."

I wondered with how many women he had soothed his needs for one, but I did not ask.

The house was filled with the smell of cooking food— that delicious odor of hot crusty bread, the savory one of pasties and cooking meats.

I knew that he would be hungry for such food after the kind of fare he would have had so long at sea.

He said: "And the boy? I want to see the boy."

He stared at me, for he had seen the sorrow in my face.

"There was no boy," I told him. "I miscarried."

"My God, not again."

I was silent.

His disappointment was bitter. He turned on me: "How is it that you could get a boy from that poxy Spaniard and not from me?"

Still I did not speak. He shook me. "What happened? You did not take care. You were stupid . . . careless . . ."

"I was neither. It just happened. There was no reason."

He bit his lips, his heavy brows drawn together.

"Am I to have no son?"

I retorted: "No doubt you have many scattered about the world. You have two under this roof."

Then he looked at me and his anger faded. "Cat, how I've longed for you!"

I was sorry for him suddenly and I said with more tenderness than I had shown him before: "We'll have sons. Of course we'll have sons."

Then he was gay again. Remembering that he was home after two years away.

In the great dining hall the tables were loaded with food. We were seated as at a banquet. At the table on the dais I sat beside Jake. The children were there too— Roberto on my left, Carlos on Jake's right, and Jacko beside him. On the other side of Roberto sat Romilly. Jake had said she should be one of the family. In two years she had grown a good deal; she was tall, still willowy, and she was attractive because of her wonderful green eyes.

Jake had greeted her warmly and asked how she fared. She had bobbed a curtsy and raised respectful and admiring eyes to his face. As Captain Girling's daughter no doubt she would have heard stirring stories of Captain Jake Pennlyon.

The servants filled the center table and there was much drinking and revelry.

It had been difficult to keep Carlos and Jacko interested in their lessons since the Captain had returned, Mr. Merrimet complained. Romilly used to go and help him in the schoolroom and as she was growing into an attractive young girl with a quiet demeanor I did wonder whether they might make a match of it. She must be nearly fifteen years of age and it would sooner or later be necessary to find a husband for her.

Roberto studied with a fervor greater than before. I think he was very anxious to do well at what he was good at; and I knew that he lived in terror of Jake.

When the Ennises came there was always a good deal of talk about affairs of state and these all seemed to center around the Queen of Scots.

She was at this time in England, having escaped from Lochleven, where she had been incarcerated, and had lost the battle of Langside. She had, foolishly it was said, come over the border to escape the Scottish lairds and so placed herself in the hands of Elizabeth.

"Our Sovereign Lady's prisoner," Jake said with satisfaction. "That will take care of her."

But it seemed she was as dangerous in England as she had been in Scotland. A casket had been found in which were letters said to have been written by her to Bothwell. Some were of the opinion that they were forgeries; if they were not and had indeed been written by her, then she was a guilty woman, adulteress and murderess.

There were arguments at our table about the authenticity of these casket letters. I grew rather apprehensive. Aubrey Ennis was cautious, but Alice declared hotly that they were forgeries. Jake, who saw all Papists as criminals of the worst degree, was certain that Mary had written the letters, that she had committed adultery with Bothwell while married to Darnley and that she had had a hand in the murder.

"She's an enemy of our Queen and country," he declared. "The sooner her head parts company with her body, the better."

I used to try to change the subject. I had heard that a strange gamble had been introduced into the country. It was called a lottery.

"People get a number," explained Ennis. "Or so I've heard. If that is one of the lucky numbers there's a prize."

"They say," I went on, "that the sale of tickets went on day and night from January to May."

"A great number of people must take part if the prizes are to be worthwhile."

"A lottery," I said. "How I should have loved to see them at the door of St. Paul's."

But we could not talk long of the lottery, novel though it might be, and the conversation drifted back to that lady who seemed to have an ability to attract trouble and supporters and to cause friction in families.

The Earls of Northumberland and Westmorland had raised a rebellion in the North, but this had come to nothing. Heads had fallen in the affair. More would doubtless follow in the years to come, for trouble there would always be while Queen Mary lived.

After such conversation Jake would often express his suspicion that our neighbors were secret Papists and I was always afraid there would be trouble.

I had become pregnant again.

"If you don't give me a son this time," said Jake, "I'll clap you in irons and make you walk the plank."

I laughed. I had a feeling that this time I could not fail.

Jake was going on a brief voyage to Southampton in connection with his next venture and proposed to take the boys. He said nothing to me but went into the schoolroom where they were at their lessons and told them of the proposition. Carlos and Jacko were wild with joy. I did not have to imagine Roberto's reaction.

I tackled Jake when he came to our bedroom.

I said: "What is this voyage I hear about?"

"A short one. I want to give the boys a taste of the sea."

"Take Carlos and Jacko by all means."

"I shall take your brat as well."

"You will do no such thing."

"You are foolish over that boy. Do you want to turn him into a good-for-nothing?"

"He is good for a great deal. He is a scholar who can put your bastards to shame in the schoolroom."

"Schoolroom! Who cares for schoolrooms! That boy needs hardening."

"You will leave me to bring up my son as I wish."

"He lives under my roof. He will therefore not disgrace me with his whining ways."

He laughed at me.

Carlos and Jacko could not attend to their lessons. They were constantly shrieking about the house. One would hear their shrill voices: "Aye, aye, Captain. When do we put to sea? We await the tide, Captain."

Jake laughed at them, cuffed them, pulled their hair and jeered at them; and they adored him.

I said: "They will be like you when they grow up."

The day came when they were to sail. Nothing more had been said about Roberto's going. I had promised him he should not go.

They were to sail at night, the winds being favorable. They would not be away very long. Jake would do his business in Southampton and then return. It would be a lesson to the boys, he said, for he was certain that Carlos and Jacko were going to sea.

That afternoon Carlos and Jacko said good-bye to me and were rowed out to the ship. Jennet, Romilly and I stood on the shore waving to them.

I went back to the house, satisfied that I had saved Roberto from an ordeal which he would have found intolerable.

The *Rampant Lion* sailed that night. I saw her go from my bedroom and I smiled to picture the boys' excitement and Jake's pride in them.

I might have guessed Jake would outwit me. I discovered from Jennet that Jake had taken Roberto on board earlier so that he could make the trip with them.

Roberto came back none the worse for his adventure and I quarreled with Jake.

He laughed at me.

"Why, it will do the boy good. Not that he'll ever make a sailor. Not like Carlos and Jacko. By God, they're boys a man can be proud of."

The summer was hot and the burden I carried exhausting. I was now very much aware of it. A lively child, more so than Roberto had been. What one would expect of Jake's boy.

Jake went away again for a short voyage—this time to London, where the Queen had wished to see him. He came back in high spirits.

"What a woman!" he cried. "She talked severely to me about sea rovers like myself. We were causing trouble with the King of Spain, she said. We were robbing them, and robbery was something she could not tolerate. And all the time she talked to me there was a twinkle in her eye."

"She has had her share of the treasure you have brought home," I said.

"So she has and so she remembers. She wanted a private interview with me and there she laughed with me and she made it clear that she liked what I was doing, liked it very much. She is the Queen and at this time it is amusing and necessary to deceive the Spaniards. 'Not always so, my good Captain,' she said. 'There'll come a day. . . .' And in the meantime she commands me to go on . . . just as I have been doing and the more Spaniards I blow into the sea and the more treasure I bring back to England, the better she likes it. Why, Cat, she loves her roving adventures and she made me feel Captain Jake Pennlyon was by no means the least of them."

He could not stop talking about the Queen.

"When she was born," I said, "there was a great to-do because she was not a boy. They say Queen Anne Boleyn would never have lost her head if Elizabeth had been a boy. Yet could there have been a better Sovereign?"

Jake conceded that there was no Sovereign nor ever

would anywhere in the world to match up to Our Lady Elizabeth.

My lying-in chamber was prepared and I was ready and waiting. It was not a difficult labor. I awoke in the morning to find the child on the point of being born. The midwife was in the house. She had been there for two weeks, so eager were we that nothing should go wrong.

In the early afternoon of an August day in the year 1570 my child was born.

I lay there exhausted, then suddenly I was filled with joy for I heard the cry—the lusty cry—of a child.

I closed my eyes. I had succeeded. My child was alive and well.

The midwife came in and Jake was with her. I smiled at him, but immediately I saw the blank disappointment that was almost rage in his face.

"The child . . . ?" I began.

"A girl," he shouted. "Just a girl."

Then he went out.

I said to the midwife: "Bring my child to me," and she was brought and laid in my arms. I loved her small, red, crumpled face. From the moment I held her in my arms I wanted her just as she was.

Jake's brooding anger continued. He had been so certain that the child would be a boy. I knew he had pictured himself bringing up a child that would be like himself and taking him to sea with him. He had wanted that boy as he had rarely wanted anything.

He did not come near me for two days. I did not care. I had my little girl.

"She's a bonny child," said the midwife. "I'll swear she knows you."

I wondered about a name for my little girl. If it had been a son it would have been Jake, of course. She reminded me in those early days of a little bird nestling against me. I called her my little Linnet. I decided this should be her name.

A month or so after the birth of Linnet, Jake was ready to sail away. For all I knew he might be away for two years. Before he left I decided to speak to him about

Romilly. The girl was growing up and was now marriage-able. I thought that she and Mr. Merrimet might have a fancy for each other. Romilly was often in the school-room and helped him there and they were suited to each other. Would there be any objection to my making a match for them?

Jake shrugged his shoulders. "If they wish it let them," he said.

"They could stay on here. Mr. Merrimet can take on the education of Linnet and other children we will have."

"It's a capital plan," said Jake. "Get them wed. I feel a duty toward Girling and I'd like his daughter to remain one of the family. The Court's big enough to hold them."

On a glorious October day, as a fresh wind was billow-ing the sails of the *Lion* and the other two ships which accompanied her, we stood on the Hoe until the ships dropped below the horizon.

Almost immediately I set about arranging the match for Romilly. I spoke first to her. She was a demure girl and had grown quite pretty. Her green eyes had taken on a fresh sparkle.

I said to her: "Romilly, it is time you thought of mar-riage. Have you done so?"

"I . . . I have thought of it," she admitted.

I smiled. "Well, you are no longer a child. I have seen you in the schoolroom and I believe you and Mr. Merrimet are quite good friends."

She blushed. "Yes, we are good friends."

"Perhaps you might feel he would make a good hus-band. I see no reason why he should not."

She was silent.

"Of course," I went on, "if you do not wish this, then we will drop the matter."

"Has the Captain said aught of this?" she asked.

"As a matter of fact, he has. I discussed it with him before he left. Like myself, he thinks it is time you mar-ried and he thinks, too, that Mr. Merrimet would be a suitable husband. If you married him you might stay in the house and Mr. Merrimet could continue to teach. The boys will need him for some time and then Linnet will be ready. The Captain feels a duty to your father and is happy at the thought of your remaining under our roof."

She was still silent and I went on: "Perhaps I have been too precipitate."

"If I could have time to consider. . . ."

"But of course. There is no hurry. It is entirely a matter for you to decide. But when you have made up your mind tell me and then we can sound Mr. Merrimet."

This seemed to meet with her approval and we shelved the matter.

It must have been about a month later when I made a discovery which rendered the plan impossible.

Jennet, whose duty it was to bring water to my bedroom, did not appear and I went to the servants' room. There was only one maid there. All the others were about their duties.

"Where is Jennet?" I said.

The girl looked scared.

"I don't know, Mistress."

"Did she get up at her usual time?"

The girl looked embarrassed. It took me some time to get the truth from her, which was that Jennet rarely slept in the servants' room. She was almost always with a lover. This was no surprise to me. I knew that one of the grooms was her lover, and she would always have her lovers.

I guessed she was in one of the rooms over the stables and had no intention of going there. I would severely reprimand her when I saw her. Perhaps I would send her to my mother, but she would want to take Jacko with her and Jake would never allow that. He was fond of Jacko. So I could not separate a mother from her son.

Some mischievous quirk of fate led me to the tutor's room. I had for some time wanted to have a word with him about Roberto. I knocked lightly on his door. There was no answer, so I went in. The sun was shining full on the crumpled pallet, and fast asleep lay Jennet and Mr. Merrimet, naked and clasped in each other's arms.

I said sharply: "Mr. Merrimet! Jennet!"

He opened his eyes first and then I heard Jennet gasp.

I said quickly: "I will speak to you later," and shut the door.

The result was that I dismissed Mr. Merrimet immediately. I thought that a man who could indulge so blatantly in sexual adventure with one of the maids was no fit tutor for the boys. I had suspected him of a certain amount of levity but not to an unseemly extent; and I had been of the opinion that marriage would have a sobering effect on him. How mistaken I had been! Now I imagined his initiating the boys into certain practices at a too early age and I did not hesitate.

He left the next day. I sent for Jennet, who was her usual coy self—like a girl caught in her first indiscretion.

She had the usual reply that " 'twere all natural-like and Mr. Merrimet being such a gentleman. . . ."

I told her she was a slut; she was a disgrace; and I was thinking of sending her to my mother, and should do so did I not have such concern for my mother and her household. She must mend her ways or she would find herself on the roads yet begging her bread.

"There's Jacko," she told me slyly.

"He shall go with you."

"Oh, Mistress, the Captain be mortal fond of Jacko. You'd have to answer to him for that."

"I answer to no one," I cried. "I manage my own household."

She was silent, remembering that the Captain was away and that I was not to be lightly flouted. She wept and said that there was some wickedness in her that would not let her deny comely gentlemen and she thought there had been little harm done and she would serve me true and faithful forevermore.

I was fond of Jennet, so I contented myself with getting rid of Mr. Merrimet and engaging a new tutor for the boys. This was Robert Elmore, a gentleman of Plymouth who was a scholar fallen on evil times and glad to have a home. He was middle-aged and of great seriousness. I felt I had made a good change.

Linnet flourished. She was a contented baby with great wondering eyes and a ready chuckle.

Everyone in the household adored her, particularly Romilly, who was a great help with the children.

I was disturbed at the behavior of Mr. Merrimet and

I wondered what effect this would have on the girl who had such a short time ago implied that she would be ready to marry him. There was a change in her, I fancied. It must have been a blow to discover that the man who may well have made advances to her had at the same time been spending his nights with such a practiced slut as Jennet.

At first she did not appear to be greatly upset, and then suddenly I knew that something was wrong and immediately suspected that her relationship with Merrimet had not been an innocent one; indeed, was it possible that it could have been with such a man?

It was some three months after the departure of the tutor when I tackled her with this. She burst into tears and told me that she was pregnant.

I cried: "What a rogue that man is! All very well for him to take Jennet to his bed. She is as practiced as a woman can be in such matters and I doubt not has had a hundred before him. But an innocent young girl . . . under the protection of myself and the Captain! He is a rogue and a villain."

She went on sobbing.

I said: "You should have told me before."

"I daren't," she said. "What can I do now?"

"You can do nothing. I can't find a husband for you now. You will just bear your shame and the child." I was sorry for her, so I put my arm about her. "You have been a foolish girl, Romilly. You have listened to promises no doubt, and now this has happened to you."

She nodded.

"But it is not the first time it has happened to a girl. You are fortunate, for the Captain admired your father and wished to repay him for his services. You shall have your child here and it will be part of our household. Now don't fret. It's bad for the child. You did wrong and must needs bear the consequences. It is the fate of women. The man plants his seed blithely and departs. It is happening all over England . . . all over the world."

I was sorry for the girl. She was so young; and so very grateful to me for the attitude I had taken. But she was an adaptable creature and in a very short time she had forgotten her unhappiness. She settled down to making garments for her baby and helping with mending the boys' clothes, for she was good with her needle.

In June her child was born. I had sent for the midwife who had attended me, so she had the best attention we could give her. She had a son—a healthy, lusty boy.

I went in to see her—she looked so young and frail and her green eyes shone more brilliantly than ever.

She thanked me affectingly for my goodness to her and I stooped over the bed and kissed her.

"A woman's lot can be a hard one in this life," I said, "and it is our duty to help each other."

"He is a bonny boy, my son," she said.

"The midwife praises him continually."

"I have so much to be grateful for. What would have happened to me if the Captain had not come to St. Austell and brought me here?"

"He was concerned, for your father had died in his service."

"I want to show my gratitude to him . . . and to you. Would you allow me to call my child Penn?"

I said: "That is a small favor to ask."

So Romilly's lovely little boy was christened.

Suspicions

It had been a year of exciting events. In January the Duke of Norfolk was brought to trial. He had been intriguing with the Scottish Queen and had hoped to marry her and set her on the throne after having deposed Elizabeth. He had little chance of survival if such were proved against him.

In May there had been a rumor of another plot, in which the Spanish ambassador was concerned, to kill the Queen and her minister Burleigh. As a result the Spanish ambassador was ordered to leave the kingdom.

An even greater animosity was growing toward the Spanish. In the last years, when more and more English seamen had been traveling the world, again and again they had come into conflict with the Spanish. Often the English had captured Spanish gold and brought it into English harbors; a fact which delighted the Queen while she made a feint of keeping up friendly relations with Philip of Spain and implying that the action of English pirates was something she deplored but which it was hard to correct.

On the other hand, the Spanish had their successes. There were stories of how English sailors taken by Spaniards were shipped into Spain, imprisoned and tortured—not because they were pirates but because they were Protestants—and some were even burned alive at the stake.

John Gregory recounted the horrors of his imprisonment and how he had only escaped death because he had acted as a spy for Don Felipe.

The Duke of Norfolk went to the block that June and at the same time a new star appeared in the sky. As a sailor Jake was knowledgeable about the stars and he took Carlos and Jacko up to the highest part of the house and there pointed out the star to them. It was brighter than the planet Jupiter and could be seen in Cassiopeia's chair.

People began to speculate about the star. It was an omen. When it appeared suddenly the theory was that it signified Spain, which had grown in might and had conquered so much of the world. That it disappeared while the well-known stars and planets remained was an indication that the Spanish empire was about to disintegrate.

On August 24 of that year, the Eve of St. Bartholomew, there occurred an event which shocked the whole world, and I could not believe it was only the Protestant world. I was sure that what happened in Paris—and was to follow throughout France—would have as deeply affronted Felipe and men such as he was.

In the early hours of the morning the tocsins had sounded all over Paris and this had been a sign for the Catholics to emerge and slaughter every Huguenot to be found. The slaughter was horrific. The streets of Paris were running with blood; the Seine was full of mutilated bodies and the slaughter continued. The great Massacre of St. Bartholomew had begun and the cry of "kill" was taken up throughout the provincial towns of France.

The effect of the massacre reverberated throughout England. In Plymouth people stood about on street corners discussing what would happen next. A rumor was in circulation that the French and Spanish were in league together with the Pope, and they planned to murder Protestants throughout the world as they had in France.

Many were saying that it was time we gave the Catholics

in this country some of the medicine they meted out to others. "Let's give them a little Paris justice," they cried.

We heard that Lord Burleigh, who had been in the country, had hurried back to London. He feared chaos in the Capital and that there would be a repetition of the massacre in London—though in reverse. There it would be the Protestants taking their revenge on Catholics. The Queen appeared in public dressed in mourning and Lord Burleigh said, "This is the greatest crime since the Crucifixion."

There was no doubt of the effect this terrible event must have on our lives. Such momentous happenings stirred the world and none of us could ignore the rumblings of impending tragedies.

Anger against the Catholics was increased. I knew that they would be hunted out with greater severity in Protestant lands, and in those which were manifestly Catholic the persecution would intensify. Increasing numbers would be taken to the torture chambers of the Inquisition; there would be more agonizing cries as the flames consumed the bodies of martyrs.

Jake came home the following year. His homecoming was similar to the last. There was feasting and we had the mummers in to entertain us.

He took scarcely any notice of Linnet although she was a beautiful child and amazingly like him; he was amused by Romilly's fall from grace and showed a little interest in the boy. He was pleased to see Carlos and Jacko, though; and he was patient with them when they plied him with questions about his voyage. He would sit in the garden while they sprawled at his feet looking up at him admiringly, while he told them of his exploits on the high seas.

If Jake could have had a legitimate son he would have been a proud and happy man; as it was he was often brooding and resentful. I would often notice him as he glared at Roberto and his anger that I could have a son by Felipe and not by him infuriated him to such an extent that sometimes I felt he hated me.

It was after his return from his next voyage that the first of the strange events took place.

I had always followed the practice of visiting the poor

of our neighborhood personally. Some women in my position would send their servants with nourishing things to eat and warm clothing, but my mother had always gone herself and I had often accompanied her. She had said that we wanted these people not to look upon the gifts we bestowed as charity but those of one friend to another.

One morning when I was about to go into the garden one of the maids came to me and told me that Mary Lee had asked specially that I should visit her.

She was an old woman who had had three sons, all of whom had been lost at sea. I used to visit her regularly. Jake was pleased about this, for he always liked the families of sailors to be cared for. Mary was in her sixties, crippled with rheumatism; she used to sit at her window and look out when she was expecting me.

I gathered together some food into a basket and set out that afternoon, but when I reached her cottage I was surprised that she was not at the window waiting for me.

Her cottage was one of those which had been built in a night, for it was custom here that if any could put up a cottage in a night the land on which it stood could be counted as theirs. It consisted of one room only.

The door was ajar. I pushed it open and said: "Mary. Are you there?"

I saw her then. She was lying on a pallet. The light was so dim that I did not at first see her face.

"Mary, are you all right?"

She spoke in gasps.

"Go, Mistress," she whispered.

I went forward. I knelt beside her. "What is wrong, Mary?"

"Go. Go. 'Tis the sweat."

I looked down at her. I could see now the fearful signs on her face.

I put down the basket and hurried out of the house.

I saw Jake in the courtyard. I wondered afterward if he was waiting for me.

I said: "I have been to Mary Lee's cottage. She has the sweat."

"God's Death!" he cried. "You have been in the cottage?"

"Yes."

"Go to your room. I'll call a doctor. You may have caught it. He can see too if anything can be done for Mary Lee."

I went up to my room and I kept thinking of that other occasion when I had pretended to have this fearsome disease to keep Jake away.

I looked at myself in the mirror. I had been close to Mary Lee. The disease was highly infectious. Perhaps already by now. . . .

"Oh, God," I prayed, "save me from that."

I knew then how much I wanted to go on living, and in this house to see my children grow into women, to have grandchildren. Perhaps one of them would give Jake a grandson. Would that serve as well as a son?

Mary Lee had died three days after I had gone to her cottage, but the disease did not sweep through country towns as it did in crowded London.

For a week I waited in trepidation for some sign that I may have been infected, but there was none.

Jake said: "It would have served you right. Once you pretended to have it to flout me." He laughed at me. "You really must have been determined to avoid me."

"What good sense I had."

"If I'd taken you and carried you off to sea with me you might have had my son instead of the Spanish bastard."

"Don't dare speak of my son in that way."

"I'll speak how I will."

"Not of my son."

"Stop harping on the fact that you got a son by that Spanish Don or I'll do you a mischief. You goad me too far."

"I know it well," I retaliated. "Perhaps it was a pity I didn't catch the sweat and die of it. Then you could have found a wife who would give you sons."

He looked as though he had been struck in the face. At that time I thought the look meant he was horrified at the thought of losing me. Later—much later—I was to remember and wonder whether I had hit on the truth.

Jake was busily engaged in preparing for his next voyage. Sometimes he would stay on board until the early hours of the morning. Carlos and Jacko worked with him. He had promised them that they should accompany him on his next voyage.

It was on such a night that I awoke suddenly, and for a few seconds wondered what had startled me. Then I saw—or thought I saw—the door close slowly as though someone were determined to shut it with the minimum of noise.

Someone had been in the room.

I leaped out of bed and as I did so I was aware of the crackle at my feet. I looked down. The hangings about the bed were smoldering and some of the rushes were alight. At any moment they would burst into a blaze.

I picked up the heavy bedcover and beat out the flames until they were smoldering. I needed help as I rushed to the door calling that the room was on fire. By this time smoke was beginning to drift around the room and out into the corridor.

There were shouts throughout the house and in a short time servants appeared with buckets of water which they threw over the smoldering hangings and rushes. The smoke was becoming uncomfortable but the fire was out.

I heard Jake's voice. "What's going on?"

And there he was, his eyes a brilliant deeper color than usual.

"We've had a fire," said Carlos.

"In our room?" said Jake and there was a strange note in his voice. He came to me and put his arm through mine.

"What happened?"

"Something awakened me," I said.

"It's not much," said Carlos. "It could have been though."

Jake ordered that another room be prepared and that wine be brought.

I felt a little better after taking that. Then he led me to that other room and held me gently in his arms.

The next morning I was anxious to discover how the fire could have started.

"Someone was careless with a candle," said Jake. "You left it burning while you were asleep. It toppled over and then there was the blaze."

"I did no such thing. Some noise awakened me."

"Yes, the falling of the candlestick. Have done. It will teach you to be careful in future." He laughed at me. "Have you got a charmed life, Cat? 'Tis but a short time you went near the sweat. And now your bedroom catches fire and you wake just in time to catch it."

A charmed life, I thought. It would seem so.

I sent for Jennet.

"Jennet," I said, "who told you that Mary Lee wanted to see me?"

She looked puzzled. "Why, Mistress, I don't rightly remember. Much have happened since then. The fire and all."

"Try to remember, Jennet."

"I can't rightly say. I was in a rush at the time. Someone called it down the stairs, maybe. Yes, that was it."

"You'd know whose voice it was."

She wrinkled her brows.

"It was one of the servants, was it?" I persisted.

She reckoned it must have been. I could get nothing out of her.

But the seeds of suspicion were sown.

I could not get a son. If he had married someone else he could have had his son perhaps. Was that the way he was thinking? I knew that once he had wanted me as he had wanted no other woman. But I was no longer fresh to him, no longer a challenge. His desire for me may have faded, but that for a son was as fierce as ever.

I tried to remember exactly what had happened. He could have told one of the servants to tell Jennet that Mary Lee wished to see me. It was possible. And the fire? Who had quietly shut the door? Whoever it was must have been in the room a few moments before.

What had come over me? It was too absurd.

Did he want to be rid of me? Was it possible that he had tried and failed?

If this were true while he was away I was safe.

Soon after that he sailed away. Carlos and Jacko went with him, though not in the *Rampant Lion*. They were to serve under one of his captains in another of the ships.

It was some three months later when Jennet rushed into my room to tell me that the ships were back. I gave orders for a feast to be prepared and went down to the Hoe.

But I could not see the *Rampant Lion*. The two ships which had accompanied the *Rampant Lion* were home, but where was their leader?

The story Carlos and Jacko had to tell filled me with apprehension. Attacked by four Spanish ships, they had given a good account of themselves and driven them off. Jake in the *Rampant Lion* had ordered the others to stay and fight while he pursued the biggest of the galleons which was attempting to escape. That was the last they had seen of him and the ship.

They had been unable to search for her, suffering much damage themselves, and so they had returned to Plymouth, expecting to find the *Rampant Lion* already there.

After that we watched continuously, but she did not come.

The Long Absence

Two years had passed, yet still we looked for the *Rampant Lion*. Day after day I would awaken with a feeling of expectancy upon me and each day when the sun went down I would feel a heavy despondency.

Not today, I would ask myself. Perhaps tomorrow.

And still he did not come back.

Every day we talked of him. We speculated where he might be. When ships came in we would go down to the Hoe to discover if there was any news of the *Rampant Lion*.

And gradually as the months slipped by, I was afraid.

What could have happened to Jake? It was impossible to imagine him as captive in enemy hands. Yet nothing but that would keep him away so long. Unless he was dead. That was even more impossible. I couldn't believe that. I had never known anyone so alive as Jake.

Sometimes a terrible sadness settled on me. I used to

think: If he is dead, is my life over? Can it really be that I shall never see him again?

Then some certainty would remind me that he was indestructible and I would watch the horizon with new hope.

"Let him come back," I prayed. "Let us fight as we did. Even let him try to kill me. But let him come back."

Had it taken this to teach me what he meant to me? For years I had let myself brood on Carey. Oh, yes, I had loved Carey with a girlish passion, but had I loved him more when he was lost to me than I had when I believed he was mine? I knew that I had loved Felipe more after he was dead than when he lived. Was it my nature to do this?

And now Jake!

There is no one for me but Jake, I thought. Oh, Jake, come back.

But the months passed and still he did not come.

Linnet was my great solace. She was lively and remarkably like Jake. She had the same startling blue eyes and coloring; more than that there was the same stubborn line to her jaw when she was crossed. I used to think: If Jake could see her now—he who so longed to see himself reproduced would realize that this had taken place in his daughter. She was more like him than either Carlos or Jacko.

We were constantly hearing tales of the rich treasures which our seamen were bringing to England—captured Spanish gold—so much of it. The rivalries between the two countries were being intensified as the years passed.

Every time I heard these stories I thought of Jake. I imagined him in all kinds of adventures. But I knew something terrible must have happened. Otherwise he would have been home.

There seemed now to be a general feeling in the household that we should never see Jake again, but I refused to accept this. So did Carlos and Jacko, Jennet too.

"Whatever has happened to him," Carlos constantly said, "he'll be back."

There was a great deal of talk about Francis Drake, a Devon man born not far from Plymouth, in Tavistock, it was said. The Spaniards regarded him as a supernatural being, the Devil incarnate, who sailed the seas with the purpose of destroying those of the Catholic Faith and stealing their treasure. They called him El Draque, the Dragon.

It was on a December day in the year 1577 when we had the great excitement of seeing him sail from Plymouth. What a glorious sight it was. For some time Drake had been preparing for this expedition. We did not know then that he was to circumnavigate the world.

His own ship, the *Pelican*, was not unlike our *Lion*. (He was later to change its name from *Pelican* to *Golden Hind*.) With him sailed the *Elizabeth*, the *Marigold*, *Swan* and *Christopher*; and in addition to the ships there were pinnaces, some of them in pieces, the better to store them; they would be put together when needed. We were all amazed at the provisions which had been carried ashore and some of the plate for his table was of silver. He took with him too his band of musicians. It had been discovered how important music could be to men who were far from home and weary for it. A concert could turn men's mind from the boredom in which are the seeds of mutiny.

I was caught up to some extent in the general excitement, but it reminded me poignantly of the occasions when Jake had left for his voyages.

"Jake, Jake," I murmured, "when are you coming home?" I refused to consider the possibility of his death.

Carlos came in one day full of excitement. He had been talking to some of the seamen as he often did and had met the great man himself. Drake had been interested to learn that he was the son of Jake Pennlyon.

He was allowed to help load the stores and Jacko who was overcome by envy went with him and begged to be allowed to help. The outcome was, because of their enthusiasm and the fact that they were Jake Pennlyon's sons, Drake himself came to the house to see me.

Such a man must always remain in the memory forever. He was not tall, but there was about him a sense of power. His limbs were strong and he was broad in the chest; he was a merry-looking man and his large clear blue eyes had what I called "the sailor's look"—so marked in Jake —penetrating as though they could see farther than most.

His full beard was fair as was his hair and there was about him a human quality. I was deeply moved that a man who had so much on his mind at this time could spare a few hours to come to comfort me. For that was what he was trying to do.

"I have met Captain Pennlyon once or twice," he said. "A great seaman. England has need of such as he is."

I glowed with pride and my eyes filled with tears, which he noticed.

"Many of us go off for years," he said, "and most people give us up for lost. But some of us are not easily disposed of, Ma'am. Captain Pennlyon is one of them."

"My great fear is that he has fallen into the hands of the Spaniards."

"He'll give a good account of himself, I'll tell you that."

"I firmly believe he will come back."

"There's a bond between you and you would know. That's how it often is with sailors' wives."

He would find places, he said, for Carlos and Jacko in his expedition if I so wished. He had, in truth, come to ask me first.

The thought of their going off into danger sickened me, but I knew I must not stop their going.

And when he left Carlos and Jacko sailed with him.

It was a glorious sight to see them sail away—exhilarating but sobering.

Jennet stood beside me.

"To think that my boy Jacko should sail with mighty Drake," she cried. "But I'd liefer it had been with the Captain."

Then she turned away to wipe her eyes, but they were bright again almost immediately.

"Think what he'll say when he comes back!"

Undoubtedly she, like myself, believed in the indestructibility of Jake.

The days passed and still no news.

The following spring Edwina came to Trewynd Grange. She was seventeen years old and was to come into her inheritance on her eighteenth birthday. Alice Ennis called at Lyon Court to tell me that she was expected.

"We shall stay here with her," she said. "It is what

her mother wishes. A young girl should not live as mistress of such a large house."

She arrived with a band of servants, whom she had chosen from Remus Castle, the home of her stepfather. I was eager to see her and as soon as the news was brought to me that she had arrived I went to Trewynd.

I could never enter the hall there without memories flooding into my mind. I looked up at the peep and long practice told me from the shadow there that someone was watching me. I remembered how Honey and I had looked down and seen Jake come into the hall; I remembered the night when I had been taken away to the galleon. But that was a long time ago and now Edwina, Honey's daughter, was here.

As she came into the hall I held out my hands to her. She clasped them and smiled.

I think we loved each other from that moment.

Edwina was a frequent visitor at the Court; she had become as a daughter to me and she and Linnet were good friends.

I could never forget Jake. I dreamed of him often and when I awoke and found he was not beside me that overwhelming emptiness would sweep over me.

On a November day in the year 1580, Francis Drake sailed into the harbor.

What excitement there was! He had brought with him a marvelous quantity of treasure such as none had ever brought before. There was gold and silver, precious stones, and pearls as well as silks, cloves and spices.

He had also brought back Carlos and Jacko.

How they had changed! They were men now—experienced sailors.

The first one they looked for when they stepped ashore was their father. I shook my head sadly, but he was uppermost in our thoughts during the celebrations for their homecoming. We were all so much aware of the missing head of the house—even Linnet, who could scarcely remember him.

Carlos and Jacko talked a great deal of their adventures. There had been storm and calm; they had visited strange lands and come near to death. They had grown up and the sea was in their blood.

The expedition would be remembered throughout the years to come because although Drake was not the first man to discover that the Earth was a sphere, he had actually been the first to encircle it, whereas Magellan, who had known this was possible, had been prevented from completing the circle by his death in the Philippines.

Drake was the great hero of the West Country and very soon after his return he sailed the *Golden Hind* up the Thames and there at Deptford the Queen herself came to knight him.

Such men as Drake, Carlos and Jacko had become the heroes of our time because they would be the leaders when the time came to face the Spaniards.

Jake Pennlyon was such a man.

He had now been away so long that it was only because he was Jake that I could continue to hope. Carlos, Jacko, Jennet, everyone who had known him intimately, refused to believe that he was dead. Such was that magic aura he had always conveyed to us.

Sometimes I used to open the cupboard in which his clothes were kept and touch the cloth of a coat. Then I would imagine I heard his laughter. "Don't dispose of them, Cat. I'll need them yet."

Once I opened a drawer and a moth flew out. I was concerned at once. I must care for his clothes and I did not want anyone else to do this. I decided I would therefore take them out, fold them afresh and put among them a powder made from herbs which my grandmother had given me and which she was convinced would preserve cloth forever against moth and insects.

It was then that I made the horrifying discovery. In the pocket of one of his jackets was a figure. As my fingers closed around it I was transported back in my mind to that occasion when I had found the image of Isabella in my drawer.

There was no doubt who this was meant to be. Myself! I could see the pinhead, a little rusty—where it had entered the cloth of my gown.

And in Jake's pocket!

It could not be. I remembered how on more than one

occasion he had raged against witches. But why? Because he believed in the evil they could create, because he believed that could kill, because he feared them?

And why should this image be in his pocket?

I studied it. The likeness was there. My thick straight hair, and the eyes were painted a vivid green. There could be no doubt who it was meant to be.

Had he consulted a witch? Had he been carrying out her orders? Not Jake! Yet this thing was in his pocket. It must have been lying there for years. Why had he left it there and gone away? Had he hoped that when he came back the witch's work would be done?

I was going to destroy that figure.

I put it into the pocket of my gown and went out into the garden. There was a hut on the outskirts of the grounds. Few people went there. I buried the doll beneath some braken and set it alight. The grass was dry, as was the braken, and I had not thought there would be such a blaze. As the wax of the image spluttered, Jennet and Manuela, who must have seen the smoke, came running out to the hut.

"It's nothing," I said. "Only a small fire."

"How did it happen?" asked Jennet. I did not answer.

As the fire died down Jennet stamped on the last of it.

Manuela knelt down and picked up a piece of charred cloth. It was the piece with the pin sticking in it.

"People should be careful of fire," I said, trying to sound matter-of-fact. "The ground is very dry just now."

Carlos and Edwina were attracted from the moment they met and two months after the return of Drake's expedition Edwina came to the Court and said she had something to tell me.

She and Carlos wanted to marry.

"You have known each other such a short time," I said.

"It is long enough," she answered. "And he is a sailor and sailors have no time to waste."

I had heard that before, I thought with a smile.

"You see, Aunt Catharine, although we have only just met, we must have known each other years ago. We were together as babies. It is interesting that we were both born far across the sea . . . both in the same place and it seems like fate that we were brought together."

"Everything in life is fate."

"But the manner in which we were brought together! Your being taken away with my mother and there was Carlos . . . and you found him and brought him to the Hacienda. My mother has told me about it."

"Are you sure that you love Carlos?"

"Oh, Aunt Catharine, there could be no doubt."

"It isn't easy to be a sailor's wife. There will be long periods when he is away and one day perhaps. . . ."

I could not go on and she put her arms about me.

"Carlos' father will come back," she soothed. "Carlos is sure of it."

"And I am too," I said vehemently. "I know that one day I shall look from my window and his ship will be in the bay. But, oh, how the years go on . . . and no news . . . no news. . . ."

There were tears in her eyes. Her love for Carlos made her understand my tragedy.

Manuela came to my room. Her great mournful eyes glowed with fear as they rested on me.

"Señora, I must speak with you."

"What do you wish to say, Manuela?"

"There was wax. It was an image. There was what was left of the gown and I have the pin here." She laid it on the table before me. "It was pierced here." She touched her left side. "It was meant to go through the heart. It must have been like the image that was made of Doña Isabella. Such images are the same throughout the world. Witches are everywhere . . . they work together in the same way."

"What are you suggesting?"

"Someone burned that. They were burning the one who was represented by the image."

"I burned that image, Manuela."

"You, Señora! You wish someone dead!"

"That image was made to look like me. I found it in . . . I found it. I will not have such things in this house so I burned it."

"But, Señora, someone made an image of Isabella and she died. . . ."

"I don't believe in such nonsense."

She shook her head at me sadly.

When she had gone, I asked myself: Was I speaking the truth? How much did I believe? I remembered how I had been sent to Mary Lee's house and how I knew someone had been in the bedroom, for I had seen the door close, and then I had discovered that my bed curtains were ablaze. I had found the image among Jake's clothes, and since he had gone away there had been no more strange attempts on my life.

Was it possible that he had attempted to be rid of me and when he had failed had gone away, temporarily abandoning his plans until his return? I would not believe such nonsense. And yet . . . the suspicion was sown and it often came into my mind.

There was to be a wedding at Trewynd.

Edwina was very excited naturally. "My mother is coming," she said. "My stepfather was not going to accompany her, but I have written saying that he must. It is after all my wedding."

I thought then: I shall see Carey. After all these years, I wonder what my emotions will be.

At Trewynd the Ennises were preparing for the wedding. Everywhere there was the odor of burning rosemary and bay leaves to sweeten the place. I ordered that the same should be done at Lyon Court, for although our rushes were replaced regularly it was always necessary to sweeten the place at intervals. We did this at the Court by moving to different parts of the house while others were being sweetened and with so many guests coming we needed to sweeten all through. I was glad of the knowledge of herbs which I had gleaned through my grandmother in the old days and I was able to add all kinds of aromatic herbs to our sweetening.

It was an exciting day when the party arrived. They had been traveling together for safety. My mother and Rupert would stay with me, Honey, Carey and their children at Trewynd.

It was wonderful to see my mother. She had aged a little, but there was such a look of serenity about her and Rupert as to tell me that they enjoyed a happy life together.

Sooner or later I must inevitably meet Carey and I did so first in the great hall of Trewynd where he stood with Honey. The years had not marred her beauty. Her kind was indestructible. The violet eyes might have been more shadowed, but they were as luminous as ever and I realized at once that because she was fulfilled as she had never been before, and was a contented and happy woman, a new quality mingled with her beauty and added something to it.

Such meetings were necessarily emotional. I kissed her warmly and all the time I was conscious of Carey standing there. Then my hands were in his, his cheek laid against mine. I felt the firm pressure of his hands.

"Catharine!"

"Why, Carey . . . it is so many years."

"You have changed very little."

He had changed a good deal. There was something haggard about the lean face which I had once loved so well and remembered through the years. I wondered whether I would have recognized him had I not known who he was.

We talked about the journey, what was happening at home and the pleasure this marriage gave them.

It was easy and passed smoothly and I could not have believed that I could have shown so little emotion on my meeting with Carey.

It was different when we met alone in the pond garden. There we could speak freely.

"Oh, Catharine," he said. "I have thought of you often."

"And I of you," I told him.

"There was nothing to do but part."

I shook my head.

"I wanted to die," he said.

"I too. But we lived."

"Well, we made a life for ourselves," he said. "When I heard that you had been abducted by the Spaniards I cursed myself for not being with you . . . for not having defied everyone and everything."

"It is long ago. And you are happy . . . with Honey?"

His face softened. "I never thought to be so happy since I lost you."

"She loved you always."

"Yes, she has told me. I have my compensation and you have your children."

"And Jake too, Carey. He will come back. I know he will."

The wedding was celebrated. Carlos went to live at Trewynd and the Ennises left with my mother and Carey and Honey.

I helped the newly married pair settle in.

I was glad of the way everything had turned out. I had seen Carey again, not without some emotion, yet I was certain now that it was Jake I wanted.

I had loved Carey; I had loved Felipe. I had lost them both. Jake was different. He was part of me. To be without Jake was like being but half alive.

That was why I had to go on believing that he would come back.

It was late February. Carlos was at sea and Edwina had spent Christmas with us. We had decorated the house with holly and ivy; we had played our games. Time was passing. Linnet was now nearly fourteen years old and I had passed my fortieth birthday.

Poor Edwina longed for children, but so far there was no sign of them; I was deeply affected by the manner in which her eyes so often strayed to the horizon; she was dreaming of the day when a ship would appear and Carlos would come home to her.

Over the years the activity at sea had increased greatly. There were six or seven ships to every one there had been in the old days. There were prizes and honors to be won at sea. The name Sir Francis Drake was on every lip. He had won riches and honors—not only for himself but the country. There were laughing references to the fear of the Spaniards for El Draque. They thought he was some mighty god—or the Devil—and they lived in daily dread of him.

One day Edwina came over to Lyon Court as she did so often. She said that friends of Carey's had called on their way to their country estates in Cornwall and had stayed a night at Trewynd. They had brought news from London.

There had been another plot which might well have succeeded; and if it had, said Edwina, we might have had a new Queen on the throne.

"That could never be," I said. "The people are firmly behind Our Sovereign Lady, Elizabeth."

"Nevertheless the Spanish ambassador has been dismissed from the Court. He is returning to Spain without delay. Francis Throckmorton has been arrested and is now in the Tower."

I said: "There have been those plots ever since the Queen of Scots came to England."

"And there will be, some say, until her death. It is a wonder the Queen does not sanction it. Mary is in her power and one hears that the Queen's ministers constantly advise it, yet she holds off."

That visit of Edwina's disturbed my peace of mind.

It was June and the gardens were full of damask roses, which I loved particularly because they reminded me of my mother. Mayflies danced over the pond in the garden and there were pyramids of loosestrife by the streams; purple nettles abounded in the hedges mingling with roses; and on the air was the scent of honeysuckle.

The weather was exceptionally calm which created a stillness everywhere as though nature were waiting for something dramatic to happen.

Soon, I thought, Jake must come home. It is on a day like this that I shall look from my window and see the *Rampant Lion* on the horizon.

The night came and I sat at my window, as I often did, looking out to sea; I was restless that night; it was almost like a premonition, for as I sat at my window I heard the sound of a horse's hoofs in the distance, then coming nearer and nearer. I could see nothing and suddenly the sound ceased. I wondered who was riding by at this hour and as I sat at my window I saw the figure below, stealthily creeping across the courtyard.

It was a familiar figure. Roberto! I thought.

I went down hastily, unbolted the iron-studded door

and stepped out into the courtyard.

"Roberto!" I cried.

"Madre!" I held him in my arms and he was almost sobbing.

"My love," I said, "you have come home. But why do you come so stealthily?"

He whispered: "None must know that I am here. I have much to tell you."

"You are in trouble, Roberto?"

"I don't know. I may well be."

With a terrible anxiety I bade him take off his boots. He must come to my bedroom as quietly as he could. I sent up a prayer of thankfulness that Jake was not at home.

We reached my bedroom in safety.

I said: "Are you hungry?"

"I ate at an inn near Tavistock," he told me.

"Tell me what is wrong."

He said: "Madre, we must set the true Queen on the throne. We must depose the bastard Jezebel."

"Oh, no," I cried. "Elizabeth is our good and true Queen."

"She has no right. I tell you, Madre, she has no right. Who is she? The bastard daughter of Anne Boleyn. Mary is the daughter of kings."

"Elizabeth is the daughter of a great King."

"By his concubine. Queen Mary is the true and legitimate heir. She will restore the True Religion to England."

"Ah," I said, "it is a Catholic plot."

"It is the desire and determination to set up the True Religion, Madre. Spain is behind us. They are ready to strike. Their dockyards are working day and night. They are equipping the finest Armada the world has ever seen. None will be able to stand against it."

"My dear Roberto, *we* shall stand against it. Do you imagine that men like your stepfather, like Carlos and Jacko, would ever be beaten by the greatest ships in the world?"

"They are braggarts, all of them." How his face contorted with contempt and hatred as he spoke of Jake. "When they see the ships of Spain have come against them they will realize they are beaten."

"That they never will."

"You cannot understand the might of these ships, Madre."

I did remember the majesty of one Spanish galleon.

"The day will come. It can come any time now. We have failed . . . but we will not always fail."

"What has brought you here?" I asked anxiously. "You are in danger?"

"I may well be. I am not sure whether it was known that I was involved. I thought it wiser to leave. None know where I have gone. They may discover my involvement. Throckmorton is in the Tower. If they should rack him. . . ."

"Throckmorton!" I said. "You are involved in this? Oh, Roberto. Roberto, what have you done?"

"I was given my post on the recommendation of Lord Remus and that may have saved me. Remus is trusted and he vouched for me. But because of this I thought I should get away for a time. So I came here. But, Madre, if they should come here to look for me. . . ."

I said quickly: "How can we keep your visit a secret?"

"Just for a while, Madre . . . until we can be sure."

I said: "Thank God your stepfather is not at home."

He laughed. "What joy he would have in handing me over to Walsingham."

"Walsingham!" I cried.

"He has his spies everywhere. It is due to him that we are discovered."

"This is like a nightmare come to life. It is what I always feared. This conflict in the family. My mother suffered from it . . . so much. And now. . . ."

There was a fanatical light in Roberto's eyes. He took my hands. "Madre," he said, "we have to bring back the True Religion to this sad country."

"Tell me how you are involved. Tell me what has happened."

"Francis Throckmorton has traveled widely in Spain. He has spoken to men of great influence there; he has seen what efforts are being made. From Madrid he went to Paris and there met agents of Queen Mary. The Queen's family, the Guises, are proposing to raise an army and Throckmorton returned to London and set up in a house at Paul's Wharf. There he received letters from Madrid and Paris and they were passed on to the Queen of Scots."

"Oh, my God, Roberto, what are you involved in!"

"In trying to bring great benefits to this country. In trying to bring the people back to sanity, to truth and. . . ."

"And to bring yourself to disaster."

"Madre, I should be dying for a great cause and what would my death matter if that cause were to succeed?"

I said angrily: "It would matter to me. What do I care for causes? I care for my son . . . for my family. What matters it to me what doctrines flourish? I believe in the simple one: love one another. It does not seem to involve how one worships, only that one behaves like a good Christian."

"You think like a woman."

"If only the whole world would do that it would be a happier place."

He said: "Walsingham's spies saw Throckmorton's visits to the house of the Spanish ambassador. He was arrested; his house searched and there was found a list of Catholics in England who were prepared to take part in enterprises to restore the true religion."

"And your name was among these?"

"It may well be."

I was silent in my terror.

"We must hide you, Roberto. But for how long? Before the household is astir we must hide you."

"Manuela will help," he said.

I knew that he was right.

I said: "I will call her. But no one must know why. Stay here. Do not stray from this room. I will lock the door while I am away."

I went down to the room where Manuela slept with Jennet. I was thankful for the promiscuous habits of Jennet, for she was not there and Manuela was alone. I was prepared to ask her for some toothache remedy if she was not, but that was not necessary.

"Manuela," I whispered, "Roberto is here."

She rose from her pallet with alacrity, her face alight with joy.

"He has come back?"

"He may be in danger."

She nodded as I explained.

"We must hide him for a while," I said. "You must help me."

I had no doubt she would do this.

We went back to my room and unlocked the door. Manuela gathered Roberto in her arms. She spoke to him softly, lovingly in Spanish. The gist of her words was that she would willingly die for him.

She turned to me: "There is a hut on the border of the gardens. Old gardening tools are kept there. Few people go there."

"The gardeners might," I said.

"Nay. They do not. They keep all they need in the garden house. The weeds grow around the hut and it is shut off by bushes. If we could lock this we could hide Roberto there . . . for a while."

"We must do it until we can find a better plan," I said. "None must know, Manuela, that Roberto is here except we two."

She nodded fiercely and I knew that I could trust her.

"We will take covering to keep him warm, and hot food. Can you do that, Manuela?"

"You may trust me to look after Roberto," she said.

I knew it. Not only did she love him, but like him, she was a Catholic and she wished to see the Queen deposed and Queen Mary set up in her place.

I said suddenly: "You came on a horse. Where is it?"

"I tethered it by the mounting block."

Manuela and I looked at each other.

"We must take it into the stables," I said. "Let it seem as though it has strayed in."

"Will that be believed?" I asked Roberto.

"What else can we do? We cannot leave it there. Moreover, if you needed it quickly it would be ready."

"I will see to it," said Manuela.

This she did and although in the stables they talked of the strange horse that had suddenly appeared they were not unduly surprised. Someone would claim it, it was said. In the meantime it would be cared for with the others.

There followed two weeks of fearful apprehension.

I could not stop myself from walking near the hut. We had an understanding that we would knock at the door in a certain way and it was not to be opened for any other. I would wake in the night sweating with fear, fancying that I heard the Queen's men in the courtyard. I was never at peace for one moment. Even during meals I would start up at the sound of horses' hoofs.

"What ails you, Mother?" asked Linnet. "You jump at every sound."

I had to be thankful that Jake was not at home, for I was sure it would have been impossible to hide Roberto if he had been.

Linnet was worried about me. She thought I was ill.

I wanted to tell my daughter that we were hiding her brother, but I dared not. I trusted her, but I was determined that she should not be involved.

We kept Roberto in the hut for two weeks. How we managed I cannot understand. Manuela was a creature of stealth. She had found a key to the hut; she locked Roberto inside it. There was a window high in the wall through which he could escape into a bush of overgrown shrubs if the need arose. Manuela thought of everything. She was a wonderful planner, and she worked zealously for Roberto.

Edwina brought the news that Throckmorton had been executed at Tyburn. He had been racked three times and had confessed that he had compiled the lists of English Catholics who would support the cause of the Queen of Scots, and plans he had made of English harbors had been found.

So Throckmorton was dead; and what of those whose names had been found on the list?

Walsingham was a man who worked in the shadows. If he knew a man was involved in plots he might not immediately arrest that man; he might have him watched in the hope that he could, through him, draw more into the net.

How could we be sure whether Roberto was one of Walsingham's wanted men?

At least we had had no inquiries for him. It was some time since he had left his post and surely if they were suspicious of him the first place they would have looked for him was at his home.

He too realized this and he knew he must pass on.

One night when the household had retired Manuela and I went down to the stables. We saddled the strawberry roan and Roberto rode away on it.

In the morning the servants would say the animal had strayed off just as it had strayed in. That, at least, was what Manuela and I hoped.

"Take care, my son," I said.

Some months after Roberto had left I awoke one morning to see a strange ship in the bay.

There was a little crowd on the Hoe watching the ship. They had never seen the like before. She was long and had but one sail and on this were strange signs. The ship appeared to be manned by numerous galley slaves.

"She's an Arab," was the verdict.

But someone said: "Nay she's a Turk."

I invariably went down when there was an excitement on the Hoe because I always hoped that I would hear news of Jake.

I watched the boats coming ashore and suddenly the miracle happened. I saw Jake. I stood for a moment staring at him. He returned my gaze and then it was as though thousands of voices were singing a triumphant anthem.

Jake had come home.

Murder in Mind

He stood before me . . . changed, yes changed. So lean
had he become that he looked taller than ever; his hair
was bleached almost white by long exposure; his face
was deeply bronzed and more lined, but his eyes were
as startlingly blue as ever.

I flew into his arms, a wild joy taking possession of me.

He held me for a long time; then he drew away from
me and looked long and searchingly into my face.

"Still the same Cat," he said.

"Oh, Jake," I answered, "it has been such a long time."

We went into the house. He looked at it wonderingly,
touching the stone, marveling at it, loving it. Over
the years how he must have dreamed of it, of our life
here, of me!

"We have made no preparations to welcome you," I
began. "If we had known there would have been such a
feast. . . ."

"Have done," he answered. "It is enough to be home."

There was so much to talk of, so much to tell and it was only by degrees that I discovered the full story of what had happened to Jake during those long years.

I learned how they had encountered the Spaniards and that in pursuing one of the galleons Jake had left the rest of his group. The Spaniard had got away and the *Rampant Lion* had not escaped unscathed, and knowing that she could not undertake a long journey, Jake had been forced to look for some place where he might get her refitted. No easy task on a coast where the Spaniards might appear at any moment. Jake knew the Barbary Coast and it occurred to him that he might persuade or threaten the natives to help him refurbish his ship.

What a story it was of frustration, misery and hardship!

I could sense the force of the fury he had known when after leaving his ship and traveling some fifty miles inland he and his men were captured by a company of Spaniards.

Proud Jake, a captive in such hands! How that must have maddened him.

He did not tell the whole of the story at once. I pieced it together as I learned of incidents here and there. Over the years, I promised myself, I should discover more and more in detail, the whole terrible story of what had kept him away all these years.

I heard snatches of how they had been chained and marched through the jungle, of the mosquitoes which tormented them and were responsible for the death of some, of the leeches which clung to their limbs when they tried to cool them in the streams. And worst of all was the knowledge that they were the slaves of their Spanish masters.

He must have spent two years in the jungle before they sailed for Spain. Jake was a prisoner with some thirty members of his crew who had so far survived. They knew what they were heading for . . . Spain and the Inquisition. There would be no leniency for a man whose main reason for sailing the seas was to rob and plunder Spaniards and to destroy them.

Fortunately for Jake perhaps—although it seems strange to say "fortunately" in such circumstances—in the Mediterranean, the galleon in which he was sailing encountered several Turkish pirate ships and in the skirmish the galleon was defeated; Jake and his men, who were chained in the hold of the Spanish ship, became the prisoners of the Turks.

My poor Jake, sold into slavery! There was one small piece of good fortune, though, because he and those of his crew who were taken with him were sent to the galleys and there they worked together, year in and year out, pulling at the oars.

He had lost count of time, but always the determination stayed with him that one day he would escape. He impressed this on his men: One day they were going to return to England.

He told me how he had dreamed of the homecoming, never allowing himself to believe for one moment that it could fail. Such vivid accounts he gave of the stinking galleys, of the endless toil, of the beating of the drum to keep them in time, of the galley-master brandishing his whip for those who flagged.

"Oh, Jake," I cried, "what has this done to you?"

But he was the same as ever. He had come back, had he not? All sailors knew when they left home that they faced fearful odds. He had been fortunate all his sea life until that ill-fated day when he had chased a Spaniard and ill luck had sent him ashore to look for native help in a place which was already occupied by the accursed enemy.

"All the time I was biding my time," he said. "I planned every waking moment. There were times when we were released from our chains. They had to keep us alive. I have a good and faithful band and we made the most of those moments."

He would tell me more later. There were many hideous details to come. But first I wanted to know how he had come home.

He, with some fifty slaves, had overpowered the captain of the Turkish craft. They had seized her and after many adventures at sea had brought her back to Plymouth.

I said he must not go away for a long time. I wanted to nurse him back to health.

He laughed at that. He was strong as ever. "Hardship never hurt a man," he told me.

But he seemed content to stay. The *Rampant Lion* was lost and he would build a new ship. He would want to watch her grow. He was delighted to hear that the boys had sailed with Drake. They should have their own ships to command, he told them.

And I think I was happier than I had ever been before. I had come to terms with myself. Perhaps, though, during his absence I had glorified Jake. I had to relearn so much about him. I had forgotten how coarse he could be, how demanding, and he had not lost his love of a fight. Although in my heart I rejoiced at his return, at the same time we argued endlessly.

He still taunted me for not giving him a boy and I was angry with him because he was inclined to ignore Linnet, and a more attractive girl and one more like him there could not be. She had taken a dislike to him too. I think when I had talked of him I had built up a picture which she now thought to have been false. They were constantly at cross purposes.

To my great joy soon after Jake's return I conceived. This time I must have a boy.

How I longed for this son who would be born of a new Catharine, a woman who had come to terms with life and knew how good fate had been to her. Jake had been brought back to me, and whatever we said to each other in our heated arguments, I was certain that I could find no true happiness without him.

It had been a wonderful realization. And now that he was back I desperately wanted him to have his son.

Jake was busily concerned with the building of the new ship. He enjoyed the company of Carlos and Jacko and Romilly's Penn, now thirteen years old, adored him.

The months passed. Jake often talked of his adventures and more and more clearly the picture of those years was built up.

Once I said to him: "Now that you are home and safe perhaps you will never want to go to sea again."

He looked at me in astonishment and burst into laughter, "Are you mad? When I am building my fine ship? How could a sailor give up the sea? I'm going out to kill many more Spaniards yet. I've a score to settle. . . ."

He had changed little.

He talked often of the boy we would have. "Our boy," he said. "He'll be the best of the bunch. We'll call him Jake after his father."

I said I would not call him anything else.

He had a name for his new ship. A *Lion* of course. The *Triumphant Lion* because this young *Lion* was going to avenge the old one. This one would be mightier, his claws would be sharper, his teeth stronger. She was going to sweep the Spaniards off the sea.

Everything was ready for my confinement. The midwife had been in residence for a week before the child was born. We were taking no chances.

And so my child was born.

I lay in my bed experiencing that strange mingling of exhaustion and triumph which will be familiar to every mother. Then I knew the truth. My child was alive and perfect in every way—except that it was a girl.

Jake came in. I saw his face puckered and distorted.

"A girl!" he said. "Another girl!"

I felt the tears on my eyes; they were running down my cheeks. I felt so weak from my ordeal and the sight of him there angrily bitter was more than I could endure.

Linnet was at my bedside. "Mother, it is wonderful," she cried. "I have a sister . . . a dear little sister. Get well soon, dearest Mother."

She stooped and kissed me, and when Jake strode out of the room she went after him.

I heard her voice. "You wicked man! You cruel man! She has suffered and you do not care. All you care for is to have a boy. I hate you!"

I heard the sound of a resounding slap and I thought: He has struck her.

I tried to get up but I could not. The midwife was holding me.

She was laid in my arms and I loved her.

I decided to call her Damask after my mother.

Jake was penitent afterward. He, a man who had never disguised his feelings, had been unable to control his bitter disappointment at my bedside.

He came to see the baby and could not hide his distaste as he looked at the crumpled pink face of my second daughter.

He said: "It seems you and I were not intended to have boys."

"It would seem so," I answered. "You made the mistake. You said that you had chosen me to be the mother of your sons. It is your fault. You should not have chosen me."

He laughed suddenly.

" 'Tis no use crying over what's done."

"Nay," I agreed, "we make our mistakes and must needs suffer for them."

"Ah, Cat, we are in agreement at last. So I have got another girl who doubtless will grow up like her sister." He touched his cheek. "The young devil," he went on. "She struck me. Upbraided me for my treatment of you and then quick as lightning she upped with her hand and hit me across the cheek. That young woman will have to be taught a lesson or two."

"Take care that she does not teach you one."

"Not only have I got me a wife who cannot give me sons, but I've begotten a virago of a daughter. By God, my household is turning against me." He clenched his right fist suddenly and beat his left palm with it. "I wanted a boy," he said. "More than anything on earth I wanted a boy."

There was a boy in the house, Romilly's Penn, and from the time of Damask's birth Jake's interest in him increased. Penn was a bright lad, fearless and showing a great interest in ships and the sea. Jake had a model of the *Rampant Lion* and the boy had been discovered taking it apart, a fact which might have earned him a severe punishment. But Jake took a lenient view of the offense and showed the boy how the ship was operated. I was amused to see them trying out this precious model on the pond in the garden.

Romilly was pink with pleasure. I came upon her standing by the pool, her hands clasped in a kind of ecstasy as she watched Jake and the adventurous Penn together. I was sure she hoped Jake would do for her son what he

had done for Carlos and Jacko. I was certain that he
would. Penn had the sea in his blood, for his grandfather
had been, as Jake had said often, one of the best captains
who had sailed with him.

As each month passed there was more and more talk
of the growing strength of Spain. The captive Queen of
Scots was a perpetual menace. There were constant rumors
of plots to set her on the throne and bring the Catholic
Faith back to England.

The Queen honored her sailors. The news of the great
fleet of ships which Philip of Spain was building was
constantly discussed. People cheered the English ships
when they came into the Hoe as though they looked to
them to save us from the terrors which the Spaniards
would thrust upon us.

Old sailors on the Hoe chatted together about the
Spaniards. One or two of them had been captured by
them. There was one man who had been taken before the
Inquisition, tortured and somehow escaped before they
had been able to burn him at the stake. He had many a tale
to tell. The people had to understand that the ships of the
Spanish Armada would bring not only guns and fighting
men but instruments of torture which would make the
rack and thumbscrews and even the Scavenger's Daughter look like children's toys.

John Gregory, who was still with us, was clearly
afraid. I wondered what would happen to him if he
were taken by the Spaniards a second time.

It was almost open war between England and Spain
at this time. Philip declared that he would seize all ships
found in Spanish waters. Elizabeth replied that reprisals
would be taken. She equipped twenty-five ships to avenge
the wrongs done to her and her brave seamen. Who
should be in charge of this venture but the great Sir
Francis and he set forth in the *Elizabeth Bonaventure*
with vengeance in his heart?

We heard stories of his exploits; how he had raided
Spanish harbors and carried off treasure. Drake sailed on
to Virginia, where he had a conference with the colonists
who had been sent there by Sir Walter Raleigh.

Very soon after that two very interesting products

were brought to England. The potato, which we found very good to eat and which we began to serve with meats to great advantage. The other was tobacco, a weed, the leaves of which were rolled and smoked, and from these, oddly enough, many people began to find a certain solace.

These were uneasy times. We could never be sure when we would look from our windows and see the Spanish Armada bearing down on us. Jake said this was nonsense. We should have warning of their coming. Sir Francis Drake and men like himself were ever watchful. We need have no fear. The Spaniards were not ready yet and when they did come, by God's Death, we would be ready for them.

He had decided that he would not go far away until the matter was resolved. He was putting his ships at the disposal of the Queen. He would make forays into Spanish harbors, but he was going to be at hand when the great confrontation took place.

Jake had changed a little. He seemed to enjoy being at home. He was becoming more domesticated. He took no notice of Damask, but he was very watchful of Linnet and the fact that she scorned him seemed to amuse him. He was Penn's hero and the boy would follow him about at a discreet distance until Jake either roared at him to be off or had a few words with him.

Jake was mellowed, I believed; there seemed a certain contentment about him. He had accepted the fact that we were not going to have a son.

On my birthday he gave me a cross studded with rubies. It was a beautiful piece. I wondered whether he had taken it from some Spanish home, but I did not ask him because I did not wish to question a birthday gift.

He liked to see me wearing it so I did often.

A few weeks after he had given me the cross I began to suffer from an occasional headache and when this was so I used to take my food in my room. Jennet would bring it to me because in spite of our differences I had always wanted her to be my personal maid.

Jake had little sympathy for physical ailments. He never suffered from any himself and his lack of imagination made it impossible for him to understand other people's feelings.

When I was not feeling entirely well I liked to be by myself and these were the occasions when I remained in my room. Linnet would come and talk to me. She was always tender toward me and had taken up a protective attitude, which amused me, because I had always been well able to look after myself.

On this occasion Jennet brought me a kind of soup dish which contained that novelty, the potato, and some kind of mushrooms and meat.

It was tasty and I enjoyed it, but in the night I began to feel ill. I was very sick and feverish and I wondered whether there had been something in the dish which had not agreed with me.

I went to see the cook who told me that others' had had the dish and suffered no ill. They were fearful, I could see, lest I had contracted the sweat after all.

I said it contained mushrooms and there were toadstools which looked very like mushrooms. Could it be that one of these had been used?

The cook was indignant. Had she not been cooking for twenty years and if she didn't know a toadstool from a mushroom she ought to be hung, drawn and quartered, that she did.

It took me some days to recover my health, but in a week or so I had forgotten the incident until it happened again.

I had eaten in my room half a chicken with a loaf which I had washed down with a tankard of ale, and as I was drinking the ale I was aware of a strange odor about it. I had drunk little of it but was determined to drink no more, for it was at precisely this time that a horrifying notion came to me.

I had eaten of the soup dish. So had others. I had been ill. Mine had been brought to me in my room. What had happened to it on the way up?

I smelled the ale. I was becoming more and more convinced that something was wrong with it.

Somebody had tampered with it on its way to my room. Who?

I found a bottle and poured some of the ale into it. I threw the rest out of the window.

I felt mildly ill and I was certain that the ale had been poisoned.

Could it possibly be that someone in this house was trying to poison me?

I took the bottle out of the drawer in which I had hidden it. I smelled it. There was a sediment.

Oh, God, I thought. Someone *is* trying to kill me. Someone in this house. Who would want to do this?

Jake!

Why should he immediately come to mind? Was it because when someone wished a woman out of the way it was usually her husband? Jake had chosen me. Yes, to be the mother of his sons. Could it be that he wanted sons so much that. . . . I would not believe it.

Life was cheap to men like Jake. I saw a vivid picture in my mind of that scene when he had run his sword through Felipe's body. How many men had he killed? And did his conscience ever worry him? But they were enemies. Spaniards! I was his wife.

Yet if he wanted me out of the way. . . .

I sat at my window looking out. I could not face him. For the first time I felt unable to stand up to him. Always before I had been conscious of his great need for me. Now I doubted it.

I went to the mirror and looked at myself. I was no longer young. I was in my mid-forties and getting too old to bear sons. One does not notice one is growing old. One feels as one did at twenty . . . twenty-five, say, and imagines one is still that age. But the years leave their marks. The anxieties of life etched lines around the eyes and mouth.

I was not a young woman anymore. Nor was he a young man. But men such as Jake never feel their age. They still desire young women and think they should be theirs by right.

I went back to the window and sat down.

The door opened softly and Linnet was there.

"Mother," she said, "what are you doing here?"

"I was looking out of the window."

She came and looked at me searchingly.

"Are you ill?"

"No, no. A little headache."

I took the bottle of ale to the apothecary in one of the little streets close to the Hoe.

I knew him well. He mixed scents for me and I often bought his herb concoctions.

I asked if I might speak to him in private and he conducted me into a little room behind the shop. Drying herbs hung on the beams and there were pleasant smells which were intensified during simple time.

"I wonder if you could tell me what this ale contains?" I said to him.

He looked astonished.

"I fancied that it was not as it should be and I thought you might be able to tell me why."

He took the bottle from me and smelled it.

"Who is your brewer?" he asked.

"I do not think this has anything to do with the brewer. The rest in the cask was well enough."

"Something has been added," he said. "Could you give me a little time and I might be able to discover what?"

"Please do," I said. "I will call in two days' time."

"I think I shall have an answer for you then," he replied.

I went back to Lyon Court and there seemed to be a sudden menace about it. The lions which guarded the porch looked sly as well as fierce, sinister as well as handsome. I felt that I was being watched from one of the windows, though through which I could not say.

The thought kept recurring: Someone in that house wants me out of the way.

I was sure now that my soup had been poisoned. And now the ale.

So much depended on what the apothecary would have to tell me in two days' time.

I was sleeping badly; I was pale and there were dark shadows under my eyes. I would lie in bed with Jake beside me and say: Does he want to be rid of me?

I thought of life without him and I felt wretched and lonely. I wanted him there; I wanted him to go on desiring me more than I desired him. I wanted to quarrel with him. In short, I wanted to return to the old relationship.

But he had changed. I had thought it was because he had become preoccupied with the coming war with Spain. But was this so?

Strange things began to happen.

Carrying a candle, I was mounting after dusk the stairs to the turret whither I had been earlier that day. I had discovered that I had lost a bow of ribbon from my gown and wondered if it was there. It was lonely in that wing of the house. Normally I should not have thought of this, but of late I had become nervous and was startled at the least sound. And as I mounted the spiral staircase I thought I heard a noise above me. I paused. The candle in my hand cast an elongated shadow on the wall. I noticed what looked like a grotesque face there—but it was only the shadow caused by the shape of the candlestick.

I stood very still. I was sure I could hear someone's breathing above me. The turn of the staircase made it impossible to see more than a few steps ahead and I felt a cold shiver run down my spine. All my instincts were warning me that I was in danger.

"Who is there?" I cried.

There was no answer, but I fancied I heard a quick intake of breath.

"Come down, whoever is there," I called.

There was still no answer.

I felt as though I were rooted to the staircase. For some seconds I could not move. Someone was waiting for me up there . . . someone who had sent me to Mary Lee's cottage, someone who had poisoned my soup and my ale.

Good sense was saying: Don't go up there. Don't attempt to find out now. This is not the time. It could be fatal if you took another step.

I thought I heard a board creak. And turning, I ran down the stairs as fast as I could.

I went to my room. I lay on my bed. My heart was beating madly. I was frightened. This was unlike me, but recent events had shaken me more than I had realized and I was not in my usual good health.

I must be strong, I thought. I must find out what was

happening. I must know if someone was in fact threatening me.

You know, said a voice within me.

I don't believe it, I answered myself. He couldn't. I know he has killed many times. He has taken what he wanted . . . always. Oh, no, it can't be.

But why not, if he no longer wanted me? Why not, if I stood between him and something he wanted? Perhaps a young woman who could give him sons.

The door of my room opened suddenly. I knew it was Jake who had come in.

Had he come straight here from the turret? What would he do now?

Could it really be that he wished to be rid of me? Fiercely he had wanted me once; now did he as fiercely want someone else. Jake allowed nothing and no one to stand in the way of his desires. The lives of others, what were they? I kept thinking of Felipe lying dead on the floor of the Hacienda.

Jake had never shown any remorse about killing him.

He was standing by my bed looking down at me. He whispered my name quietly, not roaring it as he did so often.

I did not answer. I could not face him now with these dreadful suspicions in my mind. I could not say to him, "Jake, are you going to kill me?"

I was afraid.

So I pretended to sleep and after a few minutes he went away.

I went to the apothecary's shop.

He bowed when he saw me and invited me into the room where the herbs were drying on the oak beams.

"I have found traces of Ergot in your ale," he said.

"Ergot?"

"It's a parasite which grows on grass, very often on rye. It contains poisons known as egrotoxine, ergometrine and ergotamine. It is very poisonous."

"How could it get into the ale?"

"It could be put in."

"How could it be?"

"The leaves could be boiled and the liquid added. I

believe people have died through eating bread which had been made from rye which had this parasite growing on it."

"I see. Then the ale I brought you was poisoned?"

"It contained Ergot."

I thanked him and paid him well for his trouble. I intimated that I did not wish him to discuss this matter with anyone at the moment and he tactfully gave me to understand that he realized my wishes and would respect them.

As I walked back to Lyon Court I tried to remember the little I had learned from my grandmother about the things that grew in the fields and which could be used to advantage in cooking.

I remember her saying: "You must know the difference between good and evil. That's the secret, Catharine. Mushrooms now. There's many been caught on mushrooms. The most tasty food you could find; but there's wicked growth that masquerades as good in the fields as there is with people. And you must not be deceived by looks. There's Fly Agaric, which looked wicked enough; there's stinking Hellebore, which would drive you off with its smell; but the Death Cap toadstool and the Destroying Angel are white and innocent-looking as any good mushroom."

I had been amused by the names of Death Cap and Destroying Angel and also my grandmother's earnestness. Perhaps that was why I had remembered.

Someone had put a Death Cap or Destroying Angel into my soup. Someone had put Ergot into my ale. A long time ago someone had sent me to Mary Lee's cottage. Someone wanted me dead.

If I was going to save my life I must find out who was my would-be murderer.

I laughed at myself and said: You know.

But I wouldn't believe it. I couldn't believe . . . not then. It was not until later.

How strange it is that one does not see something which concerns one deeply and would be obvious to many. And then suddenly one discovers something which can be linked with other things and the truth is revealed.

I was looking from my window and I saw the three of

them by the pond. Romilly, Jake and Penn.

Penn had a model of a ship and he was sailing it on the pond. Jake knelt down beside him and guided the ship. I could see he was pointing out something to Penn.

Romilly stood there, arms folded, the sunlight gleaming on her luxuriant hair; there was something about her which told me. She was complacent, satisfied. And I knew.

Romilly and Jake! He had brought her to this house as a young girl—was she twelve or thirteen? She had not cared when the tutor had been found in Jennet's bed, for he was nothing to her. She had been ready to marry him, though. Yes, because she knew that she was to bear a child.

Jake had said: "We must care for her. Her father was one of the best men I ever sailed with."

He did not add: "And she is my mistress."

But of course it was so.

When Jake came into our bedroom I said to him, "Penn is your son."

He did not attempt to deny it.

"So under my own roof. . . ."

"It is my roof," he replied shortly.

"She is your mistress."

"She bore me a son."

"You have lied to me."

"I did not. You did not ask. You presumed it was the tutor's. There seemed no reason to upset you with the truth."

"You brought that girl into the house to be your mistress."

"That's a lie. I brought her here because she needed a home."

"The good Samaritan."

"God's Death! Cat, I couldn't leave an old seaman's daughter of that age to fend for herself."

"So you brought her here to bear your bastard. I wonder what her father would say to that?"

"He'd be delighted. He was a sensible man."

"As I should be, I suppose?"

"No, I wouldn't expect that of you."

"You are a considerate husband."

"Oh, come, Cat, what's done is done."

"And the girl is still here. Is there another on the way?"

"Stop this. The girl had a child. It was mine. There, you know. What's to it? I was home from sea. You were having a daughter. There's little time I have ashore."

"You have to make up for you celibacy at sea of course, because raping dignified girls and sending them mad does not count. You have much to answer for, Jake Pennlyon."

"As much as most men, I'll swear. Oh, stop it, Cat. I took the girl. There's no harm done. She has a fine boy who is a joy to her."

"And a joy to you."

"Why not? I get no sons from you. You can get a son with a Spaniard and for me . . . daughters . . . nothing but daughters."

"Oh, I do hate you, I do!"

"You have said that often enough, God knows."

"I had thought that we might come to some good life. I had pictured us . . . our grandchildren in our garden . . . and you contented. . . ."

"I'm not ill content. I've got three fine boys that I know of. And I wouldn't want to part with one of them. Understand that, Cat. Not one of them. I'm proud to own them. Proud, I say."

"Proud of the manner in which they were begotten, I doubt not. One from rape of an innocent child, the other on a lustful serving girl and another on this sly creeping . . . *insect* who crawls into my house . . . who is a poor little orphan who lies about the tutor and all the time is laughing because she has your child."

"Oh, come, Cat, it's long ago."

"Long ago, is it? Is she not still your mistress? I see it all now. The ribbons she puts in her hair; the manner in which she pushes the boy under your feet. What plans has she, this sly little crawling thing? What does she hope for, to take my place?"

He was alert I fancied. "How could that be! Don't talk nonsense, Cat."

"Is it nonsense?" I asked slowly. "How do I know what is happening in the house? I am deceived all the time.

My daughters are nothing to you. But you have ever made made much of your bastards."

"They are my sons."

"Mayhap this woman . . . this Romilly could give you more sons. She has given you one. I am beginning to understand. I see so much."

"You see what you want to see. You are an arrogant woman. You led me a dance as no other woman has. You belonged to a Spaniard before you did to me. You gave him a son and what have I had?"

"Was it my fault? Everything that has happened has been due to you. You raped Isabella, Felipe's bride. It was on you that he sought to revenge himself. What have I ever been but a counter in your games . . . your wicked cruel games? Jake Pennlyon, I wish to God I had never seen you. It was an ill day for me when I met you on the Hoe."

"You mean that?"

"With all my heart," I cried. "You blackmailed me because of what you saw in the leper's squint."

"You were playing a game with me. Did you think I didn't know that? You wanted me as I wanted you."

"So that I pretended to have the sweat to escape you?"

"By God, I'll never forgive you for that."

"What does it matter, eh, now that you have Romilly? She gave you a son. She can give you sons . . . sons . . . sons . . . for as many breeding years as are left to her."

"She could," he said.

"They would be your bastards unless. . . ."

"Who cares for that?" he said. "I have three fine boys and I'm proud of them."

I wanted him then to seize me, to shake me roughly as he had done so many times before. I wanted him to tell me that it was nonsense. Penn was his son. He had gone to her when I was ill and he was sick with disappointment because I had not given him a son. I wanted him to tell me that it was all over and done with. That he had been unfaithful as I knew he must have been a hundred times . . . a thousand times during his long voyages from home.

But this was different. He went away and left me and I did not see him again that night.

It's true then, I told myself. He wants to be rid of me.

He wants to marry Romilly, who can give him sons . . . legitimate sons.

I knew instinctively that my life was threatened and there seemed no doubt by whom. My husband wanted to marry another woman and the reason he wished to marry her was that she could give him sons. This sly creature who had wormed her way into my household with her pliable ways was threatening me.

It was not that she meant more to him than hundreds of other women had. But she had proved that she could give him sons . . . and men like Jake wanted sons. It was an obsession with them. We had the example of a recent King who had rid himself of several wives—and the great theme of his life had been "Give me sons."

It was the cry of arrogant men. They must continue the family line. Daughters were no use to them.

Boys adored Jake and he was interested in them; girls mean nothing to him until they reached an age when they could arouse his sexual desires. Jake was a fierce man, undisciplined, a man who had always known what he wanted and gone out to take it.

That was what was happening now.

I was no longer desirable to him because I could not hold out any hope that I would give him sons. He wanted me out of the way.

I thought then of Isabella. I remember the calm intensity of Felipe. He had wanted me; he had wanted to legitimize our son. Isabella had stood in the way of Felipe's marriage to me as I now stood in the way of Jake's to Romilly.

Isabella had been found at the bottom of a staircase. She was not the first to die in this way. Long ago the Queen, some said, would have married Robert Dudley. But he had had a wife and she was found dead at the bottom of a staircase.

Beware, unwanted wives.

What could I do? I could go to my mother. I could say: "Mother, let me live with you because my husband is trying to kill me."

I could tell my daughter perhaps. But how could I? She hated her father already. There was too much hatred in the house. And somewhere at the back of my mind was the thought—the hope—that I was wrong. A part of me said: He would not kill you. He loved you once—oh, yes, this emotion he had for you was love. You are the same except that you are ageing and can no longer bear a son. He would never kill you. You still have the power to infuriate him, to anger him. How could he forget the passionate years, the delight you have had in each other, for it is true that you have. Battles there have been, but have not those battles been the joy of both your lives?

This was why it was so wounding and so impossible that Jake should want to kill me.

I would wake in the night trembling from some vague nightmare.

Jake was away a great deal and I was often alone. He was visiting the towns along the coast where preparations were going on for the possible coming of the Spanish Armada.

I was glad in a way. It gave me time to think. I went over many of the little incidents of our life together. I remembered vividly scenes from the past. And always afterward I would say: It is not so. I don't believe this of him . . . not of Jake.

I refused to see Romilly. She was aware, of course, that I knew who Penn's father was. Jake must have told her.

Penn was kept well out of my way and I never saw the boy. I could not bear to look at him—sturdy, healthy, his home my house, the son another woman had given Jake when I had failed to do so.

Linnet was worried about me. "Are you well, Mother?" she asked constantly. She would make me lie down and sit beside me.

Strange things started to happen. Once I awoke in the night when Jake was away and saw a figure in my room. A shadowy figure dressed in gray. It stood at the door. I could not see the face, for it was as though it were wrapped in a shroud.

I screamed and some of the servants came running into my room.

"Who is there?" I cried. "Someone came into the room. Find who it was."

They searched, but they could find no one. Jennet appeared at some time later, half-asleep. I knew she had had farther to come than the others—from the bed she was sharing with a lover.

"It was a nightmare," said Linnet. "I shall write and ask my grandmother to send something to make you well. You are not yourself."

Who had come into my room, and for what purpose? What was the matter with me? I was not the sort to be intimidated. Why was I overcome by this strange lassitude so alien to my nature?

Linnet said I was to stay in bed for a day. I had had an unpleasant shock. She brought my food to me. I felt very sleepy.

"That is good," she said. "It shows you need a rest."

I slept and when I awoke it was dusk. I saw a shadowy figure by my bed and I cried out. Linnet was bending over me.

"Everything is all right, Mother. I have been sitting with you while you slept."

Yes, I was different. Something was happening to me. I could not throw off this tiredness. I found that I was falling asleep during the day.

What is changing me? I asked myself, and once again I thought of my grandmother who knew so much about herbs and plants and how she used to talk to me when I was a child. My attention had often wandered, but my mother had said: "You must listen to your grandmother when she talks, Cat dear. She is very clever about these things and they are important to her. When terrible tragedy came to her she went into her garden and found solace there and she prides herself on her knowledge as you do on your riding."

To please my mother I tried to listen and as a result certain things she said remained with me.

"There's everything here in the ground, Catharine. There's life and there's death. There's things to cure and things to kill. There's things to make you lively and things to make you sleep."

To make you sleep. There was poppy juice, I knew. That could make you sleep.

I thought: Someone is trying to unnerve me. Who was it who came into my room? Where in this house is there a gray shroud? Who wore it to stand at my door?

Why should I, who had fought Jake Pennlyon and sometimes been the victor, why should I be gradually growing into a lethargic, frightened woman?

I was going to find out.

I was sure that someone was tampering with my food. Romilly and Jake would work together. Did they talk together of how they would rid themselves of me? Did Romilly picture herself the mistress of this house? Were they impatiently asking each other: "How long must it be?"

Felipe had never talked to me of his desire to see an end of Isabella. Yet Isabella had died and the day she died the household had gone to the *auto-da-fé* and neither I nor Felipe was at the Hacienda.

Jake was away. Was he deliberately away? Did he, when he returned, hope to find me dead . . . say at the bottom of a staircase?

Who would throw me down? Who had thrown Isabella? The man Edmundo had done it. He had confessed. But he had done it for Felipe and that was Felipe's guilt. Who would do it for Jake? Jake was surely a man who would do such things for himself. Would he creep into the house by stealth when he was supposed to be far away? Would he come to my room and drag me to the top of the staircase and hurl me down? Would he strangle me first? It could be done, I had heard, with a damp cloth pressed over the mouth. That was what was said to have been done to Isabella.

I must regain my former strength and courage. I must first find out what was changing me into a feeble, defenseless creature.

I was no longer Jake's wildcat; I was his tame mouse—frightened and caught in a trap. I was a woman who allowed others to plan her death while she waited inactive.

No more, I said.

I would never drink anything in my room. That would mean that my food could not be tampered with, for if I ate at table I would take from the dish which everyone partook of.

That was the first step. I did this and it was amazing how much better I felt.

There at the head of the table I sat—since Jake was away. Romilly was present, sly, eyes downcast. It was small wonder that she dared not look at me.

Linnet was delighted.

"You are getting better, Mother," she said.

For three days my strength returned. I laughed at myself. I even laughed at the idea of Jake's wishing to marry Romilly. How could she hold his affections? He would tire in a week of her meekness. I was for Jake as Jake was for me.

It had taken more than twenty years and threats of murder for me to realize this.

Then strange things began to happen again. I looked for a cloak in my wardrobe and could not find it. I sent for Jennet; she could not be found.

"That woman is useless," I stormed.

I went into the garden and there I found her among the herbs and lettuces we grew, for salads.

I said: "I sent for you."

"Why, Mistress," she said, "I was here, you see."

"I cannot find my green cloak. Where is it?"

"Why, 'twas there but this morning, Mistress. I saw it when I was putting your clothes away."

"Well, 'tis not there now."

"Then where can it be to, Mistress?"

I went back to my room and she came with me.

She opened the wardrobe door and there was my cloak.

" 'Twere here all the time, Mistress."

"It was not," I said.

"But, Mistress, 'tis there just as I hung it."

"It was not there ten minutes ago."

She shook her head with a disbelief she dared not utter.

This was constantly happening. I would miss something, question its disappearance and then find it miraculously in its place.

The household was beginning to notice and Linnet was distressed.

I often went down to the hut where we had hidden

Roberto. Ever since he had ridden away that morning I had been anxious about him. I had heard nothing. What was happening to him? I hoped that he was not involved in anything that would bring him to trouble.

He was young and impetuous. What match would he be against men such as Walsingham?

I would creep into the hut and look around and assure myself that he was not hiding somewhere.

There was so much talk now of plots and the Spanish menace that my anxieties had grown concerning him. I would not have been surprised at any time to find him there.

But I was feeling better. If it had not been for the apothecary's evidence I would have told myself my fears were the result of my foolish imaginings. I was certain now that Jake had had no hand in any plot against me. Romilly must have poisoned the ale and the soup. She must have sent me to Mary Lee's cottage all those years ago. Had Jake ever told her how I had evaded him long ago? Had she thought to murder me in such a way as could never be traced to her?

And then Jake had gone away and was lost to all for all those years. I was out of danger then. Had Romilly made the wax image of me? Then how did it come to be in Jake's pocket? Had she put it there—why?

Now Jake was back; Romilly's and his son was growing up. Jake wanted a legitimate son; she had borne him one; she had proved she could do so. She could give him his legitimate son . . . if I were out of the way.

It fitted.

I tried to work out what had happened. I had taken the whole of the soup and I had had a comparatively mild attack afterward. So whoever did it either did not wish to kill me or did not understand what quantity was needed to bring about the desired effect. The same may have applied to the ale. But who could want to make me ill and yet not kill me?

Romilly! She knew of the effects of these plants but did not know the extent of their deadliness. What could I do about Romilly? Send her to my mother. Send a potential murderess to my mother! I could not do that. And what of Penn? She would not go without him and

Jake would not let him go.

I must lay my own traps. Thinking thus, I wandered down to the hut. There was no sign of anyone there. The relief was great, for I could not imagine what would happen if Jake discovered Roberto in hiding.

I stood for a few moments in the hut recalling these anxious times and when I went to the door I found that I could not open it. I pushed with all my might and could not budge it.

I'm locked in, I thought, and I felt the hair rise from my head.

For what purpose? Here I was some distance from the house. If I called no one would hear me. Strange things had been happening to me and now someone had locked me in this hut. What was to happen to me now?

I looked up at the window high in the wall through which Roberto was to have escaped into the bushes had he been surprised. I did not see how I could reach it. Then I should have to break it and jump through.

I turned back to the door and hammered on it. There was no response.

I leaned against the wall.

"What is happening to me?" I asked myself.

There was a key to this hut. Manuela had found it hanging inside. She had said that we would lock Roberto in and no one would be able to disturb him. Then if the Queen's men came for him he was to jump through the window.

I went to the hook on the wall. The key was not there. Someone had seen me enter this hut often. Someone had taken the key and locked me in.

But why? For what purpose?

Was there someone lurking outside now waiting to come in and kill me?

Jake?

Jake was away.

Who had locked me in? Romilly? Would she leave me here until Jake came back . . . say, at dusk . . . and open the door? Would Jake then creep in and kill me and then go away again? A man should not be at home when his wife was murdered. Felipe had not been home and I had been sent away.

If only someone would come. Anyone. It was the quiet that was so nerve-racking. No one was about. I was all alone. I banged on the door until my fists were bruised. I called. But who could hear me? It was because the hut was so far from the house that it had provided such a good hiding place for Roberto.

It was afternoon. I felt sick and frightened. But if my murderer had come I should tackle him, I would fight for my life. Anything was better than this waiting.

I called out. But who could hear my voice beyond the thick walls of the hut? I tried to climb up and look through that window. I could not do so. My hands were grazed and bleeding and I fell twice in the attempt.

The afternoon was passing. Soon it would be night.

Night! I said to myself. Of course they are waiting for the night.

Oh, God, I prayed, what is happening to me? What has gone wrong with my life? Why was I not content with it? I had Jake, who wanted me and loved me in his fashion—as I loved him in mine. I had my beloved children. What more could I ask?

And now I was going to lose everything I treasured. Someone was trying to kill me.

Dusk fell. No sound from outside. Nothing. Let someone come this way, I prayed. Linnet will be worried. I was to have been with her and Damask. They will come to look for me. Oh, God, let the door open and Linnet come for me.

I went to the door and beat on it with my fists. To my amazement it moved. I pushed. It was open and I was out in the fresh air.

I ran to the house.

Linnet cried out when she saw me. "Mother, what has happened? We have been so worried! Where have you been?"

We were in each other's arms.

"I was locked in the hut," I said.

"In the hut? Mother. You mean that old place. . . . What were you doing there?"

I said: "I went in . . . and then the door was locked."

"Who locked it?"

"I don't know."

"They have gone out searching for you. I sent two parties of men out. We had been so anxious. But you are exhausted, dearest Mother. I'm going to bring you something warming to drink."

What a ministering angel she was! How I loved her! How could I die when I had my beloved daughter Linnet?

I could not sleep. Nor did I wish to drink the hot herb drink she had brought for me. It stood on a table by my bed.

"Try to rest," she said.

"I want to talk. Who could have locked me in the hut?"

Linnet stroked my hair; she was looking at me in a strange way as though she did not recognize me.

"Mother dear," she said, "you were not locked in. The door was unlocked all the time."

"What nonsense! It was locked. I couldn't open it. And then suddenly it was open."

"Perhaps it was jammed."

"It couldn't have been. I pushed and pushed and then it opened so easily. Someone unlocked it."

"It doesn't matter now. You must have thought it was locked. The key was there all the time."

"Where was the key?"

"It was hanging on a hook inside the hut."

"But it wasn't. Someone locked me in and put the key back afterwards."

"It doesn't matter," said Linnet soothingly.

I was so tired that I thought it didn't matter either. I was so exhausted and so glad to be back with Linnet sitting beside me.

It was only when I awoke later that I realized how much it did matter.

They were watching me. I saw their looks. My daughter, Edwina, Manuela, Romilly, the servants . . . everyone.

Something was happening to me. I had changed. I imagined that a shrouded figure was in my room. I had spent hours in the hut thinking I was locked in when the door was open and the key was on the hook all the time.

Devils were beginning to possess me, which meant that I was being robbed of my reason. This was what they believed, but I knew that some evil threatened me, that someone was trying to rob me of my reason—or to make it appear that I had lost it—before killing me. It did not seem impossible that my husband wished to be rid of me so that he might marry a young woman who could give him sons. Death was stalking me and with Death was a companion, Madness.

No one could ever have called me a weak woman. I had always been able to defend myself and I was going to defend myself now. I was not mad. I was certain that I had been locked in that hut and that the door had been suddenly opened and that the key had been put back after I had left. Someone had been lurking in the bushes outside the hut. The door had stealthily been unlocked and when I had run out and gone to the house the key had been replaced.

That was how it must have happened. That was how I knew it had happened.

And I was going to prove it.

Strangely enough that incident in the hut had given me strength. I was going to throw off this lethargy which I knew now was the result of the evil herbs with which my food and drink had been laced.

I was going to fight this with all my strength and I was confident that I could win.

Oh, Romilly Girling, I assured myself, you will find you have a strong adversary in me. I shall not step aside so that you can marry my husband. And, Jake, you have not won the last battle yet.

Linnet had left now. "I will sleep," I said. But I never felt less like sleep.

I picked up the drink by my bed and smelled it.

How could a drink brought to me by my loving daughter have become contaminated?

Still, I did not drink it. I left it there at my bedside.

I must think of a plan. I would watch what I ate. I must be alert. I must be ready at any hour of the night. The next time the shrouded visitor came to my room it should not escape. I was going to catch it, drag off the shroud and find out who it was who was playing these tricks on me.

I would stay in my room for a few days. I would feign

illness. I would have food sent to me which I would not eat. I would preserve part of it and take it to the apothecary and when I had proof from him that my food was being laced with poison I would lay my evidence before . . . before . . . before whom? Before Jake? What if my suspicions were correct and he was my would-be-murderer? How he would laugh. Before Linnet? Could I say to her: "Someone is trying to kill me. Help me find who it is." How could I? No matter. I would wait and see what I would do. In the meantime I would collect my evidence.

I took a piece of beef from the kitchen and with it a good cob loaf. These I concealed in my bedroom. I took also a flagon of muscadel wine with nuts, apples and marchpane.

Once I had pretended to have the sweat. I must have been rather good at pretense. I now feigned to a lethargy which I was far from feeling. I took my secret meals and ate nothing which came to my room, although I took several samples of what was brought to take to the apothecary.

My spirits were rising. I was at last taking an action which I felt suited my nature. I was going into the offensive.

I did not take even Linnet into my confidence, although I was on the point of doing so many times.

I wanted to be ready when my shrouded visitor appeared. And I was.

I had pretended to be very sleepy all day. I had become aware that most of the food which came up to me was laced with poppy juice, so the object was to dull me into a mood when my wits would desert me. Then instinct warned me some plan was about to be put into operation.

I was right. It was three o'clock in the morning of the third day when I was awakened by a presence in my room.

The bedclothes were being gently drawn from the bed.

I opened my eyes. Standing at the foot of the bed was the figure I had seen before—shrouded in gray. Over the head was a hood which covered the face; there were slits for the eyes to see through.

I lay still waiting. The figure moved not toward me but to the door. It stood there and I was ready to leap out of bed—tense waiting. As soon as it moved I would be after it. I would tear off that concealing cover. I would find out who was hiding beneath it.

And suddenly there came to my mind: What if it were indeed a ghost? What if the ghost of Isabella had come to haunt me? What part did I play in her sudden death? Was it murder? And if it was, was not I the motive for that murder?

And why should I think of Isabella at such a moment? How could I say except that there was something about that shrouded figure which had brought her to my mind?

Ghost or not I was going to find out. The figure moved backward. Then I saw a hand emerge. The finger was beckoning me.

I was about to leap out of my bed when my instincts warned me. If there was a murderer concealed behind that shroud it was the same person who had been dosing my food. I had feigned a lassitude I did not feel. I must behave like a person who was under the influence of poppy juice.

I rose slowly from my bed.

The hand disappeared; the figure had moved out into the corridor.

I went out. The figure was a few yards away. The finger beckoned me again.

Trying to act like a sleepwalker, I followed.

The figure had disappeared around a bend. I hurried after it. I came to rest at the top of the great staircase which led into the hall.

There was no sign of the shrouded figure.

I stood at the top of the staircase; and then I knew. Someone was behind me, hands stretched out, waiting to hurl me down those stairs.

I turned and grappled.

I heard someone shout: "I'm coming," and there was my daughter Linnet. She seized the shroud. The three of us were huddled together for a moment. I felt myself lifted off my feet. Then suddenly there was a wild scream. I found myself clinging to a piece of gray cloth as a figure went crashing to the foot of the staircase.

Linnet and I did not speak. We ran down the staircase to that crumpled figure, which lay face downward. I lifted the hood and the mask that fitted over the face.

" 'Tis Manuela," I said.

She did not die until three days afterward. Poor tragic Manuela!

She was conscious and lucid for a while before death overtook her. I was at her bedside and she was aware that I was there. She had little time left, she said, and much to say.

To think that this Spanish woman should have lived in my household for so many years and I knew so little of her! How strange that she should be so devoted to Roberto and yet plan to kill his mother.

It was vengeance. Just retribution, she called it.

"As soon as I saw the ruby cross I knew that I would kill you," she said. "Before that I just wanted to make you suffer."

"But you did not attempt to kill me until last night," I reminded her. "You gave me small doses of poison and tried to rob me of my reason."

"That was what happened to Isabella. She was ill; she was robbed of her reason; and then one day she was thrown down the staircase."

Her story was told jerkily, far from lucidly and not at one sitting. I had to piece it together to make a coherent whole. She was very weak, but she wished to tell it. It was a kind of confession. She wanted extreme unction, and I was determined that she should have it if I could manage it. It would mean running some risk, but I had known of Catholic families in the neighborhood and I would ask if a priest might come to ease Manuela's last hours.

He would have to come in secret, but I would defy Jake, if necessary, to bring her this last consolation.

I learned that Manuela was a half sister of Isabella—her mother having been a serving girl in the mansion which was Isabella's home. Manuela had been given a place in that mansion as soon as she was old enough to take it and had been sent to Tenerife when Isabella went there to marry Don Felipe.

She had been present when Jake had stormed the mansion; she had successfully hidden herself from the marauders. She had assisted at the birth of Carlos and had loved the boy. It was only when he came to England and threw off all his Spanish ways that she turned to Roberto.

But the gist of her story was Edmundo. She had loved him and they were to have been married. She had greatly admired the ruby cross which Isabella wore frequently. She had even taken it once and worn it when she went to meet Edmundo in the garden—a sin for which she had done penance.

Edmundo had said: "I would I could give you a cross like that."

Perhaps someone had heard him. In any case the cross was missing and Edmundo confessed that he had strangled Isabella, then thrown her down the stairs. He had done it, he admitted, because he had stolen the cross and had been discovered in the act by Isabella, who had threatened to have him arrested for robbery.

Manuela had accepted this because she knew he loved her and the cross was missing—until she had seen me wearing it. She believed then that it had been in my possession ever since, that Don Felipe had given it to me and that therefore I must have known that Edmundo had not stolen it and only admitted to doing so under torture which few men could stand out against.

It seemed clear to her that Edmundo had killed Isabella on orders from his master. A servant belonged to his master and if certain deeds were demanded of him he performed them, but any sin incurred was not on his conscience.

When Edmundo was arrested Don Felipe should have saved him, but he had not done so. He did not want anyone to know that Edmundo had killed Isabella on orders from him. The situation was fraught with danger because Don Felipe wished to marry me and there were rumors in circulation that I was a witch and a heretic. Therefore, Don Felipe dared not make any move to save Edmundo because by doing so he could turn suspicion on himself and I was involved. The ruby cross provided a good reason why Edmundo should have committed the murder and so Don Felipe was content for this to be the accepted version of the affair, although the cross all the time was in his possession, while poor Edmundo, tortured until he admitted that he had stolen it, was condemned to death.

When Manuela saw me wearing the cross she believed that I had had it all those years. It had not occurred to her that it was one of the valuable objects which Jake had stolen when he raided the Hacienda, that it had been in *his* possession ever since and he had only recently given it to me.

She had always hated me. She had blamed me for what happened. But for me, she was sure that it never would. In her view, I was, therefore, responsible for Isabella's death. It was she who had aroused Pilar's venom against me; it was she who had made the image of Isabella and put it in my drawer. She had taken it to Pilar and it was to have been used as evidence that I was a witch.

And then because she knew that there had been suspicion in my mind, she had sought to make it grow. She wanted me to suspect my husband was planning to murder me. She had put the image among Jake's clothes and waited for me to find it. Her revenge was slow and painstaking. She was in no hurry. She had infinite patience. All she wanted was my uneasiness—until she saw me wear the cross.

Then there was no doubt in her mind of Felipe's guilt and mine. She brooded on the happy life she might have had; on the children of her union with Edmundo who had never been born. She was fierce and passionate; she could find no satisfaction in anything but revenge.

So she had decided I should suffer as Isabella had suffered. She did not wish to murder me outright. She wanted justice. Isabella had gone mad, so should I. She had suffered over a long period, so should I. And in due course I should be found at the bottom of a staircase, as Isabella had been.

She lived for this revenge. It was the only thing which could compensate her for the loss of Edmundo.

She had put poisonous plants into my food—not enough to kill me but only to impair my health; she had locked me in the hut and then unlocked the door and hung the key inside. She had made herself a shroud and tried to unnerve me. She had meant to drive me into madness and then, when those about me began to doubt my sanity, lure me to the top of the staircase—an easy victim, half drugged as she believed me to be—and throw me to the foot of it. People would say: "She was possessed by devils. Remember, how strange she became?"

"My poor Manuela!" I cried, and I assured her that I had never seen the cross until a short while before. I now remembered such an ornament's being mentioned at the time of Edmundo's execution, but I had not connected it with the gift which my second husband had given to me.

Oh, Jake, I thought, you took the cross when you came to the Hacienda. You took everything of value you could lay your hands on. And Felipe . . . you were guilty of the murder of Isabella, just as guilty as though you yourself had strangled her and thrown her down the stairs.

I was relieved that Manuela now knew that I was guiltless of participation in Isabella's death.

"Take care of Roberto," she said. "I loved him . . . dearly."

I told her she had no need to ask his mother to do that.

I rode over to a family nearby who when the priests had come to Trewynd in Edward's time had entertained them there and hidden them.

They had one there at that time. He was brought out of the priest's hole in which they hid him whenever visitors called at the house and, disguised as one of the grooms, he rode back to Lyon Court with me.

I knew that I was doing a daring thing. If Jake had returned home at that time I cannot imagine what would have happened.

I told the priest of my fears and he answered that he was accustomed to taking risks and would not deny a dying woman her last solace on Earth.

I took him to her sickroom and he was there holding the cross before her eyes as she passed away.

She died peacefully, I think, for I had assured her of my forgiveness. She was glad that she had not succeeded in killing me and did not have to go before her Maker with murder on her conscience.

She died clasping the cross.

I felt alive again. What a fool I had been. As if Jake

would murder me and if he did it would not be by such devious methods. He would have taken out his sword and run me through. I laughed. It was good to be alive. I was not menaced. Jake was an unfaithful husband. Had he not always been and had I ever expected anything else? I had sheltered two of his bastards under my roof already. Penn was but the third. They gave him satisfaction in the sons he could not get with me.

My vitality had returned. I could fight again.

Linnet had to know what had happened. I should have had to tell her the whole story some time or other— just as my mother had told me her strange story when I was about my daughter's age. The whole household knew too that the mistress who was supposed to be going mad was not, but Manuela had been completely so because she had poisoned my food and tried to throw me down the stairs. There was no need for them to know the reasons why she had done these things. It was enough that they accepted the fact that devils had begun to possess her.

Manuela was buried in the Lyon section of the grave- yard and we laid rosemary on her grave.

I at least would never forget her.

The Fugitive

So deeply immersed had I been in my own affairs that I had not been aware of what was happening in the outside world. Now I heard the excited talk about what was called the Babington Plot, which, said all loyal supporters of Our Gracious Lady Elizabeth, had by God's grace been discovered. A young man named Anthony Babington had in his youth served as a page to Mary Stuart and, as men were wont to, fell in love with her. He had joined forces with a group of ardent Catholics and together they had made a plot to put the Queen of Scotland on the throne and bring back the Catholic religion to England. This plot had the blessing of Spain and the Pope.

The conspirators met in taverns around St. Giles' and in Babington's house in Barbican and there worked out their conspiracy. Elizabeth was to be assassinated, Mary set free and set on the throne. Catholics throughout the country would rally to her help. The Pope gave his sanction and Philip of Spain would help—with his fast-growing Armada if necessary.

Letters had been smuggled into the prison of the Queen of Scots by a most ingenious method. Corked tubes had been fabricated in which letters could be concealed and these were inserted into the beer barrels which were carried into the Queen's apartments. When the Queen had read the letters she could insert her answers into the tube and put them back into the empty barrels which would be returned to the brewer. It seemed foolproof and would have been if the brewer had not been in the pay of Walsingham as well as the Queen. Thus the letters which were inserted in the full barrels and the replies that went into the empty ones were all conveyed to Amyas Paulet—the Queen's jailor at that time—and passed on to Walsingham. In this way Elizabeth's Secretary of State knew every twist and turn of the Babington Plot as it was worked out.

He had not hastened to make an arrest as he wished to draw as many into the net as possible and his great desire was to incriminate the Queen of Scots so thoroughly that Elizabeth would have no alternative but to send her to the scaffold.

Now the arrests were being made and an excitement was running through the country because it was said that so deeply was the Queen of Scots implicated that this would be the plot to end all plots.

I was in a state of great tension as I always was when stories of plots came to light. My first thought was: Is Roberto involved in this?

We heard the names of men arrested. Roberto's was not among them, but each day I expected to hear that he was taken.

Jake had come back. He was full of excitement because he said at any time now the Spaniard would strike.

He had heard of Manuela's attack on my life and I was gratified to see that he was disturbed by it.

"Spaniards!" he cried. "I should never have taken them into my house." Then he took me by the shoulders and looked at me intently.

I said: "Are you thinking that you might have rid yourself of me?"

He laughed. " 'Tis true, I might. But I've a feeling not many would get the better of you."

"Except you perhaps."

"Of a certainty. Me of course!"

He laughed and held me against him.

I said: "At one time I thou̲ ̲ ̲ ̲ were planning to rid yourself of me and take a younger woman to wife."

He nodded, pretending to consider the idea.

"Romilly, for instance. She has borne you one son. She is young enough to bear others."

"Now you are putting temptation in my way."

"That does not have to put it in your way. And men such as you do not give themselves time to be tempted. What is there they take and to the devil with the consequences."

"It's the way to live, Cat."

"Is it? To bring your bastards to your lawful wife?"

"I brought none to you. You brought two to me and Penn was born here. Did I not allow you to bring yours?"

The thought of Roberto weakened me.

Jake put his hands about my throat and laughed at me.

"All I would have to do is press a little."

"Well, why don't you?"

"Because shrew that you are, mother of daughters, I have decided I'll not replace you yet."

Then he kissed me with a rare tenderness which moved me somewhat. He pulled my hair as he did the boys' now and then. I knew it to be a gesture of affection.

"I'm impatient, Cat," he said. "Here I am kicking my heels . . . waiting . . . waiting for the Spaniard! We've got to be ready for him when he comes. God's Death! It could be today. It could be tomorrow. Why does he delay? And now this traitor Babington. By God! He'll suffer the traitor's death and I hope they linger over it. He would have killed our Queen; he would have set the Scottish whore on the throne. It is time her head parted company with her shoulders. I would hang, draw and quarter any man who gave his sanction to such treachery."

Oh, Roberto, I thought. Where are you, Roberto?

I said: "They have caught all the conspirators?"

"Who knows? There may be others. Walsingham's sly. He knows when to pounce. He gives them a little license

. . . the better to bring in more. We have to stamp them out, Cat. Every one of them . . . traitors to England, friends of our enemy Spain! I'd like to blow that country off the Earth."

How fierce he was—his eyes blazing blue fire.

Oh, Roberto, I thought, where are you?

I knew he would come. It was a premonition perhaps. He would come at night and he would come to me as he had before. I was tense, waiting. Some maternal instinct was preparing me, so I must have slept lightly and I was ready when I heard the clod of earth thrown at the window.

I crept silently out of bed, terrified that I might awaken Jake.

I knew it of course, Roberto had come. How could he stay near London and the Court at such a time when Babington was captured and but for the ingenuity of Walsingham's spy system, the Queen might have been assassinated and a Catholic Queen set up on the throne?

If Roberto's name had been on the list found in Throckmorton's house, Walsingham would have his spies watching him. Even if he had not been involved in the Babington Plot, and it seemed he had not, he might be formulating others.

I slipped out of bed and looked down. I saw him clearly in the moonlight. He was looking up at my window.

I looked back at the bed. Jake, I thanked God, was a heavy sleeper and he was fast asleep now. I signed to Roberto. He understood and pointed in the direction of the hut. I nodded and went back to bed. He would understand that Jake was with me.

I went back to bed, shivering.

The hut was not the safe place it had been. My adventure there had called attention to it. Jake had even said he might have some building done to it and make it into a dwelling place for some of the servants.

Bushes still grew around it, obscuring it from view to some extent, and I must make my way to it as soon as possible.

I was distraught.

Carlos, who had, like Jake, not gone far from Plymouth since the threats from the Armada had grown, came over to see Jake. I was waiting for a moment to slip away to the hut with food. But I must make certain that no one was aware of this. Linnet could have helped, but I was not going to allow my daughter to be involved.

Carlos was saying that he had heard Babington and Ballard had been executed. He described the agonies of those men—hanged in a field at the upper end of Holborn near the road to St. Giles's where a scaffold had been set up. Ballard, the other main conspirator, had suffered first. He had been hung, cut down and disemboweled while he was still alive. Babington watched, then suffered like treatment.

"So perish all traitors," cried Jake.

I felt sick.

Jake was looking at me strangely.

As soon as I could do so I took some food from the kitchens and went to the hut.

I took my son into my arms and held him against me.

"Oh, Roberto, tell me what has happened."

"When they took Babington I knew it was unsafe for me to stay near London. I had to get away."

"You were with the conspirators?"

"Not . . . not with Babington. If I had been. . . ."

I understood. None who had been involved in that plot would have been allowed to go free.

"But Walsingham is determined to have more proof ready. Friends of mine have disappeared suddenly. I know that they are under arrest. If the Babington Plot does not bring the Queen of Scots to the scaffold, they will discover more plots. They are determined to. No Catholic, or any man who has ever joined in any scheme is safe. They are hunting us out, Madre."

"And they are hunting you!"

"They came to my lodging. I was fortunate. I was warned. If I go back there I shall be taken. They are searching for me now."

"The Captain is here," I said.

"I saw his ship from the Hoe."

"Oh, Roberto, we shall have to take the greatest care."

"Manuela will help."

"Manuela is dead."

I told him briefly how she had tried to murder me and for what reason.

He was silent, deeply shocked.

"Madre, how cruel life is! And now it seems that everyone's existence is governed by this hatred between Spain and England."

"It is the shadow across our times. Religion—Catholic or Protestant. It has been so for many years. It darkened my mother's life. I have not escaped. I brought a priest to Manuela when she died. She wanted it. I hope it was not discovered. One can never be sure."

He kissed my hand.

"Madre, I love you. Always through my life I have looked to you, relied on you."

"You can rely on me still, my son; not because I am Catholic or Protestant but because I am a mother. I know little of doctrines, nor do I care. But I do know of love, which seems to me of greater importance in the world."

"You will let me stay here?"

"It must not be for long, Roberto. The hut is no longer safe as it once was. After I was locked in, the household seems to have become aware of it. Before, few people remembered it was here. Soon you must go away."

"I have thought, Madre, that if I could get to Spain, I might find my own people. My father's family would know of me and I must have estates there, must I not? Did not my father make me his heir?"

"He did, but that was long ago. Others would have taken your inheritance by now."

"But I would be of their family. They would receive me."

"Roberto, how could we get you to Spain?"

"I must get away from England. I am wanted and Walsingham will never let me go free. I shall be taken as Babington was. . . ."

There was stark horror in his face and reflected in his eyes I seemed to see that fearsome plot of land near Holborn with the scaffold and Ballard and Babington undergoing excruciating torture.

Not for Roberto, I thought. Not the little boy who had lain in my arms, who had given such joy to Felipe and brought us together.

What a cruel world, where men could do such things to men. Not my son. I would do anything but allow that to happen.

I must save him. I must find some means of getting him out of the country. Who would help me? Carlos? Jacko? Jake? How ironical. If I said: Roberto is here. He is involved in plots, he must escape, what would they do, these haters of Spaniards? At best they would draw their swords and run him through; more likely they would hand him over to those who sought him that he might die the dreaded traitor's death.

I said: "I must have time to think. I must find some way. One thing is certain. You cannot stay here long. I must find another hiding place for you."

"Madre, you must not be involved. They call those traitors who give aid to Catholics."

"They can call me what they will. I shall guard my own son. I will leave you now. When I am gone you must lock the door and open it for no one but me. Eat the food I have brought. You must not grow weak and I see you are already."

"I have walked far, Madre."

"Eat and rest and I will come back." I went to the door. "Lock it when I am gone and open for no one. Remember it is most unsafe for you to remain here."

I had opened the door and horror overwhelmed me.

Jake was standing there.

"Indeed it is most unsafe," he said, "for traitors to hide on my lands."

He came into the hut and shut the door. I felt as though I would faint and leaned against the stone wall for support.

"So," said Jake, and never had I seen his eyes so brilliant, his mouth so cruel. "You are running from the law? You are a fool as well as a traitor to come here."

He towered above Roberto. He seized him by the shoulder and shook him. His hand was on his sword.

I ran forward and gripped his arm; I hung onto it with all my strength. Jake looked down at me, his mouth hard as it could only be for Spaniards.

"Jake," I pleaded. "For God's sake. This is my son."

"Your Spanish bastard," he said.

His sword was out. I saw the gleaming steel. I tried to thrust myself between him and Roberto.

Jake pushed me aside. He put the point at Roberto's throat.

"So you have come here, you dog."

Roberto did not answer. He stood very still, his face white, his Spanish dignity never more apparent. I was praying incoherently, not to the God of the Protestants or the Catholics but to the God of love. Save my son. Let him live. Whatever happens to me now let him live. Let him escape to a good life. If I never see him again I care not, if he can live and be happy.

"Jake," I cried. "Jake . . . I am begging you. . . ."

Jake hesitated. It was miraculous that he should sheathe his sword.

"You left your lodging," he said. "You are wanted. They will take you. It's the traitor's death for you. But you come down here. You would smear your traitorous slime on your mother. You would have her suspected of sharing in your evil crimes. If that were so even I could not save her. Do you know that, you coward?"

"I would not involve her. I would swear that she has never shared in my schemes. I would say she did not know I was here."

"Be silent." Jake was rocking on his heels, thinking deeply.

He took the key from the hook.

"You will stay here," he said.

And to me: "Come, Cat. Leave him."

He pulled me out and locked the hut.

I said: "What are going to do, Jake?"

"You will see," he said.

I knew that he meant he would keep him a prisoner until he could hand him over to those who would bring him to trial and sentence him to the traitor's death.

I do not know how I lived through that day. I could not think what I should do.

Jake was grim and silent, making plans, I knew. I asked myself whether Roberto would attempt to escape.

If he did he could not get far. He was exhausted. Could he manage even to climb up to the small window, break it and jump through? He was not in the same condition that he had been in when Manuela and I had sheltered him before.

Jake was vengeful; he knew no gentle feelings. He would have killed him on the spot had I not been there. At least he had not wished to do so in my presence.

He went away and I stayed in my room. I dared not go to the hut for fear of what I would find there.

All day long I waited for something to happen. I kept thinking I heard the sound of horses' hoofs—men come to take Roberto away. Five minutes was like an hour that day, one hour like twenty-four. I felt sick and ill; I could not get out of my mind the terrible picture of men's suffering on the scaffold. This must not happen to Roberto . . . not to my son, the little boy of whom we had been so proud, Felipe and I.

Jake returned home in the late afternoon. He came to our bedroom.

"Jake," I cried, "what are you doing?"

"What would you expect me to do?"

"You are giving him up?"

"He is still in the hut. He's trussed up so that he can't move and I have the key."

"I beg of you Jake . . . I have never begged for anything from you yet but I do now . . . let him go. Please, Jake, if you will but do this. . . ."

"What will you do?"

"I shall hate you forevermore if you harm my son."

"You have talked so much of hating me over the years."

"That was mock hatred. This will be real. If you harm Roberto. . . ."

"You are dramatic. This is a traitor. Do you understand that, Cat? Very soon we shall be fighting for our lives against men such as your bastard Roberto. The Spaniards are preparing to come here . . . to force their evil doctrines on us, to set up the Inquisition in this land. Do you know what that means?"

"I do . . . I know that very well. I hate it. I would fight with all my strength and will against it."

"Then you are with us, Cat, and those who are with us cannot allow those who are against us to escape . . . no matter who they are."

"Let him go, Jake. Help him. You could. You could give him a horse. He could ride far into Cornwall. He could live there in peace."

"Live in peace! Would he ever do that? He'd be trying to set up idols wherever he was."

"Jake, Jake, I beg of you."

There was silence.

He went out and left me. He went far, I knew, for when he came back his horse was exhausted.

Night came. I did not rest. I sat silent in my chair and wept.

Jake lay in bed, sleeping, or pretending to. He awoke and I was still sitting in the chair.

He came to me then and lifted me up and carried me to bed.

He held me in his arms.

"You'll make yourself ill," he said tenderly.

I did not reply. I knew words were useless now. He had made up his mind. I sensed the purpose in him.

I slept at last, worn out by my emotions.

It was daylight when I awoke and Jake had gone.

I thought I would go to the hut, but Jake had warned me so firmly not to that I did not go. I must wait in any case until I knew what to do.

There must be something. "Please, God," I prayed, "tell me what I can do. Help me to save my son."

All morning I did not see Jake.

Jennet came. She was full of chatter.

"Look, Mistress, the *Golden Fleece* be ready to sail. They say she be going on the tide."

I did not want to listen. I was thinking: Roberto, what can I do to save you?

I was afraid that Jennet was going to say that someone had been to the hut, but she did not mention it. She was full of the unexpected departure of the *Golden Fleece*. She had known a sailor who was one of the crew.

I sharply told her to be silent. I was in no mood to ponder on Jennet's emotional entanglements. If she had lost her sailor on the *Golden Fleece* she would soon replace him.

Jake came in in the afternoon.

He said he wanted to speak with me and we went to our bedroom.

"They are on their way," he said.

"You mean you have warned them?"

"No. I did not warn them. They were after him. All the suspected traitors are being hunted out. Your son is one of them. He is a fool. He should never have come here. The first place in which they will look for him is his old home."

"Oh, God, they will find him here."

"They will search the place."

"They will go to the hut." I covered my face with my hands. As I did so I heard the commotion in the courtyard.

Jake had raised me to my feet; he had taken me to the window.

"Look out," he said. "Do you see the *Golden Fleece*? She has shipped her anchor. She is about to sail on the tide. There's a fair wind. It will carry her far before nightfall."

I did not look.

I shook my head wearying, seeing Roberto cowering in the hut, trussed by Jake ready for his captors.

"I am a good patriot," he said. "All know it. I have helped to hound the Spaniards off the sea. Everyone knows I would not harbor a traitor in my household."

"You will be safe," I said fiercely.

"And I'll vouch for my wife," he answered.

"You taunt me . . . at such a time."

"Nay," he said. "You will not look at the *Fleece*. Shall I tell you what cargo she carries?"

"I am not interested in her cargo."

"Not when it is your son, Roberto."

I stared at him. "Jake! What means this? You. . . ."

He lifted his arm and clenched his fist. "He's a traitor. I never thought I'd help a traitor. But when my vixen of a wife commands me."

I lay against him.

Then I looked up into his face. "Oh, Jake, is it true? You are not tormenting me?"

"They'll go to the hut. The bird has flown. Or been spirited away. I took him out to the *Fleece* early this morning."

What could I say to this man? How could I ever show him what I felt?

I took his hand and kissed it. I think he was moved.

Then I heard the rapping at the door.

The Triumph of the Lions

The land was heavy with foreboding.

We knew that the Spaniards were coming. We knew that they had conquered a great part of the world; we knew, too, that they came, not only with fighting men and armament, but with the rack, the thumbscrews and the more deadly instruments of torture such as we had never heard of. They came not only as conquerors of our land but as religious fanatics. If ever they conquered us as they had other peoples, this would be the end to freedom as we knew it. We should be forced to accept not only them but their faith.

To men such as Jake, Carlos, Jacko, Penn, it was inconceivable that we should fail. *Their* faith was in England, the undefeatable land.

Men might talk of the Invincible Armada but we laughed that to scorn. *We* were the invincible, the unconquerable.

The memory of that Whitsunday will linger forever in the minds of those who went to church that morning. It was more than a Whitsunday service; it was a dedication; it was an exhortation; for in the Bay lay the great ships waiting. And never had the people of Plymouth seen such a glorious sight.

We came down from Pennlyon—Jake and I with Carlos and Edwina, Jacko, Penn, Linnet and Damask. The sun was dancing in the water and in the little streets people were hurrying from their houses to come to the church to see Sir Francis. For he was there: the great sailor, the terror of the Spaniards and the hero of all the Queen's loyal subjects.

We knew that soon the greatest battle in our country's history would be fought. Those of us who were sober-minded reminded ourselves that our future could depend on it. Already the Spaniards were preparing to sail.

Out in the Bay lay the ships flying the flag of England— a red cross on a white background. The wind was strong and the ships seemed to be pulling at their anchors, impatient to be away. There lay Drake's own ship, the *Revenge*, Howard of Effingham's *Ark*, Martin Frobisher's *White Bear* and *Triumph*. There were the *Elizabeth Bonaventure* and *Nonpareil*. A wonderful sight. Jake had given his services to Lord Howard and Sir Francis. Carlos and Jacko had done the same.

They would never have forgiven themselves if they had not been at hand to sail out and fight the Armada when the time came.

And as I sat in the church on that Sunday I asked myself what would the next days bring.

The *Golden Fleece* had not yet returned. I wondered often whether she had been taken by the Spaniards. If so, Roberto might well have been saved. He might be living with his father's family in Spain. Was that too much to hope for? Who could say? But it was not so very long ago since he had sailed away; perhaps the *Fleece* would return bringing him with her. And if he did, could he settle down to a peaceful life?

The Queen of Scots, deeply implicated in the Babington Plot, had the previous year been beheaded in Fotheringhay Castle, and if we could beat the Armada we might be free of menace from outside England and from within. Could we hope for a few peaceful years?

I had told Linnet of Roberto's escape. I confided in her more and more. She was now eighteen years old— a lovely, spirited girl. She was like us both—Jake and myself. I had stressed, too, how Jake had saved Roberto by sending him off in the *Golden Fleece* which was a noble act on his part, for she would realize his firm convictions.

"He did this for me," I said. "It is something I shall never forget."

Linnet with the emotional impulsiveness of the young changed toward him. She began to see him in a new light. The rough and violent man whose heart was good nonetheless. She no longer scorned him; and it was another revelation to notice that Jake was almost pathetically pleased by her change toward him.

They were wary of each other; but I think she wanted to be proud of him and he wanted her to love him.

That was how events stood on that Whitsunday morning.

The weeks that followed were frustrating—for the Spaniards did not come. The ships continued to lie in the harbor. There was friction between the admirals, so we heard.

Jake hated inactivity. He was down at the Hoe each day waiting for the signal.

News arrived that the Armada had set out from Lisbon, but the weather had so harassed the ships that it was necessary for them to shelter in Corunna for revictualing and for the repair of damage to the ships.

In England this news was greeted with delight. It showed, was the general opinion, whose side God was on.

The waiting continued. The tension was growing. I never saw a man so impatient as Jake.

"What's the matter with the Spaniard?" he growled. "Is he afraid to come out?"

We laughed and talked of how the great Invincible Armada had been unable to withstand the weather and had been forced to retire for repairs, but I was afraid of what the inevitable battle would bring. All my life there had been this conflict over religion. All through my mother's it had been the same. I knew this was the culmination. I feared for Jake and I knew that Edwina feared for Carlos, as Jennet did for Jacko and Romilly for Penn. Those of us who had men who would go out and do battle were naturally especially anxious. What would happen if the invader set foot on our soil we did not know. We did not reason as far as that. Deep down in our hearts we believed no invader could ever conquer our land.

But there would be a mighty battle.

We heard that the Army was assembled at Tilbury and that the Queen had ridden among her men.

Jake's eyes gleamed with pride when he spoke of her. "She sat her horse like a soldier and she carried a truncheon. Would to God I could have been there to see her."

"Your place is here," I reminded him.

"Aye," he answered, "with Drake, Frobisher and the rest."

I remembered seeing her all those years ago when she came to the Tower of London and had said that she would be to God thankful and to men merciful. Now she, like myself, was no longer young; and the years would have taught her much, as they had taught me.

She was a woman who could assume greatness when the occasion demanded it; and God knew this occasion did.

Her speech was circulated through the land and it did much to raise our spirits. I shall remember certain parts of it all my life.

"I come amongst you, as you see, at this time, not for my recreation and disport, but being resolved in the midst of the heat and battle, to live or die amongst you all, to lay down for my God and my Kingdom and for my people, my honor and my blood, even in the dust. I know I have the body of a weak and feeble woman, but I have the heart and stomach of a King, and of a King of England too, and think foul scorn that Parma or Spain or any Prince of Europe should dare invade the borders of my realm. . . ."

These were the words which inspired us all.

And so we waited—some in trepidation and others, like Jake, with a frustrated impatience.

Then one day—it was July by then—and the nineteenth

—the news reached Plymouth. The Armada had been sighted off the Lizard.

People came out of their houses, crowding the narrow cobbled streets. Rumor was in the air. There was excitement everywhere.

Sir Francis, playing bowls on the Hoe to while away an hour or so, said he would finish the game. There was time for that, and to beat the Spaniards afterward.

With Linnet, Edwina, Romilly and Jennet, I watched the ships sail out.

None of us spoke, but each understood the feelings of the others. Our men were going out to meet the greatest challenge of their lives. Their ships looked gallant enough with their sails billowing in the wind, but I trembled when I thought of the great galleons they must meet.

The Spaniards were in the Channel; they came with their much vaunted Armada. Our ships were dwarfs compared with theirs.

But as we stood watching them we *believed* in victory. So confident was Admiral Drake that he could beat the Spaniards that we all shared that confidence. Men such as Jake had never doubted it; and it was said that the Spaniards were aware of that strange certainty in the English ranks. They believed it was witchcraft, conjured up by the devil dragon.

I watched Jake's ship, the *Triumphant Lion*, until I could see it no more. Carlos and Jacko each commanded two of Jake's ships.

"Oh, God," I prayed, "we shall beat the Spaniard, I know, but send back our men safe to us."

All now know the outcome of the battle—how the mighty and dignified galleons were no match for the jaunty little English ships, how one of Drake's squadrons lay before the harbors of Newport and Dunkirk and stopped all transport of troops from Flanders.

We know too how the English could make no impression on those mighty galleons and craftily waited until dusk when they set small ships ablaze and sent them among the galleons, so that the Spaniards finding fire on many of their ships, cut their cables and sought to get away, whereupon the English smaller and more agile craft captured some and destroyed others, although many escaped to drift along the Channel and out to sea or be washed up on the coasts where a hostile reception awaited them.

The spirit of men such as Drake and Jake Pennlyon was undefeatable because they knew they would succeed while the Spaniard feared to fail. The Spaniards were brave men doubtless, but they were no match for the English. The English were defending their homes; the Spaniard was out for conquest. Our ships could be victualed from the shore and pinnaces were constantly making the journeys to and from them.

Against us came the greatest fleet of ships ever, up to that time, to be put on to sea. What the Spaniards called an "Invincible Armada engaged in the Great Enterprise." And it failed.

Back came the ships to the harbor. Linnet, Damask, Penn, Romilly, Jennet, Edwina, myself, we were all there waiting, our eyes strained to see the return of the ships.

Would they all return? Could we hope that all our men could come back to us?

I looked at Edwina, who was thinking of Carlos, and I took her hand. I understood her fears, for I shared them. And I thought back to my first meeting with Jake Pennlyon on this Hoe and how determined I was to fight him with all my might.

Please, God, I prayed now, let him come back. Let me go on to the end of my life with Jake Pennlyon.

What a day of rejoicing when they all came back. The *Triumphant Lion* was limping a little, but she was safe.

And her Captain? I was trembling, but there he was climbing into the boat.

The people were cheering madly. The news was all over the country. Bonfires were burning, bells were ringing. The Spanish Armada was broken and defeated. Some of those ships were drifting out into the ocean, some were being washed up on our shores. Few would return to Spain.

It was victory; and we owed it to our English seamen.

There was Jake. I ran to him and threw my arms about him. His eyes were shining.

"God's Death!" he cried. "We've done it, Cat! We've wiped them off the seas! They're finished. This is the end of Spanish power. It's the beginning of ours. We're going to be masters of the sea and the new lands. This is a day to be proud of. Yes, this is the day of triumph. The day of the Lion. . . . My family, Cat, and my ships, my *Triumphant Lion*, this is the greatest day they have known. And the English Lion too, Cat, master of the seas! This is the triumph of the lions."

I laughed at him. "You seem contented with your life this day, Jake Pennlyon."

"Never more in my life."

"If only you had a legitimate son, you'd be completely content."

He looked at Linnet. "God's Death!" he said. "I reckon my girl Linnet is as good as any son."

She came to us then and slipped her arm through his; and the three of us walked home together.